JONAS KARLSSON

Jonas Karlsson (b. 1971) writes plays and short fiction. One of Sweden's most prominent actors, Karlsson has performed on Sweden's premier stage and in several acclaimed feature films and television series. In 2005, Karlsson made his debut as a playwright, earning rave reviews from audience and critics alike. Spurred by the joy of writing for the stage, Karlsson began writing fiction. With an actor's ear for the silences that endow dialogue with meaning and a singular ability to register moods and emotions, Jonas Karlsson has blossomed into one of Scandinavia's finest literary authors, with two novels and three short story collections published to date. He has been awarded with the Ludvig Nordström Award 2018 for his short story collections *The Second Goal*, *The Perfect Friend* and *The Rules of the Game*.

JONAS KARLSSON

The Room, The Invoice, and The Circus

VINTAGE

1 3 5 7 9 10 8 6 4 2

Vintage
20 Vauxhall Bridge Road,
London SW1V 2SA

Vintage is part of the Penguin Random House group of companies whose addresses can be found at global.penguinrandomhouse.com

Penguin
Random House
UK

First published in Vintage in 2019

penguin.co.uk/vintage

A CIP catalogue record for this book is available from the British Library

ISBN 9781784702205

Typeset in in 10.5/16 pt MetaNormal
by Integra Software Services Pvt. Ltd, Pondicherry

Printed and bound in Great Britain by Clays Ltd, Elcograf S.p.A.

Penguin Random House is committed to a sustainable future for our business,
our readers and our planet. This book is made from Forest Stewardship Council®
certified paper.

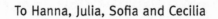
To Hanna, Julia, Sofia and Cecilia

THE ROOM

THE ROOM

1

The first time I walked into the room I turned back almost at once. I was actually trying to find the toilet but got the wrong door. A musty smell hit me when I opened the door, but I don't remember thinking much about it. I hadn't noticed there was anything at all along this corridor leading to the lifts, apart from the toilets. Oh, I thought. A room.

I opened the door, then shut it. No more than that.

2

I had started work at the Authority two weeks before, and in many respects I was still a newcomer. Even so, I tried to ask as few questions as I could. I wanted to become a person to be reckoned with as quickly as possible.

I had got used to being one of the leaders in my last job. Not a boss, or even a team manager, but someone who could sometimes show other people what to do. Not always liked, not a sycophant or a yes-man, but well-regarded and treated with a certain respect, possibly even admiration. Ever so slightly ingratiating, perhaps? I was determined to build up the same position at my new place of work as soon as I could.

It wasn't really my decision to move on. I was fairly happy at my last job and felt comfortable with the routines, but somehow I outgrew the position and ended up feeling that I was doing a job that was way below my abilities, and I have to admit that I didn't always see eye to eye with my colleagues.

Eventually my former boss came and put his arm round my shoulders and told me it was time to look for a better solution. He wondered if it wasn't time for me to make a move? Move on, as he put it, gesturing upwards with his hand to indicate my career trajectory. Together we went through various alternatives.

After a period of consideration and reflection I decided, in consultation with my former boss, upon the big new Authority, and after a certain amount of discussion with them it turned out that a transfer could be arranged without any great difficulty. The union agreed to it, and didn't put the brakes on like they so often do. My former boss and I celebrated with a glass of non-alcoholic cider in his office, and he wished me good luck.

The same day the first snow fell on Stockholm, I carried my boxes up the flight of steps and into the entrance of the large, red-brick building. The woman in reception smiled. I liked her at once. There was something about her manner. I knew straight-away that I had come to the right place. I straightened my back as the words 'man of the future' ran through my head. A chance, I thought. Finally I would be able to blossom to my full potential. Become the person I've always wanted to be.

The new job was no better paid. Quite the opposite, in fact, it was actually slightly worse in terms of perks like flexitime and holidays. And I was forced to share a desk in the middle of an open-plan office with no screens. In spite of this, I was full of enthusiasm and a desire to make a platform for myself and show what I was capable of from the start.

I worked out a personal strategic framework. I arrived half an hour early each morning and followed my own timetable for the day: fifty-five minutes of concentrated work, then a five-minute break. Including toilet breaks. I avoided any unnecessary socialising along the way. I requested and took home files documenting previous policy decisions so as to be able to study which phrases recurred, and formed the basic vocabulary, so to speak. I spent evenings and weekends studying various structures and investigating the informal communication networks that existed within the department.

All this so that I could quickly and efficiently catch up and create a small but decisive advantage over my colleagues, who were already familiar with our workplace and the pervading conditions.

3

I shared my desk with Håkan, who had sideburns and dark rings under his eyes. Håkan helped me with various practical details. Showed me round, gave me pamphlets and emailed over documents containing all manner of information. It was presumably a welcome break from work, a chance to escape his duties, because he was always coming up with new things that he thought I ought to know about. They might be to do with the job, our colleagues or decent places to have lunch nearby. After a while I felt obliged to point out to him that I had to be allowed to get on with my work without interruption.

'Calm down,' I told him when he turned up with yet another folder, trying to get my attention. 'Can you just calm down a bit?'

He calmed down at once and became considerably more reserved. Presumably sulking because I had made my feelings plain from the outset. It probably didn't sit well with the accepted image of a newcomer, but it fitted with the reputation for ambition and tough tactics that I was happy to help spread about myself.

Slowly but surely I built up profiles of my closest neighbours, their character and place in the hierarchy. Beyond Håkan sat Ann. A

7

woman somewhere round fifty. She seemed knowledgeable and ambitious, but also the sort of person who thought she knew everything and liked being proved right. It soon became clear that everyone turned to her when they didn't dare approach the boss.

She had a framed child's drawing near her computer. It showed a sun sinking into the sea. But the drawing was wrong, because on the horizon there were landmasses sticking up on both sides of the sun, which of course is impossible. Presumably it had some sort of sentimental value to her, even if it wasn't particularly pleasant for the rest of us to have to look at.

Opposite Ann sat Jörgen. Big and strong, but doubtless not possessed of an intellect to match. Pinned up on his desk and stuck all round his computer were loads of jokey notes and post-cards that obviously had nothing to do with work, and suggested a tendency towards the banal. At regular intervals he would whisper things to Ann and I would hear her squeak 'Oh, Jörgen' as if he'd told her a rude joke. There was something of an age gap between them. I estimated it to be at least ten years.

Beyond them sat John, a taciturn gentleman of about sixty, who worked on the financing of inspection visits, and next to him sat someone called Lisbeth, I think. I don't know. I wasn't about to ask. She hadn't introduced herself.

There were twenty-three of us in total and almost all had a screen or a little wall of some sort around their desks. Only Håkan and I were stuck in the middle of the floor. Håkan said we would soon be getting screens as well, but I said it didn't matter.

'I've got nothing to hide,' I said.

* * *

Eventually I found a rhythm in my fifty-five-minute periods, and a certain fluency in my work. I made an effort to stick to my schedule and not allow myself to be disturbed in the middle of a period with either coffee-breaks, small talk, telephone calls or trips to the toilet. Occasionally I felt like going for a pee after five minutes, but always made sure I sat out the whole period. It was good for the soul, character-building, and obviously the relief of finally easing the pressure was that much greater.

There were two ways to get to the toilets. One, round the corner past the green potted palm, was slightly shorter than the other, but because I felt like a change that day I decided to take the longer route past the lift. That was when I stepped inside the room for the first time.

I realised my mistake and carried on past the large bin for recycled paper, to the door alongside, the first of the row of three toilets.

I got back to my desk just in time for the next fifty-five-minute period, and by the end of the day I had almost forgotten ever having looked through the door leading to that extra space.

4

The second time I went into the room I was looking for photo-copy paper. I was determined to manage on my own. Despite all the exhortations to ask about things, I was unwilling to expose myself to humiliation and derision by displaying gaps in my knowledge of the set-up. I had come to recognise the little stress wrinkles they all got whenever I did actually ask. Obviously they weren't to know that I was aiming to get to the top of the Authority. To become someone who commanded respect. And I didn't want to give Håkan any excuse to indulge his work-avoidance.

So I checked everywhere, all the places where in the majority of offices you might expect to come across photocopy paper, but there was none to be found. Finally I made my way round the corner, past the toilets, where I had a feeling I had previously seen a small room.

At first I couldn't find the light switch. I felt along the walls on either side of the door, and in the end I gave up, walked out again and found the switch on the outside. What an odd place to put it, I thought, and went back in.

It took a moment for the fluorescent light to flicker into life, but I was quickly able to ascertain that there was no photocopy paper there. Even so, I got an immediate sense that there was something special about this place.

It was a fairly small room. A desk in the middle. A computer, files on a shelf. Pens and other office equipment. Nothing remarkable. But all of it in perfect order.

Neat and tidy.

Against one wall stood a large, shiny filing cabinet with a desk fan on top of it. A dark-green carpet covered the floor. Clean. Free from dust. Everything neatly lined up. It looked slightly studied. Prepared. As if the room were waiting for someone.

I went out, closed the door and switched off the light. Out of curiosity I opened the door again. I got a feeling I had to check. How could I be sure the light wasn't still on in there? Suddenly I felt uncertain whether up or down meant on or off. The whole idea of having the switch on the outside felt strange. A bit like the light inside a fridge. I peered in at the room. It was dark.

5

The next day my new boss came over to our desk in the big, open-plan office, with his thinning hair and cotton cardigan. His name was Karl, and the cotton cardigan wasn't very new, but looked expensive. He stopped next to Håkan and pointed out, without any introductory pleasantries, that my shoes were dirty.

'We try to think about the floor,' he said, pointing at a metal basket full of blue plastic shoe-covers hanging on the wall right next to the entrance.

'Of course,' I said. 'Naturally.'

He patted me on the shoulder and walked away.

I thought it was strange that he didn't smile. Don't people usually try to smooth over that sort of remark with a little smile? To show that you're still friends, and make me, as the newcomer, feel welcome? It wasn't nice, getting told off as bluntly as that. It had a serious impact on my work and I sat there for a long while with an uncomfortable feeling that I'd just been taught a lesson. It was annoying that I hadn't thought about the shoe-covers myself. Obviously I would have done if I'd had time to think about it.

He had managed to make me feel both stupid and insecure, when in actual fact I was one of the smartest. Besides, it was just rude to walk off like that. I counted the number of errors my boss had made during my short time there and came up with three. Plus one minor infraction. Three or four, then, depending on how you looked at it.

Håkan, who had obviously heard the whole thing, sat there unusually quietly, apparently preoccupied with some document. Carry on pretending, I thought. Carry on pretending.

I leaned down and undid my shoes even though I was in the middle of one of my fifty-five-minute work periods, and something like that really ought to be dealt with during one of the short breaks.

I looked around the room. Everyone was immersed in their own business. Yet it still felt as though they were all watching me as I walked, in just my socks, over to the small kitchen at the other end of the office and fetched a cloth. I cleaned up as best I could, fetched a pair of shoe-covers and put them over my shoes. They rustled as I took the cloth back. I tried to see if anyone else was wearing shoe-covers, but they were all wearing either slippers or normal shoes. Maybe they were indoor shoes, I thought.

I wrote a note and stuck it on my briefcase.

Buy slippers.

Then I went to the coffee-machine and got a cup of coffee. I reasoned that this fifty-five-minute period was already ruined. I would just have to sit it out and start again with the next one.

The bulb in the ceiling of the little kitchen was broken and needed changing. When I opened one of the cutlery drawers I discovered that there were plenty of new bulbs there. It would be a painless task to unscrew the broken one and replace it with a new one. It seemed odd that no one had done anything about such a simple problem.

The coffee was far too hot to drink straightaway. I had to keep moving it from hand to hand to avoid burning my fingers, so I thought I might as well take a turn around the department and try to build up my social network.

First I went over and stood beside John's desk. But as I was standing there it struck me that it might be best to start with Ann, seeing as she, in purely geographic terms, was closest to me and Håkan. If I was going to expand my contacts, obviously I ought to start at the centre and work my way outward. Like ripples in water, I thought. Besides, John made a hopelessly bland impression. What did someone like that have to offer me? That I didn't already have? It would be unfortunate for my profile to be seen with such an insipid individual from the older generation, and thus become associated with the colourless crowd.

Ann was a woman, of course, and I was reluctant to associate too intimately with women and risk seeming pushy or ingratiating, but I realised I could adopt a gender-neutral attitude to start with. It ought to help my modern image and demonstrate a certain intellectual flexibility. Besides, Ann was looking more and more like the social queen of the department. Whether I liked it or not, she seemed to be something of a spider at the centre of the web. I carried on to her desk and adopted a relaxed posture with my weight on one leg, so that she could be left in

14

no doubt that I was amenable to having a conversation. She looked up at me and asked if I wanted help with something.

'No,' I said.

She went on working.

I stood there for a while, looking at the badly drawn child's picture of a sunset, and wondered if she was aware of its flagrant inaccuracy. Maybe she was blinded by her emotional involvement? No matter what the circumstances, the child, or grandchild, deserved to be made aware of its mistake so that the error could be avoided next time. If things like that weren't pointed out, its marks for drawing would certainly be negatively impacted.

After a while I became aware that the zip of my trousers, and thus my genitals within, were on exactly the same level as her face. So I shifted my body slightly to find a more neutral position and ended up standing right behind her chair, which also felt rather awkward. Particularly as she didn't seem remotely bothered by me. I blew gently on the coffee and waited for her to say something. It was starting to feel a bit uncomfortable just standing there. Jörgen looked up at me briefly and I decided to give Ann ten seconds. Once they had passed I walked away, taking with me the clear message: I wasn't welcome.

Håkan was sitting there typing, and I wondered if he was actually writing something or merely wanting to give the impression that he was busy.

He was wearing a shabby blue corduroy jacket, which made an unusually scruffy impression. Particularly when combined with his long sideburns, which somehow seemed better suited

15

to the 1970s. I wondered why he hadn't taken it off. As I was sitting there looking at him, it struck me that his blue jacket had been bothering me since first thing that morning. Even before the business with the shoe-covers and cloth, before the incident with Ann. I seriously disliked that jacket. Once when he emptied his pockets out onto the desk I saw he had a whole bundle of crumpled serviettes. Several of them appeared to have been used. He looked tired. Maybe he was out every night partying? Either way, he ought to take care to make sure that his work didn't suffer.

I never went into the room that day. But I thought about it several times. It was as if I was thinking: I ought to go into the room.

6

That night I lay awake thinking about Karl's cotton cardigan and what sort of unfortunate consequences his attitude problem might have. I thought about Håkan and the way he got away with things. I thought about Ann and the elegant way she rejected me. I realised I would have to look out for her. She was doubtless capable of dragging a creative individual down to the semi-social state of casual interaction involving endless coffee and small talk that characterised most workplaces.

Oh well, I wouldn't let myself be affected.

Instead, I thought about the attractive woman in reception. Her smile. The way she made me feel genuinely welcome each morning with just a glance. As if she really saw me. Saw that there was something special about me. I realised that she was one of the rare breed of alert women, of whom there are fewer and fewer, and decided as I lay there to give her a little of my time. Maybe a chat early one morning, maybe lunch?

In my mind I went through material from the department. Decisions and framework documents that I arranged chronologically and put in folders. I got up, went out into the kitchen and drank a glass of milk as I read the adverts in the morning paper.

7

The third time I went into the room, I did it for no reason. That's not like me at all. I usually stick to a clear chain of cause and effect, but this time it was as if I just wanted to go there. I closed the door and stopped in the middle of the floor, in front of the desk.

The desktop was partially covered by a protective pad that seemed almost to have been stuck down. I felt obliged to lift one corner to check that it was only held in place by the anti-slip backing that stopped it shifting even a millimetre in any direction, no matter how you pulled and pushed it.

In front of the pad was a hole-punch, a stapler, a teak penholder containing two ink pens and a pencil.

All neatly lined up.

I raised my elbow and rested it on the shiny metal filing cabinet that stood against one wall. I felt a sense of calm in my body that seemed to cleanse my whole system. An intoxicating feeling of relaxation. A bit like a headache pill.

There was a full-length mirror in the room. I caught sight of myself in it and fancied, to my surprise, that I looked really good. My grey suit fitted better than I thought, and there was something about the way the fabric hung that made me think that the body beneath it was — how can I put it? — virile.

I stood there for a long while, resting my weight on one leg, with my elbow on the filing cabinet. It was a good stance. It looked incredibly relaxed. Simultaneously confident and aware.

I had never thought of myself as 'attractive'. Most of the time I used mirrors to check that my clothes and accessories were in the right place. Not to check how 'attractive' I was. The idea had never occurred to me. I never actually thought about men as being either more or less attractive. But I realised it was time to start doing so.

Because the best thing was the look in the eyes.

The man reflected in the mirror had a remarkable look of concentration in his eyes. He fixed me squarely with his pupils and followed me wherever I went. I realised at once that this was a new asset, a pair of eyes that could demand anything. And get it.

8

Inhibited people don't see the world the way it really is. They only see what they themselves want to see. They don't see the nuances. The little differences.

A lot of people – more than you'd imagine – think everything's fine. They're happy with things the way they are. They don't see the faults because they're too lazy to allow themselves to have their everyday routines disturbed. They think that as long as they do their best, everything will work out okay.

You have to remind them. You have to show people like that what their shortcomings are.

Fresh documents kept arriving from the investigators. The numbers on the title-page indicated the level of priority given to their conclusions, on a declining scale where number one was the most important. On the fourth floor we worked exclusively with three- and four-figure documents. The framework decisions from one to ten were almost never changed now, and those in double-figures were dealt with by considerably more senior administrators on the floors above. No one in my department had ever worked with a single- or double-digit decision. Not even Karl. As soon as anyone started working on a file near two or three hundred, rumours of promotion would start to circulate about the person in question.

Fortunately for everyone on my floor, there were departments lower down that worked with all the five-figure material.

9

The fourth time I went into the room I took my colleague Håkan with me. We had some questions about internal organisation to go through, and I thought it best to discuss them inside the room.

Håkan sat on the other side of my desk. We worked opposite one another. At any moment we might happen to look up and meet each other's gaze. I tried never to look straight ahead whenever I looked up from my work. Håkan carried out his duties with the same lightness of touch as everyone else in the department. He used the phone more or less as he liked, took breaks whenever he felt like it. He would spend ages gazing off into the distance without it apparently having anything to do with work. Now and then he would try to talk to me as well. I would rebuff him gently but firmly. Usually with a simple gesture of the hand. Arm out, palm raised towards him. It worked.

We didn't actually share a desk. We each had one of our own. But the desks were positioned back to back and Håkan had an irritating habit of shoving his papers across his desk every time he started something new, which meant that they eventually ended up on my side.

One day I caught him in the process of doing precisely that. In the middle of one of my fifty-five-minute periods.

It certainly wasn't my intention to sit and stare at him as he worked, but his movements were so expansive that it was hard not to. He took out a couple of weighty new files from the investigators and put them in front of him on the desk, but instead of gathering up and tidying away what was already there, he merely pushed it away from him. Towards me.

I realised at once what was going to happen.

Not now, maybe not even today, but eventually Håkan's desktop would overflow with files and papers and documents, and they would begin to eat away at my side.

I had seen the same pattern before, in other workplaces, and knew it would be a source of irritation between us. I spent a little while wondering how best to tackle the situation on this occasion.

For the time being there was nothing I could say. He could manage or mismanage his desk however he liked as long as he kept to his side. There were still a few centimetres left as yet. Almost a decimetre. What could I say?

I looked at the time. There were still about twenty-five minutes left of my fifty-five-minute period, but my rhythm had been disturbed. I would just have to regard the rest of the period as lost.

At the same time, I realised that now that the thought of what was going to happen with Håkan's and my desks had arisen, it was going to be very hard to let go of. It would be there as a point of friction, and was bound to unsettle me. Maybe it would be just as well to deal with the confrontation at once, seeing as I now, in a manner of speaking, had some time to spare? At some point Håkan would have to learn to put things away before he started on something new. Not just push it away and assume that it would disappear by itself. Maybe it made sense to make him aware of that without delay?

I got up quickly. Walked behind my chair and stood there with my arms leaning on it. Took three deep breaths. Håkan looked at me and smiled a quick, false smile that was probably meant to look polite. I spun the chair gently, back and forth, as I looked at his papers.

I was very conscious of the fact that this was properly a matter for management. Efficiency savings of this sort and solutions to potential collegial conflicts ought to be dealt with by an alert and engaged boss.

An attentive and empathetic leader would naturally have noticed the fissure that was on its way to breaking out within the ranks, and would have done something about it. Rather than waste time picking on the more alert members of staff about shoe-covers.

But perhaps I recognised that Karl really did not possess

those qualities? Perhaps I recognised even then that he wasn't management material, and that one day I instead would be taking control of this department? Perhaps this was the first step? Perhaps this was exactly the right opportunity for a rebuke?

'Håkan,' I said in a friendly but firm voice.

'Yes,' he said, looking up at me as if I were interrupting him in the middle of something important.

'Have you got a minute?'

He nodded.

I stretched, sucked in a deep breath through my nose and let it out of my mouth in small puffs as I contemplated what tactics to employ.

'Look around you,' I said eventually.

'Yes?' he said.

'What do you see?'

He said nothing for a short while as he looked around.

'No, I don't know . . .'

He went back to looking at his screen.

'I'd prefer us to deal with this at once,' I said.

'With what? What do you mean?' he said, suddenly irritated.

I fixed my gaze on him and said in a calm and friendly voice: 'Before this gets out of hand, I'd like you to listen to me. I'm sure you'll see what I mean.'

He looked at me with the tired, ignorant, slightly stupid expression that is so common in people who aren't used to seeing the broader picture in small things.

'Let's take a walk,' I said, leading him round the lift and

into the little room. I thought it best to deal with this in private, so that we could talk without being interrupted.

Inside the room the air was fresh and cool. I closed the door behind us and stood in front of the mirror with my arm on the filing cabinet. The light in the room definitely made Håkan look worse, while I glanced in the mirror and confirmed that I had retained the same crispness as last time. The man in the mirror was able to smile. He looked relaxed and spoke with a calm, deep voice.

'There's something I've noticed,' I said.

'Yes?' Håkan said, looking round as if he'd never seen this room before. Perhaps he hadn't. He didn't seem to be particularly observant. Poor fellow, in just a couple of weeks my local knowledge had already surpassed his.

I decided to get straight to the point and if possible get back in time for the next fifty-five-minute period.

'You don't put your old files back when you take out new ones,' I said.

'What did you say?' Håkan said.

'I said I've noticed that you're letting your papers spread out across your desk. Soon they'll be on my side, and then you'll be encroaching on my space. I am, as I'm sure you can appreciate, keen to have full access to the whole of my desk. I am already inconvenienced by the disproportionately large computer that takes up about a third of the space, it really ought to be possible to procure a system with more modern, smaller terminals, but never mind that, that isn't your responsibility. I would just like you to adopt new habits that don't risk disturbing my work. Do you understand?'

Håkan looked at me in surprise, as if he had been expecting something completely different. Perhaps he thought I had something private to say? Maybe he thought we had come in here to discuss personal matters? I felt a momentary satisfaction at having so quickly and concisely clarified the problem to him, presenting my demands without a lot of introductory small talk. Now the ball was in his court and he had little option but to accept my terms. After all, my wishes were in no way unreasonable. Sure enough, he made a slight nod.

'Good,' I said. 'Well, I suggest we get back to our duties, and if everything goes smoothly we need never mention this again.'

I smiled at him, opened the door and stepped out. Håkan followed me and we both went and sat down. He had a dried, white stain on his shirt, high up on one side of his chest. I noted that he sat and looked at me for a long while after we had returned to our places. Without doing anything about his papers. I let him. Things need time to settle, I thought. Eventually the message would get through to him and hopefully lead to a more proactive way of dealing with his things. Presumably he wasn't used to being reprimanded in such a clear and effective way. You might as well get used to it, I thought. I might very well end up as your boss one day.

I leaned across the desk and whispered: 'Don't think of it as a reprimand. More as an observation.'

'What?' he said, and I realised that he was playing along in our tacit understanding to let this stay between us. I nodded, leaned back, and mimed zipping my mouth shut, then locking it and throwing away the key.

10

That night I went through my reprimand sentence by sentence, word for word, and it got better each time.

I put on a CD of Mozart's twenty-first piano concerto, but soon swapped it for one of Sting's albums, only to switch to Dire Straits and then John Cougar Mellencamp. I didn't really feel like listening to any of them, but liked the idea of associating with the very best.

I went over to the window sill in the living room and looked down at the courtyard. It was getting more and more like winter out there. The ground was already white and even more snowflakes were dancing in the light of the lamp-posts. I rolled my head a little to massage my neck, and counted the windows in the building opposite.

As I was about to go to bed I noticed my briefcase leaning against the wall. On the outside was a Post-it note. The glue had probably already left a mark on the leather.

11

The fifth time I went into the room there was no reason at all. I had successfully completed my fifty-five-minute period of concentrated and undisturbed work, and felt no need of coffee or a trip to the toilet. I just went to the room because I liked it, and found a certain satisfaction in being in there.

Håkan hadn't yet found a better solution for his papers, which were still threatening to slip onto my side, even though a couple of days had passed since our conversation inside the room. Yet I still felt somehow calm about the matter. He probably didn't want to change his behaviour just like that, after being ordered to do so. Possibly because he didn't want his colleagues to connect his sudden organised behaviour with our meeting the other day, but possibly also to demonstrate a degree of independence towards me. That would pass. I couldn't deny him a degree of pride. If it turned out that he was consciously being obstructive and if things hadn't improved within a week, I would have to raise the matter again.

The open-plan office around me was full of protracted and completely unstructured discussion about the forthcoming Christmas party. It was about what games would be played. What sort of punch would be served, et cetera. Questions and ideas were tossed into the air and drifted around the office. The same individual subject was discussed in several places at once without there being any central focus, or even any contact with the actual party committee. I did my best to ignore the whole fractured debate, and naturally declined any involvement. When Hannah with the long ponytail, who seemed to have some sort of responsibility for the party, came over and asked if I wasn't going to consider attending, I used Ann's old trick of completely ignoring her and carrying on with my work. I actually thought about using her line 'Do you want help with something?', but when I turned round to deliver it she had already gone.

12

The sixth time I found myself in the room it was in the company of the woman from reception. Completely unplanned.

Late in the day I had decided to attend the Christmas party after all, because I realised that a certain amount of information of the more informal variety tended to flourish on such occasions.

'So you came in the end,' Hannah with the ponytail said as I stepped out of the lift and saw that the entire office had been transformed.

There were sheets and various fabrics hanging everywhere. The lighting was subdued. It was hard to see. At first I considered not replying at all. Hannah with the ponytail was one of those women who laugh readily and can talk nonsense for hours without a single sensible thing being said. In principle I try to ignore people like that as much as possible. I simply choose not to think about them. Make up my mind that they don't exist. And I didn't think hers was a particularly pleasant way to greet guests. Especially not if you were one of the organisers. In the end I decided to give a clipped response.

'I did,' I said.

'I mean, you didn't seem very keen,' she said.

She stood there looking at me for a while in silence. I looked back, calmly and neutrally, until she spoke again.

'Well, we can probably find you a plate,' she said, making it sound like a nuisance.

I realised a long time ago that dismissive remarks like that could easily be sexually motivated. Women of her age have that inverted way of approaching men of the same age. Particularly if you show a certain disinterest. I imagine it's to do with status and an unwillingness to show any sort of inferiority. A sort of liberation, maybe even feminism? My generation of women always have to show they're as strong as men, before finding clumsy ways of showing their affection.

I wasn't going to let myself be moved.

I got a glass of the tasteless, blue-coloured punch that matched my blue shoe-covers in a most irritating way. I realised once again that it was time to get a pair of those indoor shoes. But at the same time it didn't look like the other guests were paying much attention to the shoe-code that evening. Some of them were definitely wearing the same shoes they had arrived in. I took a stroll past the glassed-off manager's office, trying to catch a glimpse of Karl's shoes in the crowd, but I couldn't see him anywhere.

He probably wasn't there, because the office had been rearranged in a way that it would be difficult for a boss to allow. The sheets had been fastened with a staple-gun, which was bound to leave marks on the walls. Printers and phones and other electronic equipment had been covered in a way that was clearly a fire-hazard. Who knows, maybe they had also blocked the fire-escapes?

Here and there stood little clusters of candles, and someone had sprinkled some sort of glittery silver stars around them.

Somewhere a stereo was playing Christmas songs, but I never managed to identify where the noise was coming from.

People were standing in groups, noisily interrupting each other. It was obvious that they were all more relaxed than usual. Even John was participating in the small talk, which revolved around either the threat of cutbacks or the usual conversation about families and children and football.

A string of fairy-lights had been hung from one wall to the other. It was supposed to be a Christmas decoration, but the whole thing had been done in a very amateurish way and didn't feel quite proper.

I walked around among people who made various excruciating attempts to engage me in conversation. As you might imagine, it was a pointless task.

Outside the snow was still falling and after a while I sank onto one of the two leather armchairs over by the window, mainly to try out what it felt like. I'd just made up my mind to leave when the woman from reception came over and sat in the other chair. She looked very neat and clean. She had two glasses of wine in one hand and a napkin in the other. She smiled at me, the way she did every morning, and I asked why she was here, seeing as this wasn't her department.

'No, I know,' she said, slightly embarrassed. 'It's usually like this. I get invited to all the parties. I suppose everyone thinks I don't have a department of my own.'

I did a quick calculation in my head.

'Let's see, there must be, what, eight departments?'

'Nine, actually,' she said with a laugh. 'The maintenance department invite me to theirs as well.'

'That's not fair,' I said, but she just laughed.

She took the napkin and started rubbing the bottom of her dress with it.

'Have you spilled something?' I asked.

'Well, I didn't,' she said. 'The punch splashed a bit, but I don't know. It's hopeless trying to get rid of stains like that. Especially if they've been there a while.'

We sat in silence for a time as she rubbed her dress. Eventually she looked up at me.

'My name's Margareta, by the way.'

'Oh,' I said, then thought that I ought to say something more.

She looked as if she were expecting a reply, but what could

I say? What could I possibly have to say about her name? Her name was Margareta. Okay. Good. Nice name.

I looked round the room. People were laughing and it was getting a bit loud. Every so often someone would shout something. The armchair was much less comfortable to sit in than I had imagined. I shifted my buttocks slightly to find a better position. On a small table between me and Margareta there was a large bowl of sweets. I looked at them, trying to work out if I wanted one.

'Don't think much of the fairy-lights,' I said after a while, pointing at the wall.

'No.' Margareta laughed. 'I think it was Jörgen who put them up.'

'Oh,' I said. 'You seem to know a lot.'

She laughed again. There was something about her laugh that, besides indicating a certain interest in me, also managed to put me in a good mood. It was clear that she was slightly intoxicated, which made her seem – how can I put it? – more physical. It made me think of Marilyn Monroe. But I didn't think that mattered much at the time.

She raised one of the glasses and sipped the wine.

'Would you like a glass?' she asked, passing me the other.

I shook my head and reached for the large bowl of Christmas sweets instead. I fished out a toffee, which I toyed with for a while.

I recalled a man from Denmark who took me on a pub crawl once, and insisted on us drinking spirits all evening. I felt sick for two whole days afterwards.

'Come with me instead,' I said, putting the toffee in my pocket and pulling her gently but firmly with me towards the little room beyond the toilets. Somehow it felt like she appreciated the initiative, maybe even the energy behind the decision and its implementation, by which I mean the firm way of taking a decision.

We slid round the corner behind the wall holding Jörgen's fairy-lights. I flicked the light switch outside and she giggled like a little girl who was being allowed to follow the naughty boy into his secret den.

13

We entered the room just after half past ten in the evening, and I'd guess it was half past eleven by the time we emerged. What happened in between is in many ways still unclear.

Not that I was drunk. I still know what happened, but I'm not entirely sure how to interpret it.

We stood for a long time in front of the mirror. She touched me. I touched her back, but it was like she pulled my arms and hands to her, showing me round. Like a dance. I didn't have to move a muscle. She did it for me. Naturally it was erotic, but never sordid the way it can so easily be when a man and woman meet. She smiled at me but I can't remember us saying anything.

She had big, beautiful eyes and shiny hair. It was lovely. I was enchanted.

When we kissed it was as if she was me. I was me, but she was me too.

When we came out again she stood there looking at me for a long time. Charged. Changed. As if I'd shown her something entirely new. Something big. Something she hadn't quite been prepared for, and didn't know how to handle. She turned on her heel and walked away. As far as I was aware, she went straight home.

As for me, I stayed for a while sucking the sweet.

14

Someone had made a snowman in the courtyard below my window, but it wasn't very good at all. The two bottom balls were roughly the same size, and the top one was only marginally smaller, which meant that it didn't have anything like the traditional snowman-shape that a snowman ought to have. And it didn't have a nose. Whoever had made the snowman hadn't bothered to find a carrot or anything else that would have functioned as a nose, and had just left it as it was. Maybe they had lost interest halfway through? Such is life, I thought.

That night I lay in bed and went through the evening, moment by moment. Over and over again. From the frosty greeting and Hannah's strange comments, via the encounter with Margareta from reception, to my strong sense of having been master of the situation. In some ways it was a novel experience. A feeling of power.

15

Stupid people don't always know that they're stupid. They might be aware that something is wrong, they might notice that things don't usually turn out the way they imagined, but very few of them think it's because of them. That they're the root of their own problems, so to speak. And that sort of thing can be very difficult to explain.

I got an email from Karl the other day. It was a group email to the whole department. The introduction alone made me suspect trouble: *We will be putting staffing issues under a microscope.*

Anyone with even a basic understanding of the language knows that you put things under 'the' microscope, with the definite article. (Sadly, this sort of sloppiness is becoming more and more common as text messages and email are taking over.) I let it pass this time, but knew that I would have to act if it happened again. I wondered what suitable comment about the proper use of language I could drop into the conversation next time I spoke to Karl.

16

The morning after the party I got to work early.

A lot of the signs were still there. There was a sour smell, and plastic glasses and napkins on the floor. I wondered what preparations they had made for the clearing up.

'Things don't just clear themselves up, do they?' I said to Hannah with the ponytail when she arrived, still looking sleepy, a couple of minutes later. She glanced at me with annoyance, and I know she was impressed that I was there first, even though I wasn't part of any cleaning team. I sat down on the sofa by the kitchen and looked at a few newspapers, so that she would realise I had chosen to come on my own initiative rather than because I was told to.

After a while I noticed that she had chosen to start clearing up in a different part of the office, rendering my presence pointless. I folded the newspaper and went over to the lift.

I went down to reception and caught sight of Margareta hanging up her outdoor clothing in the little cloakroom behind the desk. I stopped beside the plastic Christmas tree and waited. From the other side of the counter I could see her standing in the little cloakroom adjusting her hair and clothes in a small mirror. Her skirt was nice, but she was wearing a dull-coloured blouse that wasn't at all attractive. I'd have to remember to tell her not to wear it when she was with me if the two of us were going to get together, I thought. She must have felt she was being watched, because suddenly she started and turned towards me.

'Goodness, you startled me,' she said.

'Did I?' I said. 'I didn't mean to.'

She gathered her things and came over to the counter.

'Early,' she said, meaning me.

'Yes,' I said, thinking that she seemed a little odd. She was being snappy in a way that I didn't appreciate at all.

I wondered whether I should say anything about events in the room the previous day, but decided that it would be best to maintain a certain distance at first, and simply ride the wave of the impressions I had been given yesterday. I tried to remember what we had said to each other. What kind of agreement we had reached, so to speak. Eventually I said: 'You too.'

We stood there in silence for a while. She was arranging some papers on her side of the counter. Opening a large diary. Pulling a page off the calendar. People started to stream in. Margareta greeted almost all of them in an equally warm and friendly way, which put me in an even worse mood seeing as she really ought to realise that she was devaluing the impact of her smile if she used it on everyone. Didn't she know that she ought to hold back a bit?

I tried to look as though I had business down there. Started to leaf through a trade magazine that was on the counter, and after a while I went over to the coffee-machine and pressed the

42

button to get a cup. I stood there for a long while waiting for the coffee to start trickling down into the cup. I pressed the button a few extra times, and had managed to get fairly annoyed by the time I realised that I hadn't put any money in.

I couldn't help noting how much better the organisation worked down here, where you had to pay for coffee, compared to the lax coffee-drinking that pertained up in my department where anyone, at any time, could scuttle off and get coffee without any restrictions at all.

When I was putting the coins in I realised that I was a couple of kronor short. I went back to Margareta and asked if she could lend me two one-krona coins. She was standing talking to a woman in a suit and didn't answer me at first, so I asked again. Slightly louder. Then she turned towards me with irritation and said that she could. She went into the little cloakroom and got her handbag, took out her purse and passed me the coins. I thought it impractical to keep her handbag containing her purse so far from the counter, but said nothing. Partly because I didn't think her behaviour deserved to be rewarded with my advice, and partly because I didn't want to appear too superior to her at such an early stage of our relationship. Instead, I merely smiled and decided to counter her irritation with a forgiving, worldly attitude.

'After all, two kronor isn't the end of the world,' I said, glancing towards the woman in the suit, but there was no conspiratorial smile.

They resumed their conversation and I went back to the coffee-machine, put my money in, got my coffee, then went and stood beside the plastic Christmas tree again. By now most people had arrived and the reception area resumed its usual deserted appearance. I was left alone again with Margareta on the other side of the counter.

'Well,' I said after a while, sipping the hot coffee and wondering what I ought to say.

She looked up at me from her papers, but I saw none of the respect you might expect from a receptionist of her level. It made me slightly annoyed. Maybe she was one of those people who thought it was acceptable to set aside all politeness and manners once you've been introduced and become acquainted.

'Yes?' Margareta said.

I decided to sit her out. Let her catch up and realise the situation she was in. Any moment now everything ought to click into place, I thought, but she just went on looking at me with that indirectly arrogant expression, rather like a mother looking at her teenage son.

When she didn't say anything, I felt obliged to speak: 'Well, I thought it was nice, anyway.'

She took a paperclip and fastened several documents together, then put them on a new pile.

'I have to ask you something personal,' she said after a while, as she pushed the papers away. 'Is that okay?' I nodded and she looked round. I could see she was gathering herself.

'Are you on drugs?'

At first I thought she was joking. I laughed, but then I saw that she was serious. I took a couple of steps back and noticed that

I'd spilled some coffee on the sleeve of my jacket. What did she mean? Why would she ask that? Was she on drugs? Did she want me to join her on some sort of junkie adventure?

I must have looked angry because suddenly she got that scared look in her eye that I recognised from the night before. I wasn't used to people looking at me that way. It unsettled me, and made me even more angry.

'What do you mean?' I tried to say in my usual voice, but I heard it come out much more strained than I had intended.

It annoyed me that she had so suddenly managed to throw me off-balance. I wasn't remotely enjoying the confusion she was spreading, and felt the need to create more distance. I backed away another couple of steps.

'I just mean,' Margareta began uncertainly, 'well, what are you doing down here now, for instance? In work time?'

I looked at the large clock on the wall behind the desk and saw to my surprise that it was already twenty-five to ten. How could it be so late? So quickly?

45

17

I left at once. Without a word I hurried across the granite floor and went up in the lift. I got off at the fourth floor and made an effort not to run to my desk. I slipped onto my chair and leafed quickly through my diary to check that I hadn't missed a meeting, but there was nothing written down. I glanced over at the glass doors where Karl sat, but couldn't see him. I took a deep breath and suddenly realised how tired I was. I tried to remember when I had last slept.

I should have seen through her earlier. Obviously she was a junkie. All that smiling. That optimistic outlook. It was a chemically produced friendliness. I'd walked straight into the trap. Being taken in by the surface appearance of a drug-user was one of the dangers of being an open, honest person. Never suspecting anything.

I realised that I would have to stay away from her in future.

I raised my head and tried to look straight ahead, but it was hard to get my gaze to settle on anything. I have to find somewhere I can pull myself together, I thought. I got up and felt my whole body aching with tiredness.

Without knowing how it had happened, I felt something

warm and wet on my legs. I looked down and saw the remains of the coffee on my jacket and trousers. The empty plastic cup upside down in my hand. Slowly but surely I made my way towards the corridor with the toilets, then in to wipe off the coffee. I pulled out a bundle of paper towels and pressed them against my jacket and trousers.

The room, I thought. I'll go into the room for an hour. I crept out into the corridor, past the big recycling bin, switched on the light and opened the door for the seventh time.

18

I could feel the clean white wall against my back. The gentle texture against the palm of my hand as I placed it against the wallpaper. The cool steel against my cheek as I leaned my head against the filing cabinet. The soft motion of the drawers as they slid in and out on their metal runners. Order.

I counted the lengths of wallpaper on the long wall. Five, I made it.

After a short while I felt brighter. I looked at myself in the mirror and saw that I was my old self again. I looked better than I deserved to. I adjusted my tie and went back out to the office.

19

I sat down in my place and looked at the time. I had about fifteen minutes left until a new fifty-five-minute period started, so I leaned back and stretched my arms up in the air. Then let them fall and folded them behind my head. I glanced over at Karl's glassed-in office. I didn't mind if he did see me now. See me taking time for myself. I sat for a while going through various replies to things he might say. Little hints that would slowly but surely make him realise that I was a man of the future. Someone worth keeping in with. Not the sort of person to pick unnecessary arguments with. About trivial things.

I looked over towards the little kitchen with the broken light above the stove that still hadn't been fixed. It seemed astonishing that it was still like that. Was it really so hard to screw in a new bulb?

I sighed, tilted my head back, gazed up at the ceiling and looked at the various fittings. The cables for the fluorescent lighting were attached to the outside of the ceiling tiles, fixed in place by little clamps that made the whole thing look rather provisional. A sausage-like cornice between the ceiling and the walls. I counted the lengths of wallpaper along the wall by the toilet corridor, and made it sixteen.

For some reason I thought that was rather low, so I counted them once more. And made it sixteen again. I spun gently on my chair and wondered how that could be right. Each length must be about half a metre wide. Making eight metres for the whole wall. I looked down at the bookcases and cabinets lined up against it and tried to work out the distance. Yes, eight metres – that could be about right. But there were five lengths inside the room alone? How narrow could the toilets be, lined up alongside it? I wondered. They couldn't be less than one metre? Not when you took the walls into account?

I got up from my chair and went over to the wall. I stood there for a while looking at it. Three bookcases, a filing cabinet and a photocopier were lined up against it. I went round the corner into the toilet corridor. There were the three toilets. The first one was vacant and I stood in the doorway and held my arms out to measure it. It must be at least a metre, I thought. I went back out into the corridor, past the room and the big green recycling bin, and reached the lift. I looked at it.

Then I went round the far corner and came to the wall with the bookcases and cabinet again. I backed away slightly and counted the lengths of wallpaper again. Sixteen.

I went up to the wall and put my lower arm against the wallpaper. I had heard somewhere that a grown man's lower arm and hand together make up about half a metre. That seemed to fit.

Once again I went back round the corner to the toilet corridor. Three toilets, a recycling bin and a lift, all of which combined came to about eight metres. So what about the room?

*   *   *

I went back and sat down at my desk. Took out a pad of squared paper and did a simple sketch of this part of the fourth floor.

Impossible, I thought, as I looked at the sketch. There's something that doesn't make sense.

I put down the pad and went round to the lift. I went down and got out on the third floor. It was almost as empty as the fourth floor. A man in a cap said hello to me as I went round the corner into their toilet corridor. I didn't bother to respond. I was taken by surprise, and because I didn't know him I didn't think there was any reason for us to waste time saying hello to each other. Besides, I was busy with this peculiar discovery, and I wasn't about to be sidetracked. I was on the trail of something. I could feel it in my whole body.

The layout was the same down here, toilets and recycling bin. But no room.

I went round to the other side where a large whiteboard had been screwed to the wall. I counted the lengths of wallpaper. Sixteen. Exactly the same proportions, I thought. It's all here. Except the room.

I took the lift back up again and stopped on the office side of the wall.

I looked at Jörgen's fairy-lights up by the ceiling. They stretched all the way from one wall to the other, and down to the plug-socket by the floor.

I grabbed hold of the string of lights, unplugged it from the wall and pulled it down from the ceiling. It was more firmly attached than I had expected and when I finally managed to get the whole string loose, small flakes of plaster broke away from the top part of the wall.

I tied the part of the wire that had been hanging down towards the socket, then went round and laid it out on the floor on the other side where the toilets started. It reached just past the green recycling bin.

I knew it, I thought, then said it out loud to myself so that I would be sure to understand.

'It's invisible. It's a secret room.'

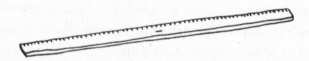

I heard someone say my name. I turned round and caught sight of Ann in the doorway to one of the toilets. Her face was completely blank. She was staring at me, so I spoke as calmly as I could to her.

'Have you got a ruler?'

'What did you say?' she asked.

'A ruler?' I said. 'Or a tape-measure?'

She shook her head.

20

I got the long ruler from Håkan's desk. It was fifty centimetres long. He'd borrowed plenty of things from me. It was only fair that I finally had a good reason to borrow something from him.

I started with the photocopier wall, in towards the office, and measured along the carpet. *8.40*, I wrote on the sketch on my pad.

On the other side I sat down and started measuring the carpet where the first toilet started. I held my thumb in place, moved the ruler, and counted the number of lengths as I did the calculation in my head.

When I reached the lift I had got to 12.20. Impossible, I thought. That makes three metres and eighty centimetres that don't exist on the other side.

I went and stood by the lift to see if the corridor was angled somehow, in a way that would distort the measurements, but the wall and corridor were perfectly parallel.

It was an excellent viewpoint. From there you could clearly see that the corridor ran parallel to the wall on the other side. No distortion, no angles. But with one room too many on one side. It was extremely professionally done.

21

'Can I ask you something?' Håkan said when I gathered up my things at the end of the day. I had just decided to stop lending him my Staedtler pens with the 0.5 and 0.05 mm tips, seeing as I had noted that he seldom, if ever, put the lids back on them. Next time I would say no.

'Yes,' I said. 'Go ahead.'

'What are you doing?' Håkan said.

I took my coat and scarf off the hanger and went round to Håkan. We were almost the only people left in the office. Lena by the window was still there, as she usually was.

'When do you mean?' I said.

Håkan folded his arms, leaned back in his chair and looked at me.

'What are you doing when you stand like that?'

'Stand? Like what?'

'When you stand still like that. By the wall.'

'Which wall?' I said.

He nodded his head towards the toilet corridor.

We both fell silent and looked at each other. I realised that this was a defining moment. A moment when I might be able to find out what was really going on in this department.

'Come on,' I said. 'Show me. Where do I stand?'

Håkan squirmed and suddenly didn't seem so interested any more.

'Oh, you know.'

'No, show me. Where do I stand?'

He hesitated. He ran the fingers of one hand through his hair, down his cheek and under his chin. He scratched his long sideburns. It was obvious that he felt unsettled.

'Look, never mind, we can talk about it some other time.'

He slowly gathered together his things on the desk. I caught him glancing over towards Lena by the window.

'No, show me now,' I said. 'What do I do?'

'Come on, surely you know?'

'No. I don't know.'

He folded his arms again and looked me in the eye.

'You stand there, completely still,' he said.

'Where do I stand?'

'Over there. By the wall.'

'Show me, Håkan. Please. I want you to show me exactly.'

Håkan looked at me suspiciously. Finally he got up and went off round the corner. I followed him. We stopped right outside the door to the room.

'Here,' Håkan said.

'What do I do here?' I said.

'You stand here. Completely still.'

'Do I?'

'Yes, it's almost a bit creepy. You're so bloody still. How can you do that, without moving a muscle? It's like you're just not there.'

'Show me.'

'No.'

'Go on, please.'

'No, damn it. You just stand here completely still.'

'Do I say anything?'

'No, you're completely gone. It's like you're somewhere else. Completely out of reach. Hell, your phone even started to ring in your inside pocket. I asked if you weren't going to answer it, but you didn't move a millimetre. It was like you couldn't hear. As if you were somewhere else.'

'When did I do this?'

'The other day. You made me come with you. And then you just stood there like that.'

'How long do I stand like that?'

'It varies. Last time it was about five minutes, but last week you must have stood for at least a quarter of an hour.'

'Has anyone else seen me like that?'

Håkan shuffled uncomfortably.

'Well, yes. People have to go to the toilets.'

'So they've seen me.'

'Yes. I mean, it's not like they stand and stare, but they can't help wondering. Me too. What is it you're doing?'

I looked him in the eye and he looked back. We looked at each other as if we were playing some sort of game where you had to make the other person laugh or look away. I thought it felt uncomfortable and somehow infantile. I felt a sudden burst of impatience. Was this the start of a message? Some sort of code that would initiate me into the secret?

Was he trying to tell me something, or was this whole thing a test?

'Can I ask you something, then?' I said.

'Sure,' Håkan said.

'What do you see in front of you here?' I said, pointing at the door.

22

Håkan was wearing his rather worn, dark-blue corduroy jacket that day, and I could feel that it was having a negative effect on me. Blue really wasn't his colour, and the corduroy was soft and threadbare. No substance to it at all. It made me think of poorly stuffed cushions in waiting rooms. It was making me uneasy and unfocused. And even more angry.

It was as if he wasn't properly concentrating on work.

There was something about him that had long made me suspect that he had a hidden agenda beyond the watchful eye of the Authority. His hair, his sideburns, and that scruffy jacket; it all suggested a set of values different to the ones that we in the department set most store by.

'Shall we go home now, Björn?' he said.

'Not before we're done here,' I said.

As Håkan reluctantly explained, for the second time, what he could see in front of him, and stubbornly denied the existence of the room, I realised that I was going to have to be more obvious. I reached out my arm and pointed, so the tip of my forefinger was touching the door.

'Door,' I said.

He looked at me again with that foolish smile and glazed expression.

'Wall,' he said.

'Door,' I said.

'Wall,' he said.

23

The following day I decided to pay careful attention to everyone going down the corridor, and I was forced to admire the elegant artistry of whoever had constructed the secret space. What had the architect done to conceal a room so effectively, when it was right in front of the noses of everyone working here? And who had managed to get them to act so credibly as if it didn't exist? Who had drilled this crazy exercise into them? And what was that room, really? Maybe it was dangerous, or did it possibly contain classified information? It seemed so unassuming, but perhaps that was the whole point? Maybe it was supposed to look innocent.

Just before lunch I went over to Jörgen. I stood there waiting until he looked up from his papers.

'Did you want something?' he asked.

I beckoned him towards me with my forefinger but he didn't move from his chair. His jaw was hanging like a boxer's.

'Have you got a minute?' I asked when he didn't obey my signal, which couldn't possibly have been unclear.

Finally he got the message and slowly followed me round the corner into the corridor. I stopped outside the door to the room, just as I had done with Håkan the day before. I made an effort to adopt a confidential tone of voice.

'Jörgen,' I said, 'I want you to be completely honest now. I want you to tell me what this room is for.'

'What room?'

'This one,' I said, touching the door with my finger.

'There's the lift,' Jörgen said. 'And there are the toilets.'

'Mmm, but what about in between them?'

'In between? Well, there's a recycling bin, if that's what you mean . . .'

'That's not what I mean,' I said. 'What's this room for?'

I slapped my hand on the door, fairly hard. Actually harder than I had expected. I realised that this nonsense was wearing my patience. I had to try to keep a cool head.

'Well . . .' Jörgen said, looking at me.

I could see that he was extremely uncertain. He was evidently disconcerted at having to talk to me.

'. . . it's a wall.'

I glared at him.

'Is that all you've got to say?'

'Yes, what do you want me to say? You're fucking weird, you know that? Why are you so interested in this wall? Don't drag me into this.'

I realised that Jörgen wasn't the right place to start. He was only a poor subordinate. Loyal, but entirely without influence. Whoever was responsible for this deception was on a different level of the hierarchy. I patted him on the shoulder and said he could go back and sit down again.

*   *   *

That afternoon I went round and led my other colleagues to the same spot and carried out the same procedure as with Jörgen and Håkan. They were all reluctant, and they all stuck to the same story: there was no door there, let alone a room, and anyway, what was I doing when I stood there without moving?

A certain anxiety spread through the department. People stood and whispered to each other. Håkan tried to put his arm round my shoulders and a number of people pointed at me. In the end I lost patience and gathered all the staff together. Apart from Karl, who was off at some meeting all day.

I went from desk to desk and summoned everyone in friendly but firm terms to a short meeting. Some of them muttered, wondering what this was all about, wanting to know in advance. Some of them literally required a helping hand to get moving. But most of them came along without any fuss, and I told them all it would be best, as well as easiest, if everyone was given the information at the same time. Jörgen and Håkan laughed rather nervously at first and tried to make a joke of it, but when they realised that no one else thought they were very funny they quietened down noticeably. I herded them like a sheepdog out to the corridor, past the toilets, towards the room.

When I stepped inside the room for the eighth time, I had the whole department with me, apart from Karl. Each and every one of them stepped through the door, and once I had them all in there I explained to them that I had seen through their little joke. I said I didn't know who was the brains behind it, but that I'd worked it out well enough to let them know.

24

That night I lay in bed, still feeling the congenial inner calm that only arises when you've discovered, grappled with and successfully resolved a problem. I read four pages in the last but one issue of *Research and Progress*, and listened to Madonna's 'Ray of Light' on the radio before I turned out the bedside lamp and fell asleep.

25

The next day the whole department was called to Karl's office. It was quite a squeeze, but Karl said it would work if we squashed up a bit. Håkan was wearing a black jacket and I felt at once that I was much happier with it. It had a decent, classic cut and looked relatively new. It made him fit in better with the rest of us, and made me feel calm.

Everyone was talking at the same time. Once the whole team had gathered Karl knocked on his desk.

'Okay, everyone. Right, Ann, there was something you wanted to discuss?'

'Yes,' Ann said, blushing. 'Not just me. I think I can speak for the whole department . . .'

She fell silent, as if she were waiting for some show of agreement from the others.

'Well?' Karl said, looking around at the others. It was clear that he found this situation uncomfortable. Never previously had we all had cause to gather inside his office. Something was obviously going on. He turned towards Ann again.

'Maybe you'd like to start, then?'

Ann cleared her throat, and it looked like she was standing on tiptoe as she talked. It made her look a bit like a schoolgirl.

Even though she was over fifty.

'I . . . We think this business is all getting a bit unpleasant, Björn,' she said, looking at me.

Everyone turned towards me.

'What's unpleasant?' I said.

'Shall we let Ann finish without interrupting?' Karl said, completely unnecessarily, because obviously I was going to let her finish. But all of a sudden it was as if his supposition that I had interrupted her were true. I could feel everyone's attention focus on me even more intently.

'Yes,' Ann went on. 'We're all getting worried. About you.'

'Why would you be getting worried?'

'Well, when you stand there like that.'

The room was silent for a long while. It was as if everyone had suddenly realised how absurd the situation was. They were looking at me; I realised that I was supposed to say something. I stood there without speaking for a few more seconds, trying to look as many of them as possible in the eye. Then I lowered my gaze and sighed.

'Didn't we deal with this yesterday?' I said, raising my head and looking from face to face. No one said anything.

'Didn't I tell you it was pointless trying to conduct psychological warfare against me? I don't fall for that sort of thing. No matter how well you synchronise your stories.'

Karl cleared his throat.

'What are you talking about, Björn?'

'I'm talking about systematic bullying,' I said in a fairly loud voice, so everyone could hear, while I pushed my way through towards Karl's desk.

'Bullying that has evidently been going on for several weeks.'

I twisted round so that the others could see me properly. I touched the collar of my jacket so that a little of the lining became visible. I thought it made a good impression.

'To start with, I've noticed that some people in here have adopted an unnecessarily harsh tone, and have demonstrated a rather unpleasant attitude towards me and not made any great effort to make me feel welcome. This is probably because you're unsettled by me. There's nothing strange about that, creative people have always encountered resistance. It's perfectly natural for more straightforward individuals to feel alarmed by someone of talent. I would imagine that this has its origins in the fact that one or more of you have observed that I have taken the liberty on two or three occasions to take myself aside and gather my strength alone. Having a short rest in that little room beside the lift. To some extent I can understand that this might strike some people as annoying. Obviously, we need to do our work and not take breaks whenever we feel like it, but I can assure you all that I have always taken care to make up for any concomitant loss of efficiency. And if it is the case that you have any secrets in there that for some reason you don't want me to see, you're welcome to tell me. Right here.'

'As I understand it,' Karl began, but now it was my turn to speak.

'You haven't understood anything,' I said. 'On the contrary, you've kept your distance. And in the meantime one or more individuals have taken it upon themselves to play some sort of psychological trick on me. Instead of coming straight out and having a normal discussion. A decision has been taken to test my limits.'

'Who—' Karl began.

'Everyone,' I interrupted. 'Who knows, maybe you yourself are involved somehow?'

'I don't think so,' Karl tried once more.

'Would you mind waiting with your analysis until all the facts are on the table?' I said, in a reasonably stern voice.

Karl fell silent again. It was obvious that he had nothing to offer in response. He stood there stiffly and listened as I went on.

'I have reason to believe that my – shall I say closest? – colleague, Håkan here . . .' I pointed at Håkan, who immediately looked down and began to scratch his sideburns. '. . . is one of the people behind this. At least he was the first person to raise it with me.'

I let the accusation sink in, then turned back to face Karl again. I fixed him with a steady gaze.

'I have no great expectation that you will be able to resolve this situation, Karl. But I presume you can't bury your head in the sand indefinitely, and that that's why you've called this meeting? It can't be any secret that you feel threatened by me, and would like to get rid of me, which is why I'm taking the liberty of uncovering this charade. This attempt to destroy me.'

There was absolute silence in Karl's office. Everyone was standing completely still. The only thing disturbing the silence was the rustling from my blue shoe-covers as I turned to inspect the stunned workforce.

'Try to see this as a learning experience,' I went on in a somewhat gentler tone. 'If we all go back to our respective duties and never mention this incident again, embarrassing as it is for everyone – if everyone can promise to be open and honest from now on, and never try to play similar tricks on me to unsettle me, then I am prepared to draw a line under the whole business. Simply because I am all too aware that intelligence and talent always upset people of more average abilities. For that reason alone, I am prepared to forgive you. Little people can't always be held accountable for the fact that they sometimes feel drawn to ruin and undermine their betters.'

There was total silence for something like twenty seconds. It was as if no one in the room had properly understood what had happened. I looked at Karl, who just stared back. This time he had met his match. After a while I realised that I was going to have to take charge.

'You can go now,' I said.

One by one they went back to their desks. A breathless procession of subdued employees dispersed around the department.

26

Karl ran his hand over his thinning hair. He had tiny beads of sweat on his brow. Almost imperceptible. He craned his neck and loosened his tie slightly. I sat down on the comfy armchair opposite him, although it was a little lower than the office-chair he was sitting on. Karl slumped down in his chair. He sat there in silence for a long time, massaging his temples with two fingers on each side. Eventually he sighed.

'How are you feeling, Björn?'

'Fine thanks,' I said.

He rolled his chair closer to his desk, leaned his elbows on it and rested his chin on his clasped hands.

'You appreciate that you simply can't behave like this?'

'How so?'

'This sort of performance. It's unacceptable.'

And then once more, as if he thought I hadn't heard him, or simply needed to repeat it to himself. 'Unacceptable.'

'The way I see it,' I said, crossing one leg over the other, 'they simply need a strong hand. This sort of collective bullying only arises when people feel lost and—'

'Björn, Björn.'

Karl raised one hand in the air. He leaned towards me.

'I'm in charge here. You do know that, don't you?'

'Yes,' I replied.

I nodded.

'Don't worry about personnel matters, Björn. I can deal with those.'

He leaned back in his chair again. Rubbed his chin with his hand and looked at me.

'Björn,' he said, 'you pulled down the Christmas decorations and damaged both the wall and ceiling.'

I nodded.

'That was careless of me.'

'And the fairy-lights themselves . . . well, they're evidently broken now.'

'I shall make good the damage,' I said. 'How much?'

'Well, the wall and ceiling will be all right. It's probably time for them to be redecorated anyway. But the Christmas lights were Jörgen's personal property.'

We sat and looked at each other for a long while without speaking. Finally he leaned forward.

'This . . . room,' he began.

'I'm glad you raised that,' I said.

He looked out at the open-plan office.

'Where do you say . . . ?'

'Right next to the lift, to the left of the recycling bin, next to the toilets.'

'In the corridor?'

'Correct.'

He sat in silence for a long time, and after a while I began to wonder if he had started to think about something else. In the end he spoke again.

'What sort of room is it?'

'As far I can tell, it's not being used, and hasn't been for some time. I haven't made a mess or touched anything. If anything shady is going on in there, I don't know anything about it. I've just gone there when . . .'

I paused for a moment, trying to find the right words, the correct way to describe what I did there. 'To recuperate' sounded feeble somehow, and besides, it was more like I was 'recharging my batteries'. I tried a different tack.

'The strange thing is that I've made some calculations. I've measured the surrounding area, and I can't quite make it fit . . .'

I wondered how much of this I ought to reveal to him. It was beyond question that I was the subject of a comprehensive and well-thought-out prank, and I didn't want to appear stupid. I tried laughing about it.

'Ha, this trick with the walls . . . I really can't work out how they've done it. In purely architectural terms. Well, it's certainly been very cleverly done . . . Very cleverly done.'

He looked at me, a whole series of lines on his forehead.

'What do you do there?' Karl asked.

'In the room?' I said.

He nodded.

'After first carrying out a visual check, I usually just . . . spend time there.'

'But,' Karl said, 'what exactly do you do?'

'Nothing,' I said. 'But I can appreciate if it upsets—'

Karl interrupted me again.

'Never mind about the others now, Björn. Why do you want to spend time there?'

'I. Well – how can I put it? – I take energy from it.'

He sat in silence for a while, just looking at me.

'Okay,' he suddenly said, leaning forward. 'Are you finding it difficult, working here for us?'

I looked at his perspiring temples and wondered who was finding it more difficult. Then I leaned back and said: 'Not particularly.'

'Is there anything you'd like to talk to me about?'

I wondered if I ought to raise the subject of correct linguistic usage, but somehow this didn't feel like the right moment. I decided to give a more sweeping answer that would be bound to arouse his curiosity and throw a spanner in the works.

'There's plenty to talk about with this department.'

'I see,' Karl said. 'Such as what?'

'Well, I don't want to mention anyone by name. But I can say that more than one person here at the Authority is a drug-user.'

'Drugs?'

'Oh, you didn't know?'

He sat for a moment just looking at me.

'Does that have anything to do with this room?'

'Not in the slightest,' I said.

'Mmm,' Karl muttered, then sighed again.

He stood up and went over to the window, and stood there with his back to me for a while. Drumming his fingers lightly on the glass. He turned round, sat back down and looked me in the eye. It was as if he was building himself up.

'There is no room, Björn.'

'Yes there is,' I said.

'No,' he said.

'Yes, just behind—'

'Listen to me carefully now, Björn. There is no room next to the lift. There has never been a room there. It's possible that you've convinced yourself that there is. Maybe it's there for you, I don't know how that sort of thing works.'

I raised a finger in the air and got him to shut up temporarily.

'If you're going to start—' I began, but he interrupted me immediately.

'That's enough!'

He stood up and came over to where I was sitting.

'Listen to me now, Björn,' he said, in a surprisingly stern voice. 'Whether or not there is a room there, I must ask you to stop going to it.'

He waited for a second or two, just looking at me. I realised that for the moment it would be best to keep quiet, but I could feel my whole body wanting to move. The situation was reminiscent of when you've spent a long time sitting in a seat on a plane and just want to stretch your legs. He carried on in a considerably calmer voice.

'You have to appreciate that it upsets the rest of the group when they see you standing like that, in your own little world. It's perfectly all right if you want to do it at home. But not at work. You're scaring the staff. Don't you think you should try

73

socialising with your colleagues a bit more? They say you hardly ever take a break.'

'I have my own rota,' I said.

'But it can be good to take a break every now and then.'

'That's when I go into the room.'

'But you can't go into the room any more. Okay?'

I looked out through the window, with its surprisingly dull view of a deserted inner courtyard. It was the same snowstorm that had been going on for I don't know how long. The sun hadn't shown its face for several weeks. I met his tired gaze.

'What you're telling me now . . .' I began, but suddenly felt my voice fail me.

I lost my flow and could hear that I sounded as if I were about to start crying. I cleared my throat and once again shifted position in the chair.

'You have to understand,' I said. 'The fact that you're saying there is no room is just as strange to me as if I were to say that that chair isn't there.'

I pointed at his office-chair.

'This chair is here,' he said.

'Good,' I said. 'At least we agree about that.'

He laughed lightly and put his hand on my shoulder.

'Since the time we agreed to have you working here, things have evidently changed dramatically. I still thought you might be able to cope with the relatively simple tasks you were given. Sorting, archiving, et cetera. We knew you were a complex character, but no one mentioned anything about you being delusional.'

He fell silent for a moment and looked out at the courtyard as well. Just like me.

'You'll just have to stop going to that "room". Otherwise we'll have to come up with a different solution for you. Do you understand me?'

He pointed at my feet.

'And can't you get hold of a pair of indoor shoes? With those silly plastic things it's like you're just asking to be bullied.'

I nodded slowly and looked through the glass at the people working out there. None of them seemed interested in our conversation. Not a glance from any of them. But they must all be aware of what was going on in here. Had they done all their talking about this – about me – already? What else had they agreed on? Karl sighed and went on.

'And I must also ask you to agree to see a psychiatrist.'

27

The clinic had turquoise curtains, and all the weekly magazines were aimed at a female clientele. I pointed this out to a nurse who just giggled and hurried on.

The little sofas in the waiting room were full of people with colds, and even though there was a space right on the end I chose to stand slightly off to one side. I rested my eyes on a pleasant picture of flowers and grasses by Lena Linderholm.

Twenty minutes after the allotted time a different nurse came out and called my name. She went with me down the corridor, knocked on a half-open door, showed me in and then disappeared.

I stepped into a sort of treatment room containing a brown vinyl padded couch with a big roll of paper at one end. In the middle of the floor was a little trolley with a stethoscope and instruments for measuring blood-pressure. There was a muddle of probes and test-tubes.

I couldn't see a chaise longue anywhere.

Sitting behind a computer was a fairly young man with one of those goatee beards that were popular for a while. He was wearing a pale-blue short-sleeved tunic with a name badge. *Dr Jan Hansson*, it said. He tapped on the keyboard and read something without taking any notice of me.

I waited politely for a good while, wondering if he was older or younger than me. I cleared my throat a couple of times, and was on the point of turning and walking out when he finally looked up.

'Well,' he said. Nothing more.

He clicked his mouse, got up from the chair and came over to me. We shook hands. His hand was wet and smelled of surgical spirit.

'Jan,' he said.

'Thanks, I noticed,' I said, pointing at the name badge.

He gestured towards a chair next to a sink. On either side of the basin were two pressure pumps with containers attached.

'Please, have a seat,' he said, sitting down on his own ergonomic office-chair.

'Thanks, I'm happy to stand,' I said.

He looked at me.

'Mmm, I'd prefer it if you sat down.'

I sighed and put my coat over the back of the chair. I sat down reluctantly, perching on the edge of the considerably more basic chair.

'Okay . . . er . . .'

He rolled over to the computer and looked at the screen.

'Björn,' he said. 'What can we do for you?'

'I thought I was going to see a psychiatrist,' I said.

'We'll start with me,' he said. 'Well?'

'I'd rather not say anything. I'd like you to make your own evaluation without any preconceptions.'

He glanced at a large clock on the wall.

'It's going to be very hard for me to help you if you don't say anything, Björn.'

'I'd like you to make your own evaluation.'

'I don't know you.'

'But you are a doctor?'

He nodded.

I thought for a moment, and then described objectively and in detail recent events in the office. About the room, and Karl, and the other staff. About ignorance, invisibility and the withholding of information. The doctor listened, but I noticed one of his legs starting to twitch after a couple of minutes. He interrupted me in the middle of a sentence.

'I don't understand what sort of medical—'

'If you'll let me finish, it might be clearer then,' I said.

He looked at me as if he were weighing up an opponent. And it amused me that for the first time since I entered the room he seemed a little dispirited. He was presumably used to harmless patients with no will of their own who just wanted medication, but here was something different for him. Someone made of sterner stuff. He leaned back, folded his arms and listened with a forced smile on his lips.

When I had finished he sat for a fair while just looking at me. On the wall behind him was an ugly picture of an apple, and another of a pear that was almost as bad.

'This room,' he said. 'What sort of room is it?'

'A normal room,' I said.

'What does it look like?'

'It's an office.'

'Where is it?'

'At work.'

'I mean, where at work?'

I thought for a while about whether it would be okay to tell him about the ingenious architectural solution, because he must have some sort of duty of confidentiality, but I decided not to trust the goatee beard entirely and instead chose a middle way.

'It's between the toilets and the lift,' I said.

'And you go in there?' he said.

'Yes, but they say I mustn't.'

'Mmm,' he said, feeling for a pen in his top pocket.

'What do you do there?' he said.

'I rest.'

'You rest?'

'Yes.'

He got the pen out and clicked it, making the point pop in and out. Back and forth.

'And you want to go on sick leave?'

'No.'

'Oh. So what do you want?'

'I don't want anything. The company sent me here.'

'Don't you work for an Authority?'

'I prefer to see it as a company. It makes my abilities sharper.'

'Really?'

'Yes.'

He looked at the computer and I wondered if he was really looking at anything or just trying to buy himself some time. I decided to try to answer his questions quickly, in order to throw the ball back into his court as soon as possible, so to speak. Clearly he was clutching at straws. Presumably he lacked the skill demanded for matters of this sort.

'Have you mentioned this to your colleagues?'

'My boss was the one who made me come here.'

'Why?'

'He said I had to see you.'

'Me?'

'Someone. He said I had to come here.'

He nodded and spoke slowly, as if he were trying to slow the tempo. But I wasn't about to let myself be sunk.

'So that you could go on sick leave?'

'I don't want to go on sick leave.'

'Because you went into that room?'

'Exactly.'

'Why?'

'He says it doesn't exist.'

'What?'

'The room.'

'Your boss says the room doesn't exist?'

I was very pleased that I managed to say 'Yes' before he'd even finished his sentence, which I felt reinforced the impression that I was one step ahead of him. He nodded slowly.

'So does it?' he said after a pause.

'It does to me.'

'Does it for anyone else?'

'They pretend it doesn't.'

80

'Has anyone else been inside the room?'

'I don't know. They don't seem keen to go in.'

'Why don't they want to go in?'

'I don't know. They say it doesn't exist.'

'But you know that it exists.'

'It exists.'

'And it's an office?'

'Yes.'

'A perfectly ordinary office?'

'Yes.'

He fell silent for a while, clicking his pen.

'Is there anything else in there?'

'Anything else?'

'Yes. Are there things in there?'

'Of course there are things.'

'What sort of things?'

'Do you want me to . . . ?'

'Yes, please.'

'Well, there's a desk . . .'

'Yes?'

'And a lamp. Computer, folders, a filing cabinet, and so on.'

'Yes?'

'Pens, paper, a hole-punch, a stapler, Tippex, tape, cables, a calculator, a desk mat, all sorts of things.'

'Yes?'

'Yes.'

A nurse knocked on the door.

'Are you nearly finished?' she whispered.

I wondered what it was we were supposed to be finished with, but the doctor just nodded at her, looked at the large clock on the wall and went on.

'Have you ever had any psychiatric treatment in the past?'

'Of course not,' I said.

'Any counselling when you were in your teens?'

'Hardly.'

'You're not on any medication?'

I shook my head.

'What about alcohol?'

'What do you think?'

'I'm asking you. Drugs?'

'No more than you,' I said.

He shut his eyes and blew the air out of his mouth. He rubbed his eyes with one hand, and I carried on looking at him so that I could look him in the eye as soon as he decided to open them again.

'Do you feel unwell in any way?' he went on, still rubbing his eyes.

'Do you?' I said.

He shook his head and sighed.

'I honestly don't know what to do with you,' he said after a brief pause.

'That doesn't surprise me,' I said.

'You don't have to be unpleasant,' he said.

'Nor do you,' I said, as quickly as I could.

We looked at each other for a while. I was fairly pleased with the way this was going. I could tell he felt a degree of respect for me. You could see in his eyes that he wasn't used to getting this sort of response.

'Why are you here?' he said.

'Because I was sent.'

'Okay, you know what? I think you should contact us again if you feel worse. It's difficult for me to do anything about any other problems you may have at work.'

He got up and went back to the computer.

'I was told I'd be seeing a psychiatrist,' I said.

He shook his head gently.

'I don't know what grounds I could refer you on . . .'

'No, of course not,' I said as I stood up and took my flattened coat from the back of the chair. 'Maybe you could talk to someone who does know?'

'Do you know what I think?' he said, in a completely different voice, almost a whisper.

'No,' I said, suddenly noticing the loud ticking sound that the big clock on the wall was making.

'If you'd like my own personal opinion,' he said, 'I'd have to say . . .'

'Yes, what would you say?'

He looked at me for a brief moment.

'I'd say that you're putting it on.'

28

Inside the room there was a calm, a concentration that felt like early mornings at school. It contained the same relaxed feeling and limited freedom. Each line seemed perfectly connected to the next. Everything messy and unsettling vanished. Precision returned.

I ran my finger over the desktop and felt the utterly straight line that was held at precisely the same plane by the flawlessly sanded and varnished veneer chipboard, which in turn rested upon the perfect frame: spray-painted legs made of metal tubing. I was sure that a spirit-level would prove the evenness of this generously proportioned work-surface.

Beneath the desktop, inside the legs on one side, was a varnished drawer unit on wheels with a cedar-wood frame. It was fronted by a matt wooden shutter that folded smoothly back along its rails as I put my palm on the front and slowly moved it upwards.

The whole room breathed tradition. There was an air of old-fashioned quality to it. Is this what monks feel like as they walk the corridors of their monasteries?

On the desk was a low-energy lamp, 20 watts, attached to a clock of shiny, stainless steel. The armature of the lamp was adjustable. One setting for the strength of light. A firm base on the desktop.

By the side of the desk I discovered a lever that could be loosened so you could adjust the exact angle of the desktop. You could tilt the whole top to get the exact angle that you preferred. I adjusted it slightly to suit me, tilting it fractionally forward, downward. And felt how my other arm, which I had left idle, ended up in a perfectly relaxed position in which each part of the arm was firmly supported. Perfectly in tune with the furniture.

As I was sitting there my mobile rang. I picked it up and answered it, and the sweetest music streamed out of it, into my ears.

29

The next morning we were summoned to another meeting in Karl's cramped office.

Karl tried to say something funny about small spaces, concluding with 'tight passageways'. No one laughed. I took this as further evidence of his incompetence as a manager. Naturally, he ought to have chosen a more neutral topic for humour, there are plenty of innocent jokes about animals or ketchup bottles that didn't necessarily have any association to the conflict in which we found ourselves, and which could function more generally as a means of raising morale. If he felt he had to make a joke. Because this really wasn't amusing.

Håkan had sat down on the desk with Ann beside him. He was wearing his black jacket, and I definitely preferred it to the corduroy one, but I tried not to look at them. Jörgen and John were squashed up against the wall, and I couldn't help noticing that Jörgen kept nudging one of the big pictures, knocking it askew.

'I think this is very unfortunate,' Ann said before Karl had even started. 'Is he really going to stay? I mean, we said—'

Karl stopped her. He went behind his desk, and spoke in a loud, clear voice.

'Björn and I have had a little talk. Björn has been to see a psychiatrist. Together we have agreed to get rid of . . .' He held his fingers up in the air on either side of his head to indicate quotation marks. '. . . "the room" for the time being. Björn has promised . . .' He turned to me. '. . . not to go there any more. Isn't that right, Björn?'

I assumed I didn't need to nod. After all, everyone understood that I was party to this anyway. But Karl insisted.

'Isn't that right, Björn?'

I nodded. Karl went on.

'I think it's very useful for us to realise that we aren't all the same, and that some people see things in a − how can I put it? − slightly different way. But we're all adults, and we should be able to get along regardless. Shouldn't we?'

He looked around, but found no sign of agreement. In the end he turned to me.

'To emphasise the fact that this is a fresh start for you, Björn, I've taken the liberty of purchasing, at the expense of the Authority . . .' He took out a bag containing a box and put it on the desk. He pulled out the box, opened the lid and held up a pair of imitation-leather indoor shoes. '. . . a small gift.'

He handed them to me. I accepted them reluctantly.

'There you go,' he said. 'Now, I hope we can concentrate on our work from now on.'

There followed five seconds of total silence. Then everyone started to talk at once.

'You mean he's going to stay?'

'Can't you see he's not right in the head?'

'What the hell is he doing here?'

'It's a health and safety issue.'

'If he's allowed to carry on like that, I should be allowed to . . .'

'He's getting favourable treatment . . .'

'But he's mad.'

'Really we ought to feel sorry for him.'

Hasse from accounts shook his head slowly.

'Now that things are so tough here at the Authority, with the threat of closure hanging over our heads constantly . . . I mean, we really need to be functioning at full capacity. We haven't got time to be running some sort of day-centre, have we?'

He looked round at the others. A number of them nodded. People starting talking all at once again. Karl managed to calm the mood temporarily, and Hannah with the ponytail tilted her head to one side as the prelude to a long-winded comment.

'It seems to me that management's way of dealing with problems of this nature indicates a certain degree of weakness.'

Karl pinched the bridge of his nose with his fingers. Everyone seemed to be getting involved in the discussion, but none of them looked directly at me.

'He's a nutter, you have to admit that!' said a young man whose name I thought was Robert. He was about twenty and quiet as a mouse normally, I'd never heard him say a word before this. But evidently he felt he had to speak up now.

'According to the medical—' Karl began.

'But he's mad!' Jörgen said. 'Anyone can see that. Surely we can't have a moron who goes and stares at the wall the minute things get busy?'

A few people laughed. Which only served to spur Jörgen on.

'I mean, he needs treatment for that.'

Hannah with the ponytail raised her voice.

'Although I do think we should all be allowed to do what we like during our breaks.'

'I'm not so sure,' Jörgen said, to even more laughter. 'I say: fire him.'

It was as if they all felt like laughing and were prepared to grab any opportunity. Even though it really wasn't funny. Karl waved him off.

'We can't dismiss someone simply because they are . . .'

'But we're talking about someone who's mentally ill,' Jörgen said.

'I'd like to point out,' Karl went on, 'that Björn has been carrying out his duties faultlessly.'

Hasse spoke up again.

'Obviously he can do whatever he likes, but he keeps dragging the rest of us over there as well.'

'Exactly!' Robert exclaimed. 'Like that time he wanted the whole lot of us to go and stand there.'

He looked round at the others, who nodded. Ann turned to address Karl with the whole of her feminine authority.

'I think it's creepy, seeing him stand there like that. He's so . . . It's like he's just not there.'

As usual, several people decided to voice their agreement,

and once again there was a hubbub of voices all wanting to have their say. Karl raised his voice to drown out the muttering.

'Hello. Hello. Hello!' he called, waving his arms in the air.

One by one they fell silent. Karl turned to me.

'What do you say, Björn?'

I took my time, seeing as I knew what he wanted me to say, but I decided to stick to the facts, unlike the rest of them.

'They say there's nothing wrong with me and that I'm perfectly capable of carrying on working.'

Several of them looked at me as if they'd only just noticed that I was still there. Hannah with the ponytail and Ann whispered something between them. Several of the others muttered among themselves, like they were still at school.

'Well, surely we can agree . . .' Karl began. 'I mean, why don't we say that it's okay as long as Björn doesn't go into the room?'

There was a long silence. Then Jörgen stepped forward. The picture rocked behind him.

'Okay, let's agree on this,' he said, fixing his gaze on Karl. 'If I see him standing like that once more. Then he's finished. Just saying.'

Karl nodded with exaggerated clarity to show that he was really listening. Then he turned to me.

'Do you think you can manage that, Björn?'

I felt a knot in my stomach. But I still opened my mouth and replied.

'Yes.'

'Good,' Karl said. 'So we're all in agreement, then?'

One by one they drifted away.

30

Late that afternoon the sun peeped out for a couple of minutes. Everyone in the department turned their faces towards the windows, but soon it was gone and shortly afterwards it started to snow again.

I kept to my desk and wondered if I ought simply to skip my five-minute breaks and carry on working. Maybe it would be best to shut out everything else in the office and concentrate one hundred per cent on work? Maybe Karl and I could come to some arrangement where we calculated how much time I saved by not taking breaks, not chatting to my colleagues, not making private phone calls or running to the toilet every five minutes, like some of the older women did, and reduce the time I spent at work by the same amount?

I took a deep breath and sighed. Getting authorisation for something like that seemed unlikely under management that was so hostile to positive developments.

I pulled open the bottom drawer of my desk and put the indoor shoes inside.

I passed the room twice that day. Once on my way to the toilet, and once when I tidied my desk and went to put two old journals in the recycling bin. I tried not to think about it. I did my best to imitate the others and pretend the room didn't exist. It felt utterly ridiculous. Of course there's a room there, I thought. After all, I can see it. I can touch it. I can feel it. I went round the little corridor once more, as if to check that the door hadn't suddenly disappeared and I'd been imagining it all. But the door was still there. It was firmly fixed in the wall. No question. Solid. As clear as day. It almost made me laugh. I nudged it with my elbow as I walked past it the second time. I heard the sound as the fabric of my jacket touched it. And when all the others were off at lunch, I couldn't see any reason not to go in there for a short while, the tenth time.

31

After lunch we were all called to yet another meeting in Karl's office. I didn't understand how it could have happened, but I assumed someone must have seen me sneak into the room even though I had taken all reasonable precautions. I prepared myself for the worst.

'Well?' Karl said, when everyone had squeezed into his office.

His gaze swept round the room and settled on Jens. I made an effort to look as relaxed as possible.

'Well . . .' Jens said from over in the corner. 'I'd just like to know . . . how much those shoes cost?'

'The shoes?' Karl said, stretching to his full height.

Jens nodded, with a self-important expression on his face.

'I mean, they weren't free, were they?'

'No,' Karl said, picking up a pen, which he drummed idly against the edge of the desk. 'I took the liberty of—'

Jens didn't let Karl finish his sentence.

'So how daft do you have to behave to get a pair like that?' he went on, to scattered laughter.

Karl gave a strained smile, holding the pen in the air.

'Let's just say that I have a certain amount in the budget for pastoral investment in personnel matters . . .'

'That's still not fair,' Ann said.

'No,' Jörgen said.

'This seems to me to be all too typical,' Hannah with the ponytail said, folding her arms over her chest. 'We didn't get any contribution to the Christmas party. But apparently there's money available now.'

'Now listen,' Karl said, leaning back in his chair with the pen under his chin. 'That's not the same thing.'

'So he can turn up and get given stuff just because he acts a bit crazy?' Jörgen said.

Hannah with the ponytail held her arms out.

'It seems to me that it's very unclear what the applicable rules actually are.'

Several people nodded.

'The question is,' Ann said, 'what sort of signals are we sending out?'

When we went back to our places John appeared alongside me. He put his hand on my arm and hissed in my ear: 'I saw what you did at lunchtime.'

I raised my eyebrows and did my best to look uncomprehending.

'Don't act all innocent,' he went on. 'I saw you. If I see you again, I'll tell. Just so you know.'

32

The snow carried on falling, and I carried on working. I tried to stick to my fifty-five-minute periods. I even tried smiling. Every time anyone happened to look in my direction I fired off a broad smile, but the whole time I could feel how suspicious everyone else was of me, trying to pretend I wasn't there. Karl came over to our desk. First he chatted to Håkan, then he turned to me. As if everything was normal.

'And how are things with you, then, Björn?'

'What sort of things?' I asked in a neutral voice.

'Well,' Karl said, and I could hear how unsettled he was. 'What have you spent the last few days doing?'

Naturally he didn't want an answer. He was asking in that pointless way that people do when they ask how you are. They don't want to hear about your health. They just want to hear their own voice, and say things they've said before. They want to make a noise in a social context.

'Why do you want to know?' I said.

'Because I'm your boss,' he said.

I looked him in the eye and had a distinct sense of being the stronger person.

'I've initiated a process for developing a set of guiding

principles for the department, identified so-called focus areas, specific targets in various sectors, and gathered a number of criteria. I have chosen to call one of my focus areas "operations in the centre".'

I clicked to open the document and pointed at the screen.

'I plan to use this to measure the benefit we deliver to customers. To that purpose I have drawn up a questionnaire intended to find out what you customers think about my services.'

He looked at me.

'Us customers?'

'I usually think of you as customers.'

'What for?'

I allowed myself a gentle sigh.

'Are you really asking me that?'

Karl looked away for a moment and gazed out across the open-plan office. He put his hands on his hips and clenched his jaw. Then he looked at me again.

'Yes, I'm really asking you that,' he said.

'I think you maximise your potential better if you imagine a customer at the other end.'

I could tell he was impressed even if he was unable to grasp the full extent of the idea and absorb it there and then. I pointed at the screen again.

'So I'd be grateful if you could take the time to fill in this customer questionnaire, which you'll find by clicking this link. The survey contains five questions dealing with the quality of our services, and one question asking if you think any other service should be provided. The questions are divided according to the various entities within the Department. Home number. Mobile number. Private mobile number, if applicable, although of course that's voluntary, but I'd be grateful if you could fill in the questionnaire as fully as possible.'

I fell silent and looked at the others. They were all looking at me now. Håkan was wearing the blue corduroy jacket. It looked streaked somehow. Stained? Karl had a terribly deep wrinkle above his nose, right between his eyes.

'But Björn,' he said, 'I asked you to compile a list of phone numbers, didn't I?'

All my energy slowly drained away. I suddenly had difficulty concentrating. I felt a chill run down my spine and a stiffness spread across my neck and shoulders. Karl disappeared off towards his glass office. Slowly but surely the others went back to work. Finally even Håkan turned away, his scruffy corduroy jacket reflecting his movements like an extra layer of skin.

33

If it's never happened to you before, it's easy to let yourself be taken in by new acquaintances. You get the impression that they're better than your old ones. You ascribe to them all manner of noble qualities, simply because you don't know them properly.

They might be nice and pleasant the first time, and the second and third. In rare instances also the fourth and fifth. But you will almost always end up disappointed.

Sooner or later you reach a certain point. An occasion when their true self breaks through.

One way of dealing with that sort of thing is simply to assume the worst of people.

Karl, for instance, probably imagines that he means well. He convinces himself that his feeble efforts to help his staff are for the good of all. What he doesn't recognise, or chooses not to recognise, is his own desire to be seen as a hero: the one who solves the problem and garners the plaudits.

Or Margareta in reception. The appealing exterior, the pleasant demeanour, but before you can say the word 'unblemished' she reveals herself to be a junkie.

More people ought to learn to see their worst sides. Everyone has a bad side. As the poem goes: 'What is base in you is also base in them.'

On the other hand, it's good to realise that we aren't as remarkable as we might imagine. We want to earn a lot, eat well and generally have a nice time. Listen to the radio sometimes or watch something on television. Read a book or a journal. We want to have good weather and be able to buy cheap food close to home.

In these terms we are all relatively simple creatures. We dream of finding a more or less pleasant partner, a summer cottage or a time-share on the Costa del Sol. Deep down we just want peace and quiet. A decent dose of easily digested entertainment every now and then.

Anything more is just vain posturing.

34

After three days without the room I started to feel unsettled deep down in my gut. I became irritable and noticed I was sweating more than usual. The most acute abstinence anxiety was starting to subside but it was as if the habit was still in my body. I constantly had to stop myself when I realised my body was on its way there of its own accord. Like a former smoker fumbling for a packet of cigarettes. I tried to think about something else, and every time I felt the urge I tried counting to twenty.

I didn't go in. I'm sure of that. I sat there clinging to my desk, thinking that as long as I sat there I was fine.

That night I stood at the window fantasising about the room. Remembering details. The mirror, the filing cabinet. The little fan on the desk. I tried to recreate something of the atmosphere in there. But it just felt odd.

35

The next morning I woke up thinking about the room. I ate my two crispbreads with unsmoked caviar thinking about the room. I walked to work thinking about the room. I was thinking about the room as I passed Margareta in reception, who hadn't looked at me for several weeks now and thus hadn't given me an appropriate opportunity to show that I was keeping my distance. I went up in the lift, got out, and was almost at the door. Very close. I crept towards the forbidden place like a child on Christmas morning. Stopped right next to it. Just stood there, feeling what it felt like to be so close. A bit further down were the three toilets. And beyond them the large recycling bin. There was some writing on it: *Not for cardboard or packaging*.

Then I caught sight of Ann at the other end of the corridor. I don't know how she got there but suddenly there she was. Our eyes met and I realised what she was thinking. I shook my head slowly, thinking, No, it's not what you think.

'He was there again,' she said a short while later when we were both standing in Karl's office.

'I wasn't,' I said.

'I saw you.'

'No.'

'I saw you. You were standing like that again.'

'No. I was just standing.'

'That's what I'm saying.'

'Surely people are allowed to stand still? No one can stop you just standing for a moment?'

'You were standing on that spot again,' Ann said. 'You were talking to yourself.'

'I was reading. I didn't go inside.'

'What were you reading?'

'*Not for cardboard or packaging*.'

'Sorry?' Karl said.

'I didn't go inside,' I said.

Karl tried to calm us both down by putting a hand on each of our shoulders. Ann pulled away. She went and stood by the large window facing the office, with her back to us.

'I think it's very unsettling. How's anyone supposed to know if he's there or not? This way we can never be sure.'

36

Word spread from Ann like a group email. During the day practically everyone had passed her desk, and before they walked on they managed to glance in my direction several times. I could see them whispering and pulling faces.

Some of them talked and pointed at me without any attempt to disguise the fact. A few didn't care if I heard them discussing and diagnosing me. No one replied when I tried to say anything. No one spoke to me at all, apart from Jörgen, who pressed me up against the wall without any warning that afternoon. He held me fairly hard with both hands on my shoulders. His face contorted, his mouth hissing, 'You're a freak, you know that?'

I went home slightly early that day because I was unsure of Jörgen's mental state and I was afraid of physical violence. I once got punched in the stomach at primary school, which made me sick and I had to go and see the nurse. The memory brought with it a series of unpleasant associations.

I packed my things in my briefcase and passed reception and Margareta who pretended not to see me again. On the way home I felt I was being watched by a whole load of people. I thought everyone was looking at me. I had to stand at the front of the aisle in the bus because all the seats were taken, so anyone who felt like it could stare at me as much as they wanted. A small child with a dummy in its mouth stared me right in the eyes for ages. In the end I couldn't help saying: 'Do we know each other?'

I got no answer. The little girl just went on sucking the dummy. Her mother gave me a disapproving stare.

When I got home I leaned my briefcase against the wall. I tried lying down on the bed but I could feel how tense I was. And scared. It was an unfamiliar feeling, and it upset me. I felt pressure around my ankles and kicked my shoes off onto the floor. The seams of my socks had left marks on my skin.

I got up and turned on the television. I started watching a film with Harrison Ford fighting Russian terrorists. At the end of the film they were fighting by the open loading-ramp of a plane while it was in the air, which isn't remotely realistic. So I switched it off and went out into the kitchen instead.

On the radio an actor was reading a novella he'd written himself. The story included a number, sixty-nine. The actor was claiming that it became ninety-six if you turned it round, which is obviously a total lie, and I suddenly felt how lonely it is, constantly finding yourself the only person who can see the truth in this gullible world.

I turned off the radio and went and stood by the window, looking out. The snow had turned to rain and for a moment I thought it might have leaked into the flat when I felt the first traces of wetness on my cheeks.

37

I hadn't cried since junior school, and I didn't like it. It was wet and messy. Crying is for weak people. Crying is a sign of not wanting to pull yourself together, and a way for people of low intelligence to get attention. Crying belongs to small children and onions.

But there was something different about this bout of crying. It was calm, factual crying. Good crying. Water cleansing the tubes, rather like clearing a gutter of leaves and pine-needles. A way to get rid of negative energy and make room for something better. It was as if I could feel all the improper thoughts flying away, and new ones taking their place. Better ones. A fresh start.

A new me.

For the first time I realised how oddly I had been behaving. My behaviour belonged in the madhouse. And that was where I would end up if I didn't pull myself together.

Thinking about all the stupid things I had done and what they had led to gave me a headache. Going through the various events of the past weeks made me feel distinctly uncomfortable, as I realised how mistaken my behaviour had been in a whole series of different situations. I was forced to recognise my limitations, and it pained me.

Still, it was nice being able to think clearly for the first time in ages. And I realised that you have to live and learn.

Whatever doesn't kill you makes you stronger.

Afterwards it felt good to have cried. As if I had once again got the better of myself and clambered another rung higher on the ladder of my personal development. How high can I get? If I carry on like this, who could possibly stop me?

I could easily have cried a while longer. Obviously I didn't. I sat down at the kitchen table and thought through how to enact my return.

38

Karl looked up at me as if he'd seen a ghost in fake-leather shoes when I went into his office and stood in front of his desk with the new indoor shoes on.

'Why are you late?' he asked.

'I overslept,' I said.

Karl raised an eyebrow.

'I'm very sorry,' I went on. 'I had trouble getting to sleep last night. I lay there thinking. Thinking about recent events. The things I've said and done, and so on. I suddenly seem to get ideas in my head, you see. So I'm lying there thinking about all that. As long as I get enough sleep, I can see it's all nonsense. These past few weeks . . . Then this morning . . . Well, I just had to sort my head out a bit. I've had a lot of new things to try to take in recently.'

Karl nodded warily. I took a deep breath and went on.

'I can see that I've been behaving oddly, and I'd like to do what I can to put right any problems I may have caused.'

Karl put his pen down on his desk and leaned back in his comfortable office-chair.

'Björn, Björn, Björn,' he said, as if he were talking to a small child.

'And I understand that my actions have caused problems, not just for me but for you too, and I'd like to ask for your forgiveness. It was never my intention to cause trouble and bad feeling. I promise that from now on there won't be any more of that nonsense.'

'Sit down, Björn,' Karl said, rolling round to the front of his desk.

I sat down on the uncomfortable little chair. Karl looked at me and I thought I could detect a crooked smile.

'You're an unusual person, Björn. I'm glad you've taken the time to think this through. Maybe it was worth a late start?'

'Obviously, I'll make up the time I've lost . . .' I began, but Karl gestured dismissively with his hand.

'Don't worry about that, Björn. If we can get you sorted out, then this little break will have been entirely justified.'

He looked at my new indoor shoes and lit up. It was obvious that he liked what he saw.

'They're really nice,' I said.

'Aren't they?' Karl said with a smile.

'Yes, that's what I just said,' I said.

He cleared his throat and turned serious again.

'So are we agreed on the rules now, Björn?'

'Yes,' I said.

He leaned towards me.

'And can we forget all about that room now?'

'Of course,' I said.

He looked at me and I realised that I ought to nod. I nodded.

'Good,' he said, and rolled back to the other side of the

desk. 'Good, Björn. No one will be happier than me if we can find a solution to this.'

'I'm pleased,' I said.

'Yes,' Karl said, and smiled again.

39

On my way to my workstation I tried to find someone to say hello to, but no one looked at me. Håkan was leafing through some papers and humming to himself. I sat down at my desk and switched the computer on.

Half an hour later I handed in a printout of the updated list of phone numbers. Karl raised his head and brightened up.

'Excellent,' he said.

He scratched his head and looked around, as if he were thinking. I stood in the doorway and waited. Most of the staff in the department had gone home for the day. I thought I might as well stay a bit longer.

'Do you know what?' he said after a few moments. 'Tomorrow, could you put together a list of which projects have been quality assured and which ones haven't? It would be good to have it on paper.'

I nodded.

'You'll be able to tell from where they've come if they've been checked or not.'

'Of course,' I said.

I returned to my place and sat down just as Håkan got up,

put some documents in his bag, slung it over his corduroy jacket and disappeared without a word to me.

I logged in and got to work at once.

An hour or so later I decided to call it a day and go home too. I was almost on my own in the office. I turned the lamp off, gathered my coat and briefcase, went out to the lift and went straight down to reception. Without passing the room.

40

I slept relatively well that night. I slept the sleep that only someone who has been down at the bottom but is now on his way back up can sleep. The sleep of someone who recognises that an inferior position is a good position to attack from. The sleep of someone with a plan.

41

You don't turn a river by abruptly trying to get it to change direction. You don't have that much power. No matter how strong you are. The river will just overwhelm you and obstinately carry on pretty much as before. You can't make it change direction overnight. No one can. On the contrary, you have to start by flowing with it.

You have to capture its own force and then slowly but surely lead it in the desired direction. The river won't notice it's being led if the curve is gentle enough. On the contrary, it will think it's flowing just the same as usual, seeing as nothing seems to have changed.

42

Uneventful days. Days without any particular character. Days which at first glance didn't appear to have led to much. Days that no one pays any attention to. Every day there came more and more documents from the investigators on the sixth and seventh floors, all of them waiting to be turned into framework decisions.

Håkan was becoming more and more anxious about the workload. He started making excuses. Moaning about the quality of the investigations. Their layout, content, incoherent argumentation.

So you're the only one who's perfect? I thought. How ironic.

Håkan and Karl had endless heated discussions that always ended with talk about the possibility of the entire Authority being closed down.

The threat of closure hung like an evil spirit over the whole department. Probably the whole Authority. I assumed this was the government's way of keeping us on our toes and not letting anyone think they were safe. But Håkan was irritated at the investigators and the work they did most of the time. He waved documents at Karl when he walked past.

'How am I supposed to formulate a clear, easily understood text from this rubbish? Do they even know what decision they've come to themselves?'

* * *

I went in to see Karl with money for the indoor shoes. At first he didn't want to take it, but I insisted, and explained that I would have bought a pair exactly like them if I'd got them myself. After a while he relented. Took the money and put it in his own pocket. I didn't say anything.

43

Later that day Karl came over to see Håkan and I heard them discussing the formulation of a new decision. I took care not to look up from my work as I listened to them talking.

Håkan was groaning and constantly scratching his sideburns, and said he couldn't produce a clearer text from that material, and that it was impossible to work any faster, particularly at the moment when there wasn't exactly a calm atmosphere conducive to work.

Without looking at them I could tell that this last remark was aimed at me, and I thought I could feel them both glancing in my direction. I pretended not to notice.

Soon I had finished my task. Sorting out the quality-assured projects was really just a matter of checking the signatures at the end of each file. One investigator meant no. Two or more control declarations with different save-dates meant yes.

I was done just before lunch and another printout was delivered to Karl's office. Karl thanked me and smiled, but I could see how tired he was.

'What shall I do now?' I asked.

Karl looked at me as if he had no idea what I was talking about. He stared blindly through the window facing the office.

'Well . . .' he muttered, sighing through his nose.

'Perhaps there's some text that . . . ?'

Karl looked at me.

'What are you thinking?'

'No, I was just wondering if I could help . . .'

'No thanks, Björn. I don't think so. It'll be fine. But you could . . .' He looked round the room. '. . . check all the printers . . . make sure they've all got enough paper and so on.'

We looked at one another, both of us aware of the menial task he was asking a civil servant to do, and I realised that my humiliation had to be dragged right down to the very bottom. I didn't mind. I was prepared. I nodded and went out to find some photocopy paper.

All the printers in the department ended up as full of paper as they possibly could be without the paper-feed jamming, or the thin plastic holding it being so overburdened that it broke.

When I saw several of the others having a coffee-break I went over to the little kitchen as well and got myself a cup.

A peculiar silence spread round the small room. They all drank their coffee, but the easy banter was missing. I tried to avoid making eye-contact with Jörgen, who still looked likely to have an outburst at any moment. All you could hear was the sound of my spoon stirring the cup.

44

When I returned to my place I saw that the inevitable had now happened. Håkan's papers had finally overflowed onto my desk.

Håkan's chair was empty but his desk was covered with files and documents, all waiting to be formulated into new framework decisions. Several piles of printouts were positioned so that they were almost nudging the back of my computer screen.

I felt a pang of my old intolerance. A gust of my old self who had been far too excitable, too guileless in purely tactical terms.

I sat down at my desk and put my hands against all his things. Then I simply pushed them back until everything was just inside the edge of his desktop. I heard one or two things fall to the floor on the other side of the desk.

When Håkan came back with a large pile of papers in his arms he didn't even bother trying to make room among the mess on his desk, but impudently parked it all on my side. He leaned down and picked up the papers that had ended up on the floor. He didn't even seem to wonder how they had got there.

Soon he disappeared again.

My initial impulse was of course to repeat my earlier procedure and this time push everything a bit further to make him realise what he was doing. But then my eyes were caught by one of the printouts. *Investigation. Case 1,636*, it said. I realised that this was an opportunity. Without even asking for it, I had been given a helping hand. An almost meditative calm spread through me.

I looked around. I took hold of the pile of papers with both hands and put what had been left on my desk in my drawer.

45

Håkan spent a large part of the afternoon trying in vain to find the missing investigations. Even if he didn't say anything, I knew that was what he was doing. He picked up books and files, looked underneath things, muttering to himself and occasionally swearing quietly.

I watched him go in to see Karl, gesticulating with his arms. Karl looked sweatier than ever. At some point Håkan gestured in my direction, but Karl merely shook his head.

I took care to participate in all the group coffee-breaks and idle conversations. No one spoke to me or even looked at me, but I was there. I was taking part. I was a physical presence among them.

To start with I noticed that everything would stop as soon as I came along. I would stand beside the others and pretend I hadn't noticed. In the end I came to assume the role of passive participant, the person no one bothers about, but whose presence is a precondition for the general character of social interaction.

By five o'clock most of the others had left, but I stayed behind as usual. I did an extra circuit of all the printers and checked that they were all full, mostly to make sure that the others had all gone home.

Then I went back to my desk. I opened the drawer and took out the top bundle of papers. *Investigation. Case 1,636.*

I put it in my briefcase, put my coat on to leave, checked once more that there was no one left, crept round to the corridor with the toilets, turned the light on and slipped inside the room for the eleventh time.

46

The fluorescent light flickered and clicked inside the room like a hot tin roof in the summer. It was quiet and cool. The desktop fan with its rotating blades inside a stainless-steel mesh lent the room an almost foreign feeling. It wasn't new, but had been extremely well maintained. Classy. Un-Swedish.

It was easy to think of bygone times in the room. A whole series of eminent decision-takers behind the perfect desk.

It felt indescribably good to be back inside this small space again. I stood there for a long time just enjoying it. Resting one hand gently on the desk.

The desktop felt completely smooth under my fingertips. You could probably rest your cheek on it if you felt like it. I didn't. I pulled out the comfortable office-chair, sat down, my back straight, and read through the entire bundle of papers.

It was surprisingly simple. Words and formulations that would otherwise take a long time to grasp flowed into my consciousness in a perfectly natural way. I understood at once.

Most of it seemed obvious. As if someone had asked me to fill in the right answers in a third-year maths book.

I looked up at the ceiling and tried to memorise a few keywords. As I was resting my eyes on the red painting with its plain motif I formulated a couple of simple phrases in my head. I realised at once that they worked well. Simple and clear.

I leafed back and forth through the material. It was clumsily expressed. I had to agree with Håkan on that. Some sections were completely unfocused, but could clearly be formulated the way I had just tried out. It was as if I had cleaned the document in order to reveal its pure lines.

Now that I knew how it ought to be expressed, it struck me as odd that no one had thought of it before. Had I missed something? Was there something I didn't understand? Or was it really this simple?

47

'Excellent!' Karl exclaimed as he came over and slapped Håkan on the back with the palm of his hand the following day.

Håkan turned round, looked at Karl and raised his eyebrows lazily.

'What?'

Karl smacked 1,636 down on the desktop. Håkan leaned over and read.

'This is exactly what I meant,' Karl said. 'This is brilliant, Håkan. Bloody hell, it's genius! Factual and concise. No room for misunderstanding.'

It was clear that he was in an extremely good mood. His whole face was beaming. Håkan turned to Karl.

'That isn't mine,' he said bluntly.

Karl's joy was interrupted and he frowned. He picked up the document and pulled his glasses down, perched them on his nose and looked at the number: 1,636.

'What?'

'This isn't mine.'

'Of course it's yours. I gave it to you.'

'Okay,' Håkan said, 'but I didn't write that.'

Karl pushed his glasses up onto his forehead again.

'What do you mean, you didn't write it?'

'Someone else must have written it,' Håkan said.

He turned back to what he was doing, leaving Karl holding 1,636 in his hand, a mass of furrows on his brow.

'But . . .' Karl began.

He went back inside his office and I saw him sit in there, inspecting the document from all angles, all the while with that bewildered look on his face.

That afternoon Karl called Ann and John into his office. I watched him show them my printout, but they both shook their heads. It was actually rather a shame, I thought. If one of them had falsely taken the credit for my work, the situation would have been even better. We would have been able to increase the bounce of my trampoline, so to speak. But evidently neither of them was brazen enough. I would have to carry on as planned.

Just before I went to lunch I felt I needed to go to the toilet. I took the long route past the lift so that everyone would clearly see that I was avoiding the room. When I came out again I took the same route back, passing several of my colleagues on their way to the lift. They could all see that I was coming from the toilet. I passed the door of the room as if it didn't exist.

48

When the working day was over and everyone had gone home, I smuggled the next investigation into my briefcase, closed it firmly and snuck into the room.

I unpacked my things on the magnificent desk and started work on 1,842.

As soon as I emerged I wrote a couple of short sentences in my notepad so I didn't forget my train of thought in there. I sat down at my computer and wrote up the text. The whole process went much quicker today. It was like I'd learned something about the way things fit together. Something about the way time and space interact.

I went over to Karl's office, opened the glass door and put the document on his desk just after half past ten in the evening.

49

The next day I repeated the process with case 1,199, the only difference being that I took the neatly typed document home with me overnight.

The next morning I went into Karl's office before he got in, making sure that Ann witnessed it. I could clearly see how watchful she became the moment I entered Karl's little glass cube. She stared at me as I left the document on his desk. And just after Karl had arrived and hung up his outdoor clothes on the hanger, sure enough, she was there telling tales.

I couldn't have arranged it better.

50

'Ann tells me you're the person who left this on my desk?' Karl said, holding up framework decision 1,199.

I nodded.

'Who wrote it?'

'I did.'

He stood there for a while, just looking at me without saying anything. As if he were trying to work out whether or not I was telling the truth. He cleared his throat and scratched an earlobe.

'You did?'

I nodded again, and couldn't help noticing that Håkan was suddenly listening.

'Who . . . who asked you to do it?' Karl said.

I raised my eyebrows and answered slowly.

'I took it for granted that it was my duty, seeing as the files were on my desk.'

'The files were on your desk?'

'Yes.'

'Who put them there?' Karl said, glancing at Håkan, who quickly looked down and pretended to be reading his papers.

'I've no idea,' I said. 'I assumed—'

'Please, come with me.'

He led the way towards the little glass box without waiting for me. I looked at Håkan, who was still pretending not to have noticed anything, but his neck was bright red. I got up and walked very slowly after Karl into his office. Karl sat down behind his desk.

'Close the door,' he said.

I did as he said and tried to adopt a concerned expression, as if I were expecting another reprimand for something. There was a certain pleasure in playing the innocent schoolboy seeing as I knew what was coming. Karl fixed his eyes on me.

'Björn, what's going on here?'

'I'm sorry if I've caused any trouble. I didn't mean to take someone else's work. I was just convinced I was meant to do it because the case-notes were on my desk and—'

'Can you tell me who wrote 1,842 and . . . let's see, 1,636?'

'I did.'

'Björn, I hope you are aware that all of us in this depart-ment . . . we always stick to the truth.'

'That is the truth.'

Karl spun his chair slightly and stroked his chin with his fingers. He picked up the documents and seemed almost to be weighing them in his hand.

'The DG is very pleased,' he said out of nowhere.

'Oh?' I said, trying to look surprised.

'He says we've finally got the right tone. That these texts you've written ought to be the template for all future framework decisions in the communal sector.'

51

I looked at the picture Jörgen usually leaned against when we had meetings here in Karl's office and tried to enjoy the moment when the new order here at the Authority slowly began to take shape. The picture was of some appetising-looking fruit. You could almost have believed it was real. I came to think of an artist who could draw an empty sheet of paper and make you think it was a real piece of paper, so you'd go up to it wondering why someone had put an empty sheet of paper in a glass frame, but then you'd discover that it was a drawing, like an optical illusion. Quite funny, actually.

The thought made me smile.

'I didn't know . . .' Karl said, and I could see he was having severe difficulty coming to terms with the idea of me as a leading light in this field. He had regarded me as a nothing, an encumbrance, someone who needed to be watched and looked after. Now that he'd made his bed he was having to lie in it.

He looked up at me and smiled. Clearly uncertain about how to treat me. It was like there was something inside him that was still fighting against the idea. I could easily draw this out a bit longer, I thought, let him squash me even further down.

I could exploit my lowly status and make the turnaround even greater, even more of a shock.

But this was where we were. At last he had realised, and maybe I ought to have been pleased that he was at least intelligent enough to recognise talent when he saw it. That isn't always the case.

'You surprise . . .' he went on, waving my texts.

I stayed quiet. And smiled. Knowing when to keep your mouth shut is an art.

'If you could imagine carrying on . . . that you might be able to take on some more . . .'

I cleared my throat and frowned gently. Taking my time.

'I'd be happy to help in any way I can,' I said, 'but bearing in mind my other duties . . .'

I glanced towards the photocopier and Karl took the hint.

'We can sort that out, Björn.'

'I just mean that it might be difficult finding the time to look after the printers and . . .'

'Obviously, you wouldn't have to do anything of that sort . . .'

'And the quality assurances . . .'

Karl raised his voice slightly to indicate that he was serious. That all that sort of nonsense was at an end now.

'I'm sorry, Björn, if I underestimated you . . .' He got up from his chair and I could see the tension in his face as he steeled himself to say what was coming. I smiled and waited. '. . . but it isn't always easy to see the skills of all your colleagues. Especially not . . .'

He fell silent and sat down on the edge of the desk. He

looked tired. He sighed and ran his hand over his hair.

'I apologise, Björn, there's been a lot going on recently.'

'Apology accepted,' I said, and made myself comfortable in his office-chair.

He looked down at me with his mouth wide open. I leaned back and folded my hands over my stomach.

'Would you like to talk about it?' I said.

52

The following morning I was able to run my finger slowly over the numbers on the cover of my first framework decision, which now had its own reference number: 16c36/1.

I had gone down to reception and asked for it the day it became publicly accessible. I could smell the fresh ink, and I let Margareta behind the counter get a glimpse of the case-manager's name on the flyleaf. You could have been a part of all this, I thought. But drugs got in the way.

'How are things going for you these days?' she asked after a pause.

I didn't answer. I didn't even look at her. I had decided to regard her as a stranger, a complete unknown. And neither condone nor condemn what she did in her own time.

53

Rumours of my success swept through the whole department like a wave. Someone had heard and carried the news to the rest of the group. I saw Hannah with the ponytail talking to Karin outside the kitchen, and via Karin I was able to follow the path of the news to John and the gang in the section for the financing of inspection visits. After a while almost the whole of Supervision stood up, talking to each other and looking in my direction. I tried to read their reactions, but it was difficult as I was constantly having to pretend I hadn't noticed and was preoccupied with my work.

In fact things were relatively stress-free, and I didn't have to rush my fifty-five-minute periods seeing as the most concentrated part, the actual formulation itself, always happened inside the room. In the evenings and at night.

One day when Håkan got back from a coffee-break I noticed that even he had been hosed down by the torrent of information about the new star in the office. He smiled when he asked but I could see the icy chill in his eyes.

'So how long were you planning on keeping your talent hidden, then?' he said.

I didn't answer. He had a large white patch on one shoulder

and going part way down his chest. Hadn't he noticed? It looked scruffy.

'Do you think it's funny going round pretending to be unstable, just so you can show everyone your tightrope routine later on?'

I said nothing. I recognised the nature of his questions. They were rhetorical. It's always best to ignore those. Treat them like they don't exist. But the stain was real.

'Don't you think you should go and change your shirt?' I asked after a while, nodding towards the stain.

Håkan glanced sullenly down at his shoulder. Then he hissed through gritted teeth: 'When did you nick those files?'

I adopted a questioning look that I had practised at home in front of the mirror. I thought it gave the desired impression.

John caught up with me on the way to the canteen. He held out his hand.

'Congratulations, Björn,' he said with a crooked smile. 'It's great that things are going so well for you now.'

I took his hand and thanked him.

'I'm sorry about all that business before,' he said. 'You know how things get in stressful workplaces. There isn't always enough time to talk things through calmly.'

I decided to hold back from responding and just gave him a quizzical look.

'I mean, places like this aren't exactly famous for taking care of their staff when they get a bit – well, how can I put it? – overwrought.'

I went on looking at him in silence. It was obvious that it was starting to make him nervous.

'But I'm really pleased you're back on track, Björn. I just wanted you to know. Even the DG is pleased, he's let us know how happy he is.'

He let out one of those exaggerated laughs, as if he was hoping I'd join in. I didn't. His laughter died out. He looked round, leaned forward and said in a confidential tone, 'Even the Minister is said to be pleased with our recent progress. You might manage to save all our jobs.'

He patted me on the shoulder and walked off.

54

I worked on the investigations in the room in the evenings and at night. I edited them during the day and found every part of the job as good as you might expect when it's done by an expert. Inside the room I found a structure for the work. I regarded the investigator's words as gospel, and through a process of elimination all that remained in the end was a clear and unambiguous decision. I found it easy.

Obviously each and every individual has different ways of reaching a decision. Some people find it hard, or think it feels strange. I discovered that I find it very easy to make decisions. It seemed to come naturally. I'm happy to decide things, and every time it felt perfectly fine formulating the way that things should be.

Jens came up to me one day fishing for advice.

'How come you can suddenly . . . ?' Jens said. 'I mean . . . we had no idea . . .'

'Hard work,' I said. 'Hard work is the father of success.'

'But how do you go about it, exactly?'

I smiled.

'I'm sure you can understand that I can't reveal my reasoning.

That would be both undesirable and impossible. The best thing for the department and for you personally would be for you to work out your own way of reasoning on your own.'

55

To start with I only dealt with four-figure cases. But as news of my success began to spread, the occasional three-figure case would land on my desk. Suddenly Karl came up to me, all excited, and asked how I would feel about taking on number 97. It was a direct request from the DG, he said. I said I'd be happy to. Framework decision number 97 was my first double-digit case.

Karl came with me up to the investigators to pick up the material. We could have done with a trolley. As he walked beside me along the corridors of the upper floors with the heavy burden in his arms, it almost felt like he was my assistant. In some ways he had started to rely on me. I remember thinking: This is your future, Karl. Stick close to me.

Jörgen was losing his temper more and more often. Every now and then one of his outbursts would be aimed at Karl, usually for no obvious reason. But Karl shouted back, which I thought reasonable. Angry dogs need to be kept on a short lead.

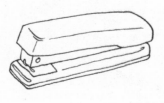

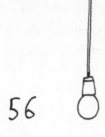

56

My days were spent writing up and editing, but seeing as that didn't fill the whole working day I soon abandoned my fifty-five-minute method and had a lot of time left over for networking in the office.

I spent long periods by the coffee-machine in the little kitchen, and noticed how people's attitudes towards me gradually changed. I was given the space to spread out in social conversation. I would declare my opinion on various subjects and could immediately identify those who agreed with me, and those who said they did but were lying.

One day when we were standing there, Hannah with the ponytail suddenly said: 'It's great that you changed the bulb in here, Jens. It was high time that got done.'

She was grinning broadly and Jens tried to look nonchalant.

'Oh, it's no big deal,' he said.

I put my cup down.

'I thought about doing that a few weeks ago,' I said.

And suddenly I realised the difference between me and my colleagues. I was ahead of them the whole time. By about two weeks. It took them numerous attempts to understand what I could see at the first go. Was it the same thing with the room? Would they stand there one day and discover what I had tried to show them such a long time before? Maybe they were just too immature to see what seemed utterly obvious to me? Was this how Copernicus felt?

57

As the days passed I began to feel a degree of irritation spread out and take hold of me.

Karl always helped me with heavy piles of documents. Sometimes he would be wholly responsible for their transportation from the investigators down to our department, if I had a lot to do, for instance. But when the work actually had to be done, I had to shift the heaps of material into the room without anyone seeing. It started to get rather wearing after a while.

Eventually I began to feel irritated at having to keep quiet about my real workplace. Besides, I was finding it both uncomfortable and tiring to have to wait until all the others had left each day before I could get any real work done.

Everyone else in the department carried on as usual. Took their breaks, chatted. Which annoyed me as well.

I realised fairly early on that there was a difference between my time and other people's. I don't just do one thing at a time. I can be on my way somewhere, but I'll spend the time thinking about other things, things that may not have anything to do with what I'm doing just then. That way I maximise the use of my time.

For instance, I don't just stand on the bus staring out of the window at things I've seen hundreds of times. I think about other things instead, calculating and thinking things through. Making decisions.

You have to apply the same principle in dealing with other people. Otherwise certain conversations can become incredibly time-consuming. I listen until I realise where the conversation is going, which in many cases can be deduced fairly early, then I switch off and concentrate on other things. There's no reason to hear the same thing twice. Or three or four times. Ordinary people listen to a huge amount of nonsense that they would be better off without.

Ordinary people can do one thing at a time. I can deal with plenty. Surely I ought to be rewarded for that?

58

'If it's possible, I'd like to go through a few practical issues,' I said to Karl in his office a couple of days later.

'Shut the door, Björn,' Karl said, parking his little trolley in the corner behind the desk.

I had asked for a private meeting to go through a list of things I couldn't help thinking about. Maybe I could put a bit of pressure on him now that I had established myself and become more or less indispensable.

Karl was sweating a lot, and I couldn't help wondering deep down about the state of his health.

'I noticed that I didn't get an email about the staff-development days,' I said.

'Didn't you get the email?' he said with a look of surprise between breaths.

'Well, that depends on your definition.'

'How do you mean?'

'Well,' I said, leaning back in the chair, 'it wasn't addressed to me.'

'But you got the email?'

'I was copied into it, yes. I'd appreciate it if my name could be included in the list of recipients. As it is, I just got it as a copy.'

Karl pulled a handkerchief from his trouser pocket and mopped his brow.

'But you did get the email?'

'Only as a copy.'

'Do you want to attend the staff-development days? If you do, I can just—'

I shook my head.

'I'd never consider that,' I said.

We both sat there in silence as he folded the handkerchief and put it back in his pocket.

'Obviously, I'm not making any demands,' I said. 'I just wanted you to know that you'd be making it easier for me to choose all of you here, if there was ever any chance of my considering anything else.'

'Considering anything else, Björn?'

'You never know.'

'Are you thinking of leaving us?'

'I can't go into that.'

Karl rubbed his head with one hand. I thought I could see a stiff smile on his lips.

'Well, go ahead. What would you like to see?'

I took out the pad on which I'd written a few reminders.

'Jörgen has to go.'

Karl looked at me, wide-eyed.

'Sorry?'

'I want Jörgen to leave. Be removed from the department. He can stay in the building, just out of my sight and hearing.'

'Björn, that sort of demand—'

'And I'm sure,' I went on, 'that my suggestions are well within the bounds of the organisation's wishes.'

'What . . . what did you say?'

'I think you probably heard what I said.'

He patted his legs and attempted a strained grin.

'You don't understand, Björn. That isn't how it works. I can't just dismiss someone who—'

'I think you can. With a bit of imagination.'

Karl shook his head. He looked at me, then shook his head again.

'Like I said,' I continued, 'obviously I can't decide what happens to anyone else . . .'

'No, exactly,' Karl said.

'. . . apart from myself.'

He looked at me, suddenly serious.

'I see. What else?'

I took my time, crossing one leg over the other. I adjusted my jacket with a pointed gesture.

'Håkan should be demoted.'

Karl held up a hand to stop me, but I carried on before he had time to interrupt.

'That can be motivated by disciplinary measures. I'll see that you get the necessary evidence.'

'You don't understand,' Karl began again.

'What don't I understand?'

'Björn . . .'

'According to the DG, I'm the only person in the department who's understood—'

'Björn, we can't just suddenly—'

'Do you want to hear my demands or not?'

Karl stared at me as if he were hoping I was going to stop joking. But I wasn't joking. I was deadly serious.

'Håkan has a wife and children . . .'

'I can't take that into consideration.'

Karl shook his head again, let out a deep breath, and looked very unhappy.

'What else?'

'Last but not least,' I said, 'possibly more important than everything else.'

'Yes?' Karl said.

'I need free access to the room.'

Karl was staring again, and I thought I could see one of his eyebrows twitch.

'You mean, "the room"?'

I nodded.

'No!' Karl said emphatically.

He stood up and started walking round the room.

'No, no, no, Björn,' he went on. 'I thought we were done with that room?'

'Not exactly,' I said.

148

59

'For God's sake, there is no room!' Jörgen said, waving his arms about and making the fruit picture sway.

He was sweating and looked like he might lose control at any moment. I thought this ought to be enough to make even Karl realise that keeping him in the department was untenable.

When we were all gathered like this it was called a big departmental meeting, but it just felt like Karl's little glass cube was getting smaller and smaller. And hotter and hotter.

Yet there was something of a different atmosphere this time. Some people – John, for instance – were sticking closer to me.

'But there is no room,' Jörgen almost hissed this time. 'Is there?'

He was staring at Karl almost beseechingly. Karl held up his hand.

'Perhaps we could agree on the formulation "the room does not exist for everyone"?'

'What the hell are you talking—' Jörgen began, but Karl interrupted him.

'I'm just trying to find a phrase that works for all of us. Can we agree . . . ?'

'But there is no room!'

Jörgen was getting close now. Jens hurriedly added: 'First there was the business with the shoes . . .'

'I've paid for them,' I said.

'. . . and now this.'

'Either it's there or it isn't!' Jörgen practically yelled.

John suddenly stood up beside me.

'Maybe we've reached a point now where the room has a certain significance. And on those terms then it obviously does exist.'

Everyone looked at John.

'Either there is a room there or there isn't,' Ann said.

'It's not quite that simple,' Karl said.

'Isn't it? So what the hell is it, then?' Jens said, glaring at Karl.

Karl turned to me. I cleared my throat, ran one finger over my chin and made no effort to hurry.

'To put it mildly,' I began, 'we can probably take it for granted that out of everyone here, I'm the one who makes the largest contribution, purely in terms of work. I have to say that it seems more than reasonable for me to have access to a space of my own, and the room is a place where I feel I can work.'

Håkan was staring at me open-mouthed, then said: 'But it doesn't exist?'

Karl looked round.

'I wonder,' he said, 'if it might be a good idea to bring in a consultant to look at this issue.'

'What would the consultant do?' Niklas said.

'It might help us find a new way of looking at things.'

Jörgen craned his neck towards Karl. He was making an effort not to lose his grip.

'You're going to bring in a consultant to tell us the room doesn't exist?'

'Or does exist,' I said. 'I can quite understand that you might be scared of bringing in an outsider.'

'That costs money,' Ann said.

'Maybe it would be worth it?' Karl said.

Suddenly there was a loud noise. Not a howl, but an almost muffled sound. It was Jörgen.

'Jörgen.'

'I think I'm going mad,' Jörgen said.

'Okay, you need to calm down,' Karl said. 'It's extremely important that we do the right thing in a situation like this. It's important for the whole Authority. We're not going to make any hasty decisions.'

I got the impression that he glanced in my direction. I stood up and walked towards the door.

'Call me when you've finished working out how to clear up this elaborate charade. I'm perfectly prepared to overlook the whole thing and move on, but I'd like you to identify one person responsible for it. Someone I can consider as – how can I put it? – the guilty party. Have you got that?'

No one said anything. Their mouths were all hanging open. Even Jörgen was sitting there gawping.

Karin looked very unhappy.

'Can't we say that the room exists a little bit?'

Hannah with the ponytail tilted her head to one side.

'It strikes me that it would feel rather uncomfortable to have a room that only Björn is allowed inside.'

While everyone was looking at her I walked out. I heard the discussion resume with fresh impetus as soon as I closed the door.

60

I sat at my desk, moving the mouse up and down over the mouse-mat. All the while I could see above my screen the heated debate taking place inside Karl's office. It looked quite funny, all those big people in such a little room. It was like they were part of some work of art. They were gesticulating and talking. I heard fragments of sentences, 'a monster' and 'ought to get help', but also 'remember that Björn is working on two-figure cases these days'.

Eventually things quietened down and I stretched to get a better view of what they were up to.

After a good while they all emerged.

John came straight over to me. The others followed him, stumbling rather aimlessly, like the flock of sheep that they actually were. No one really seemed to know where to go. No one seemed capable of going back to work.

'What's going on?' I asked.

'Karl's on his way up to the DG,' John said.

'Oh, what for?'

'He's going to ask him.'

'About what?'

'About the room. That's what we agreed. That this is a matter for the DG.'

I smiled and patted him on the shoulder.

'That's probably right,' I said.

Ann came up to us, and behind her trailed the rest of them. They ended up in a circle around Håkan's and my desks. As if they didn't really know where to go. As if I were going to read them a story.

'What exactly is it that you want?' Ann asked me.

She looked distraught. Unhappy. I wondered if she was about to burst into tears. I tried to answer in a gentle, friendly tone of voice.

'I just want to do my job,' I said.

There was muttering in the congregation.

'And what do you think we're doing, Björn?'

That was Håkan's voice. He was having trouble getting to his place with everyone crowding round my desk. I looked up. First at him. Then at all the other anxious pairs of eyes around me.

'Obviously I don't know with one hundred per cent certainty,' I said. 'I can only speak for myself. Seeing as I have noticed the room over there and find a certain joy in working there, I have no option but to accept its existence, as I'm sure you can understand. I could work on the assumption that I myself am wrong and the rest of you right, but that doesn't make much sense in my head. I simply have to assume that one of us is lying. Because I know that I am telling the truth, I draw the conclusion that the rest of you are telling untruths. That's simply the logical conclusion.'

I saw several of them lower their gaze. Ann looked nervous. Jörgen was sweating.

'What I can't help wondering is whether you've done this before? As well as which of you are involved, and how you managed the practicalities? When did you decide? At what level has this been authorised? For instance, I don't imagine that the DG has been informed about this, which is odd, seeing as you must surely all recognise that if something like this got out, it would mean the end for the whole department?'

Håkan looked at me with horror in his eyes and I had time to think: Now you get it!

'In some ways it's such a grandiose and detailed project,' I went on, 'and so ingeniously malicious that I can't help being rather fascinated.'

I leaned forward and rested my elbows on the desk.

'It's going to be very exciting to hear what the DG has to say when Karl comes back down. Taking the DG's decision as my starting point, I am going to have to resolve how we proceed with all this. Who among you will be staying, and who will have to leave.'

I saw from the clock that it had gone half past eleven and I could feel my stomach starting to rumble gently.

'The very least I can ask is that you agree to nominate one person who can take the time to go through exactly how it all worked with me: what important decisions were taken, who was the driving force behind it, who was in favour or opposed to it, and so on. That person must also be prepared to accept severe punishment and leave the organisation immediately. I suggest that you discuss this among yourselves and come back to me once you've decided upon a suitable candidate.'

I gathered my things together on the desk. I put on my coat and went off to lunch early.

On the way out I went straight to the door in the corridor, opened it and stepped inside. I stood there for a good while, thinking: Soon you'll be mine.

61

As soon as I returned from lunch Margareta in reception informed me that a meeting was about to start. I had treated myself to some sushi from the little restaurant just across the street from the big, red-brick building. I had sat there eating my raw fish and looking out across the square with its incomprehensible sculptures. I took my time, and was well aware that I was slightly late as I climbed up the flight of grey steps leading to the Authority.

'They're waiting in Karl's office,' Margareta said.

As usual, I thought, and took the lift up. I went into the glass cubicle and tried to get a glimpse of Karl. The whole department had been summoned and everyone had dutifully trotted into his office, but Karl wasn't there yet. This was starting to feel like a habit. Håkan in his blue jacket.

Håkan was pinching the bridge of his nose with his thumb and forefinger. He was sitting on the desk where Karl usually sat, and he looked at me wearily. I started to get an idea of what this was about, and tried to work out who among the staff had been telling tales and thus indirectly occasioned this improvised meeting. Without Karl. From past experience it seemed most likely to have been Ann. She went and stood beside Håkan when I walked in, ready – responsible, somehow. With a look on her face that wasn't entirely dissatisfied.

Don't they ever get fed up? I thought, and let out a small sigh.

'Ann, you had something to say to us?' Håkan began, like a sort of stand-in boss.

'Yes,' she said, tilting her chin.

'Aren't we going to wait for Karl?' I said.

Håkan shook his head firmly.

'No need,' he said. 'Well, what did you want to say, Ann?'

Ann stretched and took a deep breath.

'Björn was standing there again.'

A murmur went round the room. One of those 'oohs' you sometimes hear in American sitcoms when the audience reacts obediently to something cute said by a child. But there was nothing cute about this. This was an expression of 'What did we say?' and 'Knew it! He's done it again!'.

'And this time I've got witnesses,' Ann said.

The loaded atmosphere in there, their infernal obstinacy and united front made my cup run over. I could hear that I was speaking louder than necessary when I was no longer able to hold back the torrent of frustration growing inside me.

'That's absolutely true, my friends,' I said. 'I have made use of the room for all manner of activities. I have gone there on a daily basis in recent weeks. I have done most of my – and forgive me for putting it like this – singularly successful work in there, during the evenings and at night. And yes, I intend to carry on doing so.'

I went round the desk that Håkan and Ann were leaning against and sat down on Karl's very comfortable office-chair. The others looked at me.

'That's enough now. More than enough. You have just obliged me to meet force with force. I have no other option but to put myself up against you all.'

There was total silence in the room. You could have heard a pin drop.

'There are a couple of you that I could imagine reaching an accommodation with. You, John, have shown a degree of loyalty. And that will obviously be rewarded. The rest of you can start packing your things, because from now on the following applies: I will only stay on the condition that you go.'

I leaned back calmly in the chair.

'Now, I suggest that we wait for the DG's decision.'

62

Five, six, maybe seven minutes of intense silence passed inside Karl's office without anyone so much as moving a finger. No one could think of anything to say or do. It was like everyone was holding their breath. Finally Karl came rushing in in a very undignified manner, breathless and with beads of sweat on his forehead.

'Hello, everyone. I've come straight from the DG. We spent a long time talking. I informed him about everything . . . well, everything that has happened, and our various different opinions about . . . and I can tell you that . . .'

He paused and looked at me, slightly uncertain. Maybe in an attempt to gauge my reaction in advance, maybe to be sure he still had me with him. He went on slowly and clearly: '—The DG and I have had a . . . conversation . . . about the room. By which I mean, its existence or otherwise, and so on.'

The entire room was utterly silent. Karl cleared his throat. I saw Håkan swallow, and Jörgen loosened his tie slightly.

'The DG has shown me the plans. He was in no doubt. Very – how shall I put it? – persuasive in his argument.'

He blinked and cleared his throat again as he turned towards the others.

'The DG says that on this, the fourth floor, between the lift and the three toilets . . . there is absolutely no other space.'

63

I remained seated in Karl's chair for a while as all the others filed out and drifted back to their workstations. Slowly but surely the office resumed its usual atmosphere. As if nothing had happened.

I was trying to work out if the DG could possibly be involved in this conspiracy, or if Karl was simply lying. How could I check? I got up carefully, wondering if I ought to pay a visit of my own to the Director General?

When I came out of the office I saw that plastic tape had been set up between the walls by the lift and at the other end of the corridor. Karl came after me.

'To make things easier for all of us, Björn, we've decided that you're not to go inside this tape. Okay?'

I looked up at his shiny face.

'But how am I supposed to go to the toilet?'

'You'll just have to use the ones on the floor below. The same thing applies to the lift. You'll have to take the stairs to the next floor.'

He patted me on the back and went on: 'This will be best for all of us. It's simpler this way.'

64

Håkan wasn't sitting in his place when I got back to our work-station. Just that awful blue jacket tossed over his desk. I sat down and looked around for something to do. I ran my fingers over the pile of files of framework decisions. I picked up the stapler to fasten together the case with reference number 02c11/1, but it wouldn't go through the whole pile and I had to dig the staple out with my fingers.

Even though the paper was designed for being archived, or possibly precisely because of that, it sucked up the moisture from my hands and in one fell swoop lost its smoothness, its purity. A bit of the title-page came away with my fingers when I moved them too quickly. The reference number came loose from the framework decision.

65

I left the Authority just before eleven.

I took my coat, went down the stairs to the floor below, then took the lift from there to reception and rushed out into the sleety snow.

My suit felt sweaty and my shirt was sticking to my body in a very unpleasant way. On top of everything else, I felt a sort of pressure across my chest, and I could feel it getting harder and harder to breathe.

When I got to the bottom of the broad flight of steps outside the entrance I walked straight out into the car park. Across the tarmac to the little patch of grass with the sign showing directions to the various departments. I leaned forward and rested my hands on my thighs. Shut my eyes and tried to breathe. There was something that didn't make sense. I couldn't quite put my finger on it, but there was something. Something was terribly wrong. The look on Karl's face, the DG's swift action, his categorical denial – did he really have that level of oversight into every nook and cranny of the building? The makeshift cordon. The whole thing – it felt over the top, somehow. It reminded me of exaggerated, made-up stories designed to conceal something else.

I turned round and walked slowly back towards the building

again. This was really just a classic ruling-class tactic, wasn't it, making someone think they were mentally ill? What was I actually running from?

Down in reception it was as if I was seeing people for the first time. Even the ones I recognised. People I trusted. Now they appeared in an entirely different light. One had an earpiece in his ear. Another ran to catch up with a third. They exchanged a few intense words. The level of activity was stepping up. A black car pulled up and stopped right in front of the entrance. Two men in black coats got out and jogged up the steps and in through the glass doors. Margareta had her eyes on me the whole time, but now it was different. How can I put it? Settled, somehow. As if she understood that I had realised. Could she tell that I had seen through the whole thing? Did she understand that I was about to reveal everything?

The two men in black coats went straight up to Margareta at the desk. It could hardly be a coincidence that all this was happening at this particular moment. This stream of people with an anxious look in their eyes, the new way Margareta was looking at me, the men in the car. It was no accident that they just happened to show up on the day that Karl had been in to see the DG to ask about a room that no one wanted to admit existed.

I got into the lift and pressed the button for the third floor. I realised I still had a small advantage. For the time being they didn't know *who* they were after. The person who had dared to break the pattern and think along new lines, the person who had dared to think 'outside the box'. But I knew it wouldn't be long before Margareta revealed my identity to them.

I got out on the third floor and went the rest of the way up the stairs. A couple of people stared at me when I entered the department. I slowed down, looked around, tried to seem calm and collected, but when I reached the photocopier I darted quickly round the corner and crept under the barrier towards the room.

Someone cried out. It might have been Ann or Karin. Behind me I could hear Håkan yelling at me to stop. I got the feeling that Jörgen and Karl were somewhere there in the background. When I got to the room I opened the door, then closed and locked it behind me as quickly as I could. For a brief while I could breathe again and think more or less clearly. I leaned against the wall and let my eyes roam round the familiar space. Everything looked much the same, yet somehow different. I could hear the others outside. They were there already, knocking on the door. Banging on the wood. They wouldn't be happy to stay on the outside this time. The blows were getting harder and harder. I realised it was only a matter of time before they forced the door open and got inside and started poking about. I looked around to find somewhere to hide but couldn't see anywhere particularly good. I closed my eyes, took a deep breath, and walked into the wall. The wall closed around me, like yogurt around a spoon.

In there it was dark and soft. Surprisingly clean and free from lines and edges. No angles or corners for dirt to get into and hide. No light. No sound. The smell in there made me think of the sea, and lilacs, and St Paulsgatan by the junction with Bellmansgatan at five o'clock in the morning at the end of May.

I could hear them calling my name outside, and I thought: You'll never find me here.

THE INVOICE

1

It was such an incredible amount, 5,700,000 kronor. Impossible to take seriously. I assumed it must be one of those fake invoices, the sort you hear about on television and in the papers. Unscrupulous companies trying to defraud people, often the elderly, out of their money.

It was very well done. There was no denying that. The logo looked genuine, at least to me. I don't really know, I don't get much post, apart from the usual bills. This one looked pretty similar. Except for the amount, of course. W. R. D., it said in large letters, and the bit about conditions of payment was very convincing. The whole thing had that dry, factual tone, just like something from a genuine organisation.

But if it was genuine, there must have been a massive mistake. Some computer must have got me mixed up with a big company, or maybe a foreign consortium. 5,700,000 kronor. Who gets bills like that? I chuckled at the thought that someone might actually pay that amount of money by mistake and never question it.

I drank a glass of juice, dropped some advertising leaflets into the recycling box, all those offers and brochures that somehow managed to get past the 'No adverts, please' sign, then put on my jacket and went off to work.

I worked part time in a video shop for enthusiasts. There were two of us who took it in turns to stand there two or three days each week, placing orders, sorting films as they came in, cataloguing and putting them on the shelves. Every now and then I was able to help a customer find the right film or explain why a special edition with extra material hadn't come in yet, or possibly didn't include a specific interview that the customer had seen online and which they thought cast the director in question in an entirely new light, and which he or she (usually he) could reproduce pretty much verbatim for me if I felt like listening. Mostly, though, I just stood there thinking about other things.

The walk was a bit windy, but it was the start of light-jacket weather, and most of the trees already had plenty of leaves on their branches. As I walked I thought about the invoice, and wondered how they had managed to get hold of my name and address. Did they just pick the first one they came across? Unless perhaps there was someone else with very similar details?

The windows of the shop were covered by a greenish-yellow layer of pollen, and the door was tricky to open. It didn't seem to matter how we adjusted the closing mechanism. Either the door was hard to shift or it flew open at the slightest touch. Today it stopped halfway.

The floor felt sticky under my feet as I walked to the counter to hang my jacket on the hook beneath it. I put a pot of coffee on to brew in the little kitchen behind the desk. Something had burned onto the bottom of the jug, and Tomas – who worked the other days – said he never drank anything out of it, but I didn't think it was that much of a problem. Quite the opposite, in fact – it gave a bit of a kick to what was otherwise a pretty insipid drink.

I pushed the door of the cupboard under the sink several times because it wouldn't shut properly – it was missing its little magnet-thing. Each time it swung open again a couple of centimetres. In the end I got a bit of sticky tape, rolled it up and stuck it to the inside of the door, and that kept it closed.

Under the counter there was a basket containing the films that had been returned last week, the ones Tomas hadn't bothered to put back on the shelves. I sat there looking at them as I waited for the coffee. There was a Kubrick, a Godard and *The Spanish Prisoner* by David Mamet. I turned the case over and read the back. It had been a long time since I'd watched it. That was when I was still with the love of my life, Sunita, and we would take turns to show each other our favourite films. I'm not even sure if we managed to get to the end of it. She didn't think it was that great.

When the coffee was ready I found a bit of milk in the fridge that was only a couple of days old. I poured some in and drank as I put the rest of the films out.

As I was on my way back to the counter, I felt my shoes sticking to the floor again. I assumed someone must have spilled some Coke or something similar, because wherever I walked my shoes seemed to stick to the lino flooring. It sounded kind of funny, actually. Well, it did if you moved with the right sort of rhythm.

I sat for a while behind the counter and pondered the possibility that someone had stolen my identity – cloned it, or whatever the word was. And had then ordered something and let the company invoice me for that insane amount. But what could you order that cost 5,700,000 kronor? It seemed to me that they ought to have better safeguards in place for this sort of thing.

Sometime between eleven and half past we usually got a brief period of direct sunlight in the shop. I tried leaning over and tilting my head to see if I could work out what was making the floor sticky, and, sure enough, from the right angle you could see little islands of what was probably a spilled soft drink. I stared at it for a while. It looked a bit like a map of the world, if you removed parts of Asia and Australia. I squinted. Africa looked really good. Not to mention what were probably Greenland and Alaska. But, I reasoned, that's probably only because we're not so familiar with the geographic details of those regions. I thought for a while about which countries' shapes I knew best, apart from Sweden, of course, and came to the conclusion that it was probably still the ones in northern Europe. A short while later the sun disappeared over the rooftops. But the stickiness was still there: I could hear it clearly every time I walked across it.

I called Jörgen, my boss, and asked if we could buy a mop. He said that was fine. And that it was probably good to have one for future use, and that it would be nice if I could clean the whole floor.

'Just keep the receipt,' he said.

So I went to the hardware shop and bought one of those buckets with a strainer where you can squeeze the water out of the mop that comes with it. I filled it with warm water and realised that I should have bought some sort of floor-cleaner or washing-up liquid, then reasoned that it would probably be okay as long as the water was hot enough. I cleaned every bit of floor in the shop. It looked pretty good. The whole shop felt nicer. Almost a bit luxurious. I changed the water a couple of times, then, finally, mopped the soles of my shoes as well. Then I sat for a while, changing the background on my mobile phone. I switched it off, then on again, and changed the background once more.

Just in time for lunch my friend Roger came in. When I emerged from the toilet he was standing there talking on his phone. He nodded in my direction. Then he disappeared back out into the street. Twenty minutes later he came back in and asked if he could eat the rest of my takeaway. 'You don't mind, do you?' he said, and I told him I didn't.

He sat down on the stool behind the counter and slurped up the remaining noodles and meat. He said he'd had a cold for almost three weeks, but that it finally seemed to be on the way out.

'To start with, it was like just a bit of a sore throat,' he said as he chewed the food. 'Then it turned into a *really* bad sore throat, the sort where it hurts to swallow. Then it went down my tubes and turned into one of those real bastard coughs, the tickly sort where you can't sleep properly. I called the doctor's and said I needed penicillin, but by the time I got there my temperature had gone down and the cough was a bit better. So they refused to give me a prescription. They told me to take paracetamol instead, and come back if it got worse. But it didn't. It just got better.'

He tried to cough, but couldn't really manage it. He sighed and shook his head. Then he went on eating until the aluminium tray was scraped clean. Then he pushed it away and asked if we'd had any new films in, then, when I said we hadn't, he sighed again and looked out through the window.

'Well,' he said, 'I'd better get going.'

He grabbed a handful of the sweets we keep to offer children, then disappeared out through the door. I followed him, thinking I might as well hang up the faded red 'Open' flag.

No customers came in that afternoon either, so I had a chance to sort some invoices. I added the receipt for the mop and bucket. I punched holes and put everything in folders. Jörgen had a particular way he wanted things organised. Receipts in a green folder and unpaid invoices in a blue one. Then he would pay those himself and transfer them to the green folder.

As I was sitting there leafing through the folders, I found myself thinking once more about the odd invoice I'd received. I noticed that some companies printed the full amount, down to the last öre. That made it look like a very long number. Sometimes it was hard to see the little decimal point between the zeroes. Maybe that's what had happened to me, I thought. Maybe they'd just missed the decimal point, unless perhaps I hadn't noticed it? No, that couldn't be right. Because even if you removed two of the zeroes, it was still an insanely large amount. I certainly hadn't ordered anything that cost 57,000. I'd remember something like that. And what did W. R. D. stand for? I had a bit of a look to see if I could find anything similar among the shop's invoices, but there was nothing like it there. No, I thought. There must have been some sort of mistake somewhere, simple as that.

2

Pretty much exactly a month later a reminder arrived. With a surcharge for late payment. The amount had risen to 5,700,150 kronor. I looked at the sheet of paper more closely. There was no question that it was my name and my address on it. And there was no missing decimal point. There was no doubt about the amount. This time the invoice was from a payment clearance company, SweEx.

We cannot enter into correspondence, it stated clearly in the middle of the page. *All appeals should be directed to our client.* Then a telephone number.

I called the number that was printed at the bottom of the page and found myself listening to an automated voice that welcomed me and said: 'Please describe the reason for your call in your own words.'

I made an attempt to explain why I was ringing, but before I had finished the automated voice interrupted me and said I would be put through to an operator.

'You are currently number thirty-six in the queue. Waiting time is estimated to be two hours and twenty-five minutes.'

When I had been waiting quarter of an hour, the automated voice declared that the waiting time was now estimated to be two hours and forty minutes. I smiled at the absurdity of a waiting time that just kept growing, and seeing as the whole thing was really all a mistake I decided to let them work it out for themselves while I went out and bought myself an ice-cream.

It was a gloriously sunny day. Not a cloud in the sky, and the temperature was approaching thirty degrees in the shade. Down by the kiosk people were crowded into the shadow of the projecting roof, as if taking cover from rain. I stood and waited out in the square for a while, but fairly quickly felt the sun burning my scalp and neck, so I too pushed my way in under the little roof. People were chatting about all sorts of subjects, then suddenly I heard an older woman say to a young man of seventeen or eighteen: 'How much was yours?'

I didn't hear his reply, but her reaction was clear enough: 'Oh, well, you were lucky, then.'

The young man muttered again. It was impossible to make out what he was saying because his mouth was full of ice-cream, and he also had his back to me.

The woman went on: 'Yes, but compared to a lot of other people you've got off pretty lightly.'

I wondered what they were talking about, but it was difficult to draw any conclusions when I could only hear her side of the conversation. 'That's because you haven't been around long enough to get very old yet,' the woman suddenly declared. 'It's supposed to be worst for people around forty or so.'

The young man mumbled something, short and unintelligible.

'I know,' the woman went on, 'because they've just carried on regardless, not expecting this at all. They thought everything

179

was going to last for ever and that the state was going to pay for the whole thing. Imagine! Well, it'll only take you four or five years, then you'll have caught up. But for them ... well ... !'

She was holding her jacket over one arm, and was facing in my direction as she waited for her son, or grandson, or whatever he was, to finish his ice-cream. The young man went on muttering in a hopelessly low voice. I tried to move closer so I could hear better, but it was practically impossible to make out a single word. 'Still a lot of money,' I thought it sounded like.

Eventually it was my turn. As usual I went for a small tub with two scoops. Mint chocolate and raspberry. My two favourites.

On my way back up in the lift, I couldn't help overhearing a girl with several different necklaces on as she talked on her phone. She seemed very stressed. She pulled out a big leather-bound diary from her handbag, then leafed through it aimlessly, back and forth, making her necklaces jangle against each other, and even though her hair was tied up she kept brushing a loose strand from her face as she talked.

'Okay, could I borrow half the amount then? ... No, I realise that ... Okay, but what about half the amount? ... Yes. Right. Yes. I've checked with my bank, and they've promised ten, but that's still ... Yes.'

She made a small note in her diary.

'But if I could borrow half the amount from you, then ... Yes. The invoice comes to—'

She caught my eye and suddenly fell silent. As if she had only just noticed that I was standing there. The person at the other end went on talking as the girl murmured in reply.

* * *

For some reason these two overheard conversations left me feeling uneasy. It was as though they were talking about something that ought to concern me, something I'd missed. A bit like when you've been away and come back to find everyone talking about a celebrity who's said something funny, or humming an infectious summer hit that everyone else has heard but you've got no idea about.

By the time I got back to my flat there was hardly any ice-cream left. I scraped out the last drips, and managed to spill some on the payment reminder that was still lying there. It struck me that if you don't pay companies like that you end up with a black mark on your credit record – the sort of thing that can be hard to get rid of, even if it later turns out to have been a mistake.

The next time I called the queue was only an hour. But after a while the wait was recalculated once more, and had soon risen to two hours and seven minutes. At one point I got down to half an hour, and at worst it was up at six hours. I switched to speakerphone, put my phone down on the coffee table and left it there as the call went on. I plugged the charger into the wall while I played *Fallout: New Vegas* and listened to the Mahavishnu Orchestra.

Afternoon turned to evening, and evening turned to night, and eventually I slid into my gloomiest mood. A state that could easily last for hours. Sometimes I would put on particularly mournful music, melancholic songs by Jeff Buckley or Bon Iver, preferably some tormented young man singing about his broken heart and crushed dreams, so I could really wallow in pain and sadness. Just sit there and sink deeper into longing and misery. It had its own quite specific feeling of satisfaction. A bit like when you pick at an old wound, a scab – you just can't help it. But after a while I got fed up and dug out a couple of old magazines to reread. I managed to doze off on the sofa in the middle of a long article about projectors and wireless media players.

It was eight o'clock the following morning when I finally got through. A high-pitched, slightly hoarse female voice answered. I started by asking what the hell was wrong with their queuing system.

'It's completely insane,' I said. 'First it's an hour, then all of a sudden it's twice that. Then it halves again, but before you know it the waiting time's gone up to three hours.'

She apologised and said that the system was still under development.

'There are still a few teething problems,' she said. 'The idea was to develop a more dynamic, customer-centred queuing service. At the moment it takes the length of the current call and adjusts the estimated waiting time from that. But sometimes it can be a little misleading . . .'

'No kidding,' I said.

'Well,' she said, 'what can I do for you?'

I said I'd received an invoice, and that there must be some mistake, and would she mind correcting it? She listened carefully, then explained that everything was in order. There was no mistake, and no, I wasn't the first person to call. I said I hadn't ordered anything, or requested any services, but she maintained that the invoice was still correct. When I wondered what this was all about, she sighed and asked if I never read the papers, watched television or listened to the radio? I had to admit that I didn't really keep up with the news.

'Well,' she said, and I got the impression that she could have been smiling at the other end of the line. 'It's time to pay up now.'

3

Small strands of heat clouds were appearing in the sky through the window. It had to be the hottest day of the year so far. It looked like everything out there was quivering. Some children were running about on the pavement below, squirting each other with water-pistols. I could hear their delighted cries when they were hit by the sprays of cool water. On the balcony opposite a woman was shaking a rug. The sound of a spluttering moped echoed off the walls of the buildings. It died away, then came back. It sounded like someone was going from one address to the other, looking for something.

'Have you got Beta or Link?' the woman said on the phone.

'What did you say?' I said.

'Which payment system have you signed up with?'

'No idea,' I said. 'I don't think I got one at all.'

'No?' she said.

'No.'

'But you do have a plan?'

'A plan?'

'You've got a payment plan, linked to your E. H. account?'

I waited a moment.

'I don't think so,' I said.

'You haven't registered?' she said.

'No,' I said. 'Should I have?'

She didn't say anything for a while, so I repeated the question.

'Is that something I should have done?'

She cleared her throat.

'Well, let me put it like this: yes.'

I felt a sudden urge to sit down.

'But what . . . what am I supposed to be paying for?' I said.

'What?' she said.

'Yes?'

'Everything,' she said.

'What do you mean, everything?' I asked.

I was sitting on the floor, with my back against the kitchen wall and my legs pulled up to my chest. The knees of my jeans were starting to look a bit threadbare. It wouldn't be long before I had a hole there, whether I liked it or not. And even though I realised it probably wasn't fashionable any more, I still thought it would look a bit cool.

She hesitated a moment before answering, but even though she was silent, I could hear the weariness in her breathing.

'Where are you calling from?' she asked.

'I'm at home,' I said.

'At home. Okay. Look around you. What can you see?'

I raised my eyes from the floor and looked around the room.

'I see my kitchen,' I said.

'So, what can you see there?'

'Er . . . the sink. Some dirty dishes . . . A table.'

'Look out of the window.'

'Okay.'

I stood up and went over to the kitchen window, which was open slightly. I'd left it open all night. Maybe a few days. I couldn't remember. The heat had more or less erased the boundary between outside and in. The other day I had a bird in the kitchen for what must have been half an hour. I don't know what sort it was, but it was very pretty. It fluttered to and fro between the kitchen cupboards, then sat on the kitchen table for a while before flying out again.

'What can you see outside?' the woman asked down the phone.

'Buildings,' I said. 'And a few trees . . .'

'What else?'

'More buildings, and the street, a few cars . . .'

'What else?'

'I can see a blue sky, the sun, a few clouds, people, children playing on the pavement, adults, shops, cafés . . . People out together . . .'

'Exactly. Can you smell anything?'

'Er . . . yes.'

I breathed in the smell of the street. It was sweet and warm with summer scents. Flowers, a shrub of some sort? Some old food? A faint smell of something slightly rotten, and petrol. Typical summer smells. Almost a bit Mediterranean. I could hear the moped again now.

'You can feel something, can't you?' the woman continued.

'You're feeling feelings, thinking of different things, friends and acquaintances. And I presume you have dreams?'

She was no longer bothering to wait for me to reply.

'What do you mean?' I said.

'Do you dream at night?' she went on.

'Sometimes.'

'Hmm. Do you imagine all that is free?'

I didn't say anything for a while.

'Well, I suppose I thought . . .'

'Is that really what you thought?' she said.

I tried to come up with a reply, but my thoughts were going round in circles without formulating themselves into any sort of order. The woman on the phone went on, giving a long explanation of the division of costs, resolutions, single payments and deduction systems. It sounded almost as if she knew it off by heart.

'But how can it amount to so much?' I said, when I could speak again.

'Well,' she said, 'being alive costs.'

I said nothing for a while, because I didn't know what to say.

'But,' I eventually said, 'I had no idea it was so expensive . . .'

4

I looked at the payment reminder from the collection company. I ran my finger across the ice-cream stain. I felt foolish. Unmasked, somehow. I felt the same way I used to feel back in school many years ago when the teacher would ask questions designed to reveal how wrong your reasoning was. The children were heading off down the street, they were about to disappear round the corner. The sound of the moped was increasingly distant. A man had arrived on a bike and was busy chaining it to a lamp-post.

'But I've always paid my taxes?' I said.

She laughed. I sank back down onto the floor. Somehow that felt the most comfortable way to sit right now.

'This isn't a tax,' she said.

She was silent for a few moments, as if she were expecting me to comment, but I didn't know what to say so she carried on talking of her own accord.

'Tax. That's barely enough to cover day-to-day maintenance. Besides, I presume you don't belong to the group that—'

She stopped again, and I heard her tapping at a keyboard.

'Let's see, what did you say your date of birth and ID number were?'

I told her, and heard her type in the numbers. She drummed her fingers gently against the phone as she waited.

'Right. Let's see, you're ... thirty-nine years old. Hmm ... and you haven't made any payments at all?'

'No, I had no idea that—'

She interrupted me mid-sentence. 'Well, obviously it's going to amount to a fair sum.'

I heard her clicking, as if there were more pages to look through.

'Hmm,' she went on, 'that's a lot of money.'

Several rays of sunlight were falling across the kitchen floor. One of them reached my legs. I stretched my hand carefully back and forth, in and out of the light. Why hadn't anyone said anything? I wondered, and as if the woman at the authority could hear my thoughts, she went on in a rather strict tone of voice: 'I'm so fed up of hearing people say they didn't know anything. We've run several online campaigns over the past year, we've had adverts in the papers and handed out information leaflets at schools and workplaces. You'll have to be a bit more observant in the staffroom or canteen next time.'

'The staffroom?'

'Yes, that's usually where the notices get put up. About things like this.'

'But,' I said, pulling my hand out of the light, 'there's absolutely no way I can pay.'

She was completely quiet for a while.

'No?'

I considered the meagre income from my part-time job in the

video shop. The little that was left over from my wages, which were paid partly cash in hand, plus a small inheritance that was gradually shrinking, made up the sum total of my savings.

On the other hand, I'd never had any particularly large expenses. My flat was small and old-fashioned, and the rent was low. I had no one but myself to support, and I didn't have a lavish lifestyle. A few computer games every now and then, music, a bit of food, hardly any phone bill to speak of, and I got films free from the shop. Sometimes I would pay for a beer or lunch for Roger, but that didn't happen often these days. I always imagined I was free of extra financial responsibilities of that sort. Other people had careers and acquired houses and families and children. Got married, divorced, started their own businesses and set up limited companies. Employed accountants, bought property, leased cars, borrowed money. I was pretty happy on my own, without a big social circle, or anyone to cause any problems.

'It's completely impossible,' I said. 'At most, I've got about forty thousand in the bank.'

'What about your flat?' she said.

'Rented.'

She said nothing for a moment. Then she said abruptly: 'Hold on a moment and I'll check . . .'

She put the phone down and I heard her walk away. In the background there was the sound of keyboards being tapped, other people who seemed to be talking on the phone. A couple of telephones ringing. She was gone for some time. Eventually I heard her come back and pick up the phone again.

'Do you own anything of value?'

'Er, no . . . the television, maybe.'

'Hmm,' she said, 'television sets aren't worth anything these days. Is it big?'

'Thirty-two inches, maybe.'

'Forget it. That's nothing. No car?'

'No.'

'I see,' she said, and sighed. 'You'll have to pay what you can. Then we'll start with an inventory of your home and see what that comes up with. That will give us an idea of what level of debt we're going to end up at . . .'

'And what happens then?'

'That depends entirely on the amount.'

'In what way?'

'Well, we do have a debt ceiling.'

'What does that mean?'

'That means we can only permit debts up to a certain limit . . . I mean, in order to maintain continued access . . .'

'To what?'

'To . . . everything.'

'Are you going to kill me?'

She laughed. It was evidently a stupid question and I felt rather relieved at her reaction.

'No,' she said, 'we aren't going to kill you. But I'm sure you can appreciate that you can't carry on enjoying experiences if you don't have the means to pay for them?'

I held my hand out towards the shaft of light again and felt the heat of the sun. There really was a big difference in temperature, even though it was actually only a matter of a few centimetres. The woman at the other end of the line interrupted my thoughts.

'What on earth have you been thinking? All these years? Hasn't it ever occurred to you that you should be paying your way?'

'Well, I didn't actually know that we had to pay. Why—?'

She interrupted me again. She had obviously heard all this before. She knew it wasn't going to lead anywhere. She'd run out of patience for excuses and explanations. I could hear voices in the background, and got the impression that my time was running out.

'Let me put it like this: have you ever been in love?'

'Er, yes.'

'When?'

'A few times, I suppose.'

'More than once, then?'

'Yes. I mean, well, once properly.'

She was running on autopilot. Probably already thinking about the next conversation. But she still sounded friendly, in a professional way. 'There, you see, you must have experienced some wonderful things.'

I thought about Sunita, who I had been with for several years back in the nineties. A small wave of memories coursed through my body. A pang of melancholy.

'Yes, I suppose so,' I said.

She was obviously in a hurry to hang up now, there was no mistaking it. As if she had suddenly realised that we had exceeded our allotted time. As if it had struck her that she didn't have time to make idle conversation with me.

'Well, if there's nothing else, thank you for calling.'

'Hang on a moment,' I said. 'How do I . . . ? What can I do?'

She must have loads of calls waiting.

Maybe she could see the constantly rising number of people in the queue. She probably had a boss who was eager for her to move on. She was talking faster now.

'Have you checked with your bank?'

'No, but . . . It doesn't really seem very likely that I . . .'

'No, I suppose not.'

She sighed audibly, and someone said something in the office where she was sitting.

'Do you know what?' she said. 'Take a thorough look at your finances in peace and quiet – people usually manage to come up with something – and then call me again.'

'But,' I said, 'the queue to get through is really long . . .'

'You can have my direct number.'

'Okay.'

I got her number and wrote it on the bottom of the ice-cream tub.

'My name's Maud,' she said.

We hung up and I sat there for a long time with the phone in my hand. The sun had passed behind a cloud. The warm ray of light across my knees was no longer there.

5

I could hear ringing in my ears. The sort of sound you get after a concert or a sinus infection. I'm not sure when it started. Maybe it was just that long phone call. It was already as hot as Greece inside the flat. And I knew it was only going to get hotter when the sun moved completely round to this side of the building later in the afternoon. I wondered if it was best to carry on leaving the windows open, or if I was only letting in more heat. An overwhelming feeling of tiredness washed over me. I hauled myself up on to the sofa, thinking that somewhere at the back of my mind I'd always had an inkling about this. The feeling that life couldn't really be this simple.

I leaned back, took some deep breaths and felt a weak breeze just about reach me as I sat there on the sofa. I surrendered to the heavy, numbing tiredness and felt myself slowly drift from consciousness and into a wonderful drowsiness where time and space and thought gradually dissolved. After a while I fell asleep, and only woke up when my phone buzzed.

It was a text from Roger. *Call me*, it said. But I didn't feel like calling. Not just then.

I stretched out my legs and lay back on the sofa. The fabric was warm. I felt warm, right down to the roots of my hair. Everything was warm. For a brief moment I got the impression that everything was just a dream, until I caught sight of the ice-cream tub and the number written on the bottom. All of a sudden it felt pretty irresponsible that I'd gone out to buy ice-cream when my financial situation was so precarious.

I had a bit of a headache when I stood up and wandered aimlessly round the flat until I finally ended up in front of my collection of vinyl records. What could they be worth? There were quite a few genuine collector's items. I had a number of limited-edition Blu-ray films, and then there were my instruments, of course, but no matter how I tried I couldn't get anywhere close to the amount required. 5,700,150 kronor was more money than I could even imagine.

I toyed with the idea of simply running away. Leaving the country. How many resources would they devote to tracking down someone like me?

I could take the bus to Nynäshamn, then the ferry to Gotland, and hide out there on some pebbly beach. Or get the train to Copenhagen, then hitchhike down to Germany ... What then, though? I could get all my money out of the bank, buy a plane ticket to the USA, and stroll about Manhattan drinking milkshakes and eating pastrami sandwiches. In a way, the thought of just taking off like that was quite tempting. But what would I do once I'd actually got there? And the thought of never coming back ... No, I was happy here, after all. I had my friends here. All my memories. I liked my flat, the changing seasons. I liked lying on the sofa ... But of course if there was no other option ...

I picked up my phone and held it in my hand for a while. If Mum was still alive I would have called her. That would have cheered her up, something as simple as that, even if she'd have been worried about the size of the debt. Maybe she'd have been able to come up with a solution. She usually could. I stood for a while tossing my phone from hand to hand. In the end I rang the only number I could think of.

6

Maud answered on the second ring. She sounded much calmer now. It felt odd, after the long wait in the queue the previous evening, suddenly to get through to her straight away this time. It made me feel a bit special.

'What would you do if I just disappeared?' I asked.

'Disappeared?' she said.

'Yes.'

'In principle it doesn't really matter where you are. This applies to everyone. Top-up payments, or in your case the whole amount, can be made from anywhere. And in whatever currency you choose. You can live wherever you like, as long as you don't try to avoid your duty to pay.'

I thought for a moment.

'And if I did, what then?'

'Well,' she said, 'we'd put out an alert for you. Your bank accounts, driving licence, passport, credit cards would all be frozen or revoked. You'd be a marked man. You'd never be able to get a loan, for instance. It would be – how can I put it? – difficult. Why, are you thinking about it?'

'No,' I said, and sighed. 'I don't think I am.'

'Good,' Maud said, 'because I'm under orders to report any

suspicions about potential absconders. It would be nice not to have to do that.'

I thought I could detect a hint of a west-coast accent, and tried to work out where she was from. She was doing her best to speak a sort of standard Swedish, but every now and then a trace of a chirpy, rounded intonation crept into the end of her sentences. It sounded rather cute, somehow.

'So how are you getting on with the money?' she said.

I rubbed my face and tried to sound like I was on the case. Like I'd done nothing but play with numbers and call people for help since we last spoke.

'Not great,' I said.

'You don't have any investments or shares?'

'No.'

'Jewellery? Gold?'

'I've got a few rings, that's all . . . a couple of candlesticks. But that doesn't . . .'

I sat down on the sofa and was about to lie back again when it occurred to me that she'd probably be able to tell from my voice that I was lying down. That wouldn't make a very good impression.

'Can't I just work off the debt, bit by bit?' I said.

Maud took a deep breath. Once again I had the feeling that this wasn't the first time she'd had to explain this. She sounded rather mechanical when she replied.

'Assuming that you have a normal capacity to work, naturally we'll conduct an evaluation of your abilities, relative to the amount owing. But there are a lot of people to be investigated and of course that involves a great deal of administration – it's not at all certain that will even be necessary. And, as I said before, we do have a debt ceiling, and once that's been exceeded there's no way we can grant continued access.'

'What's the debt ceiling?'

'It's calculated according to a formula that takes account of age, place of residence, particular experiences, success, proximity to the sea. That sort of thing. Quality of home and relationships, et cetera. Taken as a whole, that constitutes your personal quantity of Experienced Happiness. Your levels will be constantly updated, provided that all information can be verified. It's all officially administered, of course, but I'm afraid I can't make an estimate as things stand ... Have you had any notable setbacks?'

I stared at a small mark on the wall opposite the sofa. It had been there for as long as I could remember, and I rather liked it. It felt reassuring. Homely. I wondered if it had been made by me or the previous tenant.

'How do you mean?'

'Okay, let me start with this,' she went on. 'Are you disabled?'

'No,' I said.

'Do you suffer from any illnesses?'

'No. Well, nothing ... no. I get a bit of asthma sometimes.'

'Asthma?'

'Yes, a bit. Occasionally, in the spring.'

'Oh?'

'And I might be a bit lactose intolerant.'

'Hmm, that isn't applicable. Not any more. Not now there are so many new products and alternatives available ... Did you grow up with both your parents?'

'Yes.'

'There you go. Yes, that marks it up ...'

Images from my childhood drifted through my head. Mum smoking a Blend cigarette under the extractor fan in the kitchen, Dad bent over the car with the bonnet up, my little tricycle, the broken doorbell. Long grass at the back of the house and the rusty lawnmower that was supposed to cut it.

'But we weren't especially rich or anything ...' I said.

'That doesn't make any difference to the experience, does it?'

'I don't know, I think maybe it does ...'

'How do you mean, exactly?'

'Well, if I'd been brought up ... I mean, it was pretty tough sometimes when Dad was the only one working ...'

'But you were happy?'

'What?'

'Was your childhood satisfactory?'

I hesitated for a few seconds.

'Well, yes, I'd have to say it was ...'

'There, you see?'

I wondered how old she was. She sounded a bit older than me, but that didn't necessarily mean that she really was. The slight hoarseness in her voice lent her a certain veiled charm, but she could have been five, ten years younger than me. That sort of thing is always hard to work out. Maybe it was just her official tone, that way of reciting things quickly, or the fact that she knew things that I didn't. It wouldn't be the first time. I often felt about seventeen years old mentally. And she was definitely older than that, no matter what.

'Like you replied to our questionnaires . . .' she went on. I closed my eyes and tried to focus my thoughts in the heat.

'Hang on a moment,' I said. 'Questionnaires?'

'Yes, you indicated . . . let's see . . .'

I sat up a bit straighter on the sofa. I had little beads of sweat on my forehead and temples. I could feel the phone getting damp and slippery against my cheek.

'What questionnaires?' I said.

'Our inquiries show that . . .'

She paused, and I heard her click to open something on her computer. Now I remembered some questionnaires and forms I'd filled in several months ago. Big things, with all sorts of different questions and boxes you had to tick. I think I did them while I was on the toilet. Then you just had to stick them in the pre-paid envelope and put them in the post.

'I'm getting several results here . . . Let's see . . .'

I stood up and started to walk round the room.

'Yes, but . . .' I said. 'I thought filling those in was just a bit of fun . . . I didn't really take it seriously.'

'You didn't?'

'No, because then I'd have thought about it a bit more . . .'

'You didn't really think about it?'

'Well, not really . . .'

'Here we are . . . Five written surveys and one telephone poll.'

I suddenly remembered a phone call, something like six months ago. A young woman. I enjoyed talking to her. She had a sexy voice, and for once she wasn't trying to sell anything. It was kind of fun, choosing between the possible answers: agree strongly, agree, disagree or don't know.

Maud went on: 'I'm getting quite a high reading from this.'

I wandered into the kitchen, then back into the living room.

'Really?' I said. 'Oh . . . I must have been happy that day.'

'But you did answer truthfully?'

'That depends how you look at it.'

'What do you mean?'

I walked up and down between the sofa and the wall, glad Maud couldn't see me.

'It changes,' I said. 'From day to day. I mean, sometimes you're in a good mood, so things don't feel so important . . .'

'Really?'

I sat down on the sofa, but stood up again immediately.

'I think it's rather unprofessional to base everything on surveys like that. I mean, how was I to know that my answers would form the basis of—'

She interrupted me again.

'Obviously that's not the whole picture. Your responses are only advisory. The calculations are ninety per cent based on absolute facts. But all the evidence suggests that self-evaluation gives a fairly good prognosis.'

I tried to remember those questions, and what I had answered. Maybe I'd been trying to make out I was more successful than I really was? After all, I did like the woman's voice. Maybe I was trying to impress her? I could even have just been messing about and making things up.

'Have you got my answers there?' I said. 'What did I say?'

'I've got a general overview. Basically just the scores. I can see the analysis of your results, which are the raw data presented in a more accessible format. If you want more information I'd have to put in a request for your file to be brought up. It could take a while.'

I told her I did want more information. She said she'd get back to me and we hung up.

7

It was late afternoon before she called back. I could tell that I should have eaten something, even if I wasn't exactly hungry. It was completely still outside, extremely hot, and somewhere in the distance a car alarm was going off.

'There's rather a lot of material,' she said. 'It's not available digitally yet, and I've only just received it, so obviously I haven't had time to get to grips with the details properly . . .'

'Okay,' I said.

I could hear her leafing through some papers. She almost groaned as she picked up something heavy. We exchanged some polite jokes about 'the paperless society'.

'You wanted the questionnaire results . . .' she eventually said.

'That's right,' I said.

'If you could just confirm your address, I can send them to—'

'Have you got them there?' I asked.

'Yes,' she said.

'Can't you just tell me what I said?' I went on.

She hesitated for a moment.

'It will take a while to dig them out.'

'I can wait,' I said.

'Er . . . well, we don't usually . . . over the phone. But if you tell me your address I can send you a copy . . .'

'But,' I said, 'can't you just read them out? I mean, I've given you my ID number and everything.'

She said nothing for a few moments.

'Well, I suppose so,' she said slowly.

'Just a few of them,' I said.

I heard her shuffling the documents again.

'Okay, you'll have to wait a moment while I go through the file.'

'I'm happy to wait,' I said.

We sat there like that for two or three minutes without saying much at all. Just the sound of her breathing as she searched through the documents. I found myself thinking that she should put the phone down, then realised that she was probably wearing a headset. She cleared her throat and went on.

'So, what do you want to know, then?' she said.

'Just the first few questions . . .'

'Okay,' she said after a brief pause. 'Question number one, then . . . let's see . . . age, gender, education . . . But I suppose what you really want to . . . okay, here it is: Do you think your life has a purpose, a meaning? And you answered . . .'

I imagined I could hear her running her finger across the page to the column of answers.

'Yes,' she continued. 'The first option, in fact. "Agree strongly".'

Yes, that was true. I had a clear memory now of having given that answer. I wondered if I might have replied with the first option to almost all the questions. I mean, it felt a bit cool to stick to the same response. Sort of like shrugging my shoulders at the questions. Not taking it too seriously.

Maud moved on to the second question.

'Do you feel that your opinions and ideas are listened to at your place of work?'

What opinions and ideas?! I could hardly have any ideas, apart from renting films to people who came into the shop. Maybe sell the odd bag of crisps or two-litre bottle of drink. Jörgen didn't give a damn about any opinions I might have. We never talked about that sort of thing. I got paid, and I kept the shelves tidy. That was all. What was I supposed to answer? Most of the time I just stood there thinking about other things, trying to keep an eye on the time and when I could go home. Sometimes Roger would pop in, and if I had time I'd stand there chatting to him. Maybe check out a few videos on YouTube. I thought it worked pretty well, and I certainly didn't have any better suggestions about how to run things.

Maud was about to read out the third question, but all of a sudden I felt I didn't want to hear any more, and said I had to go. I don't even know if I said goodbye properly.

8

With some reluctance, I had to admit that I was actually pretty happy with my life. I didn't really have anything to complain about. No impoverished childhood, no addictions or abuse or emotionally cold upper-class teenage years at a prison-like boarding school. The years I spent in our little terraced house on Fågelvägen seemed to have passed without any real conscious thought. My parents were dead now, but, to be fair, they were both well over seventy when they died, so not even that could be counted as particularly traumatic. And I still had my sister, even though we didn't see much of each other these days. The best thing about her was her kids. In limited doses. I was undeservedly happy with my tranquil existence here in my flat, and I'd never really dreamed of anything more. I hadn't had a proper relationship since Sunita, and naturally I sometimes wished I had a girlfriend, but I had to admit that most of the time I was happy on my own, and the internet came in very useful.

I didn't miss company. On the contrary, I was happy if I could avoid it. Especially compared to my sister's chaotic life, trying to juggle work and preschool and vomiting bugs and family therapy sessions. I couldn't really think of any injustice that had left any deep scars. Roger was always falling out with people. He often told me about the quarrels he had with his brother, or the National Insurance people, the Tax Office, people he owed money to, or who owed him money. Obviously I got upset and miserable sometimes, but most of the time I soon forgot about it and moved on. That sort of thing never really made much of an impression on me. I loved my parents, and of course I missed them, but I didn't actually have a problem accepting the fact that they were gone. That was just the way it was.

I tried to remember the last time I was properly angry. The previous week I swore out loud to myself when the handle of a paper bag broke and all my shopping fell out onto the pavement. I had to carry it all in my arms, and was seriously cross by the time I eventually made it back to the flat. But it passed, and I was soon in a good mood again when I realised I had three copies of the *Metro* in the flat with their crosswords still unsolved.

Maybe I didn't take problems seriously enough, and just took everything that was thrown at me without protest. Was I too gullible, too accepting? Should I set higher demands? Would I actually be better off if I was more suspicious, a better negotiator?

9

I heated up a slice of pizza in the microwave. It was good, but there wasn't enough of it. Then I sat at the kitchen table for a while, just thinking. The soft, warm summer air had become sticky and suffocating. It was difficult to think clearly, all my thoughts just bounced around. Any sense of true harmony was impossible to achieve. I noticed I was having trouble sitting still. So I phoned again. Even though it had gone eight o'clock in the evening.

'I've actually been very anxious,' I said.

'You have?' Maud said. 'When?'

I pushed my knife and fork together on the plate and suddenly realised I was thirsty. I should have had a drink before I called. I could feel my mouth sticking together with nerves.

'What?' I said. 'How do you mean . . . ?'

'What days?'

I gulped a few times.

'You mean I'm supposed to remember exactly what days—'
She interrupted me without apologising. She was fed up of me now. I could tell.

'If you want a deduction for anxiety, I need to know the precise times.'

'I can get a deduction for anxiety?'

'Provided it can be verified, or you can give us specific dates that can be compared with other activities that aren't incompatible with mental ill-health, then obviously you can set reduced mental well-being against your total E. H. score. What year are we talking about?'

I nudged the cutlery round the edge of the plate, a bit like the hands of a clock, and did a quick calculation in my head.

'Er . . . this year,' I said.

'Month?'

I wasn't used to lying or making things up. My mouth felt even drier, and I got the impression it was audible in my voice. But on some level I felt I had to make the most of any opportunity, and took a chance.

'January,' I said.

'Okay, I can't see any note to that effect,' she said.

'No, but it's true.'

'Mmm . . . And on a scale of one to five, where one is normal and five incapable of any activity at all?'

'Well, er . . . five,' I said.

I thought it was probably best to exaggerate.

'Goodness,' she said. 'What date?'

'The first.'

'The first of January?'

'Mmm. And the second and third.'

'Okay. Any other dates?'

I hesitated for a moment.

'No, that was about it . . .' I said.

'So everything was okay again on the fourth?'

'Yes, I suppose so . . .'

'Suddenly nothing?'

'Er . . . yes.'

I heard her take a sip of coffee or tea. A drink would have been nice.

'Is this really true?' she said after a brief pause.

I was a hopeless liar. I knew it. It would have been embarrassing to go on.

'Well . . . no,' I said.

'No,' she said. 'I guessed as much. How about you and I agree to stop messing about now? Then we can try to come up with a proper solution to this instead.'

'Okay,' I said, feeling pathetic. 'Sorry.'

She murmured something. And I got the impression that she didn't think it was that big an issue. That she was prepared to overlook it, and that she'd probably experienced similar things before.

'But I do suffer from anxiety,' I said. 'Honestly. I can't remember any specific dates or exactly how bad it was, but . . . well . . . I feel really bad sometimes.'

'Okay . . .'

There was a different tone to her voice now. Sympathetic, somehow. A bit like a psychologist, maybe. Perhaps they were trained to sound that way, to keep people calm.

'I often get anxious about nothing special,' I said.

'Oh?'

'And I don't know why. I get hurt easily, and I'm very sensitive about everything, without any particular reason. In the spring, for instance, when you'd expect to be happy and cheerful. I often feel a bit depressed then.'

I could hear her drinking more coffee as I talked.

'You realise that's all part of the experience, don't you?' she said eventually.

'Sorry?'

'And that it's the whole experience that you're paying for?'

I pulled my fork across the plate, knocking the knife off. It clattered against the porcelain. She went on: 'Think about it like this: when you go to the cinema – one day you might see a comedy, the next a tear-jerker. The experience isn't any the less valid as a result. It all gives E. H. points, you see. You know as well as I do that pain isn't a universally negative emotion, don't you?'

I said nothing.

'We wouldn't want to eat nothing but sweet things . . . just as little as we'd want to avoid all adversity. In fact, there has to be a degree of adversity for us to appreciate our blessings. I mean, think about the mix of ingredients in really good food dishes. Like that song Lasse Berghagen sings about Stockholm, "A mixture of sweet and salt" . . .'

I pushed the plate across the table. Raised my hand and massaged my forehead. She went on: 'Well, there's nothing I can do about it now. Your case has already been assessed.'

'Is this a punishment?' I said suddenly. 'Because I haven't mourned my parents enough?'

'What?' she said, sounding genuinely surprised. 'What makes you say that?'

I sighed and pinched the bridge of my nose between my fingers. I could feel myself getting a headache.

'Well, maybe it hasn't had time to sink in properly yet. I've just been carrying on as normal. Is that insensitive of me? I mean . . . maybe I haven't been as upset as I should have been . . . My sister did a lot of crying and screaming, then got all quiet and depressed and all that, but I . . .'

'Don't be daft,' she said gently. 'This is nothing personal. Your score is entirely experience-based.'

'Can I appeal against it?' I said.

'Of course. But that can take a long time, and it doesn't alter things as they stand right now. You see, this is more than a national issue. It's a question of the division of resources. Obviously each country pays a large portion of its total with a collective national amount. But then the bill has to be divided. Between everyone. I'm sure you can understand that. Floods, famine, starvation . . . If you compare that with – what did you say? – feeling a bit miserable in the spring?'

'Mmm,' I said. I didn't feel like thinking about it any more for the moment.

After agreeing that I would start by paying what little I had in the bank, we hung up and I realised that I was still very hungry. It occurred to me that I hadn't eaten anything all day apart from that slice of pizza. I went and made a cheese sandwich. I poured myself a glass of full-fat milk, and downed it in one. As soon as I'd finished the first sandwich I immediately made myself another one. I felt insatiable. It was a wonderful feeling to be able to surrender to hunger, instantly, without restraint. The taste of the cheese, bread and milk married to form a wonderful union. Just then I couldn't think of anything nicer.

I sat back down at the kitchen table and realised that all was lost. There was no way to change the situation. I simply had to accept the facts. So what was likely to happen?

As I had already been told, they couldn't kill me. She'd said as much. Through the open window I could hear the birds' evening song. People laughing and talking to each other. Friendly voices. It was approaching the time of day when the whole city relaxed. The sound of voices and footsteps outside kept growing. People going to the pub, sitting at pavement bars. This whole situation no longer felt so important. In a way, the feeling of acceptance that was spreading through me was actually pretty good, relaxing. I made up my mind to drink the rest of the carton of milk. It tasted good, almost all the way to the end.

10

It was late in the evening, but I still called. I'd remained seated at the kitchen table pretty much the whole time, listening to the city outside. I had watched darkness slowly settle over the rooftops as the sounds changed. A couple were arguing. I could hear fragments of what they were saying, but not enough to understand what it was about. A woman laughed loudly, for a long time. A dog barked, and a group of young men sang some football chant. Every so often a gust of cooler air would push its way into the warm kitchen, caressing my face and arms. I sat where I sat, and there was no reason to go anywhere else. Life was just so good, somehow. It was perfectly natural that it should be expensive.

I dialled the number but there was no answer, and it struck me that even Maud must need a break, maybe to go to the loo or get something to eat. Maybe she too was sitting listening to the sounds of the city? Maybe they had a roof terrace? Maybe she was sitting up there smoking a cigarette or drinking a cup of coffee in the balmy summer night? I hung up, waited half an hour, then called again.

'Yes?' Maud said, and sighed. I could clearly hear the

irritation in her voice. She knew it was me. She probably had one of those screens where she could see what number was calling. This can't have been what she expected when she gave me her direct number.

'Well, I'm sitting here in the kitchen, experiencing happiness,' I said pointedly.

'How nice for you,' she said.

'Yes,' I said. 'I can't help wondering what's going to happen with that?'

She didn't reply immediately.

'How do you mean?' she said.

'I mean, right now I feel really good, and that, along with all the coming experiences – I don't really like to admit it, but . . . well, it's going to happen again. This year, maybe next . . . What's to say that I won't owe five million all over again in a year's time?'

Through the window I could see a drooping pot plant that my neighbour had left out on the balcony when he went away for the summer. Maybe he thought it would survive on nothing but rainwater, but it was unlikely to last much longer in this sort of heat.

Maud let out a deep sigh. She was tired of me now.

'You really don't get it, do you?' she said.

I got no further than a drawn-out vowel, it might have been an 'e', and was just about to reply that maybe I didn't get it when she went on regardless: 'This is a one-off amount. That's the whole point of it. This is when it's happening.'

'What is?' I said. She sighed again.

'Surely you can't have missed . . . This is when we're going to regulate . . . implement the big adjustment. It was made perfectly clear in all the information leaflets. If you have a look through your inbox . . . I think I may even have mentioned it myself—'

'But,' I interrupted, 'it could end up being incredibly unfair. Let's say I'm one of the people paying most now, but then I go and get some disease tomorrow that might torment me for ten, twenty years.'

'Of course,' Maud said. 'But the money has to be paid now. And the past is the only thing we know anything about, isn't it? The future's . . . well, we've got no idea, have we . . . ? Neither you nor I can know if we'll still be standing here tomorrow.'

We were both silent for a while as we thought about that. I watched a fly struggling against the windowpane, constantly bouncing off it. In the end I said: 'I'm sitting down. Aren't you?'

I thought I could almost detect a smile.

'No, I'm not, actually,' she said. 'I'm standing.'

'Have you got one of those adjustable . . . ?'

'Precisely. After all, I have to spend a lot of hours on the phone.'

I suddenly felt rather sorry for her. It must be an incredibly wearing task, sitting there day after day, dealing with all sorts of agitated people and explaining something that you hadn't yourself come up with. In this sort of heat. Didn't she ever long to be outside? It was actually pretty fantastic that she was prepared to give me so much of her time. How many people could there be in the queue at that moment, waiting to get through? Perhaps she did like me a bit after all?

'What are you wearing?' I said.

It just came out. I hadn't planned to say it. It was as if my brain had gone soft in the heat. As if the whole atmosphere had changed just because it was night. Everything felt a bit unreal. I regretted saying it before I'd even finished the sentence.

'Sorry?' she said, as if she genuinely hadn't heard.

'Nothing,' I said quickly. 'Sorry. It was nothing.'

'Okay,' she said, sounding distant again. As if she didn't quite know how to behave when the conversation strayed outside the usual boundaries.

I could feel myself blushing, and it struck me how little it took for me to become keen on a woman. It really didn't take much at all. As long as she wasn't directly off-putting. Often all she had to do was be kind and pleasant. Or not even that. The unpleasant sort could also arouse my curiosity. Most of the time it was enough for a woman to show any sort of interest in me. But not even that was a necessity. I appreciated disinterest as well. In fact, I was even attracted by it. I realised that I didn't actually need anything at all to get my attention. It would probably be easy to trick me into anything at all, as long as it was done with a bit of imagination. I basically thought the best of people, and assumed that most people wished me well. And no matter what the reason, it did feel rather intimate, talking to someone at this time of day. Almost a bit exclusive. What sort of working hours could they have? In fact, wasn't it extremely peculiar that you could call pretty much anytime, and still talk directly to this woman?

I stood up and started looking for the invoice. What sort of official body was W. R. D., anyway? What did it stand for? It sounded made-up. Did it really exist? Didn't the font that the payment demand was printed in look a bit odd? There was actually something rather amateurish about the whole form.

I tried to remember what she'd said. And the more I thought about it, the more it sounded like a classic scam. A young woman with a seductive voice tells a man he owes a load of money, and has to pay it into a particular account. How many films had I seen on that theme? And wasn't there something a bit suspicious about the fact that she was devoting so much time to me? When did she look after the others? And where was she, anyway? Was she even in the same country as me? It was naïve of me not to have thought about all those gangs that operated through numerous ingenious connections and encryption systems and were almost impossible to trace. And this was exactly how they operated. What had I actually heard? Office noises. That could be anything. Maybe even a recording?

I walked about trying to find the invoice, holding the phone to my ear, but with neither Maud nor I saying anything for a long while. Why was she suddenly not speaking? Had she guessed that I suspected something? Maybe I ought to call Roger or my sister and check with one of them? After all, no one I knew had said anything about this. And there was something a bit odd about those people discussing it out in the city, wasn't there? Something not quite right, in an indefinable way. That mother and son talking as if they were reciting a script. And the way she was looking in my direction the whole time. Or the woman in the lift, jangling her necklaces and talking about her invoice and loan a bit *too* explicitly for it to feel natural . . .

Obviously they'd been told to get close to me and say those things within earshot.

I closed my eyes and tried to think. It would be ridiculously *foolish* to pay a load of money into an account without checking things out more closely. The more I thought about it, the more incredible it seemed that I would never have heard anything about this before that invoice popped through my letterbox. Maybe they specifically targeted single people with a shaky grasp of what was going on in the world, and got them to believe a load of lies?

When I failed to find the sheet of paper and neither of us had said anything for almost a minute, I went and stood by the window. A shiver of belated insight ran through my body. That was my first reaction, I thought. That was the first thing I thought: Fake invoice. I tried to remember how much information I had given away, apart from my address, date of birth and ID number.

In the end, I said straight out: 'How do I know you're not trying to trick me?'

She remained silent. I went on without waiting for her to answer.

'Maybe this is all just a trap? It's the sort of thing you hear about, after all. Have you seen *The Spanish Prisoner* by David Mamet? That conspiracy film, where everything turns out to have been fake? Or that other one, what's it called? *The Game*, with Michael Douglas. How do I know you're not trying to deceive me, and are going to vanish with all my money?'

She didn't say anything. I thought it felt like a nervous

silence. The silence of someone who had been found out. What can anyone say, once everything has been uncovered and revealed?

I couldn't deny that it was incredibly well done. Grandiose, really. Putting together such an advanced plan, appealing to the victim's guilty conscience like that, and making it sound almost plausible. In a way it actually felt a bit unkind to have to put a stop to it. I mean, I'd started to enjoy those conversations. I'd have been happy to carry on talking to her each evening. She was drinking coffee again now. Rustling papers, or tidying something in the office.

'Well,' she said eventually, 'naturally you're entitled to book a meeting and come up and talk to one of our advisors, if you'd rather do it that way.'

11

W. R. D.'s Swedish headquarters consisted of a number of adjoining buildings made of speckled grey granite. An apparently endless flow of people moved to and fro across the shiny stone floor of the main entrance. A large black sign bearing the words 'World Resources Distribution' in gold hung above a row of no fewer than six lifts. Along one wall water trickled down smooth, polished granite in a steady, even stream. The large, south-facing glass wall let in plenty of light, and there were big square pots containing what might have been fig trees at the foot of it. There may have been gentle music playing in there, unless it was just the well-judged design itself that was contributing to the harmonious soundscape. Between the third and fourth lifts was a map of the entire complex, with a large 'you are here' arrow to indicate where I was.

The advisors were on the eleventh floor, and their reception area had glass doors facing all directions, making it impossible to ignore the view. Straight ahead, opposite the lift, a woman was sitting at a desk looking through some papers and answering the phone. She asked me to take a seat. I sat down in one of the armchairs grouped to one side of her. To my left was an empty conference room, and to the right the sort of open-plan office I imagined Maud worked in. I amused myself by trying to work out which one she might be. There were a dozen or so people in there, and most of them were indeed standing at height-adjustable desks. My attention was taken by a woman with long hair in a brownish-beige dress. She looked calm even though you could see she was talking very quickly. It was surprisingly quiet out where I was sitting, considering the level of activity behind the glass doors. Only one door had frosted glass, and through it came a man with combed-over hair. He introduced himself as Georg and asked me to go with him to one of the meeting rooms.

Georg was wearing a suit with no tie, and looked like he was the same age as me, possibly a few years older. He had thinning dark brown hair with a hint of red in it, and I wondered if he dyed it. He sat down opposite me and put a thick folder on the table.

'Well,' he said, looking at me. 'You wanted a meeting in person?'

'Er, yes,' I said. 'I've got a few questions.'

He nodded and smiled.

'Hmm,' he said. 'What sort of questions?'

I held out my hands.

'How it can come to so much, for instance?'

He nodded again. He was clearly used to questions of this sort.

'Let's see, now,' he said, opening the folder. 'You've been talking to . . .'

'Maud,' I said.

223

He glanced up at me, then looked back down at the folder. He adjusted a long strand of hair that had fallen across his forehead, and ran his finger along the bottom of one page.

'Maud . . . Maud Andersson – yes, that's right. One moment.'

He went out to the young woman in reception, then came back in. He sat down and leafed through the file, apparently not bothered by my presence. He had a large pile of documents from the local council, the regional council, schools, the address register, betting companies, and so on. There was a humming sound from the ceiling, from the air conditioning or some sort of ventilation system. I noticed that there were small surveillance cameras in each corner. Simple, flat lenses, big enough to make you realise that it was no secret that every nook and cranny of the room was covered. We were probably being watched the whole time by someone sitting somewhere else. Maybe they were listening in as well.

Through the glass walls, I eventually saw a tall, thin woman in a navy blue jacket and skirt walking between the tables. She had full lips, fair hair cut into the nape of her neck, but longer at the front to form a little arc round her cheeks. She went out into the reception area, then came over towards us, tapped on the glass and pushed the door open when Georg indicated that she could come in.

'Hello,' she said to me, holding out her hand.

I stood up and was about to utter the phrase I'd thought out in advance: that she looked just like she sounded on the phone, when I realised that she didn't sound the same at all. I looked at the eyes and hair, and those lips that seemed too full to be entirely natural. And while I was thinking that she didn't look at all like I'd imagined, she introduced herself with a long, complicated surname that I didn't quite catch. It sounded like the name of a bank to me. Or a firm of solicitors. I can't remember what it was, neither her first nor last name. Neither of them was Maud, anyway.

Georg stood up as well. He adjusted his glasses and took the chance to brush an invisible hair from his eyebrow. The woman smelled faintly of some fresh, cool perfume, and she had a small brooch on the lapel of her jacket, a flower or wreath of some sort. I wondered if it meant anything, or was simply supposed to be attractive. She sat down on the chair next to Georg without leaning back in it, put a file on her lap and glanced at the papers Georg was leafing through. Now and then the corner of her mouth twitched in an extremely professional smile.

'Yes . . .' Georg said. 'It's a good life.'

'Yes, it is.'

The pair of them looked up at me, rather surprised, as if they hadn't been expecting an answer. Georg quickly went back to looking through his papers, and the woman with the bank-name looked at hers.

'It's going to be an awful lot of money,' he said.

'Yes, I suppose you . . .' I began again, before I realised that he was addressing her the whole time. This was a conversation between the two of them. Clearly they were going to discuss the material before I was given the opportunity to comment on anything.

The woman with the bank-name nodded and smiled again. Slightly indulgently this time. Then she turned back to Georg.

'Who compiled the summary?'

'Someone called Maud,' Georg said.

'Maud?'

'Yes, it says Maud Andersson here, must be someone down on the second floor . . .'

The woman with the bank-name ran her pen along the lines of Maud's report and worked her way through column after column, reading quickly in a fairly low voice.

'Okay, a clean sweep of H. C.s, across the board, high E. H. points since the age of twelve, no empathy inhibitors. Parents both deceased, no family of his own, but regular experience quotient from comparable relationships. No setbacks noted since last December. Zero poverty rating. Top score on the emotional quotient . . . A number of good friendships over the years, all high engagement. Also an uncle – full marks as a role model. The child's response regarding the subject is fully emotional. Reliable, but with no great responsibilities . . . Strong emotional attachments without any pressure to achieve.'

She moved on through the file, still pointing with her pen.

'Besides the welfare premium, whiteness premium, male premium, there's also . . . let's see . . . No problems sleeping. Workplace compatibility one hundred per cent. One old friend – Roger – who visits regularly, but no social obligations. In other words, nothing but positive attributes . . .'

I realised that none of this was really meant for my ears, but somehow it was rather wonderful to hear my life described that

226

way. Almost impressive. I thought it sounded as if Maud had summarised my life in an extremely elegant way, and I couldn't help noticing that Georg raised his eyebrows a few times.

The woman with the bank-name sat there straight-backed throughout in a way that I thought must be uncomfortable, but presumably she was used to it because she didn't look at all troubled.

She had quite a small face, which made her eyes look disproportionately large behind a pair of glasses with heavy black frames. She might not have been conventionally beautiful, but there was something about her that commanded respect, which itself could probably be regarded as attractive, I reasoned. And if her lips had been filled, there was no denying that it was a very good job.

'Art? Culture?' Georg muttered.

'High musical receptiveness,' she went on, reading out loud from Maud's report. 'Responds positively. Affected by stimuli of the simplest harmonic variety.'

'Payment capacity?' Georg said, and the woman leafed through her papers and pulled out another sheet.

'According to the report, extremely low, no private wealth, although no home inventory has been carried out ... yet ... even if the respondent declares that he has ... let's see ... "instruments".'

She put a hand to her mouth as she cleared her throat. Or suppressed a giggle.

'And a small collection of science-fiction literature. Value unknown.'

Georg turned to me at last.

'Well, then . . . And you haven't made any payments?'

Out of the corner of my eye I could see the woman with the bank-name glancing at the report, evidently unable to resist shaking her head. That could have annoyed me, but I was still too astonished that Maud knew so much about me and had summarised it so nicely in that document.

'Er, no . . .' I said.

He frowned and hummed to himself as he carried on looking through his papers.

'It's fairly unusual for people with similar scores to you not to have any money,' he finally said. 'Your category mostly consists of people with relatively large assets. Some, of course, were born with a silver spoon in their mouths, which is also one reason why their scores are so high – it all forms part of the same picture, so to speak. But even if they weren't born rich, their Experienced Happiness often gives them a certain excess of energy, if I can put it like that. This is usually reflected in financial gain. But with you . . . the situation seems rather different . . .'

'Yes,' I said, and laughed, holding out my hands.

Georg fixed his eyes on me.

'You do understand how much money we're talking about here?' he said.

I slowly shook my head and blew some air out of my mouth.

'Not really . . .' I said, and laughed again.

Georg didn't look remotely amused. The woman with the bank-name pulled out one of the documents and inspected it more closely.

'You owe 5,700,150 kronor,' Georg went on. 'The interest alone will swallow up everything you could ever earn. Where do you work?'

I stretched and tried to adopt a confidence-inspiring expression, but the situation was somehow too absurd to really take in.

'At the moment I'm working part time at . . . Jugge's Flicks.'

'*Jugge's*?' Georg said, and both I and the woman nodded. He looked at me sceptically, then turned towards her again.

'We'll have to arrange a home inventory as soon as possible,' he said.

But she didn't respond. She was fully absorbed in something in the file. She leafed back and forth, comparing different sheets. She made a note of something. In the absence of any response he turned back to me. He put down his pen, sighed and rubbed his eyes.

'How on earth could you have failed to notice you had to pay?' he said. 'You don't live in the middle of a forest, do you?'

'No,' I chuckled.

'It can be extremely hard to reach people living in isolated shacks,' he went on seriously. 'People in the desert or up in the mountains who don't have any direct contact with the outside world. Obviously that doesn't happen too often in our department, but you can imagine . . .'

I nodded.

'The information has to be gathered somehow.'

'Of course,' I said.

He ran a hand through his hair, squinted and looked at me

carefully as if he thought I was some sort of interesting aberration.

'Do you have a television?' he asked.

I nodded.

'So how could you . . . ?'

He held up a hand and counted on his fingers.

'Our information campaign, all the discussions . . . the whole debate.'

'I really don't watch much television,' I said.

'Really?' he said.

'I mean, it's not as if I've got anything against television,' I said. 'Quite the opposite.'

I thought about how easily I got distracted by practically any programme. No matter what it was about. I got drawn in and fascinated by pretty much any moving pictures. The most obscure little broadcast, the most niche interest, could capture my attention and carry me off to other worlds – the more out of the ordinary, the more interesting I found it.

'Still, I think I ought to clarify . . .' I went on. 'I mean, I really do think, if you make a proper comparison . . . I think I should point out . . .'

Even though I was trying, I couldn't really come up with a good way to finish the sentence.

'Hmm,' Georg said wearily, looking at me. 'You're questioning our calculations?'

'Well, I just think . . . er, I don't know.'

He waited to see if I had anything else to add. When nothing appeared he leaned back in his chair, crossed one leg over the other and said in an authoritative voice, 'Our calculations have been developed and refined over many, many years. This is an incredibly complex science, as I hope you can appreciate. This isn't just any old *felicific calculus*, you know.'

He smiled faintly.

'Obviously it has its roots in Bentham's early theories, or, if you prefer, Pietro Verri . . .'

He laughed again. This was obviously highly amusing.

'But in recent years we have developed a much more finely calibrated set of tools. Of course, we have access to a vast amount of information. Obviously this is all more than a mere mortal can hope to gain an overview of, but the programme deals with the constituent parts in an extremely sensitive way, and, when taken in context, each aspect can be calculated with a good degree of accuracy. For instance, we use both cardinal and ordinal measures.'

He brought his fingertips together.

'Instruments of this complexity give us the possibility to evaluate each individual's results. So when the main decision about international redistribution was taken . . .'

He held out one hand.

'. . . well, we were all ready to get going.'

I nodded as if I understood. As if I had even the slightest idea of who these men were and what their theories meant. Verri? Sounded like a footballer. Georg gathered his papers together and looked at the time.

'You'll have to stick around for the next few days and wait for the investigators,' he said, and made to stand up.

'Hold on a moment,' the woman with the bank-name said. She pushed one file towards Georg.

'Take a look at this,' she went on, holding out another sheet of paper and placing it on top of the first. 'It doesn't match.'

She and Georg both inspected the figures one more time. Looking from file to file and comparing amounts. The tips of her fingers slid silently across the paper.

'Who did these calculations?' she asked.

'Well, it came from Twelve, so it must have been the economists in . . .'

Georg started to look for a signature on the sheet of calculations as the woman talked, half to herself, half to Georg.

'Look at this, here . . .'

She pointed at one column, then moved her hand to another sheet of paper.

'And then compare it with this . . .'

They both hunched over the documents. I felt like taking a look as well, but thought it probably best to stay where I was. I had a feeling I wouldn't understand much of those numbers and diagrams anyway.

Georg ran a hand through his thin, tinted hair. The woman suddenly got to her feet and hurried out to the reception desk. She came back with a calculator and apologised.

'I'm terribly sorry,' she said, 'but there seems to have been some mistake here.'

'No problem,' I said. 'I'm not in any hurry.'

Georg took the calculator and tapped in some numbers.

'This isn't right at all,' he muttered. They stared at each other.

I felt some of the pressure in my chest ease and my shoulders slowly began to relax. On some level I had always suspected that things couldn't really be as bad as all that. The amount was obviously far too high for it to have anything to do with me. With a bit of luck everything was going to get sorted out now.

'See here,' she whispered. 'They've added those two numbers to that one. That's why . . .'

She looked up at me and smiled again. Her face looked tenser now, making her smile look stiffer, more like a grimace.

'We really are terribly sorry,' she said.

She put the pen down and tapped at the calculator.

'There's been a mistake . . . a miscalculation. The amount you need to pay isn't 5,700,000 kronor. It's . . .'

They both stared at the calculator.

'. . . 10,480,000 kronor.'

12

When I got back to the flat everything seemed to have taken on a different tone. The whole place had changed. Everything suddenly looked colourless. It was as if I could see how cheap and simple it was for the first time. Shabby. I saw the empty pizza boxes sticking out of a paper bag, waiting to be taken out to the bin. The dirty dishes in the sink, the sun-bleached curtains, the sagging sofa.

The worn old thresholds I walked over day after day. The dust on the floor, table and window sills. The old, washed-out clothes scattered all over the place. But also the things I liked best of all: my flat-screen computer, the shelves of films, the games, the rug with the Heinz logo. The Beatles mug. My Asimov collection. The M. C. Escher poster, of that waterfall that seems to be flowing upwards, and which I had been saying was my favourite picture for several years. Now it just looked banal. Clichéd and ordinary. The old mirrored picture with the Coca-Cola logo, which, admittedly, had felt old and ridiculous for years, but nonetheless held so many memories. Sketchpads and pens. Some paintbrushes. My guitars. The Indian statues Sunita had given me. The big bookcase full of vinyl records and magazines. The CD collection. The boxes of neatly arranged

234

cassette tapes. The things that had been my most cherished possessions. Now the whole lot felt dead. Lifeless. Why had I kept all this stuff?

A menu for the Thai restaurant was stuck to the fridge door, with one from the pizzeria on the freezer. There were circles round the Calzone Special and Pompeii. My favourites. The two I could never choose between, before I always ended up ordering the Calzone. The same calendar I always bought, the one I felt comfortable with, was hanging from the inside of the open kitchen cupboard, completely blank. I felt like bursting into tears.

13

The next day it was my turn to be back in the shop. It was fairly quiet. The tape in the kitchen had come loose and the door of the cupboard under the sink was hanging half-open as usual. I fiddled with it for a while until I got it to stick again, even though I knew it wouldn't last long. I made some coffee in the scorched jug as the peculiar events of the past few days buzzed round my head. It was difficult to make any sense of things. The astronomical amount of money, the strange way they talked at W. R. D. I wasn't used to that sort of thing. I couldn't help thinking that I really didn't want anything to change at all. Then I found myself thinking about the internet and changed my mind. Obviously there were some changes that were good, and some bad. But I realised it was sometimes hard to tell the difference. Dynamite, for instance: was that good or bad? I stood by the shelf of documentaries and reflected upon good and bad changes through the ages. As I thought about which ones had to be counted as the biggest changes over the years, I realised that I had a tendency to rank more recent changes above older ones. For instance, industrialisation above the invention of the wheel, or the telegraph above the shift to fixed human settlements. I ranked my personal three favourite changes in the western world during the past three centuries, and suddenly I was standing there with the BBC's documentary about the Suffragettes' struggle for women's votes in my hand. Then I came across a film called *Iron Jawed Angels*. It looked good. I must remember to watch it. And Tom Baker would soon be releasing a new film called *The Voice*, which had to be about Frank Sinatra, I thought. Unless it was about Ella Fitzgerald? Perhaps it was about that talent show? Then I came up with a new way of puffing out my cheeks and amused myself with that for a while.

After that I found the remains of an old sticker that someone had stuck to the side of the counter, now just fragments that it was quite fun to pick off with my thumb and forefinger. Twenty minutes or so later, I'd almost managed to get rid of it all.

I called and ordered a Thai takeaway, and just after lunch a red-haired girl came in with a whole bundle of films she was returning late. She was in a bad mood, and thought we should have sent a reminder. I said we usually did just that, but she shook her head and said she hadn't received one.

'Well, that sort of thing happens sometimes,' I said. 'There might be something wrong with the computer . . .'

We agreed to drop the fine for late return, seeing as there had obviously been a problem with the reminder, and she looked a bit happier when she left.

I wondered if she'd received a huge bill from W. R. D. as well. I reasoned that we should probably try to keep each other's mood up as best we could. Set a good example to each other. Eventually things would slip back into some sort of everyday routine again. Somehow it felt slightly reassuring to know that we were all in the same boat. She was pretty when she smiled, I thought. Freckles can be very attractive.

A bit later that afternoon I stuck an old video into the little television with a built-in VHS player behind the counter, and had time to watch the first half of *Blade Runner* before finishing for the day. As I shut and locked the shop I remembered that I had been planning to change the background on my phone again, but hadn't got round to it. Oh well, I thought. That's something else I can still do.

On the way home I walked past one of those big advertising hoardings. 'Give or take', it said in big blue letters. For the first time I noticed the name of the advertiser, their logo printed in the right-hand corner. Letters that were so wide and stylised that they didn't really look like text. Three cubes with just tiny differences to indicate the separate letters. The first was a very solid crown, and the other two like boxes with lines and dots on. Only if you looked closely and, like me, had spent a lot of time over the past few days in the company of that acronym, could you make out the letters W, R and D.

14

I got home just before seven, and had started leafing through the latest catalogue from an IT company when my phone buzzed in my pocket. For some reason I thought it was Maud, but when I answered I heard Roger's breathless voice at the other end.

'Hi! Have you had yours?'

'What?' I said.

'Invoice. Have you had yours?'

It sounded almost like he was running. He probably wasn't, but his way of sighing as he spoke, combined with his general poor fitness, made it sound like he was.

'Hang on,' he said, as if he'd just remembered something he had to do. 'There's someone here . . . Can you call me back?' He hung up.

Roger had always been very careful with money. Presumably he was worried about being poor or feeling exploited, unless it was just in his genes. And apart from adopting various rituals to save money – the sort all really mean people do, like never leaving tips, taking his own bags to the shops, reusing unfranked stamps and old envelopes, turning the car engine off when he was going downhill, all the usual stuff – he had also got into the habit of never making phone calls and waiting for people to call

239

him instead. No matter how urgent it was. If he ever did have to make a call, he made sure he started the conversation, then broke off quickly so the person he had called would have to phone him back.

He answered on the first ring.

'Yes,' I said, lying down on the sofa.

'It's unbelievable, isn't it?' Roger panted. 'What the hell's it all about? As if there wasn't enough shit to deal with already. Now they want even more money. It's insane. Don't you think? Completely insane.'

I put both legs up on the armrest. It struck me that I almost always lay down when I talked to him. As if I had a particular posture for conversations with Roger.

'Yes, it is.'

There was a crackling, knocking sound down the line, as if he'd dropped his phone or bumped into something. He never did just one thing at a time. He was always busy doing things that no one else really understood. He had the ability to sound in a hurry even though he didn't have a job, or anything else he had to do.

'Hello?' he said after a while.

'Yes,' I said.

'I mean, it's completely unbelievable. Isn't it? You think this sort of thing only happens to people who are well off. Now I've got to get a bank loan and all that crap. I'm going to have to mortgage the boat or something . . . Are you still there?'

I said I was, as Roger battled on with whatever he was doing. It sounded like he was out in the wind. Were there people in the background? Maybe he'd gone down to the marina to look at his main asset. At first it felt rather reassuring that even Roger was going to have to make some sort of sacrifice. It felt good to have someone I could share my worries with. A man with his attitude to money must be completely beside himself at receiving an invoice like that. It must have hit him like a bomb.

Roger had a very nice sailing boat that he took good care of. It was his passion. He would take me out on it in the summer. In return for a contribution to the cost of the petrol for the engine and as long as I brought food, beer and so on. We usually ended up floating about in some inlet somewhere. Drinking beer and watching the birds. But even though it was nice, it was still a fairly small boat. Six or seven metres at most. How much would he be able to borrow against that?

I put my legs back down and sat up.

'How much was yours, then?' I asked.

'What?' he panted as he fiddled with something. His voice sounded muffled and distant. I could tell he'd wedged his phone between his ear and his shoulder.

'How much have you got to pay?' I said.

'A fuck of a lot,' he said in a loud voice, to make himself heard over the sound of an engine in the background.

I stood up.

'How much?'

'220,000 kronor.'

15

The sun was going down over the city, casting dazzling reflections off the rooftops. It was still so warm that I had the windows wide open. I could hear the rowdy voices of children playing football or hockey down in the street. Their warning cries to each other whenever a car appeared. How could I possibly have ended up being charged so much more than Roger? There had to have been some sort of mistake. They must have missed something. Maybe they'd got me confused with some rich kid from the Wallenberg set? Or some oligarch. Admittedly, Roger was a tragic loser with no income and no prospects. Obviously I would have expected to have to pay more than him, anything else would have been very odd. But this? This was unbelievable.

I did a quick run-through of the problems and setbacks I'd experienced in my life, and decided that I was far too wretched to warrant this new amount of 10,480,000 kronor.

I lay down on the sofa and thought about how much I missed my parents. This was precisely the sort of time I'd have called them to say I was in trouble. I'd have a bit of a moan, and they would have listened carefully with the phone between them, then they'd have comforted me and said that everything would be all

242

right. And then it would have been. I felt an intense longing for
the warm, fluffy feeling that always blossomed in me as soon as
I'd dumped a problem on them. Then I could have curled up in
my pyjamas in front of the television with a bag of cheesy puffs.
I thought about all my friends. They'd long since got married and
had kids, and they barely had time to see me any more. What
had once been deep friendships and endless days of
unconditional socialising and spontaneous outings, weeks of
shared discoveries – at one time they were the only fixed point
in my life – long conversations, discussions about politics and
relationships and the world . . . All of that had soon been reduced
to a snatched cup of coffee in passing or a quick beer once every
six months. The only one left was Roger, who had never seemed
to be able to make much sense of life. He never really offered
any resistance to anything, and was no great support. As time
passed he was getting increasingly stressed about growing
older, and the fact that he never had time for anything, that
nothing ever really happened. But at the same time he never
seemed able to work out how he wanted things, and just sank
deeper and deeper into self-loathing and an increasingly
unhealthy attitude towards money.

He always managed to feel hard done by. It was as if he
assumed he was going to end up the loser, even if things actually
looked okay. With the passage of time he would turn his
successes into failures, like some back-to-front version of
Buddhism. Any unexpected moments of happiness always
carried with them a measure of unease, which eventually took
over. Once, a long time ago, his beloved boat fell off its winter

stand on the quayside, and ended up with a big hole in one side of the hull. 'It's a fucking nightmare,' Roger said. 'It's going to cost tens of thousands to repair.' After some investigation, it turned out that the crane-driver had knocked into the stand earlier that winter, and that the marina was therefore obliged to pay for the damage. A conflict flared up between the marina, the crane-driver and the insurance company. Each thought that one of the others was liable.

'Typical,' Roger said when he finally got me to call him. 'Now no one wants to pay. It's going to cost me tens of thousands of kronor.'

He spent all winter going on about how many tens of thousands of kronor it was going to cost him. Eventually the insurance company agreed that it was their responsibility and that Roger would get full compensation for the damage. When the hull was being repaired, it turned out that it made more sense to replace a good part of the deck as well. A highly professional boat company did the work very thoroughly, and in plenty of time before the sailing season began. To smooth things over, the marina offered to waive the rent for the following year. So when it came down to it, Roger had actually gained from the whole business. But he still went on referring to it as a huge disaster, and took it as proof that only bad things ever happened to him. 'Do you know,' he would often say, even years later, 'the whole thing cost tens of thousands of kronor.'

For the first time in a long time I missed having a girlfriend. I found myself thinking about Sunita, and felt a tug at my heart.

I thought about the evenings we spent in her beautiful flat in Vasastan. It was really her father's, but because he worked in Mexico and the rest of the family lived in India it was basically hers. When we were together it had almost felt like mine. Even though I always knew that our relationship was finite.

We met at the film club at the university, where she was studying. The members were mostly foreign students, and the club organised a programme of screenings of Swedish classics on Monday evenings. Bergman, Sjöberg, and so on. I was invited to come and run the sessions. The film club offered wine, and I would give a short talk about that week's director, explaining recurrent themes, showing stills and short clips, and on the whole I enjoyed doing it. Each Monday evening after the movie, Sunita and I would stand there looking at one another, and in the end I asked her where she was from, and she told me, not without a degree of pride and in surprisingly broken English, that she was from the holy city of Varanasi, but had grown up in Bombay. That pride, combined with a very fetching degree of shyness, made an indelible impression on me. She seemed so incredibly exotic. Maybe I seemed the same to her. We never spoke anything but English, but I think she knew a bit of Swedish, even if she pretended she didn't. She loved films, and Bergman in particular. I managed to get hold of special editions with extra material, and we spent hour after hour in front of the television in her big living room, on an enormous soft white sofa.

Sunita's father was a diplomat. He had recently been transferred from Sweden to Mexico, but for some reason he didn't want

Sunita to go with him. Maybe he thought she should finish her education first. It was probably also to do with the fact that she had an uncle who lived in Sweden who could act as a combination of guardian and chaperone, albeit from a distance. And presumably they also reasoned that it was safer for Sunita here. They hadn't counted on me.

Sunita was the apple of her father's eye, and the affection was mutual. Time and time again I heard about how great this father of hers was. That all Indians only wanted sons, but that her mother and father had been happy when they had a daughter. That it was extremely unusual for a daughter to be allowed to travel and study. Sunita always said she loved her father above everything and everyone else, and because he was such a distant presence I had no problem with that.

Her relationship with me had to be kept secret, under all circumstances. No one must know anything. Not our families, and not our friends. I wasn't allowed to breathe a word about our relationship to my friends or anyone else I knew. She had been granted a few years to study and see the world, but she would have to go home and get married before she turned twenty-five. That was non-negotiable. The family already had a number of candidates lined up back at home. I never really understood the point of that whole tradition of arranged marriage and the caste-system, apart from the fact that it was the father who took the decisions, and that she belonged to a higher caste than most people and that this fling with me would be regarded as absolutely inconceivable. The sort of thing that simply didn't happen. It was so far beyond the bounds of possibility that it was unthinkable.

Eventually the whole family would be reunited back in India. But in the meantime she was able to live a relatively free life here in Sweden. The only requirement was that she studied hard and was still a virgin when she returned to Bombay.

She wasn't.

She was very careful to start with. Me too. We talked a lot. Mostly about films, but gradually more and more about each other. She would light candles and incense. She had dark eyes – almond-shaped, that's what people say, isn't it? – and incredibly soft skin. Long hair, and oddly full cheeks given the fact that she was otherwise fairly slender. She often complained that her backside was too broad, and that her nose was too big, but she was actually astonishingly beautiful. I loved just looking at her. I told her, and I think she rather liked the fact that I did that. She was always beautifully dressed, in green, yellow and red fabrics that looked extremely expensive.

We took every precaution we could. We never spoke to each other in public, and rarely let anyone see us together. We never phoned each other, and came up with a special code and secret signs that no one else would be able to understand. A twist of a bracelet would mean that there was a sealed letter at the reception desk where I came and went fairly regularly to pick up films and packages for the film club. To start with they were just short messages: '9 p.m.', for instance. Which meant that at nine o'clock precisely I would step through the door on the other side of her block, cross the courtyard and be let into her apartment a couple of minutes later. Never any knocking on doors. Never any doorbell.

Once we were there we would stand for a while in the big living room, just looking at the view. We would talk about the weather and university, maybe about something that had happened. Sometimes she would offer me mineral water or juice of some sort. Then she would very slowly start to take off her thin layers of clothing, almost in passing, while we talked about something else or watched a film. When the film was over we would sit still and just wait. Breathing. Inhaling each other's scent. Looking into each other's eyes. Sometimes for several minutes. I never imagined I would ever meet a woman like her. In a way, I was just happy to be near her, but the prohibition of love and our mutual caution – the tentative way we approached each other physically – meant that the air in the room was charged with desire.

Only after a number of weeks did we actually touch one another, slow, feather-light strokes, and it was even longer before we kissed. Slowly but surely we shifted the boundary of what was permissible. Once or twice relatives or guardians or governesses or whatever they were showed up. On one occasion, the state I was in meant that I had to hide on the balcony. Otherwise, I was a special tutor who was helping her with her studies. Maybe I was given a title and name, I don't know. They would spend a long time talking. I didn't understand a word, but to judge from their behaviour it looked like they accepted her explanation. That uncle of hers never appeared. Maybe he had people who checked up on her for him. Either way, everyone seemed happy, and she remained unsullied in their eyes. None of them seemed able even to entertain the thought that anything untoward might be taking place in that apartment. Which was ridiculous – we were young, after all.

As time passed our messages became more and more refined. Sometimes the letters contained gifts. Serviettes or a box of matches bearing the address of a certain restaurant. That didn't mean that she and I were going to meet there, but that I was welcome to look in and pick up a signal about what might happen later that evening.

Sometimes I would find the place and sit down alone at a suitable distance, and watch her dine with one or more of her relatives or whoever they were. If she twisted her bracelet a specific number of times, that was a sign that it was okay to go back to hers afterwards, as long as I waited until the coast was clear before creeping in the back way and being let in for a late-night rendezvous.

As we grew more comfortable with the arrangement, she also became more provocative. Once there was a padded envelope waiting at the reception desk. Inside was a note with a time and the address of a smart restaurant, plus an item of clothing which she wanted me to understand that she wouldn't be wearing beneath her brightly coloured sarong that evening as she ate dinner with three elderly ladies and a gentleman who all looked like they were liable to fall asleep at any moment. I sat five tables away and couldn't bring myself to order anything but a Coke, which was a blessing seeing as even that turned out to cost three times as much as I thought it was possible for a soft drink to cost. At one point during the evening she glanced in my direction and looked me in the eye for a long moment. Suddenly

I began to worry that she had twisted her bracelet and that I had missed it. I was sure I had noticed some sort of movement, but perhaps she had just been checking the time? I sat there for a long while with ice cubes in my mouth, just staring at her in the hope of picking up a more obvious signal. But none came. Just to be sure, I went to her apartment anyway. I stood there on the landing, thinking I could hear her inside, but the door never opened.

She had an ability to smile with her whole face when she looked at me, as if she could see past the mask, past my ordinary, everyday self. Sometimes when we were lying in bed she would trace the features of my face with her finger. From my hairline, down across my forehead and nose, over my chin and down to my chest. It was like a film.

I was never allowed to sleep there. When it was late enough, I had to gather my clothes together and get dressed, then creep out the same way I had come in.

When Sunita had turned twenty-four and finished her degree, the anticipated command arrived from Mexico telling her to move back to Bombay to get married, and Sunita didn't hesitate for a second. She was conditioned to obey her family's wishes, and constantly surprised me with her loyalty to a system which – in my world, at least – could only be regarded as oppressive. She was utterly faithful to her father's wishes, and just got angry if I questioned any part of the arrangements. She was proud of her roots and who she was, and it would never occur to her to want to change anything. And that was something that no arguments about gender equality or fleeting erotic adventures would change.

On our last night together, we made love and cried the whole time, and the next day we stood at Arlanda Airport separated by a safe distance of thirty metres. Between us we had all her many relatives and hundreds of passing strangers.

A brief glance, then she was gone.

It took me several years before I could really think about anything else. I imbued all music with my own heartfelt sorrow, compared every sad lyric with my memories of us. Every so often I would wake in the middle of the night and imagine that she was there beside me. But each time the bed was empty. Sometimes I would walk past one of the restaurants she had sat in and imagine that I could see her, but it was always someone else.

I slowly sat up on the sofa. I ran my hands through my hair and wondered if I had ever really got over her. Since Sunita I hadn't had any long relationships. I compared all women to her. I searched in vain for that spark, that intensity . . .

I realised I was never going to experience that sort of erotic charge and intense tenderness again. Occasionally I wondered if she still thought about me. Did she remember me? Did she remember any of our adventures and secret meetings, or had she suppressed it all? On some level she must still miss what we had. A bit, at any rate. How much had she and her family had to pay to W. R. D.?

The sun had gone down. It was dark inside the flat, but I

couldn't be bothered to switch on any lamps. I alternated between lying down and glaring at my worthless possessions, and sitting up and scratching my head. Evening passed and turned into night. I ought to have gone to bed, but I could just feel myself getting more and more upset.

16

'I don't understand,' I said to Maud when she eventually picked up, sounding slightly drowsy. 'I don't think this is fair at all.'

I heard her clear her throat at the other end of the line.

'No ... hmm ... I heard that your amount had been adjusted,' she said.

It was the middle of the night. Maybe she was trying to get some rest between calls. Maybe she'd actually dozed off? Obviously even she needed to sleep sometimes. Either way, right then I didn't care. I'd been lying on the sofa for hours, getting worked up about the unfair calculation. I felt I had to vent my frustration.

'Adjusted?' I said. 'It was doubled!'

She was moving something. A duvet, maybe, or a blanket.

'Yes, I looked through your file afterwards and, well, it's an impressive result, I have to admit. They managed to get your figures badly wrong upstairs in—'

'But my friend Roger—' I interrupted her, before she immediately interrupted me, as usual with a practised harangue. She could probably do it in her sleep.

'It's best not to try to make comparisons,' she said. 'It's incredibly hard to see the differences if you haven't been trained and understand the system.'

I didn't care about that now. I felt like I'd heard enough.

'I think it's deeply unfair,' I went on. 'The more I think about it, the worse I feel. I mean, I haven't done anything at all with my life. Not a thing. I haven't travelled or studied or applied myself to anything . . . I used to drift about with my mates and talk a lot of rubbish and hang out at bars. And now I sit here every day watching films or playing games or listening to music. In the past few years I've always gone to the same supermarket and bought the same cereal for breakfast. I get the same coffee from the same café, I still work at the same place, and I basically stand there doing the same thing every day. Then I go to the same restaurant and get a takeaway. I even go to the same kiosk when I want ice-cream. I usually grab a Pizza Grandiosa, "X-tra everything, 40% more taste", and heat it up in the microwave. If I want to push the boat out I buy a Nogger ice-lolly for dessert. Two, even. I never go out. I don't see any friends. That's no sort of life!'

'Why don't you go out?' Maud said.

She sounded more alert, but her voice was still a bit hoarse. More than usual, anyway. For a moment I caught myself wondering if she was wearing night clothes. How did she prefer to sleep? At the same time, I was too upset really to think about her like that. For once, I was just too angry. Sad, even. And I noted how effectively that strangled any tendency towards flirtation.

'I don't know,' I said. 'I hadn't thought about it until after I spoke to you. You tell me I have to pay because I've had it so easy, but in actual fact I've had a really shit time.'

'But you had all the prerequisites for . . .' she began.

'That just makes it worse,' I said.

I could feel I wasn't far from bursting into tears, at the thought of all the things I could have done. Sunita – should I have chased after her? Should I have gone to India and found out where she lived and tried to take her away from there with me? Where to? Back to Sweden? To live in my flat, as the partner of a part-time shop assistant at Jugge's Flicks? Would she have agreed to that? Tears pricked my eyes, making me sound more strident. It probably came out more aggressively than I intended.

'That's the saddest thing of all. I had every opportunity, but what the hell have I done? Nothing. Nada. Not a damn thing.'

Maybe she was scared, or just worried that I was going to start crying over the phone, but she sounded much softer now.

'How did that happen, then?'

'How the hell should I know?' I said. 'It just did. The years passed. You don't think. Everything's all nice and familiar, and I suppose I'm frightened of getting hurt or something . . . I don't know . . . I've always avoided conflict, and I've always been really happy if I could get away without quarrelling with people. Before, I used to be happy when I managed to avoid things, it felt like some sort of victory, you know, like I'd got away with something and didn't have to do something I didn't want to. Like being let off homework at school, or managing not to get beaten up in the playground. But now . . . God, I don't know, it feels like I've been fooled somehow, as if everything I avoided was actually . . .'

I could feel my eyes stinging.

'Well . . . actually life itself.'

I couldn't hold back any more. I started to howl down the phone. Bellowing like an animal. I didn't care what she thought. She was welcome to think it was unattractive and awkward. Oddly enough, she didn't seem remotely worried. Quite the contrary. She said in a gentle voice: 'So what would you like to do?'

I lay down on the floor on my back. Looked up at the ceiling and tried to breathe calmly. The floorboards actually felt fairly cool.

'I don't know,' I said. 'Anything. I might have liked to travel, meet people. More girls. Tried different things . . . You know, maybe do something illegal . . .'

I closed my eyes and snorted the snot back into my nose.

'Nothing, really. I suppose I should just have been more aware of what I did have. I mean, we talked about the sun and all that before . . .'

'You said you liked the view,' she said.

I noticed that I had raised my voice.

'Exactly. So why the hell didn't I go outside? Why didn't I take the chance to enjoy everything a bit more?'

'Why didn't you?'

I stared up at the ceiling. There were cracks in it. Hard to see where they started. It was like it had cracked in several different places at the same time. I found myself thinking about really old porcelain. After a while I lowered my head to stretch my neck.

'I don't know,' I said. 'I suppose I'm just a – what do they call it? – a creature of habit.'

'Yes, we've noticed.'

'What? How?'

'I mean, our inspectors.'

I stretched my neck some more, back and forth, grateful for the hard floor that didn't move when I did. It was nice. Almost like a massage.

'Inspectors?' I said.

'They're the ones who give us information. They've also noticed that you're – how shall I put it? – a person of regular habits.'

'Horribly regular,' I said with a snort. 'It hasn't struck me before, but it's pretty damn tragic.'

I rested my head back on the floor.

'Are you being honest now?' Maud asked.

'Yes,' I said, clearing my throat to get my voice back under control.

'I mean, this isn't just something you're saying to get the debt down? Like when you said you were anxious?'

'No.'

I lay there on the floor thinking. Thinking about life. About all the times, the moments, that were gone for good. All the encounters and people. Quite without warning I realised that tears were welling up in my eyes again without me being able to do anything to stop them.

'And I miss my mum,' I said in a cracked voice. She said nothing for a while. Just waited. Let me catch my breath.

'You were very fond of your mother,' she said, more as a statement than a question. I couldn't bring myself to answer. I nodded to myself and sniffed.

We were both silent for a few minutes. I couldn't remember the last time I'd opened up to anyone like this. It felt good, in a way. Like a new me. She didn't seem to have anything against it. She could have hung up if she didn't want to listen. But she let me go on.

'We went camping one summer in Närke,' I said.

'I know,' she said. 'I saw.'

'You did?' I said. 'Yes, of course you did.'

'Let's see, 1984, wasn't it?' she said, but corrected herself immediately. 'No, '85.'

'Probably,' I said, trying to wipe the tears from my cheeks. 'It rained the whole time,' I added, for safety's sake.

'Yes, I saw that as well,' Maud mumbled.

'Mum and me. And Dad and my sister, of course . . . We hired a caravan.'

'A mobile home, wasn't it?' Maud said. 'The year before you hired a caravan. A Cabby, Model 532. In 1985 you had . . . Ah. Sorry. You were about to say something . . .'

I went and got a piece of kitchen roll to blow my nose on.

'Right, yes, a mobile home.'

We said nothing for a bit. I blew my nose as quietly as I could.

'Did you like the rain?' she said.

'Well, I don't like it when it rains non-stop . . .'

'No, of course not, but on that occasion it seemed to match your profile.'

'Really? Yes, it was nice sitting there. We didn't really do much. We just . . . Well, what can I say? We just *were*.'

I heard her leaf through her file again.

'Hmm. Yes, you score very highly for that week. Health, relationships, intensity, the oxygen content of the air ... Yes, across the board, actually.'

'We played Uno,' I said, feeling that I was about to burst into tears again.

'Sorry?'

'Uno,' I said. 'That's what we played.'

She said nothing for a moment.

'Oh. What's that?'

'Uno. It's a game. You've never heard of it?'

'No, I haven't, actually. Is it like Monopoly?'

'Sort of, but easier.'

'What's the point of it?'

I couldn't help smiling.

'What's the *point* of it?'

She sounded suddenly bewildered.

'Yes?' she said bluntly.

'I can't actually remember any more. I think you have to get rid of your cards or something. Well, it's not important. You've never played Uno, then?'

'No.'

'We should try it one day,' I said.

She didn't answer.

17

It was somehow easier to talk to her now. It felt more like talking to a friend. Even if she was still using that factual tone of voice. I realised that to her ears I must sound like an extremely sensitive, intuitive person. She was so correct. So definite. I suddenly got the impression that I was the opposite. But what did that mean? Wrong? And abstract?

'You're good at Sporcle,' she said. 'You get very high scores. Especially on film titles and directors.'

'Too right!' I said. 'I'm right up there . . . well . . . somewhere in the middle.'

She laughed.

'You don't have to cover up anything,' she said. 'Anyway, we've already got the information.'

'Mmm,' I said. 'Okay, I'm pretty good.'

I ran my hand across the floor. I ended up with a pale grey strand of dust on my fingertips. I really should get the hoover out.

'Is it fun, your job?' I asked after a pause.

'I'm not sure about fun,' she said. 'It's exciting to be part of the big change, and the work feels useful . . . I mean, it's an important task . . .'

'That Georg,' I said.

'Yes?'

'He's . . . What's he like?'

She thought for a moment.

'I don't know the people up there very well. But as far as I know, he's smart, and knows the procedures very well. Out of everyone at W. R. D., he's probably the one who's best at—'

'Does he dye his hair?'

She fell silent again.

'Hmm . . .' she began. 'Does he dye his hair? I don't actually know.'

'I bet he does,' I said. 'He reminds me of a character in a film.'

'Oh?' she said.

'I just can't remember which one.'

I crumpled the piece of kitchen roll into a ball and dabbed my cheeks again.

'Have you always liked films?' she asked after a brief pause.

I sniffed a yes down the phone.

'How long have you worked in the video shop?'

I thought she ought to have that in her files, but took a deep breath and thought about it. I cleared my throat and made an attempt to steady my voice.

'Er,' I said, 'it must be nine years now.'

She said nothing at first, as if she too was wondering if this really sounded like a ten-million-kronor life.

'So what's your favourite film?' she asked eventually.

'My favourite film? Oh, I don't know, it's so hard to choose. I almost always think there's something good in every film . . .'

261

I could hear her smiling at the other end.

'I could have guessed that,' she said.

'I mean, it's so hard to pick just *one* film.'

She muttered in what could been agreement, or just an indication that she knew I was going to say that as well.

'But there is one scene,' I said, after a pause. 'In a Bosnian film called *The Bridge*.'

'*The Bridge*?'

'Yes, it isn't a very well-known film. You probably haven't seen it, but ... it's, I don't know ... I often think about that scene.'

'Why do you do that?'

'It's ... How can I put it? It's good. It's a good scene. Anyway, what's your favourite film?'

She coughed.

'Mine?' she said. 'Oh, I don't watch a lot of films.'

I was on the point of saying I could have guessed that, but stopped myself.

'But you must have seen some?'

'Well,' she said, 'nothing very memorable.'

'So what do you do, then?'

'Me?'

'Yes.'

'I work,' she said quickly, and laughed.

I joined in. These conversations of ours were starting to feel fairly intimate. As if we'd crossed a boundary. As if we could talk about things that really mattered. Openly and honestly. Without embarrassment.

'No, but seriously?' I said.

She didn't reply at first.

'Well, I do work a lot, you know.'

We both fell silent.

'So, what do you like most?' I eventually asked. 'Films? Music?'

She laughed again. Unless it was more of a giggle.

'Art? Theatre, maybe?' I went on.

'No, not theatre,' she said.

'No?'

'No, I don't know . . .'

'Books?'

More silence. It was obvious that she wasn't used to this sort of role reversal. She wasn't at all comfortable answering questions, and would much rather do the asking herself.

'What do you do to relax?' I persisted.

'Well,' she said, 'I like reading the paper . . .'

Another silence, and I didn't really know what to say. I let my eyes drift from the ceiling to the sofa with its threadbare cover. She made a rustling sound, then drank some more tea or coffee. I tried to imagine her at home. The silence was still fairly comfortable.

'What amount did you get?' I said.

'No,' she said firmly. 'We don't discuss our personal amounts with . . .'

She didn't finish the sentence, and I never found out what she was going to call someone like me.

'Okay,' I said, 'but you could still tell me, couldn't you?'

'It's completely against the rules for an employee to divulge . . .'

'How about bending the rules a bit?'

She didn't answer at first.

'Like I said, it's best not to make comparisons,' she said. 'It's not helpful.'

'Maybe,' I said. 'But . . . ?'

She was breathing through her nose. I imagined I could see her smiling.

'Well, it came to a fair bit,' she said.

'How much?'

She laughed.

'Look, I really shouldn't . . .'

I could almost see her top lip curl. She was probably hoping I would leave it at that, that I would realise I had gone too far and drop the subject, but when I didn't say anything she finally came clean:

'700,000, more or less.'

We were both silent for a while as the amount hovered in the air between us.

'But,' I eventually said, 'that's nothing!'

'Like I said, it's extremely difficult to make direct comparisons . . .'

I sat up.

'So what is it about you that means—'

She raised her voice as she interrupted me.

'Sorry, it was stupid of me to agree to this. I really don't want us to discuss my private—'

'But that's incredible,' I went on. 'What have I got that you—'

'Like I said, it's hard to see how everything fits together . . .'

'Why didn't you end up with a higher—'

She interrupted me again, loudly.

'I got a low score in affirmation! Okay?'

'Okay.'

'My muscarinic cholinergic system doesn't allow for high results in certain areas,' she said, then fell silent as if she thought I should make do with that as an explanation.

'Mmm,' I said. 'And in the sort of language you can actually understand?'

'I scored very low in the individual aspect. Low durability in the reward section.'

I pondered those words for a moment.

'What does that mean?'

'That I'm bad at . . . Oh, I don't know . . .'

Then it was like she suddenly lost patience.

'What do you want me to say?! How am I supposed to explain this to you? There aren't any easier words! I'm just bad at . . .'

'Rewarding yourself?' I said.

She said nothing for a long time.

'You need to learn to *Experience*,' I said.

She laughed.

'Like you?' she said.

'Like me,' I said.

'Hmm. And look where that's got you . . .'

18

The windows were open while we talked. The night outside was still and warm. Nothing but the sound of a party in the distance. Funny how you can always recognise the sound, no matter how distant it is. Young people, perhaps thinking of going off for a swim in the moonlight, maybe staying up all night. Getting hold of some wine or beer and falling asleep together in a park somewhere as the first light of morning started to appear.

I asked if she sang, and at first she sounded irritated, as if she thought I was making fun of her. But when I said she had a good voice for jazz, and that it would be exciting to hear her sing, she laughed and said she'd think about it, that she didn't know much about jazz, and that there was absolutely no way it was going to happen that night. I don't know how long we talked to each other, but my cheek was starting to feel very hot, and I had to switch the phone to my other ear. It felt odd hearing her voice on that side.

'I think you should go to bed now,' I said.

She laughed.

'Well, I tried that, but someone called and woke me up.'

'So why do you always answer?'

She didn't say anything to that.

'You don't have to pick up,' I said.

She still said nothing. But I could hear her breathing softly. Perhaps she was lying down. It felt like she was. I imagined I could see her in front of me, lying on her side, more or less the same as me, with the phone pressed against her cheek, her eyes closed.

'You've handled this really well,' I said. 'The other day I thought you'd written a really nice report about me. I'm very happy with the way you've dealt with me. I feel both informed and well looked after.'

I heard her take a deep breath.

'Yes,' she whispered. 'But you're happy with so little . . .'

I pressed the phone closer to my ear.

'I think you deserve to switch that phone off now,' I said.

Silence.

'If you don't want to talk, I mean . . .'

Another long silence. I put the phone in my other hand and carefully brushed some hair from my hot forehead.

'But if you do want to talk to me,' I said, 'we can do that. I think that would be lovely. I really like talking to you. But if you'd rather not, that's fine too. But I think my case has been dealt with now, to put it in professional terms or whatever it is. You just have to hang up and go to bed. I wouldn't think any the worse of you if you did.'

She didn't make a sound. But she didn't hang up.

I lay down on the sofa and put the phone to my normal ear again.

'In *The Bridge*,' I began, 'close to the end of the film, it's so moving. They see each other in a café. Well . . .'

I wasn't sure if I should describe the scene, but something in the atmosphere, now that we were just sitting and listening to each other's silence, led me to carry on.

'They were lovers before ... but they haven't seen each other for several years, for the entire duration of the war. Then suddenly, one day ... She's there in the café and he just happens to pass by. There's something going on, I think they're both due in court ... They can't let on that they know each other. The atmosphere is strained. Neither of them dares to speak. They're about to go to court. They're on different sides of the case. She's there with her family, who are the accused ... He's there to give evidence against her brother or uncle or something. He catches sight of her from the square outside. And, as I said, they haven't seen each other for ... actually, I'm not really sure. I don't remember the rest of the film that well. But it's been a while, anyway. Quite a long time. Several years. And suddenly there they are. He's standing. She's sitting down. Yes, that's it. She's sitting at a table in the café. And suddenly they catch sight of each other. They look at each other. Neither of them says anything. Neither of them does much at all, in fact. There's no big reaction, but rather the reverse: almost no reaction at all. But it still means so much. It's like a perfect example of a really good film-scene. If you watched it out of context you wouldn't understand a thing. You'd just see two people staring at each other. Not even that, in fact. Because they really don't do much. They look at each other and realise who the other is. I think he looks at his watch at one point. He realises that there's still plenty of time before the trial starts. He decides to sit down on the spare chair at the same table. And, well, a worse actress could have made a right mess of it by overacting and trying to show her old infatuation, anxiety, anguish or excitement, sadness, anything at all. But she doesn't. She doesn't move a muscle. Yet we still know exactly what she's feeling. And that's precisely why we know. They sit there for a long time, on either side of the table, next to each other, but both facing away. Watching people go past in the street. She raises her cup of tea or coffee or whatever it is at regular intervals. His arm is resting on the top of the table. He's holding a packet of cigarettes, and turns it every so often, standing it on end, then laying it down again. At one point a waiter comes over and takes an order, and then an old man comes over and talks to her. Presumably a relative. We don't hear what they say because there's music throughout the scene, but he's probably telling her it's time to head off to the courthouse. Once again, a less talented actor could have spoiled things by acting out too much anxiety or angst or whatever. But the man just sits there.

'Once the other man has left they just go on sitting like that, facing away from each other. Him with his arm on the table, holding the packet of cigarettes in his hand. She's still holding her coffee cup. Suddenly he lets go of the cigarette packet and moves his hand a couple of centimetres towards her. Neither of them says anything. They both seem fully absorbed in watching the street. Gradually she moves her hand towards him, and for a moment the backs of their hands touch. One of her fingers trembles slightly. He takes a breath. Her little finger nudges his.

That's all. It's so well done. It's so sensual. I mean, bloody hell, I can feel myself shiver just describing it.'

Maud let out a laugh at the other end of the line.

'It sounds very good,' she said.

'I know, it really is!' I said. 'It's bloody brilliant!'

She laughed again.

We carried on talking until early in the morning. The sun rose slowly above the rooftops and shone its rays into the flat. Birds twittered as Maud talked more about her work. She revealed that she was hoping to get a position on the distribution committee, in phase two, when all the money was going to be shared out. I understood that she had been aiming for that the whole time, that that was what motivated her. I ended up listening to long descriptions of how the redistribution process would work, and tried to ask interesting follow-up questions.

We played a quiz on the subject of 'me'. Maud was unbelievably good at it, even if I suspected that she was cheating and looking at her files occasionally, although she claimed she was lying in bed and didn't have any professional material to hand.

'It's been a while,' she laughed. 'But I really am in bed now.'

'Good!' I said.

We talked a bit about Roger, and Maud wondered if he was really a particularly good friend, and I had to explain that he did have his good sides, even if it was hard to spot them at first glance.

At some point in the early hours of the morning I asked if I could have her mobile number, so my calls wouldn't have to be redirected to her, but she said that was against the rules, they weren't allowed to give out any private numbers.

'They're very strict about that,' she said.

Eventually the early birds began to emerge from their doorways down in the street. I could hear their rapid footsteps. The street-cleaners drove around, and slowly it got warmer and warmer inside the flat as we carried on chatting about all manner of things. We debated, laughed, disagreed with each other, fell silent, listening and waiting for the other to speak, the way I thought only teenagers did, and I could feel my head getting more and more fuzzy. The conversation became increasingly fragmented. I lurched from one emotion to the other. Laughed and cried. Lay there quietly and listened. Argued calmly at times, and held long, vaguely philosophical monologues. Every now and then I would lose my train of thought and stop abruptly in the middle of a sentence. Maud just seemed to get more and more giggly. It was nice to hear her like that. I began to worry about how she was going be able to cope with a day's work when she hadn't had any sleep, but decided not to broach the subject in case it led to her hanging up, because I didn't want that. Not now, when we seemed to have crossed some sort of line and anything seemed possible. Besides, she was a grown woman. Anyway, what did I know? Maybe she was on some sort of flexitime. She certainly gave the impression that she was perfectly capable of looking after herself. Considerably better than me, for instance.

I might have dozed off on the floor for a nanosecond. Perhaps

Maud did as well. I felt tired, but in a good way. Drowsy, almost like being drunk. Every so often I would make an effort to pull myself together, and when Maud finally began to hint that it might be time to end the call, I got it into my head to try to summarise what I had meant to say at the outset.

'Okay, well, er . . .' I began, letting out a big yawn. 'So, what now, then . . . ? Do you think it would be feasible to . . . ? I mean, it ought to be possible to correct my, er, E. H. score?'

I barely managed to get the sentence out, and Maud just giggled at me.

'Hmm . . . you mean change it?'

'Yes?'

'Based on what you've told me tonight?'

'Yes?'

'Hmm . . . No, I'm sorry.'

We sat in silence for a while, and eventually I couldn't help laughing too. It was all just too much. I rolled onto my side and ended up with the phone pressed between my cheek and the floor.

'Oh, what the hell!' I said, and sighed. 'I don't know. I suppose my life isn't that bloody awful.'

'No?'

Now she sounded both amused and surprised.

'Well,' I said, 'I mean, it depends entirely on what expectations you have, doesn't it?'

'I think it sounds pretty good,' she said.

I sighed again.

'Yes, but ten million kronor? Come on, I'd have thought you'd get a bit more for that sort of money . . .'

I got up on my knees, looked out through the window and caught sight of the pot plant on my neighbour's balcony. It was barely recognisable. The leaves were drooping over the edge of the pot, and there was something brown sticking up from the middle. I went and got a glass of water from the kitchen and tried to reach it with a few quick throws. Most of the water missed, and I wasn't sure if I was doing any good at all or just making the situation worse for the poor plant. I lay back down on the floor, took several deep breaths and suddenly felt a fresh wave of tears rising up inside me.

'And I can't help thinking about Sunita,' I said. 'It seems so incredibly tragic.'

'Sunita?' Maud said.

'Yes, it was all a long while ago now, but I still find myself thinking about it the whole time. It still hurts . . .'

Instinctively I put my hand to my heart. As if she could see me. As if it could somehow emphasise the pain I felt.

'Sunita?'

'Yes.'

'Who's Sunita?' Maud said in an entirely different tone of voice.

'Sunita. She was the great love of my life. We could have—'
Maud interrupted me.

'Hang on. We don't have any information about . . .'
'What?' I said.

I rolled onto my stomach and leaned my elbows on the floor.

273

Down the line I could hear her get out of bed and tap at her computer.

'I haven't got anything about a Sunita,' she said.

I got up on my knees, rubbed my eyes and tried to think straight.

'You're kidding?!' I said. 'You mean to say that you've managed to miss Sunita?'

I stood up, my body felt sluggish. Every step I took seemed jerky, like an ultra-rapid film sequence. But I couldn't help feeling a glimmer of hope. Had they really missed Sunita? Was it even possible that they hadn't taken account of the greatest sadness in my life? Maybe there had been more mistakes.

'She broke my heart, for God's sake,' I went on, in as reproachful a voice as I could muster. 'That's affected my whole life. There's not a day goes by without me . . . I mean . . . Have you really not taken that into account?'

I could hear Maud's breathing speed up as she clicked between various documents.

'Er . . . Not as far as I can see.'

'Holy shit,' I said. 'No wonder the invoice ended up being so expensive.'

'When was this?' she asked.

I wondered if she was typing on her laptop. Had she logged in from bed? Or was she taking notes the old-fashioned way with pen and paper?

'1998,' I said. 'To 2000. January 5, 3.25 p.m. We first met in '97, but didn't start seeing each other until the following year.

Okay, hang on a minute, something like this has to be taken into account, even retrospectively, surely?'

I heard her moving at the other end.

'You're sure you're not getting mixed up with some film you've seen?'

'Are you kidding?' I said. 'This is the biggest tragedy of my life.'

She tapped at her computer again.

'But this has to be taken into consideration!' I said.

I was pacing up and down in the flat now.

'This could . . . Bloody hell!' I said.

She was breathing hard. I could tell things were serious this time.

'Yes. I think it would be best if you came back in again,' she said.

19

On my second visit to W. R. D. a man came down and met me in the vast entrance hall. Everyone seemed extremely troubled by the mistake with Sunita. I was assured that a thorough internal investigation would be carried out, and led to believe that such occurrences were extremely unusual, and that it must have happened because she was a foreign citizen and the relationship hadn't been registered anywhere, as well as being kept secret from family and friends. Correspondence with their south Asian office hadn't been entirely without friction, and the systems there probably needed to be reconsidered. It had long been a problematic area.

On the way out of the lift by the reception desk on the eleventh floor I was met by an older woman in a jacket and tight skirt, who made a rather girlish impression in spite of her age. She smiled and tilted her head as she spoke. She had a little scarf tied round her neck, a bit like an air hostess. She thanked me for my cooperation, and promised compensation for the intrusion into my working hours. I didn't mention the fact that I had simply swapped shifts with Tomas, who wanted all the extra hours he could get before he went off on holiday to Torremolinos. It was no problem at all. He had told me I could have the following day off too.

The woman in the scarf handed me an unwieldy bundle of forms, which she told me to fill in before the meeting. She led me through the open-plan office to the far end of the building, to another small room with glass walls. In one corner was a plant that looked like it was made of plastic. She pulled out a chair for me and asked if I'd like anything to drink while I went through the paperwork.

'I don't know,' I said. 'Some water, perhaps?'

'Still or sparkling?'

'Er . . . sparkling.'

I sat down on the chair and began to fill in the forms.

The questions were concentrated around the years 1997 to 2002. I made a real effort to answer as truthfully as possible this time, and not exaggerate.

After a while the woman returned with a bottle of mineral water, a glass and a coaster. She put them down on the table a short distance from my papers.

'I'll be back shortly with a bottle-opener.'

I thanked her and went on answering the questions as best I could.

It got quite warm in the little room when the sun came out, and I had to take off both my jacket and sweater and sit there in just my T-shirt. I checked a few times to see if I could smell sweat. It was much quieter in there than in the last meeting room – presumably at the expense of any ventilation. Every so often I looked around to see if I could catch a glimpse of Maud, but then I remembered that they had said something about her working down on the second floor. Anyway, I had no idea what she looked like. Even if I imagined that I'd know who she was as soon as I laid eyes on her.

The woman in the scarf stayed in the vicinity the whole time after she'd brought the bottle-opener. As soon as I was ready with one of the forms she would come in and get it. Otherwise she stayed outside the room. At one point Georg appeared and exchanged a few words with her. They both looked in my direction and I nodded slightly, but he showed no sign of returning my greeting.

After an hour or so inside the stuffy room I started to get tired. The questions were of various sorts: Describe an event. What happened first? What did you do next? Option 1, 2 or 3, and so on. There were various scales I had to make marks on. Circles and semicircles that I had to fill in or tick in the appropriate place. The questions kept probing into greater and greater detail. And into increasingly peripheral events. In the end my head was spinning and I was no longer sure if I was describing the truth or just a fantasy. How much of this had actually happened, and how much had I constructed in hindsight?

I tried to remember as many setbacks as possible. I made sure to give high points to anything related to pain and suffering.

Most of it was to do with my relationship with Sunita, but I also managed to squeeze in some of my and Roger's failed attempts to pick up girls.

Roger often dragged up 'that disastrous night' many years ago when he and I had met Linda and Nicole. To him this was just more evidence of all the hardships he had to endure, but I wasn't sure if it ought to be regarded as entirely negative. We had been sitting in a bar and caught sight of two attractive girls a few tables away. We were both focused on the tall blonde with the incredibly pretty smile, whose name turned out to be Linda. During our discussion of tactics about who was going to go for which one, Roger argued that he should go for the blonde – the one we both liked most – because, as he put it, he deserved something nice for once. He thought I ought to be prepared to support him in this, and set my own sights on the brunette in the cap, and maybe even put in a good word for him so she could pass it on to her friend later.

I pointed out that it was a bit difficult to sort that out when we had no idea of their opinion on the matter, and that we should probably count ourselves lucky if they wanted to talk to us at all. Roger said I was just trying to make excuses, and in the end I agreed to try to set things up as best I could for him and the tall blonde.

After a couple of beers we plucked up the courage to go over to them, and luckily they asked us to sit down. I stuck to the agreement and mainly talked to Nicole, who turned out to work in comics and was great fun to talk to, while Roger and Linda had a separate conversation. All in all it was a very pleasant evening, and a couple of days later we started dating our respective girls.

I liked Nicole more and more. She taught me all about drawing and comics. She was very engaged with the environment and animal rights. She was a vegan too. Ate soya mince and You-can't-believe-it's-not-chicken, but occasionally her concentration would lapse. Sometimes she was halfway through a bag of sweets before realising that they contained gelatine. She would check the list of ingredients, then go and spit them out in the toilet. I enjoyed the afternoons and evenings I spent in her flat, lounging about on her sofa talking to her while she drew her cartoons. Sometimes she answered, sometimes she didn't. Sometimes she went off on long rants about society and Swedes and people in general. Her cartoons weren't all that nice to look at, or even particularly comprehensible. They weren't very realistic, but they were produced with passion and care. I loved them. We ended up getting it together, and went out for at least a month.

Roger and Linda embarked on a relationship as well, but I soon started to get reports about her failings. She talked too much, laughed too loudly, devoted too much time to her appearance. She was far too interested in his background. She would 'interrogate' him, as he put it. Wanted to know what he thought about all sorts of things. She wanted to go out a lot too, and do fun things in the evenings, but these rarely turned out to be all that much fun, although they still cost a great deal of money. When she eventually – after Roger, on my suggestion, had told her that he wasn't comfortable doing all those expensive things and proposed that they stay at home and do things there instead – floated the idea that they experiment with more adventurous sex, he dumped her.

He came round to see me and Nicole and went on about how awful it was for him. He sat there on the sofa claiming that the world was against him.

'I was always going to end up with the nutter!' he said.

'Typical. You had all the luck, as usual,' he said to me, glaring at Nicole over at her drawing desk.

He also went into great detail explaining the difficulty he had had telling Linda that he didn't like cream in spray-cans, or blindfolds, and then – once he'd told her – finding a decent way to end it. He later declared that at least I hadn't had any of those problems, seeing as Nicole dumped me a few days later.

Once I'd described a number of occurrences with the help of an outline of the body on which you had to indicate where you felt your emotions were based, I had to fill in a load of forms with pre-printed questions where you had to rank different types of experience. Once again, they began with general issues and gradually became more specific.

I might have exaggerated slightly. Maybe I answered a little more negatively than I would have done under different circumstances.

For instance, in the column marked 'Social Competence / further ed.' I ticked the options connected to alienation, bullying and deficient group dynamics.

Under 'Social Competence / dating / early rel. / sex. exp.' I took the opportunity to emphasise as much insecurity and performance anxiety as I could. They could probably work everything out themselves, down to the smallest detail, but I couldn't be entirely sure, seeing as they had missed the whole story of Sunita. Besides, I reasoned that it wouldn't do any harm if I added a bit of extra confusion with condoms and colliding front teeth.

Under 'Work life / prev. empl.' I ticked lots of boxes relating to irregular working hours, poor conditions and unpaid overtime.

When I was something like halfway through the pile of forms I went to the door and asked if I could have another bottle of water, but the woman in the scarf just shook her head. As if someone had told her not to leave her post on guard outside the glass box. I struggled through the rest of the questions and handed over the completed forms, by which time it was long past lunch.

'Can I go now?' I asked.

'No,' she said, looking rather excited. 'You have to come with me.'

She led the way to the reception desk and left my forms there. I sat down in the same armchair as before, and the woman in the scarf went and stood by the lift. A few moments later Georg emerged from the frosted-glass door. He went over to the desk, collected my bundle of papers, then disappeared into the secret room again. The woman and I were left in reception.

She must have stood there by the lift for two hours while I tried to find a comfortable position in the narrow armchair. I stretched out as far as I could, but it was obvious the chair wasn't made for long-term use. I felt tired and sweaty and a bit dazed after all those questionnaires. There were posters on the wall next to the lift, and the table in front of me was covered with all sorts of information leaflets from the campaign I had evidently missed. 'Time to pay – have you checked your E. H. score?', 'Give or take?', 'Time to even things out!', in large, slanting blue lettering printed over colourful pictures of children and adults. They were in a number of different languages. As I looked at them, it dawned on me that I may well have seen those leaflets at home somewhere, but had thrown them in the recycling without ever thinking that they concerned me. They looked disconcertingly similar to all the other advertisements that I usually ignored. I picked up one of the brochures and leafed through it. There was a short history, and an account of the big international agreement. Various politicians and leaders from different areas of society were quoted: short, punchy sentences.

It went on to give a description of the next step: the process of redistribution, when those with negative scores were going to receive compensation, and how this was going to happen. Towards the end were contact details for anyone wanting to lodge a complaint or who thought they had been unjustly treated.

From time to time, as I sat there reading, people went up to the reception desk. Some had similar questions to mine. Some wanted more detailed repayment proposals, some were angry. Some came to plead their case, others swore and gesticulated wildly. I wondered if my amount was higher or lower than the average.

A couple of times I almost dozed off, and once I was roused by a voice that seemed strangely familiar. After a while I realised that it was the girl with the necklaces from the lift in my building, the one whose phone call I had overheard a few days before, standing and talking over at the desk. She seemed really on top of things as she spoke to the receptionist. She took out some papers and a loan agreement, and explained the repayment schedule she had worked out for herself. I couldn't help but be a bit impressed by her proactive attitude. I was struck by the advantage people like that had in society. She was probably already saving for her retirement, compared electricity suppliers, and had registered her children – born or unborn – for the best schools. And now she was here to get the lowest interest rate possible. For a moment I felt a little envious, and thought that I ought to be more like her. The sort of person who could look after themselves and sort things out. Then I would probably never have ended up in this situation. As it was, I had to stake everything on Sunita.

Eventually the woman with the bank-name appeared.

'Hello! We've met before, of course,' she said, and it occurred to me that it wouldn't be a good idea to ask for her name again, so I was none the wiser this time. She was dressed in a mauve jacket and skirt, the same severe cut as before, but now she had a large artificial violet-coloured flower attached to her lapel. She was holding a folder to her chest, and led me into the big conference room. She asked me to take a seat. The woman in the scarf stayed outside.

Shortly afterwards Georg arrived, bringing with him an older man with bushy eyebrows and a dimpled chin. The three of them stood in a little group on the other side of the table, and the woman with the bank-name gave the new arrival a brief summary of my case. Every so often Georg interrupted with a clarification. Sometimes they very nearly talked at once. I recognised some of the terminology this time.

'Maximal E. H. score . . .'

'High values for euphoria, harmony, sorrow and pain, melancholy . . .'

'Sensitivity?'

'Maximal, as far as we can tell. But without lasting trauma . . . and, well, you know what that means. The resulting experiential charge shoots up . . .'

The woman held up a graph that the other two studied very carefully.

'Bloody hell, that's the highest quotient,' the man with the eyebrows said.

'Definitely. I've got nothing but fives here . . .'

They bent over another document.

'And the curve for shortcomings?'

'Latent,' she said.

'To take one example, he's only declared life-enhancing humiliation,' Georg said. 'Nothing but character-forming setbacks. All according to the progression framework. There's no deviation from the development model. He's almost a textbook example of the *Live for today* template.'

'The only infections he's suffered occurred at exactly the right time to cause the least possible problems and the mildest symptoms, yet with optimal results for his immune system. Just look at this graph . . .'

They lowered their voices and I could only hear fragments of what they were saying, because they were trying not to be overheard. Occasionally they covered their mouths with their hands.

'. . . almost absurd levels of pleasure . . . And full access to his feelings. According to our contact, on certain occasions the subject has the ability to forget basic simplifying acts in daily life which on sudden recollection give a two-fold increase to his E. H.'

'And now . . .' the woman with the bank-name said, picking up a new folder. 'Now a hitherto unknown relationship has come to light. With a woman named Sunita.'

'Look here,' Georg said, pointing with his pen at the new folder. 'Post-Sunita, life-affirming results all the way.' He leafed forward a few pages and pointed again. 'Here again . . . life-affirming.'

The others nodded.

'Excuse me,' I said.

All three of them looked at me, aghast. As if they'd forgotten I was sitting there, or didn't know I could talk.

'I thought I was going to be seeing Maud,' I went on.

The man with the eyebrows looked quizzically at the woman with the bank-name.

'Maud?' he said. 'Who's this Maud?'

'Maud Andersson,' she replied. 'Apparently she works down on the second floor. He has indicated . . .'

She turned to a different page.

'. . . here that he thinks "She is doing a very good job."'

The eyebrows were suddenly fixed on me.

'I see,' he said, shaking his head at me. 'No,' he said. 'No, no, it will just be the three of us.'

He put one hand to his mouth as he leafed through the file with the other.

'Intellect?' he muttered to the woman.

'Intact,' she replied.

'Here again,' Georg said, still looking down at the file. 'Look, same as before . . .'

As I sat there watching these three people my attention was taken by the new man's build. His body looked out of proportion. At first I couldn't work out what it was, then I realised that his legs were far too short. Which meant that he had an extremely low waist. The end result was about right. He was more or less of normal height, but now that I came to think about it he was almost entirely torso. It looked a bit odd when you saw them standing next to each other.

The woman with the bank-name took out another diagram. Georg interjected from the other side: 'We can't possibly allow continued access as things stand,' he said.

'No,' the man with the torso whispered. 'He's past the debt ceiling, so we'll have to impose a 6:3 on him.'

The others reacted sharply.

'A 6:3?'

One of them took out another document. The meeting moved further along the table as the paperwork spread out. They slowly sat down as they carried on talking.

'He can't request any deductions either,' the woman said. 'He hasn't really had any grounds on each of the . . .' She fell silent for a moment. Almost as if she had lost her train of thought.

As if on a given signal, all three stopped and looked over at me. Astonished.

I realised that I was something special. Georg broke the silence.

'But,' he began slowly, 'as I understand it, his repayment capacity is practically zero?'

The woman and Georg took turns tapping new numbers into a calculator.

The man with the bushy eyebrows and short legs was still staring at me. He very slowly leaned across the table and held out his hand, as if it had only just occurred to him that he ought to shake my hand. I took hold of it, and he pressed my hand, at the same time as continuing his conversation with the other two.

'Have we carried out a home inventory?' he said, still not taking his eyes off me. As if the handshake was taking place in a parallel world.

Georg and the woman both shook their heads. The man with the eyebrows replied with a low rumble of disapproval.

'See that it gets done as soon as possible.'

He leaned back and sat down on his chair again.

'Well . . . ,' he said, looking through the file until he found my name. Then, when he evidently realised it was too late to get personal, he didn't bother to say it. He simply nodded, as if he were content merely to know what my name was.

'Your debt has just been increased to 149,500,000 kronor.'

20

The inspectors came early the next day. I opened the door and let them into the flat just after half past seven in the morning. They were large and taciturn. Careful and thorough. They worked efficiently and almost without speaking to each other. They went through my belongings quickly and methodically, rather like customs officers. A woman in the same sort of uniform looked through my clothes and registered the things in the bathroom. I tried to help them as much as I could, but soon realised that they were best left to their own devices.

For each item they made a small mark in a pad. They pulled out my kitchen drawers, opened my cupboards. Checked my pictures and photographs. They dealt with some things in bulk. One of the men looked at only a couple of my vinyl record collection, for instance. And not even the two most valuable. None of them noticed my copy of Jimmy Smith's *Softly as a Summer Breeze*, for example, no scratches, original pressing. The one checking the records merely shook his head and made a note.

An hour later they were finished. One of them handed me a 'next-of-kin form' that he said I should fill in. They thanked me and left.

I sat on the floor looking at my things. Now that the men had gone, they felt even more worthless.

It was oppressively hot inside the flat. The kind of sticky heat that clung to your body. Like having a tight helmet round your brain. It was as bad as trying to breathe in a sauna, and it didn't get any better when I opened the windows even wider. The sultry air outside was completely still. Swallows were flying low. I looked at the piece of paper in my hand and wondered who I should give as my next-of-kin. Jörgen? Roger? In the end I wrote my sister's name and address.

I paced up and down in my boiling-hot living room and tried to make sense of my thoughts. Had I presented everything wrong? Was there something I'd missed? Was it really possible to claim, as W. R. D. were, that I had taken the best from my relationship with Sunita? Okay, so our relationship was already starting to feel a bit tired when we separated. We didn't really share any interests beyond film, and we didn't agree on most things. She had a rather spoiled way of looking at the world, but at the same time she could seem pretty helpless. She was provocatively uninterested in other cultures, and declared on one occasion when we were having a row that I was more or less insignificant. That what we had together was only a parenthesis, something that didn't count, and, quite regardless of what she might feel now, would have absolutely no impact on her future. It was as if she didn't really value her own feelings. As if everything she had with me, all the films and her education, our entire culture, was just one long dream. Soon enough she would be going back to reality. She was Daddy's little princess, and when I once pointed out that he didn't seem to have been in touch for several years it was enough to make her expression freeze and break the spell between us.

It wasn't that great standing outside in the winter and shivering in different places, waiting for a sign that might or might not come. Towards the end she had almost seemed a bit bored, as if she had had enough. I dare say we both realised that it wouldn't have lasted much longer, but the fact that we were forced to split up suddenly made the whole thing feel incredibly sad. And the pain. The pain! I could still feel it as I walked about sweating between the window and the living-room table.

As soon as I'd pulled myself together I called Maud again. At first I couldn't get through to her. They said she was busy, and had therefore redirected her calls to reception. Did I want to leave a message?

I said I needed to talk to her, and that it was urgent, and I must have sounded persistent and difficult and aggressive enough, because in the end they put me through anyway.

'So, are you done with me now, then?' I said.

'I don't know,' she said. 'Have you got anything else sensational to report?'

I yelled that this was completely unreasonable, and how the hell did they actually work things out? But Maud managed to stay calm and said that I was the one who had withheld information. I begged and pleaded and shouted in turn. I wondered how the business with Sunita could *increase* my debt when it ought to have done the reverse. For the first time she sounded tense and rather nervous. I realised that she was under pressure. Perhaps because of all the miscalculations and mistakes. She said I shouldn't think I could judge things like this better than some of the country's most prominent experts and psychiatrists and psychologists, the people who had developed the system.

After a while I calmed down and felt stupid. After all, it wasn't her fault that things were the way they were.

'How serious is it?' I asked after a brief pause.

'Well,' she said, and even though she was making a real effort to sound calm, I could tell that she was upset. 'You should have told me about Sunita . . .'

'I assumed you already knew—'

She interrupted me before I could finish, and sounded very apologetic.

'Of course, that was our fault,' she said. 'I don't understand how we could have missed such a . . .'

'So what happens now?'

'I don't know. You're now registered as a so-called 6:3, and I can tell you that you've already gone through the debt ceiling . . .'

I got up from the floor, waving the next-of-kin form in my hand. I was breathing hard down the phone.

'But . . . we were going to sort this out . . .'

She didn't let me finish.

'That was before Sunita,' she said. 'And from what you told us, that only raises the credit side.'

'How can it do that?' I said. 'It was one of the worst experiences of my life ...'

'The way you described it, you had a fantastic time.'

I noticed that I was shouting again. 'Until she was snatched away from me! We were forced to ... well, separate, under extremely ... extremely painful circumstances. How can that be counted as something positive?'

She snapped back at me.

'Come off it!' she hissed. 'It's pure Hollywood! How many people do you think ... ?'

Her voice was almost trembling. She fell silent for a moment, as if to compose herself, but soon carried on.

'How many people do you think experience anything like that? Ever? Anywhere?'

She tried to revert to cooler, more formal vocabulary, but her tone of voice gave her away. 'And you still had your self-esteem intact at the end. According to your declaration, you could have drawn the experience out ... so to speak ... even after the conclusion of the relationship involving physical contact.'

She flared up again. Sounded properly angry for the first time. Almost as if she were lecturing me.

'And you tried to make out that your life was more or less a waste of time? Well? Isn't that what you did? Wasn't that the whole point of your last phone call? I almost fell for it. You're actually a perversely happy person!'

I didn't say anything at first. Then I mumbled something about unfair calculations and other more successful people around me, but Maud dismissed all my objections.

'It's not as simple as that. You understand that, surely? It's impossible to make generalisations ... It's all about the combination ... and your specific combination of experiences in life has turned out to be extremely happy.'

'Fine! What about everyone else, then?' I exclaimed.

For a moment there was total silence. It was like she was thinking hard.

'You really don't get it, do you?' she eventually said.

'What?' I said.

Quiet now. Almost a whisper.

'People are extremely unhappy. Most people feel really bad! They're in pain. They're poor, sick, on medication, depressed, scared, worried about all sorts of things. They're stressed and panicked, they feel guilty, suffer performance anxiety, have trouble sleeping, can't concentrate, or they're just bored, or constantly under pressure, or feel that they're being treated badly. Deceived, unsuccessful, guilty – anything and everything. At most, the majority of people experience a few years of relative happiness in their childhood. That's often when they build up their score. After that it's pretty bleak.'

She sighed, making the line crackle, and I thought I could hear her shake her head.

'If only you knew,' she said.

I sat down against the wall again. She took a deep breath and went on: 'You see, we look at life as if it were a classically constructed play. The one with the most whistles and bells isn't necessarily the best. Things have to happen in the right order, too, otherwise there's no point ...'

I realised I'd never heard Maud talk like this before. And I recognised that there was a sort of trust, an honesty between us that it would be hard to manage without now that these conversations were drawing to a natural conclusion. Because even if I was upset about the way things were, I really didn't want anything else but to sit and talk to her on the phone. Talking about stuff. Listening to her voice. But I said nothing. I realised that it would hardly work in my favour.

I could hear her rustle some paper again. For the first time I suspected that she was doing it to make it sound as if she had more important things to be getting on with. Maybe she just did it when she couldn't think of anything to say.

'So . . .' she said after a pause. 'That film, what was it called? I watched it.'

She fell silent, but I couldn't hear any paper rustling this time.

'*The Bridge*?' I said. 'You watched *The Bridge*?'

She sighed. And once again that strange warm feeling spread through me. She had taken the time to get hold of a Bosnian film from the turn of the millennium for the simple reason that I had recommended it.

'I rented it,' she said. 'And that scene you talked about. The one in the café. It was, well, I don't know how to put it . . .'

'You rented *The Bridge*? How did you manage to get hold of it?'

'I got hold of it, okay?!' she said irritably. 'So I sat down and watched it. I waited for that scene, and it eventually came. But, well, there was none of that stuff you were going on about. It was just two people sitting there. In a café. So what? It was pretty boring. Terrible lighting.'

'Oh, come on,' I began. 'No, I don't think that's—'

'Don't you get it?' she said. 'You're the one who read all those looks and touches and everything into it,' she said. 'They're all in your head.'

I stood up and went over to the window.

'No, I don't think . . .'

She went on: 'But I ought to have realised that by now. It's typical of you. You think you're discovering a whole load of things, but they aren't really there. No wonder you got such a high E. H. score.'

'But they touched each other,' I said. 'You must have seen them touch each other!'

'It's all one single scene, no editing. The camera's a long way away. The whole time. It was all done in one take. You can hardly see anything.'

'Okay, but *that's* what's so . . .'

'Sure, they put their arms next to each other, but that's all there was to it.'

I tried to find the right words.

'Yeah, but you still understand . . .'

'What is it you understand?' she said. '*What*?'

'Their little fingers touch . . .'

'Yes, but what is it you understand?'

'You see how—'

'What do you see? You could hardly even see their hands.

296

What's so special about it? Grainy and black-and-white and all in long-shot. To me it was just an endlessly drawn-out scene where practically nothing happened.'

'How can you say that?' I said. 'It's completely magical . . .'

'It's impossible to tell from that distance. If they'd filmed a bit closer, maybe, but it was just one single, drawn-out shot.'

I really wanted to say something, but couldn't get the words out.

'No,' she said, and this time I'm sure I could hear her shake her head. 'You filled in all those details for yourself.'

'But all great art . . .' I began.

'It's brilliant that you can extract so much emotion from that scene, but I have to look at it practically,' she said. 'To me it was just unbearably dull.'

The two of us said nothing for a long time. The only sound was the noise of her colleagues in the background. The next-of-kin form in my hand was damp and crumpled now.

'If I could just watch that scene with you . . .' I said.

'You won't have time to watch anything,' she said. 'They're probably already on their way to you now.'

'What? Who . . . ?' I said. 'What's going on now?'

She took a deep breath and began speaking in a low, confidential voice so that no one else in the office would hear her, as if she were telling me something I really shouldn't know.

'You're about to be picked up by one of our teams—'

'Picked up?' I exclaimed.

'Shhh! Yes, what did you expect? You can't possibly have further access under the circumstances.'

I could definitely hear emotion in her voice now. Even though she was really trying to sound businesslike.

'There's nothing I can do as things stand . . .'

I let the phone slip slowly down my cheek, until it hit my shoulder and fell to the floor. I heard her call my name from down there several times.

21

Clouds were gathering outside. Big, lead-grey billows were rolling in over the rooftops. The sun passed behind them and soon there was a flash of lightning, like a momentary camera-flash lighting up the whole city. There was a thunderous rumble and the first heavy drops were in the air. Soon the rain was pattering on the window sill and bouncing in onto the floor. I should have shut the windows, but I just sat there paralysed, staring at the cloud of dancing droplets.

What did she mean by 'picked up'? What did 'no further access' mean? In my mind's eye I saw myself being segregated, with one of those cones you put on dogs, to stop me absorbing any more experiences. Light, sound, birds, wind, all the things I liked, even rain and stormy weather. I tried to think of really dull days, but suddenly everything seemed so wonderful. I really did try to imagine a properly grey day, but without meaning to I found myself thinking of water gushing out of the bottom of a drainpipe. So wet. The water in general. The whole principle of water. What the air is like when it rains. Drops against my skin. Girls I'd seen out in the rain. The way their clothes stuck to their skin, and that film, *The Umbrellas of Cherbourg*, which Sunita had made me watch, and which I honestly hadn't appreciated at all until afterwards, in hindsight, when she was gone. When all I had left were the things she opened my eyes to. A whole load of things that I now loved. The measured pace of Rachmaninoff's sonata for cello and piano, for instance. Bloody hell – there was no escape!

I shook my head and tried to conjure up images of terrible monsters and horrible demons. I tried to make them as vicious and dangerous as possible, but no matter how hard I thought of tails and tongues and teeth, they never ended up as anything but colourful characters in a computer game. I looked round the room in an attempt to find something really grim, tragic, or at least depressing, but everything I could see felt secure and beautiful and held only happy associations. My beloved old sofa, my lovely cushions, the wonderful poster of M. C. Escher's perfectly mathematical illusion. The damp, and the tiny drops of the liberating, oxygen-rich rain that occasionally reached the tops of my arms . . . I was still hopelessly happy.

For the first time I was struck by the unsettling thought that the true value of my Experienced Happiness might have actually been seriously undervalued.

22

Ten minutes later, when the men from W. R. D. knocked on the door, I was still sitting there, leaning against the wall in the same position. I had just thought of a summer some years ago when I'd borrowed Lena and Fredrik's cottage. At first I felt a bit lonely, but as the days passed I felt more and more liberated. And weightless. In the end I stopped noticing the passage of time, and even forgot how old I was. I would cycle slowly down to the lake through warm, gentle summer rain, and I was all ages at the same time. I got to my feet and went to open the door.

They said hello politely and waited for me to go to the toilet and get changed before we headed off to the vast granite complex, where we drove down into a large garage. We got out and went up in the lift to the same reception area where I had been twice before. Rain was lashing the big windows, sounding like hundreds of little drums.

Georg met us at the desk. He nodded to the guards and indicated that they could go now. This time he had with him two very well-dressed foreign gentlemen who didn't speak Swedish. He introduced them in English, and I was told that they were from head office in Toronto, and the Calgary subsidiary. They smiled at me and seemed pleasant enough. Neither of them said much. They mostly fiddled with their phones while we waited. I couldn't help wondering what was going to happen.

I held the next-of-kin form out to Georg, who looked at it with surprise and hesitantly took it.

'Of course, yes, this . . .' he said slowly. 'I don't really know who . . . This is really just a trial, so far . . .'

After a while another man came and got the two foreign men. Georg remained standing over by the desk and I sat down in an armchair while the others disappeared into the conference room with the noisy ventilation. He looked at my form for a while, then put it down on the desk beside him.

'Well, then.' He sighed, and shook his head.

He sat down in the chair next to me and gave me a sympathetic look. I realised I was sweating. I looked round to see if I could see any handcuffs, or a cage, or anything like that.

'What are you going to do?' I asked in as relaxed a voice as possible.

He shook his head.

'No,' he said. 'I'm not going to pre-empt anything, but it doesn't look good. Not good at all . . .'

Everyone who walked past looked completely normal, and seemed preoccupied with their own concerns. No one looked at me oddly, so I assumed that only a small group there at W. R. D. knew about my situation and what was likely to happen to me.

I was having trouble sitting still. I turned round and tried to look into the glass office where meetings were usually held, and where a large number of people were now leaning over something on the table. Some of them were gesticulating with their arms. It was like they were waiting for a particular signal, or perhaps another participant. I took a deep breath and tried to stop my hands shaking on my lap.

'Why me?' I asked Georg, almost in a whisper.

He shrugged his shoulders. As if it was a question that couldn't possibly be answered easily.

'What about all the millionaires?'

He smiled and ran his hand through the hair that may or may not have been dyed.

'Believe me, we're taking care of them as well. Most wealthy people will obviously receive a fairly hefty invoice. But it isn't always so simple. To take just one example, let me tell you about . . . hmm, let's call him Kjell.'

He sat up in his chair and leaned towards me.

'Kjell worked at a factory in Stegsta and lived a quiet life in all respects. He mostly kept to himself. He did his job, saved some money, and was eventually offered the chance to buy some shares in Stegsta Ltd, which shot up in value shortly afterwards. Two or three years later they were worth five times what Kjell had paid, and he sold the shares at an impressive profit. He ended up with a small fortune, which he looked after carefully, whilst still going to work as usual. Each year his capital grew in various funds and investment accounts. When I asked if he wasn't thinking of doing something fun with the money, he always said he was planning to take early retirement and have his fun then. I couldn't help thinking that if anyone had the strength of character to do that, it was Kjell. Sure enough, he retired at the age of fifty-five. The day after he left work he called and said triumphantly: "At last, I'm free!"

'I didn't hear from him for six months. There was nothing unusual about that. He wasn't the sociable type and I assumed he was in the Bahamas or on some luxury cruise or whatever someone with plenty of time and money might come up with. But the next time he called he was in an acute psychiatric treatment centre.

'He had ended up having severe anxiety attacks. He was depressed, but not just feeling a bit low and thinking that life was a bit miserable. He was depressed in a way that didn't mean finding new ways to think about things or to get going with his life again, or eating better and enjoying the little things, nothing like that. For him it was about whether he could be bothered to get out of bed in the morning. And not give up and put an end to it all. It was about deciding at each moment to go on living. Resisting the easy option for one more day, one more hour, one more minute. He said when it was at its worst, he just sat there breathing and looking at the time. Waiting for the relapse into darkness to pass.'

Georg leaned back again.

'The E. H. score he had gained because of his financial success fell away, like cherry blossom in May, when there was no longer anything to push against.'

He looked at me to see if I'd understood.

'Naturally there are special cases,' I said. 'But what about all the others? The ones whose lives are a never-ending party. The ones with loads of friends and acquaintances. Fast cars. Lovers. I haven't got anything like that.'

'A large social circle can be a good thing, of course,' he went on. 'And lots of parties. But it's the quality that's important. Too many contacts can lead to stress – it actually reduces E. H. scores. Increased financial assets also raise expectations. And some things that at first glance can look like negatives actually end up raising the score dramatically. Take your own case, for instance, and everything connected to pain and pleasure. How do you think we deal with the BDSM community?'

He raised his eyebrows. I couldn't think of anything to say.

'Children, then?' I said after a while. 'I haven't got children. And that must be the meaning of everything to some extent . . .'

He sighed and rubbed one eye with a finger.

'You keep picking out individual things. None of them need necessarily mean anything by itself. There's no such thing as an unambiguously positive event. Or an isolated state of happiness. Besides, I seem to recall that your sister has children . . . ?'

I shook my head and sighed.

'You're very smart,' I said.

He laughed and looked at me. And held up his hands in a way that said, *I rest my case*.

'You see,' Georg said, 'that way you have of being impressed by everything you experience. In our formulas . . . well, what can I say? It quickly mounts up.'

'I've always been so cautious,' I muttered, slowly shaking my head. 'I've never really pushed for anything . . .'

He looked at me as if he wondered what I was getting at. As if he couldn't really work out if I was actually heading somewhere with my argument, or just drifting about aimlessly in an attempt to gain time.

'Yes,' he said, 'there are advantages and disadvantages to everything. But in your case ... well, it certainly looks as if the advantages have the upper hand.'

He looked me in the eye again.

'You must realise that very few people even come close to a score like yours?'

I nodded and looked over at the window, where the rain was forming thick lines on the glass. Like little rivers. He narrowed his eyes slightly.

'You've maintained a very constant level,' he said. 'And with so little personal effort. It's very odd. Fascinating, actually.'

'I suppose so,' I said. 'It's just that I probably expected ...'

'What?' he said. 'What did you expect?'

He fixed his eyes on me.

'More?' he suggested.

I squirmed.

'There must be people who have lived – how can I put it? – far more passionately. People who've followed their desires. I don't know. Fucking around. Taking drugs.'

'Most narcotics also have drawbacks,' he said bluntly. 'I presume you know that.'

I nodded.

'That's also a typical masculine trait,' he said. 'Men always assume that more money means more happiness.'

'Really?' I said. 'Still ... a friend of mine ...'

He shook his head dismissively.

'Let's not start making comparisons.'

'I know. But we did,' I said. 'And the woman who ... Well, I happened to find out how much she was being charged, and it seems quite unreasonable that she should have such a lower amount than me.'

'Like I said . . .'

'I just don't get it,' I said.

He folded his arms.

'What does your friend do?'

'She works h . . . I mean . . . She . . . she has a similar job to you . . .'

Just as I was thinking that I mustn't give anything away with my body language, I realised that I'd already glanced over at the conference room. He looked at me. He suddenly became very serious. He was silent for several long moments, studying me without blinking.

'I don't mean what job she has,' he said slowly, also glancing over at the glass-walled room containing the others. 'I mean, what does she *do*? How does she act? How does she pass her time, and how is that connected to her well-being?'

'Oh,' I said hesitantly. 'Well, I don't really know her like that . . .'

'No,' he said quickly, and leaned closer to me again. 'You've got no idea, have you? You don't know what psycho-social effect her work could have on her, for instance. Or how many negative interactions she may have in her life.'

I shook my head and tried to find the right words.

'She . . . well, she doesn't seem depressed,' I said. 'We get on pretty well, actually . . .'

He wasn't listening to me, and went on: 'And you don't know

anything about her daily life, about the depersonalising impact of her work. And do you know what?'

He moved closer to me and lowered his voice to a whisper.

'If I were you,' he said, 'I'd keep very quiet about this "friend".'

He looked over at the meeting room, where the others were preparing for my arrival.

'If only for her sake . . .'

The man who had shown the foreign gentlemen in some time ago was suddenly standing next to me.

'We're ready,' he said. 'You can come in now.'

I turned round and felt my pulse speed up. Georg was already on his feet, and I was about to stand up when I realised that I had to take my chance. Who knew if there would be any more chances at all? I leaned back.

'I want Maud to be here,' I said.

They both stopped and looked at me.

'Maud?' the man said. 'Who's Maud?'

'Maud Andersson,' I said.

He looked round.

'There's no Maud here,' he said.

'Yes, there is,' I said. 'Maud Andersson. I want her here.'

Georg turned to the new man.

'She works on the second floor, apparently,' he said. 'She's been his contact here.'

'Oh?' the man said uninterestedly, as if he were wondering how this could change anything.

'You could get them to call down and see if she's there,' Georg said.

'Yes, do that,' I said. 'I'll wait here.'

The new man stood there for a moment looking at me, then he went over to the desk and spoke to the receptionist.

Georg sat down again and looked at me. After a while he leaned over.

'A little tip,' he said. 'If it turns out that your "friend" here has interacted with you in an inappropriate way, it may well be that we won't be able to retain her services. Do you understand? I can't imagine that you want that. You want her to keep her job, don't you?'

I think I nodded. He leaned back in his chair. We sat there in silence for a while.

Eventually the new man returned.

'She's on her way up,' he said.

23

This time there were four of them. Plus the two foreign gentlemen. Another man, slightly overweight and with very little hair, just some above his ears, had taken a seat at one side of the table, where a number of documents relating to my case had been laid out. I sat down on the same chair as the previous two occasions.

The bald, thickset man introduced himself as Pierre, and he must have been superior to all the others, because whenever he spoke they all listened breathlessly. He frowned and fixed his eyes on me. He sat there for a long time just staring at me.

'I hear you've had a decent life?'

I nodded.

'Without paying your way.'

I nodded again. He called the two foreigners over to him. He pointed at something in the documents, and the other two men raised their eyebrows. One of them let out a whistle. 'Wow,' the other one said, and nodded appreciatively in my direction. When they had returned to their seats, Pierre turned back to me.

'And you've built up quite a sizeable debt,' he said.

There was a modest knock on the door.

And there she was at last.

* * *

Outside the glass stood a woman with dark blonde hair in a ponytail. She was wearing a black polo-necked top and a jacket with plenty of practical little pockets. A dark corduroy skirt and black tights. She had her arms clasped in front of her stomach, her hands clutching the handle of a briefcase. They opened the door for her and she took a couple of steps into the room, nodded to her colleagues, and when Georg went over to say hello I saw her straighten up and almost stand on tiptoe, so that the heels of her matt black shoes with white buckles lifted slightly off the ground.

She turned towards me. I found myself getting to my feet.

Georg indicated a chair next to mine. She walked towards me, put the briefcase in one hand and held the other one out to me.

'What's this person doing here?' Pierre hissed to the woman with the bank-name.

'She's his contact here,' she said. 'He's requested that she be here.'

Pierre looked sceptically from Maud to me.

'Really?' he mumbled.

'Maud,' she said quietly, and I realised that I was smiling as I heard her voice. She was smiling as well. It was like she was smiling at my smile, and I at hers, then she was smiling back at mine a bit more, and so on, ad infinitum. The smile revealed a neat but slightly irregular row of teeth. One of them was crooked and seemed to be winking at me as she smiled at me. A short curl of hair that wasn't tied up hung down one side of her face, and looked as if it was gently tickling her soft, slightly blushing cheeks whenever she moved her head. She smelled vaguely of coffee and deodorant.

'Nice to meet you,' she said to me.

'Same here,' I said.

She had a small necklace outside the wonderful polo-necked sweater, I guessed it was probably half cotton, half polyester. The necklace had what looked like a silver dolphin on it, but it could have been any fish really. The skin just under her chin moved slightly when she spoke. It looked soft, smooth. I wanted to touch it.

'So,' Pierre said. 'Are we all ready, then?'

He tapped his pen impatiently on the tabletop, evidently extremely put out by the small delay. He pursed his lips silently as he waited for Maud to take her place beside me. She put her briefcase down on the floor next to her chair, took out a pen and notepad, and did a quick scribble in one corner to check that the pen was working.

'As I was saying,' Pierre said to me as soon as she was ready, 'you've built up a fairly sizeable debt, to put it mildly.'

He looked round the room.

'You are now what we call a 6:3. For that reason we have conducted a home inventory, which came up with . . . nothing.'

He gestured lazily towards one of the documents on the table, it was impossible to tell which one. 'Absolutely nothing,' he said to the gentlemen at the other end of the table, and to make his point even more clearly he addressed me in a rather loud voice and with exaggerated pronunciation: 'You own nothing of value.'

I wasn't sure how to respond, so I just nodded slightly to indicate that I'd heard what he said.

'No education, so no immediate prospect of increased earnings . . .'

'If I don't win the lottery,' I said, in a nervous attempt at a joke.

I looked at Maud, who registered no reaction.

Pierre gave a supercilious smile and adopted my tone.

'Quite. And of course we can't kill you,' he said.

He smiled towards the foreign representatives, and they smiled back. All of a sudden I became aware that my palms were sweating. He leaned across the table towards me.

'Are there any more people you've socialised with but not declared?' he said.

I shook my head.

'You're sure about that?'

I couldn't help glancing at Maud, who was looking straight ahead the whole time.

'Not as far as I'm aware,' I said. 'Is it important?'

Pierre maintained eye contact the whole time he spoke. As if he really did want to see how I reacted to what he said.

'With this type of positive perception, there's reason to suppose that people in the immediate vicinity will register a certain – how can I put it? – passive gain. It could raise their E. H. score dramatically. After their cases have been re-evaluated, of course.'

I noticed that one of the surveillance cameras up at the ceiling suddenly moved slightly. Presumably there were even more people watching us. Maybe via direct streaming to other countries?

He sat and fiddled with his pen for a while. Suddenly he clapped his hands together, and gestured to the other people in the room, who all stood up. Then he turned to Maud.

'Would you please stay here with the subject while we have a short meeting in private?' he said.

Maud nodded.

They all walked out, leaving just the two of us alone in the room. As soon as they had gone I turned to face her, but she quickly cleared her throat and glanced up at one of the cameras as if to remind me that we were probably still being observed, and that this wasn't a place where we could talk freely. So I turned back and we sat there in silence, next to one another, like passengers on a train, listening to the sound of the ventilation in the ceiling.

After a while she put one arm on the table to adjust one of the documents. The sleeve of her jacket had slid up towards her elbow, so most of her lower arm was lying bare on the table, right next to me. I waited a while, maybe thirty seconds, before putting my arm alongside hers. Not close, but not too far away.

We sat like that for a bit. Nothing happened. Maud leafed through the papers in front of her with her other hand, and I understood how the rustling sound I had heard over the phone was made. She would fold back a few pages to check something, then let them go again before checking something else. All with the same hand. The arm next to mine remained still. We could both hear the discussions taking place outside. Several voices, in a number of different languages. It wasn't possible to see any of the people speaking, but it sounded as if more or less the whole department was involved in the same noisy conversation. Only inside the room containing Maud and me was everything calm and still.

Eventually she pushed one of the documents closer to me, and the arm nearest to me joined in. We were now very close. I took a deep breath and turned my hand over, so that the back of it touched the back of her hand. At that precise moment she stopped and remained absolutely still. There was nothing but the voices outside, the faint drumming of the rain, and the dust drifting slowly through the air. Neither of us said anything. We kept looking forward, into the frosted-glass wall in front of us, as if there was actually something interesting to see there. And then a tiny movement, barely visible to the naked eye, and absolutely impossible to detect from a surveillance camera up by the ceiling, for instance, as her little finger slowly touched the back of my hand, and our breathing synchronised in the same rhythm.

The doors opened and the delegation came back into the room. Our hands moved apart as quickly and silently as they had come together. Everyone but Pierre went back to their previous places. Pierre folded his arms and wandered up and down along the side of the table. When he had done this a couple of times he sat down opposite us and smiled at Maud. Then he looked at me and his smile died away.

'Sorry to make you wait,' he said, then took a deep breath and slowly blew the air out again, as he leaned forward and clasped his hands together above the table. He rested his chin on the knuckles, and sat like that for a while just looking at me, waiting for all movement in the room to stop before he resumed speaking in a calm, confidential tone of voice.

'You see, we are faced with an extremely costly investment which would appear to stand very little chance of collecting any significant repayment.'

He looked around the table at the others before his eyes settled on me again.

'Naturally we could carry on and impose further ... but I can't really see that that would be worthwhile ... can you?'

I nodded. It seemed best to agree with him.

'Unless,' he went on in a more light-hearted tone, 'you see any possibility of promotion at, er ... "Jugge's Flicks"?'

I shook my head. He smiled, but his eyes remained cold.

'No, I thought as much,' he said.

He closed his eyes for a moment, as if he were trying to work out how to phrase something. Then he snapped them open again and looked straight at me.

'The cost of keeping you isolated – and yes, I see here that you have an ability, even in the most trying of circumstances, to maintain a certain, how can I put it ... ?'

His eyes flitted about, trying to find a particular document. The woman with the bank-name and the others hurried to find the right one, but when they eventually found it and put it in front of him, he waved it away and went on staring at me.

316

'You know what people say: if you owe the bank a million, it's your problem, but if you owe a hundred million . . .'

I nodded. Yes, I'd heard that one. He lowered his voice even more and sharpened his tone. Everyone in the room held their breath.

'So what I'm going to suggest must stay between us. Do you understand? Under no circumstances must this get out.'

He fixed his eyes on me and I wasn't sure if I'd stopped nodding from last time, so I nodded extra hard to show that I was keeping up.

Without looking away from me, he gestured to a woman outside who, with some help, pushed a wheeled trolley into the room. On top of the trolley was a pile of papers twenty centimetres thick.

'Please be aware,' he said, as the trolley laden with documents was parked immediately next to me, 'that the debt remains. In case you were, against all expectation, to win the lottery . . .' He gave me a wry smile.

'But for the time being . . .'

He leaned forward even further. I could feel his breath. A faint smell of curry and gastric acid. He stroked his chin with one finger, as if he still hadn't quite made up his mind.

'. . . we won't make any efforts to call it in. It will simply be frozen. Do you understand?'

I said nothing.

Pierre went on, 'Are we in agreement?'

I glanced at Maud, but she was sitting there straight-backed, writing something down, so I turned back to Pierre. I could see a trace of sweat on his top lip, shimmering in the glow of the fluorescent lighting. I noticed that Maud had started to gather her papers together, and she might have brushed against me briefly under the table as she leaned over to put some documents back in her briefcase. I'm not entirely sure.

'Does this mean . . . ?' I began.

All three men were looking at me now, and I could feel Maud tense up next to me. It was as if they were suddenly all worried that I was about to throw a spanner in the works. The two foreign gentlemen straightened up.

'Does this mean that I can carry on with my life more or less as before?' I said.

Pierre looked at me unhappily. Then he slowly nodded.

'If you could just . . .' he said, passing me a pen. 'If you could just sign this. On each page. You understand, this must remain utterly confidential.'

I looked down at the first sheet of paper.

24

Down at the ice-cream kiosk that evening I caught sight of the girl with the necklaces again, the one I recognised from the reception desk and whose phone call I had overheard in the lift. She was walking quickly away from the bus. She looked harassed, frowning deeply as she passed by in a hurry. She didn't buy an ice-cream. Maybe she was having to save money?

It was a magical evening, the air clear after the heavy rain. The sky, trees and people were all reflected in little puddles that were gradually drying in the mild evening sunlight. It was as if everything had been given a fresh start.

My phone buzzed in my pocket. I pulled it out and looked at the screen. Roger. I wondered if he'd sold his boat. He only let it ring once, then he hung up. He did this a couple of times, then a text arrived.

Call me!

I realised that it was urgent. This was the second time in a week that he had gone to the expense of sending a text. I'm not sure I'd ever received a text from Roger before that. Apart from the time he was on a course in personal development and I suddenly received a message out of the blue, saying, *I find you attractive, exciting, and I think of you as a very good*

319

friend. Fondest wishes, Roger. Roger's brother, Eric, had booked and paid in advance to attend the course himself, but at the last minute was unable to go. Food and lodging were included, which is why Roger agreed to go in his place. The tender message turned out to be the last part of an exercise in showing your appreciation of other people. It was some sort of group message sent free of charge from one of the course computers. 'I had to adapt it slightly so it would work for everyone,' he said afterwards when I asked what he had meant by 'attractive'.

I called him and he answered on the first ring.

'Listen,' he said, 'I've had one of those forms now.'

'What forms?' I said.

'From W. R. D.,' he said. 'Obviously I appealed against the amount. And now I've finally got them to agree to look at my case again. And I've got one of their forms to fill in any "gaps" or "blank periods", or whatever the hell they call them. Presumably they've got things missing from their records that you have to give them information about . . .'

'Okay,' I said.

'You have to tell them who you saw on certain days, and so on. Then I suppose they double-check against the records of the people you mention.'

I pulled on my jacket. Not because it was cold, but because I wanted to look a bit smarter. Among the receipts and old sweets in the pocket I found a new scrap of paper. I pulled it out and saw that it contained a phone number and a name. *Maud*, it said. I looked at the number and saw that it was different to the one I had called before. A mobile number.

'Well,' Roger said, 'I thought I'd give them your name.'

I ran my thumb over the numbers on the piece of paper. She had written them very neatly. Her handwriting leaned forward slightly, and looked rather ornate and old-fashioned.

'What did you say?' I said.

'I just thought it was simpler that way. And you don't have to come up with anything. You just have to say yes if they ask you.'

I folded the piece of paper with Maud's number on it and tucked it into my inside pocket instead. A ball came rolling towards me, and a small boy ran after it. I stopped the ball with my foot and the boy picked it up without looking at me.

'Hang on,' I said. 'What did you say?'

'Look, I'm not so stupid that I didn't realise they give you loads of points the more people you mention, and the more fun you say you've had. So I thought that . . . Well, I thought I'd give your name, for everything.'

I didn't reply at first.

'Hello? *Hello?* Are you still there?' Roger shouted down the phone.

'Look . . .' I said hesitantly. 'I don't think . . . No.'

He was panting the way he usually did, and I wondered if he was on his way somewhere.

'There's nothing funny about it,' he said. 'If they call and ask, you just have to say: Yes, I was with Roger. That's all.'

'No,' I said. 'I don't think that's such a good idea.'

'What? Why not?' He let out a sigh. 'Look, it's not like you'd have to lie. You'd just have to . . . confirm what I say.'

'No,' I said.

'God, you're really touchy all of a sudden. I mean, we *have* met, haven't we? And I can't list everyone else I've . . . Hang on, are you ashamed of me or something?'

'Of course I'm not,' I said. 'I just think . . . How can I put it? This business of us spending time together . . . well, it might increase your score.'

He was quiet for a few seconds. I could hear him breathing through his nose.

'What do you mean by that?' he eventually said.

'Oh, I just think . . . Look, can't you try to remember what really happened instead?'

He snorted.

'Are you worried about your own score going up? Because you've spent time with me? But it's true, though, isn't it? We do know each other. Don't we? Or are you denying that?'

'No,' I said. 'Of course I'm not. I just mean . . .'

'Ah!' Roger said, as if he'd suddenly worked out what I was thinking. 'You think you're going to end up with a much higher score if they find out you've been spending a lot of time with me. That's what it is, isn't it?'

'No, that's not what I think . . .'

'It is! Admit it!'

'Please, Roger, just . . .'

'What?' he said impatiently.

'Just don't do it!' I said.

322

He said nothing for a while, as if he was thinking. He sighed.

'I'm going to,' he said. 'I can't keep making allowances for you the whole damn time. I'm sorry.'

'But surely you could ... Maybe you could say we mostly speak on the phone?' I said.

'What's wrong with you?' Roger yelled. 'Christ, you could at least try to help me out once in a while.'

The ball came back again, followed by the boy, but this time it was too far away for me to be able to stop it. It came to a halt with a splash in one of the puddles.

'Okay, okay,' I said. 'Do as you like.'

We hung up without me finding out what had happened to his boat.

I took out the piece of paper with Maud's number. I ran my fingers over the numbers again before putting it back in the pocket I had first found it in. I tried to work out if I dare ask her round to mine. Was that allowed? Would she dare to take the risk? How would that affect her career? But she herself had said that only things that had happened up to now counted. And the men in the meeting had indicated that I could carry on with my life as though nothing had happened.

I wandered slowly and aimlessly through the city, looking at the people around me. Young people, middle-aged people. A little girl rode past me on a big, red woman's bicycle. Somewhere a radio was playing 'Clouds' by Frank Sinatra. A flock of birds was wheeling through the air like a single entity. Did they do that, I wondered, to pretend that they're bigger than they are to predators, or so that a predator wouldn't be able to target a particular individual?

I looked at all the familiar things in my life. The buildings, streets, trees. The ice-cream kiosk and shops. The lunchtime crowds in restaurants. The posters on the walls and the newspaper flysheets. My fingers toyed with the note in my pocket. Of all the people around me, only I knew that I was probably the happiest person in the country. And at absolutely no cost. I took a deep breath of the mild summer air. It occurred to me that I could have some ice-cream. Mint chocolate and raspberry, my two favourites.

THE CIRCUS

1

It all started with the usual discussion: is it possible to be friends with someone who listens to 'Fix You' by Coldplay? Then it broadened out and turned into a debate about friends and friendship in general. For a while I thought there was something wrong with the phone, like when you get a crossed line and find yourself talking to someone else. Dansson had told me you could find yourself talking to a complete stranger. Obviously I should have learned never to trust Dansson. Nor Jallo, come to that. Look, I'm getting this all muddled up. I'm not actually sure what order things happened in, to be honest. But I do know what happened. What happened when Magnus Gabrielsson disappeared at the circus. And by that I don't mean he got lost in the crowd. I mean he disappeared and didn't come back.

2

An old friend of mine, Magnus, had called me and asked if I wanted to go to the circus with him. I didn't particularly like circuses, but Magnus said this one was worth going to.

'They've got clowns,' he said.

I was standing in front of my record collection holding my phone between my ear and my shoulder. In one hand I had Fun Boy Three, and in the other one of Terry Hall's solo albums, which I was trying to squeeze in between the albums by the Specials and those by the Special AKA.

I'd already spent all morning lying on Jallo's couch, drinking coffee and talking crap about all sorts of stuff. Music, old memories, the usual gossip. On and on we went. The atmosphere was pretty strained right from the start, and by the end we'd fallen out badly. It began with a discussion of 'Fix You' by Coldplay, but soon developed into a wider debate about 'real friends'.

'So what is a "real friend", then?' Jallo asked, scratching his chin.

The whole thing was ridiculous. I had no desire to get bogged down in that sort of pseudo-philosophical nonsense. And the question sounded like a bit of a guilt trip. Are you a real friend? What do you mean, a *real* friend?

'Maybe your real friends aren't always the ones you think they are,' Jallo went on, and started talking about a bully from back at school called Dennis, who had the worst music taste in the world.

'We become new people all the time,' Jallo said.

'What do you mean by that?'

'We change. There's nothing weird about it.'

In the end I got so angry that I stood up and shouted at him. I slammed the door behind me and walked all the way home. Right now all I wanted was to be left alone for a while.

Magnus went on talking about the circus, about the different acts. He gave me a long spiel about who was doing what, and what order it would be happening in. I was only half-listening, and let him go on while I sorted my records and checked that they were grouped together properly. Madness next to the Selecter next to the Specials next to Elvis Costello. Lucinda Williams next to Jolie Holland next to M. Ward next to She & Him. When Magnus noticed I still sounded dubious, he added, as if he'd suddenly remembered, 'My treat, obviously.'

Magnus Gabrielsson always made me feel guilty. We were old childhood friends and nowadays only met up every couple of years out of duty. We'd sit and stare at each other in awkward silence, saying it was good to see each other, that we really must do this more often, that we ought to go bowling some time. Then we would go our separate ways, relieved that we didn't have to go through that again for another year or so.

I suppose we still had a few things in common. Music, of course, but there were other things that made us both a bit different. Neither of us had bothered to get a mobile phone, for instance. Not out of any particular point of principle – I was actually one of the first to get a cordless phone – but when mobiles appeared for some reason I never caught up. Suddenly everybody had one. And getting one then would mean being last. So neither Magnus nor I bothered. That's made things a bit difficult, and to be honest I have thought about getting one, but it's become a matter of saving face now. So we called each other on our landlines. Just less and less often. It had been over a year since we last spoke, and now he wanted me to go to the circus with him.

I thought about all the things I'd rather do: look round record shops, rent a film, browse the latest IKEA catalogue, poke about on the Ginza music website, clean the bathroom, do the sudoku in yesterday's paper. Or just carry on sorting my records. After thinking about it for a while, I decided I'd go. Not because I wanted to, but because it felt like a good opportunity to get a meeting with Magnus out of the way. Maybe that discussion about 'real friends' had something to do with it as well.

3

The circus was called Hansen and Larsen's Magic Company, and it was more of a theatrical 'happening' than a traditional circus. We passed a big neon sign on which bright red and yellow letters lit up one at a time, from the top down, until you realised that the letters formed a top hat. I was following Magnus. A band was already playing when we arrived, but the whole thing felt shabby, haphazard and not particularly well organised. The woman standing by the entrance was busy with her mobile phone. She didn't even look up when she we showed our tickets. We headed down a corridor made of bright orange curtains, walking on a cheap, crumpled blue carpet. A string of lights ran along one side of the carpet, curling around itself in places. You had to take care not to trip over it. All over the place were things that had clearly been taken from someone's living room: a dresser, a standard lamp with a fabric shade, an extension lead running across a hand-woven carpet. It all helped reinforce the illusion that we were indoors, even though we were outside. I was already regretting coming because the moment we entered the main arena I started humming Frank Sinatra's 'Love and Marriage', and whenever I get that stuck in my head I always know things are going to turn out badly. It's like a premonition, a way for my subconscious to let my conscious mind know that something isn't right.

The tent wasn't very big, and felt cramped and homespun, with draped material forming tunnels leading off in different directions. The floor sloped. Everything sloped. Even though there wasn't much room there were lots of people there, but somehow Magnus and I still managed to get good seats. In the middle of one of the benches, fairly close to the front.

The lights dimmed to leave a spotlight shining on a little red velvet curtain. Magnus stretched out beside me, tapping his foot and very excited. Almost as if he was nervous. Like a child. I wondered if maybe he'd never been to a circus before. I'd been a couple of times when I was little. Even if they were nothing like this one.

The ringmaster welcomed us all and I wondered if he was Hansen or Larsen. He waved a staff in front of our faces. I could smell the acrid stench of his old tailcoat when he raised his arm.

The ringmaster introduced a trapeze artist, supposedly the best in Europe, and she entered the ring to loud applause. The trapeze artist turned out to be a very sturdy woman with a mane of hair and big muscles. She spun some plates with cakes and pastries on them while she was balancing on the wire. But the wire was only suspended a few centimetres above the ground, so they might as well not have bothered. It could have even touched the ground as she walked along it. Either way, the audience was very enthusiastic. Magnus clapped several times, even in the middle of the act. After the trapeze artist two clowns in blue hats came in and started to build a tower out of old musical instruments while a third clown in a red hat sabotaged their efforts. They had planned the routine very cleverly so that the first two clowns never saw the third. None of them saw the others, because as soon as one went out the other two came in, and so on. The clown in the red hat hid behind the instruments and kept rearranging things when the others had left the ring. When he had wound the other two up so much that they started shouting at each other, he switched strategy and began to help them instead, and without any of them seeming to realise how it happened, in the end they succeeded in building some sort of tower. The clowns in the blue hats shook hands and congratulated each other while the clown in the red hat toppled the whole thing over and the instruments fell to the ground with a great crash. The first two clowns chased each other out of the ring with rubber mallets.

The whole act made me feel uncomfortable. But Magnus and the children in front of me laughed so hard they could hardly breathe. Magnus looked at me, but I just shook my head.

After the clowns the ringmaster came back in to introduce a magician.

'Ladies and gentlemen,' he said. 'I present to you Mr Magic Bobbi!'

Bobbi was wearing a long cape and dazzling white gloves. He started off with some tricks involving rabbits and doves and playing cards, all the things magicians usually do. Then, after a while, he pulled off his gloves and said he was going to make a member of the audience disappear. He asked for a volunteer. A deafening silence followed, and I wondered if anyone was going to offer themselves. Then I realised that Magnus was raising his hand right next to my head. Everyone turned to look at us.

The magician pointed at Magnus and gestured to him to come forward. I tugged gently at his jacket but he just grinned and stood up.

When Magnus reached him, the magician asked what Magnus's name was, and he told him, speaking into a red microphone.

'So, Magnus, what do you think about being spirited away?' the magician asked, and the audience laughed.

'No problem,' Magnus said.

'Are you here on your own?'

Magnus wasn't used to speaking into a microphone so he answered before the magician had time to hold it out. Mr Bobbi asked him to repeat what he had said so everyone could hear. Magnus leaned towards the microphone.

'My friend's sitting over there.'

Everyone looked at me again. I didn't know what to do, so I didn't do anything.

'So what's your friend going to say if I make you disappear?'

'I don't know,' Magnus said.

As they were talking, Mr Magic Bobbi reached one hand behind the red velvet curtain and pulled out a door on wheels with a big mirror on it. The mirror ended up right behind Magnus and the magician. The lights went out again, leaving just a spotlight shining on Magnus and Bobbi.

'Well, look at that!' the magician said. 'You're already starting to disappear.'

He turned and pointed at the mirror. Magnus turned as well. There was no sign of his reflection. The magician, the microphone and everything else in the spotlight was visible. But not Magnus. The audience laughed and applauded. Magnus made a few little movements, but nothing showed in the mirror.

'I know,' the magician said into the red microphone. 'What if you try walking around it?'

He gestured to Magnus to take a look at the back, and Magnus walked around the mirror at the same time as the magician turned it the other way. Now Magnus's image appeared in the mirror. The magician spun the mirror again and showed it to all sides of the audience.

'OK, you can come out now,' the magician said.

The audience applauded again. I saw Magnus try to say something, but because the magician had the microphone only his voice could be heard above the clapping and cheering of the audience.

'What a very vain fellow!' he said. 'Sneaking inside the mirror like that. Well, it's time to come out now!'

Everyone laughed and clapped. I could see Magnus standing inside the mirror. He had his hands in his trouser pockets and was grinning sheepishly. I felt rather sorry for him then, standing there while everyone laughed.

It had always been easy to feel sorry for Magnus Gabrielsson. He never really fitted in. We came from the same suburb, from similar families. Hard-working dads you never saw much of, mothers who took care of everything, wishing they were somewhere else. Comfortable enough to wish for something a bit better. No fancy holidays, but maybe a couple of weeks at a campsite in the vicinity of some moderately interesting attraction. Enough of an income to run one or even two second-hand cars, some smart clothes to show off in, and maybe even some basic improvements to the house. Enough for the kids to keep up with whatever was in fashion, more or less, or ignore it and spend all their pocket money on records and tapes instead.

We went to different schools but saw a lot of each other for a few years, drifting around the industrial estate and the marsh behind it. He used to pick his nose, and he had a weird hairstyle as a teenager. He never talked much, kept himself to himself. There wasn't anything remarkable about him apart from the fact that he never belonged, never quite managed to figure out the things that mattered.

It felt odd sitting there watching him being mocked by the magician down in the ring. Everyone in the audience assumed that the subject of the trick was a grown man. Only I saw little Magnus Gabrielsson, who, when we were children, had sometimes wet himself when he got really scared.

4

The magician kept turning the mirror so that everyone could see it was completely flat. When he turned it in my direction it looked like Magnus was waving at me.

'Well, then,' the magician said. 'If you won't come out of your own accord, I'm going to have to take you backstage!'

He picked up the mirror frame with Magnus inside it, tucked it under his arm and walked out. Everyone cheered and clapped. To my surprise I realised that I was laughing along with them.

The lights went up and the ringmaster reappeared.

'Mr Magic Bobbiiii!' the ringmaster cried, and Bobbi ran back in to take the applause. There was no sign of Magnus.

After Bobbi, some acrobats came in on a little motorised cart. Because it was so small, they had to take turns riding on it. Hansen, or Larsen, came in and drove around on it as well.

The curtain closed and rest of the lights went up. We had reached the intermission.

I sat for a while waiting for Magnus to come back as a succession of rustling anoraks brushed past me to leave. When he didn't appear I headed to the little lobby to buy a can of drink from a machine.

There was quite a long queue, and my fingers grew cold as I stood there waiting, even though it was almost June. I kept looking round to see if I could see Magnus. I thought I caught a glimpse of him behind a woman with curly hair and two children pulling in opposite directions. By the time they'd got out of the way he was gone again. Oh well, I thought. I'll see him when we go back to our seats again. I got my drink just as the band started to play again. I hurried back to our seats along the uneven blue carpet with the strip of lights running alongside it.

The second half began with acrobats crawling in and out of various tunnels and holes, disappearing in one place only to reappear a moment later somewhere else entirely.

The audience was even more enthusiastic now, roaring with laughter at everything in the ring.

At one point one of the acrobats came very close to me. He was wearing a false moustache and glasses, but I could still see that it was Mr Magic Bobbi behind the disguise. In fact all the acrobats looked a lot like Mr Magic Bobbi. I tried to work out how many of them there were and concluded that – purely theoretically – it would be possible for him to be playing all of them, if he moved fast enough between the holes and switched hats and moustaches when no one could see. When the act was over the ringmaster came back in, and it struck me that he looked a lot like Mr Magic Bobbi as well. On reflection, all the performers bore a striking resemblance to each other. Even the rather butch trapeze artiste at the start.

I sat through the whole of the second act, waiting for Magnus. I had trouble concentrating on the circus. The finale was a sailor – definitely Mr Magic Bobbi – singing 'New York, New York' through the tinny red microphone. It was unbearable. But I still thought it was odd that Magnus hadn't come back. Didn't he want to see the other acts?

When the show was over and everyone left, I lingered to see if Magnus would appear among the benches. Perhaps he'd found something interesting at the back or had got talking to a member of staff. Unless he'd got fed up and gone home? I stood around for a while, but eventually I started to feel silly so I left. On my way out I saw some security guards laughing. I couldn't help thinking they were laughing at me.

When I got home I kicked my shoes off so hard that they hit the wall. I screwed up the circus programme and stuffed it in the bin, swore to myself and went and lay on my bed with my clothes on.

I wasn't going to call Magnus Gabrielsson to ask where he'd got to. I thought it was very rude of him to disappear like that, especially when we'd arranged to go somewhere together. And it annoyed me that whenever we met I was always the one who ended up having to take care of him. Because that's exactly how it was. I always ended up helping Magnus Gabrielsson. The very first time we ever met I had to help him up, brush the leaves off him and carry his ugly old rucksack all the way home.

5

I woke up early the next morning to the sound of rain pattering against the windows and the feeling that something wasn't right. I lay in bed for a while trying to remember if I'd had any strange dreams. Then I got up and phoned Magnus Gabrielsson. The line was engaged. Which meant that at least he was home, I thought. But the same thing happened when I tried again an hour later, and an hour after that, so I started to wonder if it wasn't a bit odd after all. He couldn't still be on the phone, surely? Unless he'd left it off the hook?

I ate a bowl of muesli and thought about the previous day's visit to the circus. It was like trying to remember an unpleasant nightmare. Everything seemed just as peculiar today as it had the day before.

When I finished eating I put the bowl in the sink and went back into the bedroom to call Magnus again. I got the engaged tone once more, but when I tried again the call didn't even connect. I stood in front of my records for a while, feeling stupid. I swapped Antony and the Johnsons and Joan As Police Woman round, then called Magnus's number again.

When there was still no answer I went out into the hall and put my shoes and coat on. I thought I might as well drop by

Magnus's flat. It must have been ten years since I was last there.

I stepped out into the street and realised I should have taken an umbrella with me but couldn't be bothered to go back up and get one, so I pulled my hood up and kept close to the buildings in an attempt to stay out of the rain as best I could.

By the time I reached the door to Magnus's building I was soaked through, and realised that even if I had been able to remember the code to get in, they would have changed it by now. I stood beneath the porch, which barely sheltered me from the rain, peered through the glass and saw the list of residents a little way inside the hall. I thought I could make out the name Gabrielsson shown as living on the first floor. I stepped back out into the rain and looked up. There was no sign of life on the first floor.

I stood there squinting through the rain until I felt the water slowly but surely soak through my jacket and sweater. I spotted a 7-Eleven a little way down the street and set off towards it at a run. There were a few plastic tables inside, as well as a counter and a couple of bar stools from which you could get a good view of Magnus's building. I bought a cup of scalding hot tea and sat down. I shrugged off my jacket and hung it over the radiator beneath the table. I was the only person there apart from the cashier, and I considered taking my sweater off as well and sitting in my shirtsleeves but decided against it. I wiped myself down with some paper napkins. It didn't make much of a difference.

'They've turned the taps on full today,' the cashier said, nodding towards my jacket.

I smiled. The cashier clattered about behind the counter. There was a badly tuned radio playing one of those Bryan Adams ballads whose titles I took a certain pride in not being able to identify. I tried to concentrate on Magnus's doorway, but the heavy rain was like a wall outside the window, which was getting more and more steamed up. After a while a figure appeared out of the rain. He rushed towards the shop door and shook himself like a wet dog when he came in. He looked at me, seeking an exchange of knowing glances about the terrible weather. I looked back towards Magnus's door again.

The cashier repeated the line about taps, and I wondered if he had only the one stock phrase.

A woman holding a newspaper over her head was heading straight towards the window, presumably to get as close to the building as possible. It struck me it was probably the first time I'd ever seen anyone do that with a newspaper in real life. It felt like a thing they'd do in – I don't know – France, say. Suddenly she was standing in front of me and we looked at each other. It felt a bit uncomfortable, realising that we were so close to each other, with just the pane of glass between us. I thought about turning away, then remembered I was supposed to be keeping an eye on Magnus's door. I wasn't the one behaving oddly. She was.

We stayed like that for a moment, staring at each other, then I turned my attention back to Magnus's building again. The heavy door was swinging shut on the other side of the street and I realised what I had just caught a glimpse of: someone had gone in through the door.

I could have sworn it was Magnus.

6

I considered running over, but couldn't see any point. The door would still be closed. Whoever had gone inside would have vanished into the stairwell by the time I got there. I needed to keep a closer eye on people heading towards the building if I was to catch someone who could let me in. I stirred the hot tea with a plastic spoon.

The new customer came over to my table with his mug of coffee. He stopped so close that I realised he was going to say something to me. The moment he put his cup down on the table a light went on in one of the rooms on the first floor.

'Did it catch you by surprise?' the man beside me asked, nodding out at the rain.

I looked up at him, wondering what he meant. He gestured towards my wet clothes. I nodded and pointed at my jacket on the radiator under the table as I pondered asking if I could borrow the man's mobile to try Magnus again.

'Smart,' the man with the coffee said.

'Yes,' I said, and leaned over to feel my jacket. It had dried a little, and had a damp warmth, like clothes in a tumble drier before they're quite done. It felt nice now, but I knew it would be cold again the moment I put it on. When I sat back up the light in the flat had gone out.

343

'Dry?'

'No,' I said, pulling the jacket on anyway before running out of the shop and over to the door.

I'd catch him on the way out.

It was still impossible to shelter under the porch of the building, and gusts of wind kept blowing fresh sheets of rain into my face. I huddled against the door as hard as I could.

No one came out, but after half an hour or so a woman appeared and let me in without any questions. She probably felt sorry for me when she saw how cold and wet I was, so I didn't need any of the excuses I'd been making up to help pass the time.

I squelched up the stairs and rang the doorbell. It sounded like someone was moving about inside the flat, but it was hard to tell because of the noise my wet clothes were making. A big puddle started to form around me. I tried to stand completely still and hold my breath so I could hear better, but there was no sound at all now. Maybe I'd imagined it. I nudged the letterbox open.

'Magnus?' I called. 'Is that you?'

It sounded stupid. The sort of thing someone would say in a film. So I didn't bother shouting again, and knocked instead. No answer.

After five minutes I walked slowly back down the stairs and stopped in the entrance hall. It was still raining just as hard, and I decided to wait until the weather eased.

While I was standing there, leaning against the wall and looking out at the downpour through the glass, I caught sight of Jallo. He was walking along the other side of the street without a coat, and made a sudden dash across the road. Just before he reached the pavement it occurred to me that he might get a fright if he saw me standing perfectly still in the gloomy hall.

Sure enough he came to an abrupt halt when he caught sight of me. He screwed up his eyes and squinted as if he couldn't quite see if it really was me. He tapped on the glass and pointed at the door. I opened it for him.

'Bloody hell,' he said, shaking off the worst of the water.

He looked at me as if he was expecting me to say something.

'What are you doing here?' he said.

I first met Jallo at a camp we attended each summer between the years of thirteen and fifteen. He was a little older than me and went to Berg School: a hyperactive hippie kid who had moved from Finland with his mother a few years earlier. We spent a few summers together at that place – there were horses and a garden and you could paint, all that sort of thing. For a long time I thought we were in love with the same girl, but I don't remember us ever falling out about it. 'People like us need to stick together,' he had said. By that he was probably referring to the fact that we both liked synthesiser music, and it was important we stuck together because things weren't easy if you were into synth music back then. But I can't say I ever heard him play any music, and he knew surprisingly little about the subject when we talked about it. Then again, it was always difficult to get much of a handle on him. Admittedly he was older than me, but he seemed even older than his years. He got on well with grown-ups and was occasionally allowed to help the staff, and he was able to talk in that grown-up way that sometimes made it hard to say if he was one of us or one of them.

We only really started to spend more time together when we got to high school. After Dansson, he was the person I socialised with most — not that there was much competition. But I did genuinely enjoy his company.

'I thought I'd look in on Magnus,' I said.

'Magnus?' Jallo said and sighed.

'Yes. What about you?'

'Oh, I don't know,' he said with a shrug. 'Do you want to do something?'

Despite having been friends for so long, Jallo often annoyed me. He spoke in a drawl that made me feel restless and irritated at the same time. His clothes looked as if he'd made them himself and he used to go on personal development courses in Holland, coming home with rosy cheeks talking about the more important things in life. It often felt like he lived in a different reality and that rules and regulations didn't apply to him the way they did to the rest of us. Everything seemed to be relative, conditional, as if it all could just as easily have been the other way round.

He never bore grudges. He was bound to have forgotten our row about 'real friends' already. Nothing ever seemed to bother him. He just brushed himself off and carried on. He regarded every setback as an exciting challenge, and was only interested in how to move on from any given situation. He could turn on a sixpence and go off in completely the opposite direction without slowing down at all, as if it was the most natural thing in the world. Success didn't seem to affect him either. Everything was just 'exciting' or 'cool', and nothing was too insignificant not to warrant in-depth exploration. He could spent ages staring at you in silence, as if he was expecting something more. As if nothing was ever quite enough for him. As if there was always something he wanted to change.

Magnus didn't like Jallo. He said there was something weird about him. And of course there was. He always popped up just when you least expected it. He stood way too close. Didn't have any of the usual inhibitions. Always asked question after question, trying to get under your skin. It was as if no answer was ever good enough for him. It didn't matter what you said, he always followed up with another question.

'Why are you in such a hurry?'

'I don't want to be late.'

'What for?'

'A class.'

'Why not?'

'I don't want to miss the start.'

'What difference would that make?'

'I'd get a black mark.'

'Why would that matter?'

'It's not a good idea to get black marks.'

'Why not?'

'Leave off!'

Whenever you said something, he would nod, and you'd assume you'd reached some sort of agreement. Then he'd make a completely different decision instead. Maybe he was just shy or being polite, but it always made me feel a bit stupid. As if he always knew more than me in any given situation.

Before he even graduated from high school he had developed an entrepreneurial spirit. He registered as self-employed and set up a phone line for people who 'wanted to get things off their chest'.

'This is the future,' he told me. 'The service sector! The soft economy, human issues. Contact, interaction, interpersonal values. Industry,' he said with a snort. 'Industry is so over, you know. There's no future in *stuff*. No one wants more *stuff*. What society needs now is someone to take care of all the lost souls industry has left behind. You need to take care of your brand, construct your own style, your own way of dealing with other people, understanding and appreciating them. That's the future. Communication. You're home and dry if you know how to communicate. But if you don't, then ...'

Over the next few years self-employment became a private company, and the private company became a public limited company. These days he was renting office space to run some sort of clinic, as well as various other questionable activities. He had customers he called clients, but not so many that you couldn't show up there pretty much whenever you felt like to drink coffee and talk rubbish while Jallo proudly showed off his latest purchases, notwithstanding his proclamations against 'stuff'.

'Take a look at this! Velvet!' he said, patting a couch he'd placed in the middle of the room.

He had furnished the room with heavy red curtains, hand-woven rugs and big, annoying, garish pictures that didn't seem to be of anything much, but which he was still very proud of. He always said the way things looked was vital.

'It's more important than you'd think,' he said. 'People often pass judgement at first sight.'

I don't know what he did to the poor fools who went to see him, but they must have been happy since they kept going back.

He had long hair, sometimes loose, sometimes in a ponytail. If you saw him out in the street you could easily think he was a dropout, a 'resting' rock musician or some other unemployed hedonist who had been taking a few too many drugs, whereas he actually ran that clinic as well as a number of other businesses. He'd just applied to register a new form of therapy and was, if you believed what he said, 'on his way to becoming a real player'. If he was on his way to an important meeting you might see him with a suit hanging off his lanky frame. But it was as if he didn't care what other people thought when it came down to it. He did exactly what he liked, when he liked.

He was perfectly capable of talking crap about Magnus, for instance.

'Forget him,' he might say before dragging you off somewhere, even though you'd made other arrangements. As if what you were doing really didn't matter, and whatever new thing he had going on was bound to be way more interesting.

I told Jallo that Magnus wasn't home but there was something strange going on seeing as I had heard noises inside the flat. And his phone was engaged the whole time. Jallo listened and nodded.

I told him how I'd seen the lights go on and off. In the end we both went back upstairs and knocked on the door. No answer.

'So he's not home,' Jallo said.

'What d'you mean?' I said.

'If he was home he'd open the door.'

I looked at him and he looked back at me. As if it was as simple as that.

I told him that Magnus and I had been to the circus and I hadn't seen him since.

'OK,' Jallo said, nodding. 'So?'

I looked at him.

'So I thought I'd try to get hold of him,' I said.

Jallo tilted his head a few times with an expression that could be taken to mean that he'd been hoping we could do something more entertaining.

'Why don't you write a letter?' Jallo asked.

'To Magnus?'

'Yes,' Jallo said.

I sighed.

'You know what I think you should do?' he said after a pause, brightening up as if he'd just had an idea. 'I think you should check out this place.'

Jallo found an old till receipt in one pocket and a pen in the other. He scribbled something on the scrap of paper and handed it to me. I took it. He stuck his tongue out and caught a raindrop that was trickling from his wet hair. Then he stiffened and raised his eyebrows. He pulled something from the pocket of his hoodie and held it up triumphantly.

'Toffee,' he said.

I glanced at my watch while Jallo unwrapped the toffee with his long, thin fingers and put it in his mouth. He smacked his lips as he sucked it, still looking at me. As if it was down to the pair of us now. As if I had to decide what we should do.

'Bought any records lately?' he asked as he chewed the toffee.

'Yep,' I said.

'"Sail Away" by Enya is pretty good,' he said.

I didn't respond to that.

We stood like that for a while, and the only thing that happened was that the toffee in his mouth got smaller, and the obscene slurping sounds came faster and faster. Every so often he held up his hand and looked at it. It looked chapped and red.

'I've started getting dry skin again,' he said. 'Need to remember to wear gloves.'

Eventually I realised I had no choice but to leave. Jallo stood where he was, still looking at me in that forlorn way, and I thought it was just as well to get going before he asked if he could come with me. I pushed the front door open and felt the relentless rain on my face. I held up the receipt Jallo had given me. It came from the Gryningen health food shop on Folkungagatan. Jallo's handwriting was as bad as a doctor's, and the rain was already washing some of it away. But I could just about make out the address: Bondegatan 3A.

I stood there a while, shuffling from one foot to the other. Then I went home.

7

Bondegatan 3A? What was that supposed to mean? I didn't like the way Jallo went about things. He always saw so many different ways of approaching a subject, the possibilities seemed endless. If you lost your wallet, for instance, and the police couldn't help you, why not try hypnosis? Or a Facebook group? Everything seemed equally valid to him.

He would muddle brand new research findings from the Karolinska Hospital with long-forgotten medieval remedies. Grumble that a lot of conventional psychology was too rigid.

For a while he tried to cultivate oyster mushrooms in a garage on Kungsholmen. He had a load of cardboard boxes that looked like little red cottages lined up along the wall behind the cars.

'Low rent,' he said. 'Decent margins.'

I don't know what happened, if it just wasn't profitable after all, or if there was some sort of problem with the garage or people driving over the boxes. But he seemed to have put the project on hold, anyway. It had been a long time since he had mentioned anything about the 'mushroom industry'.

More recently he had embarked upon a proper psychology course.

'Having a bit of paper that says you can do stuff seems to be so important,' he said.

I agreed that it might not be a bad idea to acquire a bit more evidence-based knowledge if you were serious about setting yourself up in that line of business. So he had applied, been accepted, and decided to study enough course units at university to get himself a certificate, but it was highly doubtful that he'd stick at it for long enough.

'Takes a hell of a long time,' he said.

Predictably, his studies ended up taking a back seat in favour of his other activities. Being 'certificated' no longer seemed so important, as Jallo put it, with air-quotes. People would still come to his clinic.

The last time I was there he showed me a karaoke machine. He said he'd got it to help his clients 'lower their guard'.

'The atmosphere can get a bit too tense,' he said, looking through the songs on offer. 'And of course it's pretty cool, too!'

Maybe he used rocks or crystals, or did some sort of CBT treatment? I don't really know what he offered his clients. Apart from karaoke, of course.

It was impossible to get any real grip of all his plans and activities. Maybe even he didn't know. He seemed to collect slightly dodgy people and together they would come up with unconventional ways to earn money. His ideas often seemed to involve telesales.

Bondegatan 3A. There could be anything there. But perhaps it would be silly not to make use of his contacts, I reasoned. Whoever they might be.

353

8

That evening Magnus's phone was still engaged. I called five times and never got through. I watched some TV, had a cup of tea, then went round the flat turning the lights out before I went to bed. I knew I should get to sleep just after eleven in order to be vaguely awake for work early the next morning. There was nothing good on after the late news anyway. The programmes would only get worse and worse until eventually I was left watching repeats of *The Fall Guy* from the early 1980s or staring at the rolling news on TV Vision. Even so, I still found myself sitting on the sofa with the phone in my hand. Why was the line still engaged? Did he have that many friends to talk to? Or had he pulled his phone out of the socket? Why hadn't he called me? I put the phone down next to me on the sofa and listened to the engaged signal for a while before I pressed the red button.

Sure enough, SVT was showing a documentary about a school orchestra tour, Channel 5 had an American poker programme, TV3 a reality programme in which the participants pretended to be friends before voting each other out in the hope of becoming the World's Biggest Loser. By the time *The Fall Guy* finished it was two o'clock. I picked up the phone. Looked at it. It rang. I answered at once.

No one said anything, there was just a faint hum, but I could hear someone breathing on the other end. I switched the television off, and the flat plunged into darkness. And complete silence. I stood up and walked over to the window.

'Hello?' I said.

Still no response, but I sensed someone there. I tried to breathe as quietly as possible even though I could hear my heart beating faster and faster.

'Hello?' I said once more. 'Who am I talking to?'

Not that there's anyone talking back, I thought, listening to the silence on the line. Down in the street a billboard advertising men's underwear was lit up, casting a faint streak of light across the building opposite, where all the lights were out. I pressed the phone closer to my ear and tried to imagine the person at the other end. The silent caller. It felt decidedly unsettling.

'Is that Magnus?' I said after a while.

There was a noise – it sounded like fabric or possibly a hand. Unless it was just static on the line. It was impossible to tell. I stood perfectly still in my pitch-black living room, feeling the warmth of the phone against my cheek.

'What ... Is that you, Magnus?' I repeated. 'Is everything OK?'

When there was no answer to that either, I decided to stay quiet as well. I walked slowly back and forth in the darkened room, waiting. It felt like the two of us, the caller and I, were each waiting for the other. I stood for a long time leaning against the frame of the kitchen door. I rested my head gently against the wood and heard a slight tap as the phone knocked the frame. I angled it away from my mouth.

I ended up in the hall, in front of the mirror. Because the flat was in total darkness I couldn't see anything in the mirror. There was nothing for it to reflect. I wondered for a moment if you could say I was in the mirror even though I couldn't see myself. I pressed the phone to my ear and because neither of us was speaking it was almost as if I was listening to myself. I got the sense that the silence was somehow betraying how anxious I was and did my best not to breathe into the receiver too much. It wasn't nice, listening to your own anxiety.

'Where's Magnus?' I said.

I imagined I could hear that the breathing at the other end was just as nervous. As if there was something stressful, discomforting about the whole situation. As if he or she had been about to say something but had thought better of it. Perhaps they were frightened and didn't dare speak?

In the end there was a click and I realised that the other person had hung up. I paced the flat for a while. I switched the bedside light on and sat on the bed staring at the phone. If it was him, why hadn't Magnus said anything? And if it wasn't him, who was it? Could there have been something wrong with the microphone on his phone? That sort of thing sometimes happened. No, because I could clearly hear someone breathing. So why hadn't he said anything? Was he afraid to?

I lay back and opened the IKEA catalogue on my chest, but the usual undemanding joy of idle browsing wasn't there. After ten minutes I got up and dialled the same number again. No answer.

9

Being awake at night can have its advantages. As long as you can manage to suppress all thoughts of sleep and the tiredness you're bound to feel the next day. The night offers a stillness, a concentration that can make you think you've found a gap in time.

I put my headphones on and listened to Prefab Sprout's *Jordan: The Comeback*. I clicked to get to 'Moon Dog' and sat in the armchair next to the stereo listening to the intro, which always calmed me down and made me feel I was going somewhere. Even if that just meant onward through the night. Somehow I managed to fall asleep like that.

10

I hate it when people disappear inside mirrors and don't come back. It's a real pain. You just don't do that sort of thing. But if people still insist on doing it they usually come back sooner or later, and you find out what happened. Then you both sit and laugh about how gullible you were, and at the entertaining but slightly humiliating fact that you fell for such a simple trick. But if they disappear and don't come back, then in my opinion the joke stops being funny. It makes you question the way you see the world, and I really don't like doing that. I'd be perfectly happy to keep hold of the way I see the world right now, with a tolerably good understanding of how things work. I'd prefer to keep hold of my friends and be able to trust my senses.

11

I worked behind the bakery counter of the NK department store. I would stand there wrapping bread and pastries, literally imprisoned in a glass cage under the gaze of the customers, all of whom had just one and the same wish: that as soon as I was done serving another customer, I would press the button so that their number should finally come up on the ticketed queuing system. If I took too long someone would call out, 'Young man, what do you think you're here for?'

The boss had told us we should just smile if that happened.

All things considered it was a good, reliable job. I mean, people are always going to want bread, and they're always going to want to buy it from NK. I was fairly happy there and did the job well enough. But I was due to start at nine o'clock on Monday morning, and when I woke up in my armchair it was already quarter to. I got up and pulled my headphones off, and it was only when the noise disappeared that I realised I had slept all night with last night's music in my ears. It echoed in my head as I brushed my teeth and pulled on my shoes and coat.

I arrived at work at half past nine and got some pointed stares from the girls who had had to cover for me. Fortunately the boss was nowhere in sight, so I clicked to the button for the next customer and tried to compensate for my late arrival by smiling even more than usual. By lunchtime it felt as if that smile had eaten its way into my features and become a grimace that was more frightening than welcoming.

I tried calling Magnus twice from work, but there was no answer. No answer-machine message. Nothing.

As the day went on, the trays from the bakery emptied, and they had to be cleaned before they were returned. I usually tried to get that job, which meant twenty minutes or half an hour at the sink in the back. Without an audience. After lunch I hauled all the trays into the kitchen and turned the tap on. I pulled off the fake bow tie that was part of the bakery-counter uniform. The girls had to wear frilly aprons and have their hair up. I had the male equivalent: a shirt with a bow tie on an elastic band that pinched your throat. It was fixed to the top button, and would snap off when you unfastened it. I stood there staring into space for a while. What on earth was going on? Magnus had gone missing, and now someone I didn't know was calling me in the middle of the night and not saying a word.

The more I thought about it, the more I felt sure that the silence on the line was in some nebulous but undeniable sense – a bit like the way Lou Reed is connected to David Bowie, or Jonas Bonetta to Josh Garrells – connected to Propaganda's third single, 'p:Machinery'.

12

There was no good reason for 'p:Machinery' by Propaganda to pop into my head. Even so, I listened to the whole of their *A Secret Wish* album when I got home, trying to figure out what it was about the silence on the phone line that had made me think of Propaganda. Sure, that was the sort of music we listened to most, me and Magnus. But what was it about that particular track? The computerised bleeps at the start, or just the dark, foreboding atmosphere? Listening to it again didn't help. When I was putting the record back I wasn't sure if it ought to move along a few places, closer to China Crisis and Heaven 17, who admittedly had more of an acoustic sound but still belonged to that same part of the synth music scene.

That evening I swapped the Pixies and the Ramones, which meant that there was no room for the Sex Pistols and Andy Hull's solo album, so they had to be squeezed in on the shelf below, which didn't feel great seeing as that was the shelf I had been happiest with up until then. I stood there for a while wondering if that meant I couldn't buy any more albums in that subgenre, or if I would just have to expand it instead. There wasn't room on the wall for any more shelves. Maybe I'd have to sell some records or use those plastic sleeves. I didn't want to put my records in plastic sleeves. It felt tacky. Disrespectful. As if all records could be reduced to a flat disc with no spine. Besides, it ruined the whole idea of a record collection if you couldn't see which records were lined up next to each other. In that case I might as well give up and switch to Spotify, I reasoned, and end up left with everything and nothing. An undefined mass of tracks on a computer where you could sneak a listen to individual tracks without any sense of the integrity of the album and the culture of album sleeves. No structure.

That was pretty much how people used to listen to the *Chart Show* at school. Listening idly and never learning names and album titles. Never knowing where the different tracks belonged. As if music was just one big river, something you couldn't influence, like fog, or pollution.

There were two schools in the area where Magnus and I grew up. One good, one not so good. Berg School and Vira Elementary.

Berg School was notorious for its thugs, bullies and genuinely criminal students. It was widely regarded as a 'bad school'. A big, old-fashioned slum school where kids ended up if their families lived in the wrong place or didn't have the right sort of influence, the right contacts in the council, didn't have the energy to keep nagging and writing letters to the education office. A place for kids with no ambitions.

The more fortunate of us went to Vira Elementary School. A modern school in nice buildings that had a 'salad bar' and flower beds in the grounds and guaranteed good grades. Those of us who went to Vira didn't socialise with the kids who went to Berg. We were told – by teachers, other pupils and not least our parents – that they were all either illiterate, hooligans or drug addicts. The papers had written about the 'situation' at Berg School, where violence and threatening behaviour were part of daily life. Our headmaster appeared on local television, tilting his head thoughtfully and lamenting the way things had developed at Berg while simultaneously declaring that there was no bullying at Vira Elementary.

Vira only had well behaved pupils who were motivated to study. Our headmaster said that at our school we helped each other and put all our efforts into our studies. And if there was ever any bullying, he crowed on that television programme, the bullies would have him to answer to.

I always imagined life at Berg School like a prison film, where different gangs were in charge, doling out punishments and demanding bribes and protection money.

Panic broke out when there was talk of transferring some of us from Vira to Berg School. The intake had been too big and the classes were too large. Unless this was just an attempt by the council to mix up the socioeconomic groups a little in order to reduce segregation and create a more equal society. Vira was considerably smaller, and in order to make space some of us might have to be moved to Berg School.

The parents, led by Dennis's dad and Mia Lindström's mum, attended a crisis meeting with the headmasters and representatives of the council. Rumour had it that Dennis's dad had torn a strip off the people from the council and told them they were incompetent and how he'd see to it that they lost their jobs and never got another position with any authority. Anna Hamberg's mum said that if her daughter was going to be transferred to Berg School, they may as well put her in a young offenders' institution there and then. Several of them, parents and teachers alike, wept openly. In the end nothing came of the whole thing. Our parents were able to draw a collective sigh of relief, content in the knowledge that we could carry on going to the very best of schools.

I didn't know anything about Berg School apart from what Magnus and Jallo told me and the rumours that used to do the rounds. I was just immensely grateful that I didn't have to go there, because I was a 'special' child, as my teacher put it. The sort who can find the social side of things a bit difficult, as he told my parents.

'And obviously that's a bit of a challenge for the rest of the class,' he said.

I didn't say anything. I rarely did in those days. I did what I usually did. Waited until it was over so I could put my headphones on again. I learned at an early age that most things only got worse the more you talked. After a lot of nagging and sulking I had finally got myself a Walkman, partly paid for by my parents, and spent almost all my free time making mix tapes that I wandered about listening to. The best part of the day was in between lessons when I could put my headphones on and disappear into my own soundtrack, drifting along listening to one song after the other and seeing the world more as a sequence of moving images set to music.

At Vira Elementary there were two musical genres you could choose between. You either liked synth music or hard rock. There was nothing in between. We'd heard of people who listened to reggae, and older people who listened to all sorts of things, jazz, for instance, but the choice at school was simple: synthesisers or hard rock. If you didn't make the choice for yourself, someone else would do it for you. If you weren't into rock, you were automatically a synth fan.

The hard rock kids were the overwhelming majority, but that was just as much to do with the whole image as the music. Torn jeans and studded belts, long blonde curly hair or dead straight black hair. Armbands with skulls on, that sort of thing. Some of them wore battered leather boots and shark-tooth necklaces, but they were still pretty tame compared to the rockers from Berg School you used to run into down at the shopping centre. They had tattoos, carried ghetto blasters on their shoulders and knew people who were real punks. At Vira all you needed to be a rocker was an Iron Maiden T-shirt. Dennis had permed hair and usually wore a clean, unblemished tennis shirt, but every so often he would wear a leather bracelet to discreetly indicate which group he belonged to. He talked a lot about W.A.S.P., chainsaws, Twisted Sister and women being crucified on stage. Synth-pop was a term of abuse.

In our class we muddled along well enough, but there was a definite hierarchy, with Dennis at the top and the rest of us in descending order, with me close to if not right at the bottom. It didn't bother me. It wasn't something that was ever spoken about. That was just how it was. And it somehow made a lot of sense, everyone having clearly defined roles. There was never any need for fighting or threatening behaviour. Things sorted themselves out of their own accord, with glances and whispers and the number of chairs between me and the others in the cafeteria. I was always aware of the situation and stuck to the rules as well as I could.

Most of the time I wasn't bothered by it. I had my music. As soon as I put my headphones on they could push me about however they wanted without it mattering at all. Sometimes they stood on my heels so my shoes would come off, but it wasn't exactly hard to put them back on again. Sometimes I was just unlucky. Like the time a note with a vulgar – extremely vulgar – sentence on it ended up on my desk, and Eva, our English teacher, spotted it. I wasn't sure I understood all the words, and certainly not what they meant, but because the note contained Eva's name I was summoned to see the headmaster.

The same thing happened in Year 9 when they composed a fake 'love letter' in my name to Maddy, which she showed to her teacher, who brought it to the attention of the headmaster because of the coarse language and threatening, chauvinistic tone. The headmaster said it was deeply insulting to women, and I would have to apologise to Maddy in person. He also said that if I wanted to have any contact with the opposite sex in the future, I would have to learn that that sort of language simply wasn't acceptable. It was far too much bother to try to explain what had happened, so I did as they said and apologised. That seemed the simplest solution, and it was all over fairly quickly. A few short platitudes by Maddy's locker, then I could put my headphones back on and retreat into the world of music again.

The times I ended up battered and bruised, or my schoolbooks got ruined, were almost always the result of a prank or an accident. Like the time I came out of the shower after PE and all my clothes had gone, and I had to cover myself with paper towels all the way to the headmaster's office, where they let me borrow some clothes from the lost property box. That was probably my fault. Maybe I hadn't heard something because I had my headphones on? That happened quite a lot. Things usually got sorted out after I got told off or had to go and see the headmaster. It was just how things had always been for me.

Once I'd slotted Lotte Lenya and Ute Lemper back in next to Kurt Weill again I was left standing there with an old Madness album in one hand and a Starsailor single from 2003 in the other. Still no solution to the Sex Pistols and Andy Hull dilemma. I pondered the possibility of getting rid of some records and wondered where to draw the line. That Starsailor single, for instance: it was pretty good in its own way, even if I never played it. I was reading the back of the sleeve to see if it featured any names I recognised when the phone rang. I picked it up.

'Hello?' I said.

There was obviously someone there.

'Hello?' I tried again, a bit louder this time.

Still silence.

I turned the stereo down and walked over to the window, making up my mind to wait. Several minutes of silence followed. I pressed the phone closer to my ear to see if I could hear any sounds in the background that might give me an idea of where the person was, but there was nothing. After a while I went on leafing through my records and almost managed to forget there was someone at the other end of the line.

I pulled out my records and laid them in piles. It started to feel almost natural to have that sort of mute company in my ear. Whoever it was, we had now spent a while in each other's company, and if it was Magnus I wasn't going to do him the favour of making any more stupid pleas. There was a good chance he'd burst into laughter and make me feel ridiculous. I wasn't going to give him that pleasure. If he wanted to play at not speaking, he was welcome to. I was just going to carry on as usual.

'Silence is easy,' I heard myself say in English.

I looked down at the Starsailor single and saw that that was the title of the song. There was complete silence at the other end of the line, but I reasoned that I might as well say that as nothing at all. So I put 'Weird Fishes' by Radiohead into the CD player and turned the volume up. I held the phone up to the speaker. When the song came to an end I clicked to end the call.

13

The next day I called my friend Dansson. It was a perfectly ordinary phone call, where both people talk, sometimes interrupt each other, agree on something, neither person just disappears, you say goodbye and hang up. You don't make the call and then not speak. No mysterious silence, no weird musical excursions. A perfectly normal phone call.

We agreed to meet up in Record King after work.

Because I was the only guy on the bakery counter and people prefer to be served by pretty girls, I always got the sense that people felt they had drawn the short straw when they ended up with me. Especially older men. Sometimes women got it into their heads that they were going to have to teach me a thing or two, or at least check if I knew the names of the different loaves and what spices they contained. Every so often people would tilt their heads and patronise me. But occasionally someone would ask to speak to me because they assumed I was the girls' boss. I'm not sure which was more embarrassing.

That day people kept buying bread and pastries, and I took orders for five identical student-graduation cakes.

'You see,' a man in late middle age said to me after telling me to fetch a pen and paper 'I was thinking of something a bit special, if you follow?'

I assured him that I understood.

'I thought it would be nice if the cake looked like a graduation cap, if you get what I mean?'

I nodded and he gave me a knowing smile.

'A traditional princess cake, but with white icing instead of green, and with a black ribbon round it. And I thought it might be possible to give it a little peak on one side. Do you understand what I mean?'

I nodded once more. Evidently that wasn't enough.

'The cake *is* a student graduation cap. Do you see?'

14

Record King was located in a basement at the bottom of a short flight of steps. The building had a lot of potential. The little sunlight that penetrated the dusty windows up by the ceiling served mostly to bleach the pale yellow vinyl records lined up as a vague sort of display, but really they just declared: we've given up.

Dansson and I were regulars there, but these days I couldn't help feeling a bit uncomfortable as I browsed through what was probably the weakest aspect of the whole enterprise: the stock. The same old records in the same places they had been the year before and the year before that, and where they had perhaps always been, in dusty rows in the home-made racks the Record King himself had constructed some time in the early 1980s.

Dansson was already standing over by the vinyl when I arrived. He looked up and nodded to me when the doorbell rang. I went down the steps and walked over to him to stand the way we usually stood, lost in covers and track lists.

Dansson was actually called Dan Hansson, but everyone had called him Dansson since high school or national service or whenever it was that someone was hungover enough to come up with the ingenious idea of combining his first and last names and ending up with Dansson.

I didn't know how many people called him Dansson, but that's what he said the first time we met: 'Call me Dansson – everyone does.' It was just after we'd tossed a coin for a Human League single. He won and probably still felt a bit guilty about it.

We used to stand opposite each other in Record King, flicking through the racks back in the days when new stock would arrive each week. Back when there was always a queue of expectant teenagers wanting to listen to twelve-inch singles and albums on the record player on the counter. Back when there was still a three-minute limit to trials and Dansson and I would listen together. Now you could listen as long as you wanted. The way I saw it, they were just happy to have anyone who wanted to listen to anything at all. I'd never met up with Dansson much outside Record King, except a few times at concerts or in clubs. Who knows, maybe I was the only person who ever called him Dansson? I'd never met any of his friends. I might even be Dansson's only friend.

He had a particular ability to tell a story, and then tell it again with a few minor adjustments, which gave the impression that he was constantly tweaking the truth. Sometimes he said the same thing a third time, usually recounting what had happened to people he knew, things they had done or tried, pop and rock stars and celebrities and inventors they had met. I often got the feeling that if they weren't actually imaginary friends, they were certainly exaggerated versions of real people. Possibly people he'd read or heard about. Unless he just made everything up on the spur of the moment? It didn't really make any difference. I'd stopped paying much attention by then. I just used to mumble and nod as we wandered around looking at records.

I pulled out a Simple Minds double album that I must have looked at and decided not to buy at least a dozen times before. I turned it over, then put it back again.

'All right?' Dansson asked after a while.

'Yeah,' I said.

I saw that Rufus Wainwright's *Want One* was among the new arrivals, even though it had been out several years. I thought about buying it for the final track, 'Dinner at Eight', but decided it was too expensive.

The doorbell rang and the Record King himself came down the steps with a microwave meal and a small carton of juice in a transparent plastic bag. He said hello and disappeared into the little room behind the counter. We could steal anything we wanted in here, I thought. But which of all these records would either of us actually want to steal?

'He's DJing in The Bar the day after tomorrow,' Dansson said, nodding towards the back room.

'Oh,' I said.

'Are you going?'

'Not sure,' I said.

Dansson was examining a Prince picture disc. He ran his finger gently across the vinyl to feel if it was scratched.

'Do you remember Magnus Gabrielsson?' I said after a while.

'Roxette?' Dansson said.

'Yes, that's him.'

A memory flashed through my head. On one occasion in Dansson's company I happened to demonstrate a surprisingly comprehensive knowledge of Roxette, which had left him staring at me open-mouthed. He demanded an explanation. I had to confess to having spent a number of hours in the company of Roxette. But I explained that it had been a very long time ago, and it was all Magnus Gabrielsson's fault. Which meant I had to tell him all about Magnus Gabrielsson.

15

When I was at high school I always used to wait outside the classroom for two or three tracks so I could go to my locker in peace and quiet, after most of the others had gone. Then I would pack my things together and walk down towards the shopping centre, still with music in my ears.

There, for a brief period each afternoon, the kids from both schools merged to form a sea of children which quickly overflowed past the bus station and newsagent and spread across the neighbourhood. As if someone had poured a bucket of kids onto the streets, which ran in and out of the shops and across the squares, kicking bins and lamp posts and anything else that wasn't tied down, until a last trickle dispersed on the outskirts of the community. It was nice to be a bit behind everyone else. Even if it was impossible not to bump into someone from Berg School. They seemed to belong to a different species. Bigger, rougher, noisier.

Among them was one guy who didn't seem to belong. Who always kept out of the way. I always expected them to shove and hit him, but that never happened. Quite the opposite, in fact. They all avoided him. It was as if he smelled. Of loneliness and isolation. No one wanted to get too close to that. Often he was just standing at the street corner by the post office. It was hard to see why. It was like he'd been dumped there. Left behind, abandoned. Like he was waiting for his mum to come and pick him up. Rescue him from this strange world. As if his whole life was just a mistake. A parenthesis.

But no one ever came.

I don't remember the first time I noticed him. He was just there. As if he'd always been there. Like part of the furniture. You got used to him. He was often left standing by the post office, waiting, looking at his digital watch.

When he eventually started to move I noticed he was walking the same way as me. Walking without any expression at all on his face. Nothing about him stood out. He probably thought he was invisible, but in actual fact it was impossible not to notice his thin figure sliding along the facades of the buildings, backing away to make sure he didn't get too close to anyone. Sometimes he and I were the only people around, but he still stayed at a safe distance of at least ten metres from me. When we emerged from the shopping centre and I set off along the path, he often walked a little way into the forest and tried to keep out of the way by deploying a number of tactics that were impossible not to notice. As if he wanted to emphasise the fact that he didn't belong. At first I just felt sorry for him and assumed he wasn't all there. But as time passed it started to feel more like self-imposed exclusion. Something he was almost proud of, and clung to with irritating meticulousness. He never looked up, never spoke to anyone. Just kept looking at his watch almost obsessively, as if he was hoping we were about to enter a different time. That this would all be over, in the past. Long ago. He never showed any emotion and kept his distance with impressive persistence. As if the rest of us could never catch him. Even if we'd wanted to.

For several weeks we carried on like that, skirting around each other. After a while I began to wonder if he had started waiting for me. It felt almost as if he was trying to attract my attention with his weird way of keeping to himself. I wondered if he was hanging about by the post office simply so he could set off at the same time as me. Hiding and making a big deal of it. As soon as we reached the path he would always walk parallel to me in among the trees. Even if he never looked in my direction, it was as if he was constantly keeping an eye on me with that expression of self-proclaimed inferiority and idiocy. Big eyes, mouth open. Rucksack slung over both shoulders. Nobody normal ever used more than one strap.

One day I stopped and looked straight at him with Alphaville's 'Forever Young' in my ears. He stopped too. Red-cheeked. Runny nose. He wiped his nose on his coat sleeve. Everyone else had already gone off ahead of us. He and I were the only ones left on the path leading to the blocks of flats. I don't know what he was thinking. Perhaps this was the moment he'd been waiting for. Perhaps he wanted me to make contact? Either way, he didn't do anything at all. Just stood there staring stupidly at me. In the end I stuck my middle finger up at him. I don't know why I did that. I'd probably just had enough. Unless I wanted to show him which of us was in charge. He stuck his finger up back at me and I don't know why that annoyed me so much. Maybe I was just surprised that he had the nerve to do it. Perhaps I thought it was childish, unimaginative, unless I was just confident that I could deal with him – that he was playing with fire. What on earth was he thinking? Without realising what I was doing, I jumped across the ditch, ran over to him and shoved him hard in the chest, knocking him to the ground.

It was so easy. No sooner had my hands struck his thin frame than he tumbled back, his woolly hat falling off. He didn't make any attempt to defend himself. Just tumbled into the undergrowth with a look of surprise. I regretted what I'd done at once and crouched down to see if he was OK.

'What the hell …' he muttered.

'Just take it easy,' I said, pulling my headphones off. 'Are you hurt?'

'Oh, not too badly,' he said as he sat up and rolled his head about as if to check he hadn't injured his neck. As if he was used to it. If felt like he knew exactly what to do after that sort of attack.

'What did you do that for?' he said.

I shook my head and mumbled an apology.

I helped him to his feet and brushed the leaves off him, the way I'd seen adults do with other kids. I picked up his rucksack and carried it for him as we set off along the path again, side by side.

'Do you like synth music or hard rock?' I asked after a while.

'I don't know,' he said.

'That means you like synth music,' I said.

He nodded, and after that we didn't say much. He kept quiet, and I had my headphones on. In the end I started to talk about the music I was listening to. I explained the running order. Why they'd been arranged like that. The thinking behind it. He nodded and seemed to want to hear more. I told him about the different groups, how they fitted together, what the differences were between them, and who did what. I described the splits in different bands, who had been in them and how they had changed over time.

We ended up walking together most days. I would pick him up outside the post office, then we would walk out of the shopping centre together. When we got to the path we usually branched off and went in among the trees instead.

I explained that the difference between synth music and hard rock was mostly about attitude, a feeling that could be hard to describe to the uninitiated. I explained, for instance, that someone who liked synth music could pretty much listen to any sort of music, as long as it wasn't metal. It just had to have a synthy feel to it.

'You have to steer clear of monsters and crucified women, and chainsaws ... stuff like that. Definitely no chainsaws. Not too much guitar distortion. But ordinary guitars are no problem. A lot of people are needlessly frightened of guitars.'

'They are?' Magnus said.

I nodded.

'There are quite a lot of guitars even in synth music,' I explained.

'Are there?'

'Sure, just think of groups like Spandau Ballet or Duran Duran. They use a lot of guitars.'

I gave him a few moments to absorb this information. Perhaps he'd never thought of them as synth groups until now. Perhaps he didn't even know who they were. He was clearly a novice and needed to be educated.

'Just from the way they look, some groups can be hard to distinguish from hard rock groups,' I went on. 'Dead or Alive, for instance. I know a lot of people who wonder about them.'

I didn't know any, but I'd been a bit unsure myself at first.

'You have to look at the details,' I continued. 'Then when you listen to them it's obvious, of course.'

I played one track after the other to illustrate the differences.

Sometimes he had to hear a song several times before he understood properly. He nodded and smiled when he realised what I meant. I used the Cure to explain the direct connection between synth music and miserablist rock, which was nothing to do with hard rock. Magnus soaked up the information like a sponge. After a while he began to ask intelligent follow-up questions, and I could see he was keeping up. He seemed genuinely interested. The lost kid outside the post office had turned into a true connoisseur, thanks to my musical instruction. He was learning to tell the difference between fakes and originals, one-hit wonders from artists with real staying power.

The good thing about Magnus was that he was such a quick learner. You never had to browbeat him or explain things too many times. I thought he was an excellent pupil.

Magnus went to Berg School. But probably not all that regularly. I didn't know anything about the state of his education, but he always showed up, whether or not we'd arranged to meet. I got the feeling that he was neglecting his schoolwork in order to hang out with me. Who knows – maybe he'd stopped going to school altogether?

Besides listening to music we used to run around the patch of land behind the industrial estate where the spring meltwater made its way down to the marsh. We wandered about in the big, tranquil forest with its tall firs and deep moss in almost perpetual motion. We slid down rocks and clambered up slopes covered with slippery grass, low branches scratching our faces.

The marsh was treacherous. Everyone knew that. According to local legend, there was quicksand beneath it that would suck everything down into it. Some of the businesses on the estate, which seemed to change hands regularly, were obviously dumping their rubbish there. There were all sorts of things – empty oil drums, tins, old crates, rags, scraps of metal, lamps and cables, all squelching among the branches and mounds of grass which stuck up like islands from the brown sludge. In the middle of a clearing, on top of a pile of leaves, or what had once been leaves – half leaves, half soil – there was a big velour armchair which oozed water if you pressed it. With each passing day the garbage would sink a little deeper into the marsh, and after a while it swallowed everything. Its appetite seemed insatiable. By the edge of the marsh we found some sodden pages torn from porn magazines, which we hung to dry in the trees and tried to put back together. The water had stuck some of the pages together, making them impossible to prise apart no matter how hard we tried. But we spent most of our time down there just wandering around, kicking the rubbish sticking out of the water and trying not to get our feet wet, passing the time by talking about all manner of things.

We used to race each other, commenting on our performance like sports presenters. It was always more of a game than a real competition. Not like PE lessons at school. We got up to everything and nothing. Walked. Talked. Often we didn't have to say much. We seemed to understand each other intuitively. And there was always music. Anything could be interrupted at any moment for a discussion of which albums Trevor Horn might end up producing next year. We could go from jumping from rock to rock to a conversation about Kraftwerk's early albums with Ralf and Florian. Before Kraftwerk were Kraftwerk. Unless they were actually already Kraftwerk even then?

It soon became apparent that the whole music thing was more than a casual interest to Magnus. He wanted to learn everything, he said. About what was happening now, and what had gone on in the past. Every so often he would ask me to run through the various line-ups of different groups and tell him what I thought might happen in the future. Was Alan Wilder likely to stay in Depeche Mode, or would he leave after the next album? And maybe Martin Gore never really felt like a fully fledged member of the group, seeing as he replaced Vince Clark, who'd been there from the start? What buildings was Jean-Michel Jarre going to perform on next? What was going to happen to the Fun Boy Three now that Terry Hall had started working with the Bananarama girls? Which producers were lined up to work on which groups' next albums? And were they good choices? Was the background you could see on the cover of *Gosh It's ... Bad Manners* actually a live recording studio? And if so, was that where they recorded 'Don't Be Angry'? Did I think we could expect the follow-up to be a live album?

I tried to answer as comprehensively as I could and couldn't help thinking that some of my guesses were pretty well informed.

After a while I started to make special mix tapes which I would mark with different colours. Then I would run through them with Magnus down by the marsh.

We hardly ever spoke about school. But from time to time we would compare our experiences. And I soon figured out that everything was much, much worse at Berg School. In comparison, life at Vira Elementary seemed almost comfortable.

For me it was mostly a question of annoying pranks. For instance, I was given the nickname Ant because I once suggested that ants were one of the strongest animals in the world, which was based on a misunderstanding but caused much hilarity among teacher and pupils, and was later used as a recurrent example of the dangers of mixing up *relative* values with *actual* ones.

But everything was always worse for Magnus.

The same day I got whipped with wet towels in the shower at my school, Magnus got beaten up at Berg. And by that I mean properly beaten up.

In my case it was mostly just high jinks that got out of hand. Dennis or Sören or someone had seen somewhere that if you twisted a wet towel you could make a decent whip, so they tried it out on the Ant while they discussed the best way to get most force behind their blows.

Obviously they weren't out to get me. But seeing as I was the last person in the shower, I was the only person they could practise on. And they clearly didn't have any idea how much it hurt. I jumped out of the way for as long as I could until they got me so many times that I slipped and fell over. I hit my knee on the tiled floor so hard that I felt something inside crack.

I had to go and see the school nurse, and was sent to the health centre to get my knee checked out. The upshot was that I got told off by the PE teacher for running on the slippery tiled floor in the shower.

'We've talked about this enough times,' he said as the rest of the class nodded. 'Running in the shower can be lethal. You were lucky it was only your knee this time. Next time it could be this.' He slapped me across the head to indicate what he meant.

When I limped over to meet Magnus that afternoon he was in much worse shape. They'd beaten him with sticks in the car park behind the school cafeteria. He was a mass of bruises. One of them had brought his stick down right on Magnus's head. He lowered his head and pointed to a large bump with a nasty cut across his scalp. I stared at his battered body.

'You don't think you should go to hospital?' I said.

'No,' he said. 'It'll heal.'

'Why did they do it?' I asked.

'They're frightened.'

'Of what?'

'Me.'

'Why are they frightened of you?'

'I don't know. There's just something about me.'

'What?'

He shook his head.

'I don't know. Something. What about you?'

'What about me?' I said.

'Yeah?'

'Nothing.'

'So why do they hit you?'

'They don't hit me.'

'No?'

'Not the way they hit you.'

In the end we got bored of the marsh and spent more and more time in my room, sitting on the bed listening to music. Record after record. Looking at album covers and discussing the running order. Analysing titles. Singing along at the same time, as out of synch as Adam Green and Kimya Dawson in 'Steak for Chicken'.

It was around then that he showed up with that Roxette album, *Look Sharp*. He thought it had 'rhythm'. He thought Per and Marie sang well together. That they were kind of 'adventurous'. I asked if he had learned nothing from me, but he persisted, saying it had its good points and pointing out that I had said it was OK to listen to some chart music. I didn't have the heart to deny him those stupid songs. So we listened to them as well. After a while I got used to it, and even started to appreciate some production aspects, at least on the first album, *Pearls of Passion*.

But I made no mention of this to Dansson.

16

'What about him?' Dansson said as he piled records up beside him.

The Record King was still in the little room behind the counter.

'Oh, I don't know,' I said. 'He's disappeared.'

Dansson looked up at me.

'Roxette? Disappeared?'

'Yes.'

'Disappeared, how?'

'I can't get hold of him.'

'Really?' Dansson said as he started to look through the jazz section. 'Maybe he's killed himself?'

I pushed some records back and leaned against the display.

'Why do you say that?'

'People do it all the time. It's more common than you'd think.'

I ran my finger over the records and glanced at Dansson, who was still looking through the jazz.

'So why would he take me to the circus, then?'

'The circus?'

'Yeah ...'

He looked at me.

'You went to the circus together?' he said, frowning.

'Well, he asked me to go. Then he got involved in one of the acts.'

'What sort of act?'

'The magic act, obviously.'

'He took part in a magic trick?'

'Yes.'

'Did he get sawn in half?'

'No.'

'What sort of trick was it, then?'

'Just a normal magic trick.'

'With knives?'

'No, mirrors.'

Dansson nodded seriously. He repeated what I'd said.

'Mirrors?'

'Yes. Then he didn't come back. And now I can't get hold of him.'

Dansson nodded silently to himself. Then he came round to my side of the racks.

'Did he volunteer?' he said.

'How do you mean?'

He looked at me sternly.

'Did he volunteer to take part in the magic act?'

I nodded.

'You know what that means, don't you?' he said.

'No,' I said.

'He wanted to make a statement.'

388

The Record King came out behind the counter and put a record by the National up above the till. I did my best to look like I was interested in the stock and tried to spot something I might want to buy, but I couldn't find anything.

As we stepped out onto the street Dansson turned to me and said, 'I knew someone who disappeared.'

'Oh?' I said.

'And I mean properly disappeared,' Dansson went on, fastening his camouflage-green army-surplus jacket. 'He became invisible.'

'What do you mean by invisible?'

'He stopped being visible.'

I could feel a laugh bubbling up inside me.

Dansson gave me an affronted look.

'What, don't you believe me?'

'Well … like the invisible man or something?'

'I swear. He could disappear. Just like that. When we were at a concert, for instance. One moment you could see him. Next moment he was gone.'

'OK …?'

'I've got proof, if you still don't believe me.'

'What proof?' I said.

'Photographic proof.'

Dansson dug about in the inside pocket of his army jacket – he seemed to have a lot of things tucked away in there – and eventually pulled out a battered photograph of several people.

'Take a look at this,' he said, pointing at the picture. 'This was at Hultsfred. When I was there with Nasim, Jovan, Lena and Tom. Here we all are in front of the Main Stage.'

'So?' I said.

'You can see for yourself. Tom isn't there.'

I looked at the picture, and sure enough Tom wasn't there.

I suddenly remembered the note Jallo had given me, and felt for it in my pocket. Yep, there it was, the receipt with Bondegatan 3A on the back. Perhaps it was worth a try?

17

There was no Bondegatan 3A. There was a Bondegatan 3, an unassuming doorway with a coded lock, but I could see no sign of a 3A.

Next door was a dry cleaner which might well have the same address. I went in.

The shop's owner was a man in his fifties, with his hair pulled into a little ponytail with a beige hairband. I caught sight of him towards the back in another room. He waved at me to indicate that he'd seen me but waited a while before coming out. There was a bench next to the counter with a pile of papers and a portable CD player on it. Next to that was a unsteady stack of CDs that looked like they'd topple over if you so much as touched the bench. I put my head to one side and counted seven Absolute Music albums.

In spite of the limited material he had to work with, the shop's owner still managed to give the impression that he had lots of hair, and when he turned towards me I saw how pale he was. It looked almost like he never left his shop. Perhaps he didn't?

He was wearing one of those pale blue shirts that never look creased no matter how much they've been worn. The sort of shirt that looks like it came from a discount store, or has been worn and washed so much it has ended up looking like a cheap shirt. Or one that might have been part of some sort of council uniform. White, or very pale blue. The sort of shirt you know is sweaty under the arms even if you can't tell by looking at it. Even if they're covered by a thick jacket, you just know they're wet with sweat.

That sort of shirt only exists for people with sweaty armpits.

The shirt in the back room, with its armpits and associated body, and the head with the long thin hair slowly began to move, until eventually the whole package was standing in front of me, breathing heavily.

'Yes,' he said.

'Is this Bondegatan 3A?' I asked.

The man in the shirt nodded.

'I'm looking for someone called Magnus,' I said.

'Magnus?' the shirt said.

'I was told he was here.'

He looked at me and scratched his chin.

'Do you want something cleaned?'

'No.'

'Oh. There's no Magnus here.'

'Magnus Gabrielsson?'

'No.'

A short, thickset woman was pulling thin plastic bags over freshly laundered white shirts which had a papery look to them. She was wearing an outfit somewhere between a dress and a cleaner's tunic. I could see her bra through the fabric as she hung the garments up and attached labels to them. She hadn't deigned to look in my direction at all.

These people looked utterly unruffled, but that didn't necessarily mean that they didn't know what I was talking about. Perhaps you had to give some sort of code word, but Jallo hadn't mentioned anything about that. I sighed at his habit of always giving incomplete information and just assuming that things would work themselves out. It was so typical of him, that whole *mañana* attitude. There was no such thing as a problem. Only opportunities. How many times had he tried to recruit me to the telesales business that formed the core of his activities? It covered everything from selling socks and mobile contracts to acting as a kind of emergency psychological helpline.

'You can choose,' he kept saying. 'Whatever you fancy doing.'

With the premium-rate numbers the main point was to keep people talking for as long as possible. According to Jallo that didn't require any special qualifications or experience. All you had to do was keep talking, but that wasn't exactly my strong point.

'Doesn't matter,' Jallo said. 'If you like you can do the tarot cards. You'd be good at that.'

'I don't know anything about tarot.'

'You'll soon pick it up. You just have to sit there with the cards and say stuff. The more cryptic the better. That could be your thing ... quiet and mysterious.'

'But it wouldn't be real.'

'What the hell is real? Trust me, you'd soon pick it up. They just want someone to talk to.'

I looked around the dry cleaner. There was a picture on one wall, the same sort of messy, incomprehensible thing that Jallo had in his office. I found that sort of picture unsettling. I didn't want to spend too long looking at them. They always felt a bit like an optical trap. Colourful patterns which could turn into anything at all when you least expected it. Perhaps the whole dry-cleaning business was just a front? A cover for an entirely different sort of business.

I leaned forward in what I thought was a pointed, conspiratorial way. Like I was trying to let on that I knew what was going on. That I knew about everything, but that they didn't have to worry about me saying anything. I raised one eyebrow.

'Look,' I said slowly. 'Jallo said it would be OK.'

'Jallo?'

I winked and nodded. The man in the shirt stared wearily at me.

'That's nice,' he said, equally slowly. 'But if you don't want to have anything dry-cleaned, I'm afraid I can't help you.'

He turned round and started to sort through some plastic-wrapped suits.

'Isn't this Bondegatan 3A?' I asked.

'It's number 3. There's no A here.'

18

That evening I took a walk past Magnus's flat, but it still looked empty. Abandoned. I stood outside the 7-Eleven for a while looking up at the dark windows. I realised that the window where I'd seen a light go on a few days before might not belong to Magnus. After a while I went into the shop and bought some chewing gum. I sat down in the same place as before and noticed the cashier watching me surreptitiously. Veronica Maggio was playing from the speakers, that song with the line 'this situation is so sick'. I thought about the girls on the bakery counter, who had asked if I wanted to go to a party this evening. They always asked me when they were going to do something because they knew I had the good sense to decline any offer of socialising with girls who were ten or fifteen years younger than me.

In the street was the same advert that was outside my building. The guy in white underpants. Presumably an ad for an underwear company, though it could have been for aftershave or deodorant. Unfortunately for the advertiser, there was a tear in the poster just where the company's name was, so it was impossible to know what brand they wanted you to buy.

I looked up at Magnus's flat again and wondered if he was the sort of person who might commit suicide. Why would he do that? And it would seem odd if he'd done it now. Unnecessary, somehow. At school maybe, but now?

I remembered the badge Magnus used to wear on his breast pocket, LIVE HARD AND DIE YOUNG. That was so wrong. Having a badge like that was ridiculous. Because everyone knew that if there was one thing Magnus didn't do, it was live hard. He didn't drink, didn't smoke, and had hardly ever ridden so much as a moped. He ran around the marsh with me, or sat on my bed listening to records. LIVE HARD AND DIE YOUNG. But it was only a badge. I tried to persuade him to take it off, but he kept wearing it.

A couple came into the shop and bought a bottle of Coke, which they shared between kisses. I sat for a while, feeling tired, and thought of the way Magnus could stand and stare at couples like that without the least embarrassment. He thought it was cute. Sure, when you're a teenager, but you soon learn better. You realise what a nuisance it is once the first flush of infatuation is over, when everything goes back to normal. At best, it might be exciting to begin with, but then the nagging starts, and you have to change your habits, and before you know it the jealousy and arguments start. And even if you think she's attractive and fun, it always ends up leading to loads of problems, no matter how you try to deal with it. Arguments about what to eat and who to see and why you don't want to merge your record collections. If she's got one. And if she hasn't there's always a load of talk about why you have a collection and why can't you just download whatever you feel like listening to? Before you know it you're standing there with tablecloths and curtains and wondering if it's really what you want. You start to row, get upset, and whatever happiness you once felt turns into pain that's many times worse.

Magnus kept falling in love with girls in a very unhealthy way. He would associate them with a particular type of music, confusing the lyrics of love songs with real life. He saw the lyrics as a way of expressing his love, but hardly ever dared to approach anyone. Then he would see them with other guys and be mortified. Many was the time I had to sit with Magnus trying to comfort him and running through my own thoughts on the subject, usually getting caught up in the horrifying example of my own parents. A long-term relationship that was always on the brink of disharmony, like a drawn-out Allan Pettersson symphony. I kept telling him he needed to learn how things worked. How you make yourself tougher. Untouchable. Otherwise you risked being destroyed. I don't think he ever really learned that.

It soon occurred to me that I ought to go back to the circus and talk to someone there. Maybe they knew where he'd gone. I remembered the old rule from school outings in the forest: that if you got lost or didn't know where everyone else was, you should make your way back to where you last saw them and wait there, hugging a tree or something.

Then I realised I wasn't sure where the circus was. I'd gone there with Magnus, and we spent the whole way talking so I wasn't paying attention. But presumably it was out on the field a few stations away, where circuses usually pitched their tents.

Live hard and die young. Well, that depends on how you look at things. I slid off my chair and went out into the cool spring air, put my headphones on and switched on my portable CD player, then set off towards the station. When I went inside I saw that they were working on the escalators down to the platform. A man in a hi-vis jacket gestured to me to take my headphones off.

'What line?' he asked.

I looked down at the CD player.

'Two,' I said.

'OK, that way,' he said, pointing to a temporary flight of steps.

I walked down it, got on a train and went the three stations to the circus. I emerged from the end of the station closest to the field, barely even noticing that I had the road to myself. I didn't look up until I reached the grass, when I saw that it was gone. The field was completely empty, the grass standing tall, swaying in the breeze. There was no trace of any tents or caravans.

It was as if the circus had never been there.

19

That night the phone rang again.

'Magnus?' I said, but there was no response. Just the nervous breathing again. Was it someone from the circus?

'Magnus, is that you?' I asked again.

No response.

I went and sat down in front of the television without switching it on. I sat there for a long time looking at my own shadow on the screen, feeling the presence of the silent person on the telephone line. After several minutes, during which neither of us said anything, I went over to the stereo and put on 'Lilac Wine' by Jeff Buckley and held the receiver up to the speaker.

When the track ended I hung up and walked into the bedroom, lay down on top of the bed and leafed through the latest issue of *Uncut*. Nothing in it really caught my attention. I was having trouble concentrating. How could the circus be gone all of a sudden? Was it possible to move a entire cavalcade of people and vehicles in such a way that they didn't leave any trace of having been there? Surely the grass at least ought to have been flattened? Shouldn't there be a few scraps of circus detritus about the place, a bit of tinsel or a plastic cup and a few napkins from the kiosk? Why didn't the person who kept calling me say anything, and what had Magnus meant when he waved like that in the mirror?

I must have dozed off, because the next time I opened my eyes it was dark inside the flat. I sat up, stared at the pitch-black room and wasn't altogether sure if I was asleep or awake. But I thought it was odd for the phone to be ringing in a dream. It rang and rang and rang – an old-fashioned ringtone. I answered. It was Magnus.

'Hello?' I said.

'Hello, this is Magnus Gabrielsson. But a long time ago.'

'Oh?' I said.

'I was wondering if you've got Kurt Cobain's number. From when he was a child?'

20

The next day was a day in which nothing happened. Nothing out of the ordinary, anyway. Only the sort of thing you might expect to happen on a Wednesday.

I woke up, went to work, worked, had lunch.

It was the sort of day when I saw stir-fried noodles and thought they looked tempting, and then saw stir-fried noodles and thought they looked disgusting, and in between those reactions nothing much happened apart from me eating rather a lot of stir-fried noodles.

I tried putting Sheena Easton between Prince and Wendy and Lisa because it ought to work – theoretically, anyway – but it didn't feel right at all.

In the end I decided to do what Jallo had suggested and try writing a letter. I got a pen and some paper and sat down to write.

'Dear Magnus!' I began, then wondered if that sounded too pompous, before concluding that it didn't matter. I couldn't let myself get bogged down in that sort of detail. The important thing was to get in touch with him. Not the tone of the letter itself. Besides, I thought it sounded rather nice. 'Dear Magnus!' Kind of ceremonial. It felt good to write it. I concluded with 'Best wishes'.

When I was finished I dug out an envelope, wrote his address, stuck a stamp on it and went and posted it.

I spent the rest of the afternoon with Dictaphone and their album *Poems from a Rooftop*.

It was the sort of day that passed like any other, and I reasoned that Magnus Gabrielsson couldn't possibly have committed suicide. I got confirmation of that the following day.

21

I spent all of Thursday behind the bakery counter humming 'Dinner at Eight' by Rufus Wainwright as I served the old women who wanted pastries and cakes in the shape of graduation caps. I was glad it wasn't 'Love and Marriage' and wondered if perhaps 'Dinner at Eight' might have the opposite effect.

When I got to Record King after work I spent a while searching for the Rufus Wainwright album I'd seen the other day but couldn't find it anywhere. Could it really have been sold? Had Record King had a customer?

I walked home and sang out loud to myself in a Rufus Wainwright style as I changed into a shirt that I soon discovered smelled of sweat, so I had to change back again.

I tried moving the whole Motown section down three shelves but quickly realised that that messed up the other end, where part of old-style hip hop ended up next to Americana, so I had to move the whole lot back again.

Then I wolfed down some sweet corn straight from the tin I'd opened the night before last. It tasted a bit metallic but not too bad. I shook my head and chuckled at the thought of She & Him next to Young MC. I didn't really feel like going out but felt I ought to for Dansson's sake.

A bit further along the same street as Record King lay what, back in the glory days of vinyl, used to be the Record King Bar but was now an Irish theme pub. It wasn't called the Record King Bar any more, but it still had pretty much the same clientele and fairly decent music, and it was where the Record King was apparently going to DJ.

I ordered a beer and sat down at the bar beside an empty stool to indicate that I was waiting for someone. I hoped Dansson would show up soon.

I was left sitting there on my own for a long time, listening to the music. I thought about asking the Record King to play 'Dinner at Eight' if he had it, but decided against it. I'd never asked a DJ to play anything, and I wasn't about to start now. I got another beer and thought about an article about vinyl collectors I'd read in a newsagent. I'd just started to get annoyed at the memory of the phrase 'airy quality to the sound' when someone interrupted my musings.

In the middle of Jeff Beck's 'You Had it Coming', Janne Markstedt was suddenly standing in front of me waving his hands. I lit up the way you do when you meet someone you haven't seen for several years and are expected to want to know all about them.

'Janne?!' I said.

'That's me.' He grinned. 'It's been a while!'

There was something so familiar about him, something that had always been there and probably always would be. The way he moved his head and spoke, his whole body language.

The hard-rock attitude. But I could see how old he'd got. A proper grown-up with grey hair and a receding hairline. When did that happen? I'd always assumed we were the same age. It felt like it, especially as we'd been in the same class and everything.

I didn't know what to say, so I asked loudly, 'You doing OK?'

'Good,' he said. I noticed that he was swaying slightly to the sound of the guitar from the speakers.

'Good to see you again,' he said after a while. 'Do you still see anyone else from school?'

'No, not really,' I said. 'You know how it is.'

I thought about how I did my best to avoid anything connected to the past and only saw Jallo and Magnus from those days. I thought about what Janne had meant to me at school. Essentially nothing, aside from being part of the crowd of hard-rock fans who always trailed after Dennis and his gang. The ones who kept quiet and watched.

Janne nodded as if he understood. Even if he couldn't possibly have heard what I'd said. Then he frowned and pulled a face.

'Shit, I heard about that guy, your friend Magnus!' he yelled.

'What about him?' I yelled back.

'That guy, Magnus. He was a friend of yours, wasn't he?'

'What d'you mean?'

'Awful business.'

'What?'

'Him committing suicide,' he said.

I choked on my beer and started to cough. Janne leaned forward to slap me on the back, but I held up my hand to stop him.

'What?' I yelled when I'd stopped coughing.

'Not that I really knew him or anything, but it's terrible, isn't it? Hadn't you heard?' Janne yelled back.

I stared at him.

'How?' I said. He leaned forward.

'At the circus.'

I grabbed hold of the table, took a swig of beer and shook my head.

Janne went on shouting in my ear.

'Cut himself on some glass.'

'Glass?'

'Yeah. From a mirror.'

'Where?'

'At the circus. Apparently he walked out into the middle of a magic trick and did it there and then. Can you imagine? The magician was distraught.'

'How do you know all this?'

'Well ... from what I heard, it was supposed to be some sort of political statement.'

22

I couldn't stay after that. I was too upset to sit in the pub, so after another few minutes of Janne shouting about former classmates right next to my ear I said I had to go to the toilet. I took my jacket and walked out. Dansson still hadn't turned up. Why didn't I have any normal friends?

I wandered along the pavement in the darkness, in and out of patches of light of varying brightness as they reflected off the puddles, and felt my skin tighten. Janne was clearly a bit of a gossip, and it wasn't hard to figure out who he'd got his information from, but Magnus Gabrielsson *was* missing. That was a fact. So where was he, if he hadn't killed himself?

I could feel I was a bit drunk and wondered if I was going to start crying. Poor Magnus, I thought. Where have you got to? My heart was pounding. I realised I was almost running. I slowed down and took a couple of deep breaths. Tried to think about my record collection, but not even that could improve my mood. Was this how it had started for Magnus as well? I wondered.

I didn't notice how odd Magnus was until Year 7 or 8. I knew he was a bit unusual, but up until then we had our own world where nothing ever needed to be compared to anything outside it. Where everything seemed normal, no matter how peculiar it was. But somewhere around the start of secondary school it finally dawned on me that Magnus was different. More different than even I was.

To start with, he was genuinely frightened of other people. Almost reclusive. I started to wonder if he ever went to school at all. His old rucksack usually hung slack, as if it was empty. I never saw any schoolbooks, and he was never in a rush to get home and do his homework. If I ever suggested we meet up with anyone else he would glance at his digital watch and say he had to be somewhere else. If we ever had anyone else with us he never said much and would always come up with some excuse and hurry away.

His personal hygiene wasn't great, and sometimes he smelled. The carefree, undemanding, fun existence we shared slowly changed into a sort of mutual boredom. He never wanted to try anything new, just carry on doing the same childish things we'd always done, even though we were getting older and older. In the end it felt embarrassing. We started to annoy each other. Started arguing about stupid things. What groups it was OK to like, that sort of thing. His firm views about what was synth music and what wasn't began to feel more and more stifling.

'But we listen to lots of different things,' he said in an accusing tone.

'We listen to things that are good,' I said.

'That means you can listen to all sorts of things,' he said.

'Not any old thing, only things that are good,' I said.

'So how do you know what's good, then?'

It usually ended with me getting my way, but even that never felt great. Magnus didn't seem to have any will of his own. It was like he was happy doing nothing and just letting me decide. In the end we would just sit at either end of the bed in my room listening to records, neither of us saying anything. There wasn't much to say. It was nice and non-threatening, but got kind of boring after a while. Even if Magnus didn't seem to think so.

'Can we listen to the whole of *Tubular Bells* again?' he said.

'I suppose so,' I said.

So we did.

It felt a bit like being married. Or what people say being married is like. That you always have to stay at home, sit at the kitchen table talking about the same old things you've already talked about a thousand times before. Never going out with friends, and if you did feeling guilty for spending time with other people. And I thought I was too young to be married. To someone like Magnus, anyway. It annoyed me that he always had to be so antisocial. So timid.

As time went by I started to wish he was a bit tougher. Or at least a bit more extroverted. It was hard to meet girls, for instance. If I had Magnus with me, anyway. He had very firm views on the women he wanted to meet and how this should happen, and who should say what and in what order. But if an opportunity ever arose he always walked away. And most of the time he wanted me to go with him.

He didn't have any choice, of course. He didn't know any better. He didn't have anyone else but me. Even so, I ended up seeing less and less of him. Sometimes I took my headphones off and talked to someone at school instead. Discussing homework, or telling them what was on the lunch menu that day. Stuff like that. There was another life outside the claustrophobic little world Magnus and I had constructed. Even if it wasn't always easy. In my case it tended to involve a lot of recurring practical jokes. Nothing too terrible. It was more like a form of shorthand. I was the one everyone made fun of. And with time I learned to deal with that a bit better. I started to play along, basically.

There were times when I felt accepted, if not exactly popular. Sometimes it was even quite fun. Not that I ever made jokes or anything like that, but I could get others to laugh. I came up with silly stuff like letting them pull my braces until they snapped back and hit me. Or running into a wall. I did that a lot, and it would get a laugh from someone. I would simply run as fast I could straight into a wall.

Once when we were standing by our lockers I punched my clenched fist into the door of my locker as hard as I could. People began to stare. Dennis and Sören cheered each time the door buckled, and I was so buoyed up by the response that I kept doing it until the blood from my knuckles began to smear across the door.

Magnus never understood any of that. He couldn't understand that you sometimes had to give away a little bit of yourself. He thought that was selling out. Whenever I told him about something like that he would give me a derisive glare. As if he had some sort of right to judge me. As if he had the right to look down on me just because I was adapting and making a bit of an effort. Unlike certain other people. Even though he never said anything, I could hear what he was thinking. I didn't share his attitude. Sometimes I ended up shouting at him because of it. And then I'd feel guilty. As if I'd done something wrong. As if I'd let someone down.

Either way, it did seem to work.

One morning I got a chance to talk to Dennis. We arrived at one of the school entrances at the same time; the doors were supposed to be open but for some reason they were still locked. Dennis banged on the glass. He asked what sort of music I listened to. I mentioned a few names. He probably didn't know any of them. We stood there together for a while. A couple of minutes at least. In the end he asked if he could listen to my headphones.

I quickly checked which tape was in the Walkman and decided that it would probably be OK. I passed him the headphones. Ideally it would have been one of the hardcore compilations, but it was the Blue Mix. Propaganda, Yazoo, Bronski Beat and Soft Cell. Well, it would just have to do. Dennis nodded. He took hold of the Walkman and put the headphones on his big head. He swayed a little in time to the music. Seemed happy.

'Decent sound,' he said, slightly too loudly. 'Can I borrow this?'

No, absolutely not. Under no circumstances. No one was allowed to borrow it. My Walkman was my refuge at school. My

411

own space. My sanctuary. I'd rather have lent someone my mother or Magnus or all my savings if I had any. But not my Walkman. My Walkman was an extension of me. That music and those songs formed the whole structure of my existence.

But this was Dennis asking, and obviously that changed everything.

Others were bound to be impressed that Dennis was borrowing things from me. He looked so happy as he stood there with the headphones on. Almost expectant. It was as if the music – *my* music – had got through to him. Had changed his attitude to synth music. To me. It was impossible to turn him down. Maybe this was the start of ... well, if not friendship, then at least a form of admittance into the gang.

Because of course I could see a parallel. This was exactly how my friendship with Magnus had started. Now things weren't so great with Magnus, maybe this was the natural next step? Maybe it was going to be me and Dennis from now on? The thought of him walking around with my Walkman and mentioning my name in relation to the tracks he was listening to made me ecstatic. And it would mean we had a reason to meet up again soon.

On the other side of the glass the caretaker was hurrying to unlock the doors with his big bunch of keys. This was my chance, and I had to decide quickly. The doors would soon be open and the encounter would be over.

'OK,' I said. 'But I need it back after school.'

'Sweet,' Dennis said and slipped in through the doors before we had arranged where and when I was going to get it back.

I spent the rest of the day on a peculiar high. I felt naked without music in my ears. All sounds seemed unnaturally loud and intrusive. It made it hard to think. I was having to feel my way through a whole new world, but I still felt oddly carefree. Because I had a secret understanding with Dennis now, even if we didn't actually talk at all – of course we didn't; everything was more or less the same as usual, you can't change things that quickly – but it still made me see him in a different light. In a lot of ways Dennis was a far more rounded person than Magnus. Sociable. Talented. A natural leader. Top grades in maths and science. All the subjects I was worst at. I was best at the humanities. He and I could be a really good combination.

I felt like I'd been given an invitation. To a tougher world, sure, but one that was also more complicated and interesting. Wild and unpredictable. Maybe I needed to make my way out into this noisy, messy, stormy world in order to take my place in … real life?

At the same time the music would start to work from the other direction. The tracks that Dennis was listening to now, they were a potential bridge between us. They would slowly bring us closer together. He couldn't help but be swept along by the percussion intro to 'Sorry for Laughing'. Or the grinding bass of 'p:Machinery', which just kept going until it eventually gave you goosebumps. If he listened to the recurring brass riff at the end of the track he'd never be able to forget it. Or when Dave Gahan sings 'It's just a question of time' on the *Black Celebration* album. I could offer to make him some mix tapes of his own, I thought. I could do that for him. I saw myself explaining the greatness of one track after the other. The unlikely combination of the two of us could be positive for him too. Maybe that was what he'd had in mind when he approached me that morning. Even if he might not have been aware of it himself. Maybe it was a subconscious desire on his part to expand his taste in music. After all, he'd taken the first step ... Was this the start of us becoming civilised adults who socialised properly and learned from each other? Who saw the differences between us as something positive, as opportunities to expand our horizons?

We could share the Walkman, I thought. Have it every other day. Obviously the days without it would be tough, but it would be fun to make mix tapes if I knew he was going to go around listening to them. And he could make tapes too. Was this the moment when synth and hard rock met? The first step to a musical dialogue? After all, I had already started listening to a bit of Rush and Van Halen, in spite of Magnus's protests, and to my ears they sounded like rock. So I'd begun to sound out the terrain, so to speak. I'd have to remember to mention that to Dennis. And of course I'd have to identify some synth tracks that could build a bridge to hard rock. I started to think out a suitable playlist for the first mix tape.

During break I saw him demonstrating the Walkman to some girls in the class and realised that it would be easier to gain access to them now as well.

It was a delicate situation, one that needed to be handled correctly. I had to do my bit to make it easy for him. Not push myself forward too soon. Not try to snatch victory too early. He had his reputation to think about, after all. Obviously he couldn't be seen with someone like me. He stood to lose everything from a change of that sort. In the short term, anyway. The transition needed to happen gradually, almost imperceptibly. That wasn't the sort of thing you can change overnight, so the best thing for the time being was to lie low for a while and let the friendship between us develop so slowly that no one would notice how the two of us came to be in each other's proximity. Swapping mix tapes and discussing different tracks.

I kept my distance all day. As did Dennis. Even if he made it look like he wasn't trying.

At the end of the day I went down to the lockers at the same time as everyone else for a change. I hung back slightly, looking for Dennis. When he showed up with the headphones around his neck and the Walkman on his belt I went towards him. I wasn't planning on hanging around. I just wanted to see if it was time for him to give the Walkman back. It could have happened almost unnoticed. Almost without words. Then obviously I'd have walked away. But before I got that far Sören Ranebo was standing in front of me.

'What do you want?' he said, pushing me back. Not hard, but enough for me to sway and lose my balance slightly.

'I'm just going to collect something,' I said.

'What sort of something?' he said.

'Something that … belongs to me,' I said.

'No you're not,' Sören said and pushed me again.

Not hard, but enough to let me know that my path was blocked.

I could see Dennis up ahead, and waited for him to turn towards us and say that it was all OK. That the rules had changed. As soon as he saw who it was he'd come and sort it all out. Give me back my Walkman, and the whole thing would be something of a triumph. (Eventually even Sören Ranebo would come to terms with the fact that synth and rock were on the point of a rapprochement.) But people kept going up to Dennis and talking to him. He was surrounded by admirers. I saw them fiddling with the Walkman and headphones.

'Get lost!' Sören said.

'But ...' I said.

'Something wrong with your hearing? Get lost, I said!' Sören said, pushing me again. Harder this time, making me stumble and fall on my backside. He probably didn't intend it, but I landed on my coccyx and jarred my spine.

I sat there as the others moved on, thinking to myself that it was probably best to hold off a bit longer and try to make contact with Dennis when there weren't so many people around him.

I followed them at a discreet distance. Saw them go in and out of shops. Maybe they did a bit of shoplifting in Åhlén's? The headphones kept getting passed around the gang, but Dennis kept hold of the Walkman, which I thought he seemed to be handling carefully.

In the end there were only three of them left, and when they were sitting on a bench in the shopping centre I ventured closer. I saw Dennis look in my direction, and before I realised how stupid it was I'd already raised my arm in a far too enthusiastic greeting. I lowered it at once and walked towards them.

Sören had gone, but one of the boys in the parallel class, I think his name was Johan – his dad had a Commodore 64 – stood up as I approached.

'What do you want?' he said.

'Er ... I thought I'd pick up my Walkman,' I said.

'What did you say?' Johan said, raising his eyebrows.

He turned his ear towards me as if he couldn't hear properly.

'I'd just like my Walkman back,' I mumbled.

'Who's got it?' he said with a grin.

I glanced at Dennis and the other boy, who were sitting on the bench looking at us. I thought that maybe this was Dennis's style, keeping you on tenterhooks. Sending one of his minions to test you, like a sort of initiation rite. You just had to make sure you passed it. Stayed cool in front of his friends. Even so, I was unable to keep as cool as I would have liked. I tried to smile, but it felt more like a nervous twitch.

'Where's your Walkman?' Johan asked again.

I looked at him, then at the other boy. In the end I pointed to the Walkman in Dennis's hand.

'No. That's Dennis's Walkman,' Johan said, shaking his head. 'You can't have that. That would be stealing, wouldn't it? You know the difference between "yours" and "mine", don't you?'

'Er,' I said. 'Look ... it's mine.'

'Dennis's Walkman is yours?' Johan asked with another grin.

I was still waiting for Dennis to give some sort of signal, but he just sat there looking idly in our direction. Every so often he said something to the guy next to him. As if he was commenting on what was going on between me and Johan.

'See for yourself,' I said. 'That's my tape in it.'

'Really?' Johan said. 'What tape is it, then?'

I didn't want to say out loud.

'It's got a label on it ...'

'What tape is it?' he asked again.

'"Blue Mix",' I said, almost in a whisper. 'That's what it says on the label.'

He brightened up.

'"Blue Mix"?'

I nodded. He grinned at me. Then he turned to the others.

'The tape in the Walkman, is it called "Blue Mix"?'

They opened it up to reveal an original Iron Maiden cassette.

'Sorry,' Johan said. 'No "Blue Mix".'

They closed the lid and Johan shrugged. What had they done with my tape? I wondered. Had they thrown it away?

'But it's mine,' I squeaked.

Johan's smile vanished and he looked at me as if he was bored now.

'Are you saying Dennis stole it?'

'No,' I said, shaking my head. 'I let him borrow it, but now I need it back.'

'You need it?! Dear oh dear, these are very serious allegations,' Johan said, turning to the two boys on the bench.

He called to Dennis.

'The Ant says you stole it from him.'

'Er, no ...' I muttered.

I cursed my own impatience. This was the very situation we were supposed to be avoiding, Dennis and I. We were supposed to do this slowly. Let it develop naturally. (Letting synth and hard rock slowly but surely get closer to each other.) That was what I'd been telling myself all day. If only I'd been a bit more patient, this could all have been avoided. Who knows, maybe Dennis had his own idea of how we should proceed? Maybe he'd been thinking of an even slower pace, which I'd now gone and ruined with my impatience. Now he was bound to realise what a mistake it had been to trust someone like me. I'd made a fool of myself, but it occurred to me that I didn't care about him, and I didn't care about any big change. I just wanted to curl up inside my music again, as usual.

'I just want my Walkman back,' I whined.

I could hear that I sounded like a little kid.

'But that isn't your Walkman.' Johan spelled out very slowly. 'You're making it up. It's just your imagination.'

He tapped my head with his finger.

'You need to learn to tell the difference between fantasy and reality,' he said.

The boy who had been sitting next to Dennis stood up and came over to us.

'Are you accusing Dennis of stealing?' he said.

He stopped right in front of me and stared at me hard. I didn't know what to say.

'Are you? Are you accusing Dennis of stealing?' he said again.

Without blinking he slapped my face hard, making my ear sting. I gasped. Everything was happening so quickly. Now he was talking again.

'Are you standing there accusing Dennis of stealing?' he said in a very calm voice.

My cheek hurt badly. I was having trouble thinking.

'I want—' I started to say, but before I could finish the sentence he'd hit me again. I had to crouch down, and felt tears spring to my eyes.

I could have run off, I could even have walked away calmly. No one would have stopped me. But the Walkman in Dennis's hand belonged to me. And that was more important than anything else just then. So I didn't move.

'Please, I only want—'

He hit me on the same cheek again. I screamed like a baby as he went on speaking in the same calm voice. As if his voice had nothing to do with his hand. As if one person was talking to me and another one hitting me.

'I just want to know,' the soft voice went on. 'Are you accusing Dennis of stealing? Is that what you're doing?'

Even though my cheek was burning, I couldn't just walk away and abandon my Walkman. I couldn't see clearly. I realised I was crying. I was about to say something but thought better of it.

In utter panic I tried to run forward and snatch the Walkman, but there was obviously no point. Johan and the other boy dragged me away without any difficulty at all. One held me while the other punched me in the stomach, then told me I had to apologise.

23

It had been a long time since I last thought about those events. They weren't the sort of thing I chose to dwell on from day to day. But on the way home from the Record King Bar I was unable to keep all the memories and images from coming back to me. Instead of going straight up to my flat I went out into the back courtyard and sat down on one of the benches in the play area. I just sat there. As if I was going to smoke a cigarette. It was still light even though it was the middle of the night. I could hear the distant rumble of the motorway mixed with the sounds of students celebrating their graduation at parties in various flats nearby. It was a lovely early summer's night, perfect for balcony drinking and skinny-dipping in murky water. I slid part way off the seat and rested my neck on the back of the bench. I half-lay like that, looking up at the light sky, where I could just start to make out a few stars.

For the first time I felt that I not only had a life ahead of me, but one behind me as well. A life I could never get back. Summer nights swimming with girls and graduation caps and dreams of the future. Youth unemployment, happiness at getting a first job, all the anxiety and expectation. It wasn't only my childhood that had passed, but the start of my adult life.

I tried to remember the names of as many constellations as I could. What were they called again? Ursa Major and Minor. The Plough. No, that was something else. Besides, it was the wrong time of year to be able to see those.

I was struck by the immense distances between the stars out in space. They only look like they belong together when you see them from a distance. They could hardly be aware that they form part of a constellation, I thought. If stars were conscious, that is. It takes one hell of a distance to be able to see the connection. From the perspective of the stars, Magnus Gabrielsson and I must look like one single indistinguishable little dot, for instance. And if you didn't know better, you could probably say I had a certain type of connection with the person who kept calling me.

24

Mum yelled at me for losing my Walkman. She said I caused them more than enough expense as it was. I couldn't bring myself to explain that I'd lent it to someone. Besides, she made it very clear that there was no question of me getting another one. We didn't have that sort of money, she said. Then she added that it might not be a bad idea for me to get used to not having headphones glued to my head the whole time.

'You need to get out into the real world a bit more,' she said.

'We can get it back if there's two of us,' I said to Magnus the next day.

We were sitting by the marsh with empty silence ringing in our ears. Throwing stones in the air and listening to them plop wearily into the water. Magnus was leaning against a tree trunk with his knees pulled up to his chin, his nose resting on one knee. The days without my Walkman were completely different. It was like entering an unknown world with different rules. Nothing made sense any more. Even Magnus was different. Smaller, paler. Scared and nervous. I hadn't seen as much of him recently. He missed the music, obviously.

'We can overpower him,' I said. 'If we work together.'

'What about the others?' Magnus said.

'We'll have to wait until he's alone.'

'When?'

'He has to be one his own at some point,' I said.

'It won't work,' Magnus said.

'Why not?'

He shook his head.

'It just won't. There's no point.'

'Of course there is. If there are two of us and one of him. We overpower him and take it back.'

Magnus buried his chin between his knees.

'But what if it *isn't* yours?' he said. 'I mean, it wasn't your tape in it ...'

'Of course it's mine,' I said. 'I let him borrow it.'

He sighed.

'Can't you just buy a new one?'

'With what?'

'Steal one.'

Magnus sometimes shoplifted. I never did. No one ever noticed him. It was as if he was invisible. Magnus was far too unassuming for anyone to suspect him of committing a crime. He could calmly pay for his one-krona sweets without anyone suspecting that his pockets were full of chocolate bars, lollipops and batteries. Sometimes even music magazines.

'No,' I said. 'Of course we could take him. If we work together.'

I kicked at an old metal locker that was floating at the edge of the marsh. Magnus frowned. He sighed and let out a groan.

'If we do it together,' I said, 'he won't stand a chance!'

Eventually he agreed for us to have a go the following day. We planned the whole thing in minute detail. Worked out what order everything should happen in. Jump him, ideally without him realising we were coming. I'd hold him while Magnus grabbed the Walkman. Once he had it he'd give me a signal and we'd run off. We practised a few different kicks and punches behind the old paint warehouse. Told each other it was vital to withstand any counterpunches he might manage to throw if he tried to defend himself. Withstand the pain and not buckle under the first blow.

'It's going to hurt,' I said, but somehow that didn't feel so bad any more.

It would just have to hurt. After all, everything hurt.

'Blue Mix!' Johan yelled when he caught sight of me the next day.

I started and looked at them. I wondered if they could tell I was planning something.

'Hello! Blue Mix! Have you found your Walkman yet?'

I didn't answer.

Dennis was still going around with the Walkman on his belt. It did actually look newer than mine. Brighter yellow, somehow. So what? Maybe he'd polished it. I tried to keep out of their way for the rest of the day.

When school was over I met Magnus at the usual place outside the post office. He was nervous and paranoid. Kept looking at his watch and talking non-stop. I kept having to tell him to be quiet.

We found Dennis and his gang and started to follow them. There was a big group of them for a long time, all walking in that assured, confident way they had. It was hard to maintain the right distance – either we hung back too far and risked losing them, or else we risked being seen.

'Look,' Magnus whispered. 'Why don't we just go home instead?'

'No chance,' I said.

Eventually some of them drifted away, but Dennis and Johan seemed to live in the same area, because they continued walking together. They were heading down a long road of detached houses, each one bigger than the last, looming over the road. They were talking and laughing, and pretend-fighting in a pretty rough way. We crept after them. At regular intervals Magnus prodded me and said we ought to give up.

'It's never going to work,' he said, twisting his watch. 'Let's just leave it.'

There was something so utterly helpless about him. So defenceless. Evasive. Almost as if he wanted us to fail. That annoyed me and made me even more irrationally determined to go through with the attempt.

'Not a chance!' I said as sternly as I could.

'It's never going to work,' he went on muttering, like a mantra.

'Of course it will,' I said.

The sun was starting to go down over the big detached houses and their neat gardens and Volvo estates parked out in the street next to big mailboxes or in the drives and big garages in gardens adorned with hammocks and flagpoles. Some even had tarpaulin-covered swimming pools.

Eventually the two boys ahead of us high-fived each other and Dennis play-punched Johan on the shoulder. Then he carried on along the road alone. It was fairly late by now and Magnus and I were able to creep pretty close to him under cover of the growing darkness.

'Now!' I whispered. 'Now, fuck it!'

Magnus stopped and shook his head.

'No,' he said.

I stared at him.

'Come on! Let's do it!' I hissed.

Dennis was already walking off. Maybe he lived nearby? If we hesitated now he'd be gone. The opportunity would be wasted and everything would be lost.

'Come on!' I said, a bit louder.

But Magnus just stood there shaking his head. Terrified. Paralysed. He was actually shaking. He wasn't even looking at his watch, just shaking his head and clenching his hands in front of his groin. He was pressing his legs together. I realised that he'd wet himself. A dark patch spread across his jeans. I realised I was never going to persuade him to go along with this. It wasn't going to happen.

There was no way I could deal with Dennis on my own. He'd make mincemeat of me. But I was too full of adrenalin. And my Walkman was so close. I watched Dennis as he moved slowly but surely further and further away, then took a snap decision and ran after him on my own.

I caught up with him just as he was turning to walk through a tall hedge surrounding a large house.

'Dennis!' I shouted, and when I reached the drive I saw that he'd stopped in front of the carport.

He turned. Stared at me, and I thought I could detect a hint of anxiety, or at least surprise, before he realised who it was.

'What the fuck are you doing here?' he said.

We stood there for a few seconds while I wondered if I should launch myself at him or wait and try to gain some sort of advantage. He was only a centimetre or two taller than me, but the odds were still heavily stacked in his favour.

'Did you want something, or what?' Dennis said after a while.

The Walkman was strapped to his belt, shimmering yellow. Only a metre or so away from me. I could have reached out and grabbed it. It would all have been so simple if that bloody traitor Magnus had been there. He wouldn't even have had to do anything, I thought. Just be there. If only he'd been there, I thought.

'I just want my Walkman back,' I said in the end.

Dennis merely grinned. A broad smile that showed both rows of teeth. Then he turned, walked up the steps and went inside the house without another word. I was left standing on the drive. I stood there for a long time after he'd gone.

I didn't see Magnus again that evening. If he'd shown his face I would probably have punched him. Hard. I walked back the same way and thought I heard rustling in the bushes. I called out a few times so that he'd hear me if he was nearby. 'You're so fucking useless!' I yelled. 'Completely fucking useless!'

I ignored Magnus after that. I walked past him outside the post office, pretending he didn't exist. At first he left me alone, but after a few days he ran up alongside me on the path home from school, whining for forgiveness and coming up with all sorts of pathetic excuses. His foot had started to hurt, he said. It had been too dark. He had been unsure of the plan, thought we were going to wait a bit longer. It hadn't turned out so badly, had it? And so on. Every so often he tried to grab me to make me stop. He was crying and snivelling, but I pulled loose and walked home, without so much as looking at him.

Dennis carried on wearing the Walkman on his belt. There were moments when I couldn't help thinking that I'd made a mistake, that I'd imagined the whole thing. That I'd never lent it to him. Or that I'd lent it to him and then got it back, only to lose it myself and blame it all on Dennis. In which case it was hardly surprising that he and his friends were pissed off with me. I started to get used to the idea, until it almost seemed more likely than the alternative. I could hear Motörhead and Slayer playing on it. Mine had never played groups like that. Eventually I managed to persuade my mum to get me another one – a different make, and a more basic model, but still: it worked. Whenever Magnus appeared I turned the volume up and pretended not to see him. As time passed it got easier and easier to ignore him. In the end it was almost as if he'd disappeared.

25

After sitting on the bench for a fairly long time I started to feel cold and went up to my flat. I realised I was waiting for the silent caller to phone me again. I sat there staring into the darkness, clutching the phone like a stuffed toy or a rosary. It was a long time ago now. It was all such a long time ago. In a way it had been surprisingly easy just to ignore Magnus back then. I simply made my mind up and tuned out the frequency on which his voice was audible. I concentrated on my music instead. If I decided he didn't exist, then he didn't. I soon realised what power I had over him. Without me he was nothing. Sometimes it was almost comforting to know that he was suffering on his own. Because obviously I could take him back at any moment. If I wanted to. Back then I was the one who decided what the rules were.

Now it was him. And he was gone.

I'd just made up my mind to call Magnus again, even though it was after three o'clock in the morning. I caught sight of myself in the black screen of the television. It almost felt like it was him in the television, about to call me. It looked like he was waiting for something. He'll call any moment now, I thought.

Sure enough, the phone rang a short while later. I was raising my hand to answer when I saw that the man in the television already had the receiver pressed to his ear. I did the same.

I was about to ask if he was still alive when I heard a click at the other end, then some crackling, and then 'Dinner at Eight' by Rufus Wainwright played on a poor-quality sound system.

26

I listened. To the whole track. I sat there perfectly still and enjoyed it. Like when you're given a present you've always wanted or a genuine compliment or a big hug. Eventually the song came to an end. There was a click, then there was no one there. I hung up, almost certain that the person at the other end was a friend.

But was it Magnus Gabrielsson? And how could he play Rufus Wainwright if he was dead? And if he wasn't dead, which seemed more likely, why would he be playing Rufus Wainwright? Did he even know who he was? Magnus had clung to a fairly fundamentalist line when it came to what music he listened to. There was no place for Rufus Wainwright there. Whoever was playing music at the other end of the line wasn't the Magnus I knew. It was a different one. Unless it was someone else altogether? In which case, who?

I went over to my computer and did a search for Magnus Gabrielsson.

I tried typing in Magnus's phone number, and found both his name and address. So he does exist, I thought rather stupidly. But the person on the phone didn't feel like Magnus. Magnus would never sit in silence and then play 'Dinner at Eight'. Anyway, how could anyone else know about 'Dinner at Eight'? I hadn't mentioned to anyone that I'd been thinking about it. Coincidence? Maybe, but it was more likely that someone had picked up on me humming it. The girls at work? A customer? Dansson? Anyway, how loud was my humming? Did I really walk about singing to myself?

After a while the phone rang again. I answered on the first ring. Neither of us said anything. I went over to the stereo, switched it on, then held the receiver up as I played 'Who Are You?' by Scarlett Johansson.

27

The next morning I called Dansson from the phone at work. I waited until I was alone in the employee changing room, then sat on the bench leaning back against the lockers. I had a headache and could feel the sweat on my back.

'Have you heard anything about Magnus Gabrielsson?' I said as soon as he answered.

'Roxette?' he said blearily.

'What have you heard?' I said.

I heard Dansson breathe heavily into the phone.

'That he committed suicide, you mean?'

'Who did you hear that from?'

'You. Among others.'

'Who else?'

'Well ... you, anyway.'

My head was throbbing, and I thought I'd better try to find a painkiller.

'I didn't say that,' I said.

'No? What did you say, then?'

'I said he'd disappeared.'

'Oh?'

'That's one hell of a difference.'

I closed my eyes and tried to calm down.

'Has anyone else said anything about him?' I asked after a short pause.

'Don't think so,' Dansson said.

'Seriously, has anyone said anything?'

'No,' Dansson said. 'What the hell – can I go back to sleep now?'

28

That evening the phone rang again. At first the line was silent. Just that same breathing. It felt simultaneously creepy and exciting, kind of forbidden. As if Magnus and I, if it was him, had found an entirely new way to communicate.

This time I was ready. I'd made it a bit of an occasion. I'd bought a bar of chocolate and broken it into squares, but left it in the wrapper so I could have some whenever I felt like it. I popped a piece in my mouth as I went over to the record shelves, wondering what to play.

I pulled out both Fink's *Sort of Revolution* and Matthew E. White's 'One of These Days', but before I had time to choose a track I heard noises at the other end of the line, then 'This Is Killing Me' by Skid Row started to play.

I concentrated on listening. What did he mean by 'This Is Killing Me'? What was killing him? Was he in some sort of dangerous situation after all? Was that why he couldn't talk? Maybe he could only play music and was using it to send coded messages to me? Should I inform the authorities? Or was it his kidnapper playing the music?

Skid Row? I thought for a long time before finally putting on 'Who Am I Talking To' from Andy Pratt's eponymous album.

A long silence followed, then Anthrax's 'The Devil You Know' started to play.

I stared into space. What did that mean? Was whoever it was trying to scare me? I didn't feel particularly scared. It was all far too weird, first spending several evenings sitting in silence, breathing into the phone, before finally playing 'The Devil You Know'. And there wasn't anything frightening about listening to the disc being taken out and carefully put back in its case. So it was someone with a CD player. Who handled their music carefully. It must be a friend, I thought.

In the end I decided to play 'About Today' by the National: 'Today, you were so far away,' Matt Berninger sang in his deep, cracked voice.

When I went over to the chocolate bar there was only one piece left. Where had the rest gone? I looked around as if expecting to see someone else in the flat.

Just to be sure I went and checked the front door. It was locked.

29

'There's someone at the other end,' I said to Dansson when I phoned him from work the next morning. 'But they don't say anything.'

'Are you sure?' he said. 'Because sometimes there can be a delay on the line. You know, when you hear your own voice, only much later.'

'Hmm,' I said. 'This isn't like that.'

'Maybe it's a sales call,' Dansson said.

'It's not a sales call,' I said. 'It's ... someone who plays music.'

'Music?'

'Yes.'

30

Just before lunchtime I looked up to serve a customer and saw Jallo on the other side of the glass counter. I said hello, but it was impossible to tell if he'd come to see me or just to buy bread. I didn't like him standing so close to the bread with his chapped red fingers, but I had to go to the other end of the counter with another customer to fill a box with vanilla slices, so I didn't say anything. Then, on top of everything else, the customer claimed I'd squashed some icing against the side of the box and demanded that I swap the slice for an undamaged one, so I had to put it back in the display and carefully replace it with another one.

For some reason I happened to look past the customer, and some way off, standing behind a pillar by the tables in the café, I saw a figure in a blue anorak who pulled his head back the moment I looked in that direction.

I could have sworn it was Mr Magic Bobbi, the magician from the circus.

I looked over to where Jallo had been standing, but could no longer see him. I made an instant decision.

I swung round the end of the counter and set off towards the pillar. I pushed as fast as I could through the sea of surprised customers clutching their queue tickets as they waited to buy bread.

In a matter of seconds I was at the pillar, flew round it and collided with a man in late middle age who apologised even though it was obviously my fault. No Mr Magic Bobbi.

I mumbled an apology as I looked around. It occurred to me that this was the perfect crowd in which to disappear. A large number of very slow-moving customers wearing a garish array of colours. Like the one good song on a compilation album.

I glimpsed the blue anorak over by the stationery department. The figure's long hair had been tied in a ponytail. I headed towards it, weaving between the café tables. It didn't take long to catch up. I was about to slap my hand on the man's shoulder and ask what the hell he'd done with my friend – I actually had my hand in the air – when I realised that it was clearly someone else. Someone much shorter. Who also happened to be a woman.

I followed her for a short while, and when she stopped at a display of notebooks I pushed past. Mostly because I couldn't just turn round.

I carried on through the doors that led to the underground station, trying to think of a good reason why I had left work and run off like that. But nothing I came up with sounded even vaguely plausible.

31

'Do you feel like telling me what happened?' my boss asked later when we were sitting in his little office to discuss my odd behaviour. I thought for a moment and then decided that honesty was probably the best policy after all.

'I thought I saw ... someone.'

He looked at me in surprise.

'What did you say?'

'Someone who ...'

I hesitated. How was I supposed to explain this in a factual way? I began again, in a slightly more steady voice.

'I thought I saw a magician,' I said, nodding slowly as I attempted to adopt a convincing expression. I quickly realised it was hopeless.

Have you ever heard the Bob Dylan song 'Hurricane' on the *Desire* album, about the falsely accused boxer? My boss told me off so emphatically that it was all I could think of. I was briefly close to tears. The bow tie was pinching my throat, and I loosened it with a couple of fingers. During the rest of the reprimand I thought about my recurrent dilemma of where to put compilation albums. What do you do with an album featuring two equally big names when it isn't obvious that one of them is making a guest appearance on the other's album? Some are obvious of course: Frank and Nancy Sinatra get filed under Frank. Besides, they're related, which makes the decision even easier. But what about the Travelling Wilburys, for instance? Or *Grimascher och telegram*, which features both Jan Johansson and Cornelis Vreeswijk? Cornelis's name is more prominent on the cover, but it's perfectly obvious that it's a Jan Johansson album.

32

Jallo was gone by the time I got back to the bakery counter after my dressing-down. Perhaps he assumed I was going to be gone for a long time? Perhaps he thought that was how I usually went for lunch? He doesn't usually have anything against waiting. Either way, he was gone when I got back. I stood there for a while looking for him before I heard a familiar remark from the other side of the counter: 'Young man, what do you think you're here for?'

I clicked to bring up another number, then went over to the woman and took her ticket.

'I'd like to place an order,' she said. 'And it's rather special, so you'd better fetch a pen and paper.'

I fetched the order book from the till.

'I'd like to order a cake. Completely white, like this.'

She moved her hands in a circular motion.

'And with a black ribbon around it. And a little peak on one side. Can you guess what it's supposed to be?'

I shook my head slowly.

33

According to the rota I finished work at 4 p.m., which meant I could start to get ready at quarter to. If you wiped the counter and did a bit of rearranging towards the end you could manage to spend the last five minutes tucked away in the kitchen. I swept the crumbs and flour from the large marble counter behind the till. Made up some boxes for cakes until I realised I'd done far too many, so I piled the rest up beneath the counter: they could always be used later. Then I rinsed some tongs and tried to avoid serving any more customers for as long as I could by making myself look busy. I checked the time, but it was still only ten to, so I sneaked into the kitchen.

The dishwasher was loaded and running through its cycle. The worktop alongside it was empty. All the cutlery and implements were carefully arranged in the plastic tray next to the sink; I sank onto the little plastic stool by the door. Some of the girls thought the big industrial dishwasher was hard to handle, but I'd learned to use one at the summer camp Jallo and I went to years ago. It was part of the daily routine there for residents to help with the cleaning and washing-up. I used to think it was a pretty easy job even back then.

The last summer at camp Jallo had signed up as one of the leaders.

'Much better,' he said. 'And you don't have pay the enrolment fee. Besides, I already know how to do it all. And they say personal experience is a bonus.'

Even if he was the same person, it was more like talking to an adult. Suddenly he was taking part in self-awareness sessions and discussing things in a mature way. Asking about my social life, my routines, school, if I still saw Magnus – that sort of thing.

'Isn't there a youth club or something?' he asked.

I shrugged.

'Maybe you could set one up,' he said.

I muttered something about that probably being quite hard to do.

'Oh,' he said, 'you just need to find premises. There must be somewhere that's not being used?'

I shrugged again.

'There must be,' he said. 'There always is. Look, do you think you could take those headphones off?'

Magnus didn't like Jallo. I don't know why. Maybe he thought he was a slacker. A poseur. Unless he was jealous because we had a different kind of relationship thanks to the summer camp? Maybe he saw him as a potential threat to our friendship. For good reason. Since the business with the Walkman things had settled down a bit. I suppose I'd forgiven him and realised that I was just going to have to accept him for what he was: a coward.

But things between us were still frosty. Jallo wasn't particularly pleasant towards Magnus either. One autumn he bumped into us after school.

'Hey, hi there!' he called. 'How's it going?'

I had almost reached the post office, where Magnus was waiting, when Jallo ran up to me and pulled my headphones off. I put them back on at once. I could still hear him perfectly well as he walked backwards along the pavement ahead of me.

'Do you fancy coming along to a thing with me?' Jallo asked.

'What sort of thing?' I said as we carried on walking awkwardly along.

'Esperanto!' Jallo said breezily. 'An Esperanto course!'

'What's that, then?'

I saw Magnus standing in his usual place and slowed down. Jallo continued walking backwards ahead of me.

'It's the new global language,' Jallo said. 'A new language that everyone in the whole world will understand, right? D'you see how cool that would be?! I'm going to do the course. You can come too ...'

We had reached Magnus now and I nodded briefly in greeting, but Jallo didn't bother to acknowledge his presence.

'No, I can't,' I said. 'Magnus and I are—'

'Oh, forget about him,' Jallo said wearily. Without so much as looking at him. Without bothering about him at all, in fact.

'Don't you see how brilliant it'll be when the whole world starts talking the same language?' he went on. 'You know what this will mean for world peace?'

447

He leaned closer.

'And you know what an advantage it'll be to know it properly before everyone else?! We'll have one hell of a head start!'

I glanced at Magnus, who was standing right behind Jallo, unassuming as always, unwilling to take up any space.

'Look, Magnus and I are—' I began again.

'Oh! Never mind Magnus!' Jallo groaned.

He took a couple of steps and noticed, entirely without embarrassment, that he was standing right next to Magnus. He looked at me as if he was simply waiting for me to go with him.

'Well?' he said.

Magnus looked down. Waiting for me to made a decision.

'Are you coming or what?' Jallo cried.

I shook my head.

'Fine. Don't, then,' Jallo muttered and walked off.

Magnus glared at him as he went. And there we were, together, again.

It annoyed me that Magnus always had to be so defensive. That he always let me make the decisions without contributing anything but a guilty conscience. But he never really wanted much. He never wanted anything new to happen. Everything was supposed to be the way it had always been. As if it was possible to stop time. Which of course it wasn't. In fact he was becoming more and more peculiar. In the end I started to feel uncomfortable in his company.

For him everything was perfectly clear. We were two outsiders who belonged together, and we would always belong with the outcasts and rejects. Naturally I was grateful for his loyalty, but it was starting to feel more and more of a burden.

Perhaps he noticed, because he did try to change as time passed, adopting a rather more provocative tone and suggesting we try more challenging things.

Like the time we walked across the railway bridge. We had been walking all evening without saying much, just wandering about kicking stones. He'd started wearing black clothes and had got hold of that stupid badge, live hard and die young. It felt like a hard-rock thing to me. I said as much. Asked if he was planning on becoming a rocker instead. He just grinned and stopped next to the railing.

'Let's climb along the outside,' he said.

'What for?'

'Are you too scared?' he said, swinging over the railing.

'Course not,' I said.

I climbed over and clung on to the outside of the railing next to him. There was a drop of maybe five or six metres to the railway line. I felt the wind in my hair. In the distance we could hear the train approaching. Magnus looked at me. It was only a game, but I got the feeling that he would have jumped. If I'd asked him to, he would have done it. Without hesitation.

The teachers at Vira Elementary told us to be careful about socialising with kids from other schools. Which basically meant Berg School. Especially if they offered us drugs. Magnus didn't do drugs, but he did develop a sort of unpredictable side to his character. Sometimes I imagined that he came up with things

like that to impress me. But in actual fact he just became more
and more tragic.

A few weeks later I met Jallo again. By then he'd given up on
Esperanto. He said he'd got a part-time job as a buddy at Berg
School. Why didn't I visit him there some time?

I told him that according to Magnus Berg School was hell on
earth, but Jallo said he'd never seen Magnus there.

'Never?' I said.

'Nope,' Jallo said.

'Not once?'

He shook his head.

I never broached the subject with Magnus. That was his
business. Somehow I had already realised that he didn't spend
much time at school. He had a world of his own. He grew less
and less engaged in music, and more and more peculiar. He got
interested in magic and some homespun version of numerology.
He saw a connection between the number of records in a box
and good or bad events. He had a weird period when he was
interested in magic tricks and magical thinking. He said he was
going to become a magician. I tried to explain to him that all
magic acts were based on different types of illusion, and that
the people who performed them spent hours practising, but he
seemed to think it was more to do with formulas and codes
rather than tricking the audience into concentrating on
something else. It was like he wasn't at all interested in hearing
what I said. Unless he just thought it didn't matter.

He kept coming up with increasingly strange suggestions. Once when we were standing by the marsh he suggested jumping in.

'Let's do it,' he urged.

'Are you mad?' I said. 'What for?'

'Why not?' he said with a grin.

'Idiot!'

Why not?'

I sighed.

'Because we'd get sucked down and die.'

'So?'

I looked at him, but he just glared back with that provocative expression. As if it was all a bit of fun. As if we might as well walk into the marsh and see what happened. No matter what the consequences. As if nothing mattered. As if nothing made any difference.

'You'll have to do it on your own,' I said.

'Then you'll be alone.'

I snorted.

'So? I'd just have to find someone else to hang out with.'

'Who?'

I snorted again.

'Anyone,' I said.

'You haven't got anyone. Who?'

I shrugged.

'Jallo.'

'Jallo's an idiot,' he said. 'He's dangerous. Can't you tell? He doesn't understand anything.'

'But you do, I suppose?'

'More than you and him do,' he said.

'*He*,' I said. 'More than you and *he* do.'

'Are you the grammar police now, then?' Magnus said.

'No,' I said. 'That's just the sort of thing you learn if you go to school.'

Magnus didn't respond to that.

'Jallo's trying to manipulate you,' he said. 'Haven't you noticed? He keeps trying to get you to think you're someone, you fucking loser.'

'Says you, just because you're a loser.'

'No more than you and him are.'

'You and *he*.'

Recently he'd started to adopt a tougher way of talking. It didn't suit him and was just embarrassing. I tried to get him to stop and act normally instead.

Sometimes I wondered if I should tell him what people said about him when he wasn't around. At school. The way they made fun of him. Saying he was crazy and disgusting and an idiot. Not just that, but that he was sick in the head, and that people were scared of him because he'd evidently done all sorts of weird stuff that people loved to talk about.

There were any number of stories about Magnus, each one worse than the last. People were only too happy to gossip about him. Not when I was around, obviously. They knew we were friends, so they always stopped the moment I appeared. But I couldn't help hearing anyway – it would have been impossible not to. Magnus was something of a sobering example, a myth. And in a way some of that rebounded on me. I ended up being automatically associated with him and all the stupid stuff he got up to.

Perhaps I should have said something to Magnus. Tried to make him realise how strange he was getting. Tried to get him to wake up and show him the guy I kept having to protect and look after. But I could never come up with a good enough reason. What good would it do? It would only make him even sadder. Even more alone. Even more weird.

More and more often I found myself wondering what sort of person I would have been if Magnus hadn't existed. Who I might have become if the two of us hadn't hung out together all the time. I could have been someone completely different.

'No, you couldn't,' Magnus said. 'You are who you are. You can't just become someone else.'

'Can't you?' I said. 'Surely we choose who we are for ourselves?'

He snorted.

'You're not the type.'

'What type?'

'Someone like that ...'

'I could have been.'

'Hardly.'

'Just because you get bullied doesn't mean I have to. I could have gone out with Maddy ...'

'Hardly.'

Why not?'

'Do you know what you are to her?'

He pulled his hand out of his pocket and formed his thumb and forefinger into a zero.

'And how the hell would you know?'

'I just do.'

I took a deep breath and leaned my head back against the wall. I looked at the time and realised it was five minutes past four. I pulled the bow tie off and undid my top button. Went off to the changing room, hung up my uniform and got changed into my own clothes. I put the padlock on my locker, picked up my rucksack and walked out.

34

Dansson was waiting outside the staff entrance when I came out.

'Do you want to come to Record King?' he said, and I very nearly nodded before I realised that I didn't want to. I was tired of Record King and wanted to try something new. Not that there was anything wrong with Dansson, but hanging out with him every day in the record shop had started to feel like being strapped into the back seat of a car, out of reach of the radio and unable to influence the choice of music.

I wondered if there was any good reason for me not to go. I felt in my pockets and found Jallo's note on the health-food shop receipt.

'I need to find an address,' I said and showed him the scrap of paper.

Dansson took it and read.

'Bondegatan 34,' he said.

'No,' I said. 'Bondegatan 3A. That's an A. It's just Jallo's …'
I snatched the receipt back.

'Right,' Dansson said, sticking his hands in his pockets.

'It's … He was in a hurry when he wrote it … It's just Jallo's …'
I said, looking at the writing. 'It's supposed to be 3A.'

'OK,' Dansson said.

I looked at the note again.

'You can see it's supposed to be an A?'

'Sure,' Dansson said.

'You can, though, can't you?'

35

Bondegatan 34 was nothing more than a door. In the middle of a wall. No sign. No windows. Just a door, nothing else.

And it was open.

Right inside the door hung a bead curtain, the sort you see in Asian films, usually with a pattern on them. A sunset or a beautiful woman. Walking through it was like walking through water, a slow shower. I let myself be washed by it and emerged on the other side. I found myself standing at one end of a very long corridor with the curtain still swaying behind me.

The walls, ceiling and floor were covered in dark blue plush. There were small but fairly powerful wall lamps every ten metres or so. I took a couple of steps forward and ran my hand along the soft wall. It felt lovely.

The air smelled of synthetic bananas. Sweets.

I took another couple of steps and realised that walking was surprisingly easy. As if the passageway sloped gently down, extending as far as the eye could see. I walked a bit further and felt how nice it was to stretch my legs, to let go and stride along.

I carried on down the soft, soundless carpet. The slight slope gave me a bit of extra momentum, and I was swept on by the seemingly endless row of wall lamps. They were relatively bright, but the distance between them was great enough to leave pockets of darkness. You walked out of the light into darkness, then back into light again.

Gravity led me on down the corridor. I just had to keep walking and take long enough strides to stop myself from stumbling.

After a while I started to make out the outline of a door at the other end of the corridor. It looked like an ordinary office door, but as I got closer I saw that it was padded, with round buttons studded across it in a diamond pattern. The handle was wood, perhaps teak. I tried it. The door was locked, but the lock was on my side of the door. I turned the lock and walked into a large dark room with a flickering light in the distance. I could hear soft music. The hall was full of hundreds of people who suddenly burst into synchronised laughter. Blue light enveloped everyone sitting in the auditorium. I turned and reached for the handle to sneak back out again, but the door wouldn't open. The lock was on the other side.

'Don't you see? It's a message?' a voice said in English from the loudspeakers. I decided to walk past all the rows of seats. It got darker again and thunderous music started to play. Before the flight of steps was illuminated by an explosion of light I managed to trip on one of the treads and almost hit my head on the carpet, which smelled of popcorn. I got to my feet, pushed through some swing doors and emerged into a foyer.

A very short fair-haired man in a red cap nodded to me as he handed a customer their change across the counter. A young man was sitting on a bench beside the popcorn machine, scribbling in one of those free film magazines.

Behind him, a little further away, stood Dennis.

36

The same broad shoulders and large head. The permed hair was gone, but he still had the same thick, heavy eyebrows. And saggy cheeks. It was definitely Dennis. In one of those cinema uniforms.

I stood by the doors, and the music grew louder again behind me.

The young man on the bench glanced at me idly, toyed with his pen and appeared so bored by the whole situation that he couldn't help yawning. I noticed that he'd drawn moustaches on Angelina Jolie and Brad Pitt.

The foyer was calm and very quiet. It was warm. The sun was shining through the windows facing the street, dividing the foyer into sunny and shaded areas. The line between them ran across the floor like a boundary. The customer walked off and the very short man went and sat down beside the young man, close enough for me to see that he had gone back to filling in the football pools. I couldn't help noting that he was taking a chance on an away win for Crystal Palace against Arsenal, which seemed pretty risky. Perhaps he knew something than no one else did? No one was paying much attention to me.

I looked over at Dennis again. It had to be him. It couldn't be anyone else. I closed my eyes for a moment. When I complained to Jallo about all the weird things that only seemed to happen to me, he said that I ought to challenge my own experiences from time to time.

'You can ask the question yourself. Ask yourself: is this really plausible?'

I opened my eyes again. And there he stood. Dennis, the bully who had stolen my Walkman all those years ago. It seemed plausible. In spite of everything. The only particularly odd thing was that someone like Dennis was working in a place like this. A cinema? He ought to be an estate agent or a solicitor, maybe even a doctor by now. I couldn't imagine Dennis's parents congratulating him on getting a job as a cinema usher. But on the other hand, it was a job. An income. Times change. Everything changes. Perhaps something had happened. It often does. He was holding a can of Coca-Cola in one hand, and took a sip as he turned in my direction.

His face froze. He recognised me instantly. We stood there looking at each other, and I realised it was too late to turn away. After a while he raised his head slightly. With the absolute minimum of effort. Barely noticeable and surprisingly calm. He didn't even seem particularly surprised to see me. Almost as if he'd been expecting me to show up. As if he knew I'd be coming. He began to walk towards me. I felt my heart beat faster and had to make a real effort not to run away.

It must have been at least ten, fifteen years since I'd last seen Dennis, at some school thing. Back then I was far too preoccupied with trying to walk straight, not hyperventilate and show that that sort of reunion wasn't a problem for me. That my time at school hadn't left any scars. I was far too absorbed in my own behaviour to notice anyone else. Some of them had their partners with them, I recalled, and I spent an hour or so mingling until I told someone I had to get going. I tried my best to come across as an unbroken individual who had dealt perfectly well with his schooldays, just in case anyone happened to think otherwise. I walked from group to group with exaggerated calm, raising my plastic glass in toasts and counting the minutes until I could safely escape with a breezy smile glued to my face. I remembered that Dennis had worn an earring. And hadn't his face been a bit fatter even then? Had he looked a bit worn down? I wasn't sure.

Now here he was, standing in front of me holding out his hand. I shook it.

'Hi there!' he said.

I wondered if I had ever held his hand in mine before. It felt soft. Smooth and a bit flabby. Surprisingly limp. There was something subdued and nervous about him. From close up I could see that he had worry lines on his forehead. The last time we met I had been far too self-absorbed to notice him properly, but things were different this time. Did he feel that? Could he tell I was looking at him closely? In a way it was like I was seeing him for the first time. He had a few grey hairs, some crow's feet around his eyes. He had a mole on his forehead that he should probably get checked out. I saw that his shirt collar was bit too tight around his neck, beneath his bulging double chin. Maybe he was seeing me for the first time too? We stood like that for a while, without saying anything. Those moments were rather strained yet oddly lucid. And possibly more awkward for him.

'Well,' he said eventually. 'Yeah ... he said you'd be coming.'

'Who did?' I said.

'Jallo.'

'You work here?' I asked.

He nodded and took his cap off. Folded and unfolded it a couple of times as if to prove that he had permission to do that. That he didn't have to wear it if he didn't want to.

'Usher,' he said. 'How about you?'

'Oh,' I said, trying to shift my weight nonchalantly to the other leg. 'I'm in the bakery business.'

He nodded again and took another sip of Coke. It was like we were both trying to normalise the situation and pretend that this wasn't a strangely unreal occurrence at all.

'You got a lot going on now, then?' he said.

I shrugged my shoulders. Didn't know what to say.

'I mean, a lot to do,' he went on, stifling a burp.

I didn't know how to respond to this sort of talk. Nothing unusual about that. It occurred to me that I never talked much about work. To be honest, I never noticed much difference in the seasons. You just stood there, pressed the button and served the customers. I would have liked to have been able to say something funny and smart to prove that I knew a lot about the industry, while simultaneously demonstrating that I wasn't that bothered about it – just that I was aware of it, in spite of the fact that it was him I was talking to.

'Well, of course it's school graduation season,' I said eventually. 'Lots of cakes ...'

He nodded knowledgeably, as if he really did know something about it.

'I've got a good idea for a graduation cake,' he said.

'Really?' I said.

'Mmm,' he said. 'Imagine, a white princess cake—'

'Hang on,' I said. 'Let me guess. With a little black peak—'

'Exactly!' he said, breaking into a grin. 'On one side, made of marzipan, so that ...'

We said it at the same time: '... the cake itself looks like a graduation cap!'

He looked delighted.

It could have been far more uncomfortable to find myself eye to eye with Dennis like that. But for some reason it was getting easier and easier with each passing second. I don't know why, but in the end I was almost enjoying standing there. I could have carried on for a good while longer, just looking him in the eye. He looked tired. As if life had treated him roughly. He didn't seem to have anything against standing there like that either. It was clear we weren't going to start socialising. We were never going to be friends. I didn't want that at all. Nor did he, presumably. We weren't going to go out drinking or bowling together. It wasn't the slightest bit dramatic, and the notion that I had once been desperate for his friendship felt very distant indeed. I thought about saying as much to him, but it felt a bit too much. Too big, somehow. And possibly also rather cruel. It was like we'd both woken up from an unpleasant dream and realised that although the waking world may not have been that great, at least it was different to what we thought back then.

He rubbed his hand across his face a few times, screwed his eyes shut and frowned.

'Look,' he said after a while. 'I know I'm supposed ... What's it called? I'm supposed to atone ...'

'What did you say?' I said.

'Atonement,' he said. 'What am I trying to say?'

He took a deep breath. Closed his eyes again.

'Look ... I admit my guilt and would like to apologise for the way we treated you.'

He breathed out. Opened his eyes again and looked at me in a way that was both anxious and expectant. I stared at him. Neither of us spoke for what felt like a long time. We stood there in silence. Dennis with his cap in his hand and what he had just said hanging in the air, looking sheepish now, afterwards, as if he was expecting some sort of response from me. I almost burst out laughing. What the hell did he mean? Did he really think that we could draw a line under everything, the whole of our teenage lives, and move on? As if it was possible to forgive something like that, to wrap up that whole period, everything that had happened at school, and put it into words. Sort it out, put the pieces back in the right place and start afresh from the beginning. As if we, if we felt like it, could erase it all and do everything differently.

I just gawped at him. Even so, it was good to hear it, and provided at least some small measure of relief.

After a while of neither of us saying anything he started to glance sideways. As if he was wondering how long this had to go on for and wanted to check the time to see when it could be regarded as done and dusted.

In the end I was the one who broke the silence.

'Can I ask you something?' I said.

He looked at me with those tired eyes as though he had an idea what was coming. As if he had prepared for this. The attack. Revenge. All the difficult questions I was going to ask. He was making a real effort to take responsibility without losing his temper or going to pieces. But I didn't want to ask any of those questions. I wasn't expecting any answers. Not from him. Absolutely not from him. There was only one thing I wanted to know.

'Was it my Walkman?'

Whatever he'd been expecting, this wasn't it. That much was obvious. He looked like he didn't even understand the question.

'What?' he said.

'That's all I want to know,' I said. 'Was it my Walkman you took?'

'Yes, of course it was,' he said. 'So, yeah ...'

465

I nodded. He nodded back.

'Christ,' he went on after a while, giving me a look of pity. 'You were so alone. You didn't have anyone.'

'Well ...' I began to say, 'I had ...'

I suddenly felt that I wanted to get away from there.

'But you were, though,' Dennis went on. 'You were always utterly alone. It's no fun being on your own. It's fucking horrible. I can see why you wanted your Walkman.'

'Oh, it's just ... I always wondered if it was really mine, or if I was imagining it ... Jallo suggested that—'

Dennis brightened up.

'Do you go and see Jallo as well?' he said.

I stared at him. Shook my head.

'No ... He's just a friend of mine.'

Dennis looked at me, winked and nodded. Almost as if we shared a secret. Was he implying something about me and Jallo? If so, what? Maybe he just felt relieved. He certainly looked much less tense now that he'd got the apology out of the way, and it was impossible to tell what he meant by his expression. I felt the urge to get out of there even more strongly now.

'What film are you showing?' I asked.

Dennis glanced towards the cinema.

'Something experimental,' he said. 'About some friends. Although it's hard to know who the real friend is ...'

I nodded. I didn't know what to say.

'Is it any good?'

Dennis frowned.

'It's kind of deep,' he said with a shrug. 'But the music's good. You've always liked music, haven't you?' he said.

He looked happy again, the way you do if you remember something about someone else that makes you look like a more considerate person. Or less arrogant, anyway.

'I listen to quite a lot of stuff myself,' he went on when I didn't say anything.

'Oh,' I said. 'I suppose it's easy these days, with Spotify and SoundCloud and all that.'

I glanced at the door. He put his cap back on. It sounded like the end titles were playing inside the cinema.

'Well,' he said. 'I'd better get back to work, but it would be good to meet up and talk a bit more.'

'Hmm,' I said. 'I'm afraid I don't have a mobile, so—'

'Nor do I,' Dennis said. 'How about tomorrow? What do you say, dinner at eight?'

37

I left the cinema by the main entrance.

I walked over to the pedestrian crossing on Götgatan and when the light turned green realised that I should actually be actually going the other way. I turned round and managed to get back to the other side before the lights changed again. I walked until I came to a bus stop, looked up at the sign and saw that the bus was going my way. So Dennis was seeing Jallo? Why would he be doing that? What did they talk about? Me? Did Dennis have psychological problems? I couldn't help thinking that it was probably his turn to have some now. As if there was some sort of force in the universe that balanced things out. But what had happened in his life to make him think he had to go and see someone like Jallo? And why had he mentioned 'Dinner at Eight'?

'You always have to look at new ways of communicating,' Jallo once said when we were sitting in his office and he was telling me about some sort of mime course he was thinking of setting up. 'Because of course language is mainly just a barrier to understanding.' I'd stopped listening to him when he said that sort of stuff a long time ago. I mostly just nodded and agreed with him while I thought about other things.

Eventually the bus showed up, and as soon as I sat down I fell asleep and managed to have one of those dreams that feels like a whole lifetime. Someone was walking behind me and I couldn't see who it was. Just as I was about to turn round I woke up and realised that I'd gone at least three stops too far. I looked out of the window and saw that I was right outside the door to Jallo's office. The big illuminated sign was already switched on even though it wasn't quite dark yet. The red and yellow neon letters lit up one after the other, from the bottom, until eventually the man was visible, with the letters forming his hat.

I got off, thinking that I may as well stop in to see Jallo now that I was there. I could take the opportunity to ask him what the hell he was up to.

I went up the narrow stairs with the creaking steps. I kept hold of the handrail because if felt like the wooden steps might give way every time you put your foot down. The receptionist had her face buried in her phone as usual. She didn't bother to pay me any attention, so I didn't say hello to her. I knew my way. I'd been there enough times. I wound my way through the narrow corridors with their bright orange textured wallpaper and the uneven floor that bulged in places and smelled faintly of mould, past the drinks machine, following the trail of lights laid out along the edge of the cheap blue carpet. Just before I got to Jallo's office I stumbled over that wretched strip of lights and fell on the floor. I only just put my hands out in time. Jallo looked up from behind the desk in his room.

'Magnus?' he said with a look of surprise.

He came out and helped me to my feet. He brushed me down and carried my rucksack into the room. He turned his arm to look at his watch.

'I'm seeing a client in twenty minutes, but grab a seat and we can have a quick chat.'

I followed him into the small, windowless office, tucked between the toilets and the recycling bins.

38

He folded a newspaper that was lying open on the desk. Waved it in the air.

'Interesting article here,' he said. 'They've come up with a new way to measure happiness. They're going to debate it at the United Nations. *Happiness*. Can you imagine? Ridiculous.'

He laughed and shook his head. I sat down on the chair on the other side of the desk.

'All nonsense, obviously, if you read between the lines. But you have to admire their nerve. Pushing it as far as that, I mean. Like they say, "The bigger the lie ..."'

He tossed the newspaper on the floor, picked up a pen and put the top back on. He leaned back.

'So, my friend,' he said.

I ran my hands along the armrests.

'What's all this business with Dennis?' I said.

He put the pen to his lips and tapped it a few times without replying.

'Why did you send me to see him?'

He still didn't say anything. Just looked at me with that lazy, inscrutable gaze.

'You knew he'd be there, didn't you? At Bondegatan 34?'

He threw his arms out.

'I thought it would be good for you to meet,' he said at last. 'Good for both of you.'

I leaned back and heard music playing very faintly from the computer in the middle of the desk. The same old Sinatra playlist that Jallo always played. The very worst way to listen to music: a barely audible carpet of background noise that you really had to concentrate on if you wanted to make out any of the details. How could he bear it? He must have it on the lowest possible setting. I stopped mid-movement and tried to sit as silently as I could.

I was well aware that some music has the ability to put me into a trance-like state. I did things without thinking about it. Or imagined that I was doing things that never actually happened. Jallo had once pointed that out to me, and had suggested that I try applying that plausibility test of his. So this sort of music that you could hardly hear always felt a bit sneaky. I wanted to know what sort of music was being played so I could figure out how it affected me.

'I gave him your number a while back,' Jallo said. 'But I don't suppose he could bring himself to call you. I've asked him several times, but he keeps saying he hasn't got round to it. Then he said that he had called, but hadn't dared say anything. He said he'd call the following week, but a week later he said the same thing. So I thought it would be just as well to send you to see him. Did it go OK, then?'

'What?' I said, suddenly thinking that perhaps I ought to have been listening to him and not the music. So I tried to remember what he'd said and listen. Sometimes you can hear what someone has already said: as if the words still hang in the air for a while, and you can pick them up after they've been spoken.

'Seeing him again?' he asked.

I raised my head and stared at his sly-looking face. That little smile that kept playing at the corners of his mouth.

'I suppose so,' I said.

He nodded thoughtfully. Looked at me intently, as if he was waiting for me to say something else. Perhaps I ought to. After all, I was the one who'd raised the subject. I didn't know why though, now. I looked around the room.

'He's scared,' I said.

'What of?' Jallo said.

'Of me.'

'Why is he scared of you?'

'I don't know. There's just something about me.'

'What?'

I shook my head.

'I don't know. Something. What about you?'

'Me?' Jallo said.

'Yes.'

'Oh, there's nothing about me.'

'Why would you and him be seeing each other, then?'

'*He,*' Jallo said

'What?'

'You mean, you and *he.*'

We looked at each other for a few moments. Jallo sat there quietly, smiling, as if he was waiting for me or had taken a vow of silence or something. It felt like it was my turn to talk.

'He said it was my Walkman,' I eventually said.

'Your what?' Jallo said.

'Don't worry; it doesn't matter,' I said.

Sinatra was singing 'In the Wee Small Hours of the Morning', and I could just make out the lyric about a lonely heart learning the lesson.

I took a deep breath and tried to get back to the conversation.

'Why did you tell me where to find Dennis when you knew I was looking for Magnus?' I said.

Jallo tapped his pen against his lips. Then he put it down on the desk and rubbed his face with both palms.

'I gave you an address I thought you needed,' he said.

'What does that have to do with Magnus?'

He leaned back in his chair. Blew out his cheeks and let the air slowly escape from his mouth.

'Well,' he said. 'Nothing.'

'Nothing?'

He shook his head.

'OK, then,' I said. 'Look, this business with Magnus is driving me mad. I can't figure out where he's gone.'

Jallo nodded. The song came to an end, and 'Learnin' the Blues' started to play instead.

'I can't help worrying,' I went on, shifting in the chair. I leaned over one armrest, but that wasn't at all comfortable so I sat back the way I'd been sitting before.

'And then there's the thing with the phone,' I said. 'Someone keeps calling me.'

'Oh?'

Jallo raised his eyebrows in that nonchalant way, as if he wasn't the least bit taken aback but still wanted to look surprised.

'Yes,' I said. 'Which is kind of OK, I guess ... We play each other records.'

'You play *records*?'

'Yes! But I don't think it's Magnus.'

'Why not?' he said.

'It doesn't feel like him.'

'No?' Jallo said, nodding thoughtfully.

He leaned his head back and looked up at the ceiling. He tapped his pen against the desk in time to Sinatra.

'Look, to be honest I don't know that much about Magnus,' Jallo went on.

'Oh?'

'Seeing as I've never met him.'

He stopped tapping the pen and made a vague gesture with the other hand. I watched him. Tried to work out what he meant.

'Yes, you have,' I said.

He looked me in the eye and shook his head.

'Of course you have,' I said. 'You always say—'

'I know what I always say,' he interrupted. 'I can't help having an opinion about him, based on what you've told me. But I've never actually met him.'

'Yes, you have ... The two of you—'

'When?' he interrupted again. 'Give me one occasion when I met him.'

I had to laugh. I opened my mouth to speak but couldn't think of what to say. My laugh sounded nervous. I could hear that for myself.

'Well, the other day,' I said eventually.

'No,' he said, shaking his head. 'You were standing in your doorway, and you said you'd seen him. I never saw him.'

'OK, a long time ago, then. Back at school.'

He shook his head again.

'You went to the same school as him,' I said.

'So you keep saying. But he was never there.'

We were both sitting upright now. Our eyes locked together.

'He was,' I said.

'Not as far as I'm aware,' he replied.

'OK, maybe not in class, but afterwards ...'

Jallo was still shaking his head.

'I've never met him,' he said.

'Well,' I said. 'He's not exactly the sociable type.'

Jallo picked up his pen again and tapped it against his lips. I took a deep breath. Leaned back as relaxed as I could and tried to breathe normally. I felt like I needed to hold on to something. Jallo waved the pen in the air as if he was wafting a strand of hair or mote of dust away.

'You know what I think?' he said, and the pen stopped moving. 'I think you should stop worrying about him.'

39

There are some things you just know. If anyone were to ask 'How do you know that?' you'd reply 'I just do.' It's as obvious as the sky being grey and the grass brown. If the weather's been bad and the summer dry. The question itself seems almost provocative. Something similar happened when Jallo leaned back in his fancy office chair, the one he loved to rock backwards and forwards in, with his elbows on the armrests and his fingertips touching under his chin. There was something ridiculous about the whole situation. Even so, somehow he had managed to get to me, and I was breathing fast.

'What are you trying to say?' I said.

'I'm just saying what I see,' Jallo said.

'This is absurd,' I said. 'Magnus ... Magnus is just Magnus.'

He held the palms of his hands up, and moved them up and down as if he were weighing something in them.

'So tell me,' he said, swivelling in his chair again. 'Does it seem plausible?'

I snorted. I tried desperately to think of something smart to say to put a stop to this ridiculous situation.

'If you stop and think about it ...' Jallo went on, 'doesn't it seem a bit strange that you've both got the same name?'

'What's strange about that?' I said.

'It's a remarkable coincidence, though, isn't it?'

'I'm called Magnus, and so are lots of other people. Plenty of people have the same name.'

He nodded.

'But ... don't you think it was very convenient that he first showed up all those years ago just when you needed him most?'

I shrugged.

'That was a good thing, wasn't it?' I said.

'And then he vanished when you put him to the test.'

'OK,' I said. 'That wasn't quite so good.'

'Why didn't he stand up for you then, that time with Dennis, when you really needed him?'

I felt myself getting angry. What did he know about Magnus? What did he know about what he was like?

'He couldn't,' I said. 'OK? He just couldn't!'

'Fine,' Jallo said, holding his hands up as if in surrender. 'I'm not trying to force you to see things a particular way. But perhaps you could try thinking about it.'

I got to my feet. Anger had freed something inside me. It felt almost refreshing. I glared at Jallo and tried to maintain the accusatory tone in my voice.

'That he doesn't exist, you mean?' I said.

Jallo didn't answer. He didn't nod. He didn't move at all. He just sat there looking at me calmly as I stood there breathing hard.

'That he's *never* existed?' I went on.

He shrugged as if we were talking about something random, like a PIN number or a postcode.

'You could try it out as an idea,' he said, then reached back so that his elbow touched the red velvet curtain behind him. It was sloping. The whole room was sloping.

'Are you saying that the circus never existed either, then?' I said after a pause.

Jallo peered at the window.

'I don't know. I'm sure you know better than anyone.'

Jallo raised one of his fingers to his mouth and bit the nail. He pulled a face and stopped. He opened the top drawer of his desk and very carefully pulled on a pair of bright white cotton gloves.

'Maybe try looking at it like this,' he said after a while. 'We become new people all the time.'

'What do you mean by that?'

'We change. There's nothing odd about that.'

I found myself looking at the dresser and standard lamp in the corner, on top of the hand-woven rug. The extension lead was curled up beside them.

'We try to create order,' Jallo eventually said. 'But the natural state is chaos. You know what Shakespeare said?'

'No. What did he say?'

'"All the world's a circus"!'

'"A stage", surely?' I said.

Jallo waved one white-gloved hand in the air impatiently.

'Doesn't matter,' he said. 'That's what he meant, anyway ...'

He looked tired, as if he was trying to bring the discussion to an end, but suddenly he raised his eyebrows and held one gloved finger up in the air as if he'd just thought of something funny. He turned and hunted through his drawers. He pulled out a cable, then a red microphone, and held it up in front of me.

'Karaoke?'

40

After a while I began to hear the sound of voices out in the waiting room. Jallo cleared his throat. He put the microphone away and glanced at the door, stood up, walked over and closed it. As he did, I noticed the full-length mirror on the back of the door. When he started to close the door only the table, part of the floor and the bookcase at the other end of the room were visible in it. But as the door closed, first my clothes then more and more of me came into view in the mirror. Once it was shut I was standing there.

Jallo went back to his chair. He closed the drawer containing the karaoke equipment, sat back down and reached over the desk, and dropped his pen into the desk tidy.

'So what happened at work?' he said.

'What?' I said, looking at myself in the mirror.

'The other day. You ran off.'

I nodded.

'It was Mr Magic Bobbi,' I said, still staring at my own reflection in the door.

Jallo frowned.

'Who's Mr Magic Bobbi?' he asked.

'And you were there,' I said.

'Yes,' Jallo said.

I could sense him leaning towards me even though I couldn't see him.

'Magnus, your imagination is a great asset,' he said. 'It's a gift. You just need to learn how to manage it. Do you understand? You need to learn how to use it properly. Think of it like this – you're like a superhero who just needs to learn to control his superpowers.'

I looked at myself in the mirror. Raised one arm slightly, as if to make sure that the arm in the mirror moved at the same time. It did. It waved. That was plausible. It was all plausible. Even so, it still felt like I'd walked into a dream world. Where everything worked differently. It was as if words meant different things now. Unless they meant the same as before but in a different way. Unless they meant exactly the same things they had always meant, but that I had always thought they meant something else. I felt I ought to say something in order to stop myself from going completely mad.

'But ...' I began. 'What about the person who keeps phoning me? Do you think that really happened?'

Jallo shrugged his shoulders.

'Once again,' he said, 'does it seem plausible?'

I didn't say anything for a while.

'Someone's definitely playing stuff,' I said.

'Playing?' Jallo said.

'Music. There's someone at the other end playing music.'

Jallo frowned.

'Mmh ... no,' he said, shaking his head. 'That sounds odd.'

'But I can hear it,' I said.

Jallo nodded slowly.

'Yes,' he said. 'But who the hell would be playing music for you?'

41

The phone rang again not long after I got home. I let it ring a few times, properly listening to the sound. I heard it echo in the room, so I was sure it was real. When I pressed the green button to take the call, neither of us said anything at first. Almost like a greeting. As if we both wanted to assure ourselves that the same rules – no words, just music – still applied. I clutched the receiver extra hard. Tapped it gently with my fingertips to make absolutely sure this was really happening. I decided to wait this time. Let him start. If nothing happened, then so be it. But I didn't have to wait long before I heard a click of a disc being inserted.

'Here We Go Again' by Whitesnake.

When it was finished I held the receiver up to the speaker and played the short instrumental piece 'I Know You' by Dislocated Timeline, from *Memories from Tuesday*. (He could always google it if he didn't know it. Or use one of those music apps that tell you the artist and title with a minimum of effort. If they actually covered a track like that. I wasn't going to make things easy for him.)

After it finished there was a bit of crackling on the line, then he played 'How Do You Feel' by Jefferson Airplane. I thought that was a bit unimaginative. I let out a deep and very audible sigh. So that the person at the other end would realise that I thought he needed a bit more instruction.

I responded with 'This is Hardcore' by Pulp.

He played Metallica's 'Sad But True', which I reluctantly had to admit had a good, heavy intro and stirring verses. The bridge was OK as well, but the chorus wasn't up to much. I replied with 'U Think U Know, But U Have No Idea' by Eps. In response I got 'All That I Have Done Wrong' by P-Dust, which – as far as I was aware – only existed on SoundCloud and possibly some obscure website. That made me think. There weren't many people who knew about P-Dust. And it was almost as far from hard rock as you could get. Impressive. A bold move. Unconventional. But the more I thought about it, the more I realised that the combination wasn't all that unthinkable. In a way it was perfect, because it was as elegant as it was unexpected. On my shelf P-Dust would have stood a long way from both Eps and Pulp, but now that I had heard it with my own ears, I saw the connection. It struck me that the choice between A and B could just as well be C.

I played Ben Wilson's 'What Will Happen Next'.

He played Robert Palmer's 'Can We Still Be Friends?'.

Tasteless. But still. Something had happened.

I responded with Andrew Bayer's instrumental 'All This Will Happen Again'. Daring, I know, but sometimes you have to take a risk. I was feeling courageous.

He replied with 'It's Going To Be Fine' from the same album. I sat there listening to the calm, repetitive piano music and synthesised voices. Looked out through the window. It was raining outside. Once again I found myself looking at the advertisement showing the guy in his underwear. The tear was even bigger now. Like a big, heart-shaped hole.

'It's Going To Be Fine' had finished a while back, and I quickly dug out Erik Ruud's 'How Can You Be So Sure?' and played it.

There was a long silence at the other end, then some rustling and clicking sounds. And then: 'Fix You' by Coldplay.

42

The next day there was a letter lying on the doormat. I knew at once what it was. I took it to the kitchen table. Got myself a bowl of cereal. Opened the envelope and read the letter, written in that familiar handwriting.

Dear Magnus!
Probably easiest to reach you with a letter.
I just wanted to say – thanks for everything.
Best wishes,
Magnus

I turned the sheet of paper over and scrutinised it. That was all there was. I read the strange note three times. Sat for a while looking out of the window, then read it a fourth time. In the end I put it on the pile of post next to the fridge. I didn't have time for that sort of thing just then. I had to plan my selection of music for that evening's phone call.

penguin.co.uk/vintage